"One of my favorite authors."
—*Huntress Book Reviews*

Raves for Jacquie D'Alessandro

"Trotting at the heels of Julia Quinn and catching up fast, D'Alessandro should win new fans with her exuberant offering."
—*Publishers Weekly*

"A delightful tale of honor and duty, curses and quests, treachery and betrayal, love and passion."
—*Romance Reviews Today*

"A delight from start to finish...Romance at its enchanting best!"
—*New York Times* bestselling author Teresa Medeiros

"Fresh, funny, and loaded with charm...This entertaining romp is on par with some of the best works from seasoned authors like Julia Quinn and Stephanie Laurens."
—*Publishers Weekly*

"Ms. D'Alessandro has the nimbleness of a thief when it comes to crafting relationship dynamics."
—*Heartstrings Reviews*

"Puts a brand-new spin on a popular plot, with an entertaining and engaging result."
—*Romantic Times*

"An entertaining, often humorous Regency romantic romp that also provides a lesson in sticking to one's values even if it hurts to do so."
—*The Best Reviews*

continued...

SEDUCED
At MIDNIGHT

Jacquie
D'Alessandro

BERKLEY SENSATION, NEW YORK

THE BERKLEY PUBLISHING GROUP
Published by the Penguin Group
Penguin Group (USA) Inc.
375 Hudson Street, New York, New York 10014, USA
Penguin Group (Canada), 90 Eglinton Avenue East, Suite 700, Toronto, Ontario M4P 2Y3, Canada
(a division of Pearson Penguin Canada Inc.)
Penguin Books Ltd., 80 Strand, London WC2R 0RL, England
Penguin Group Ireland, 25 St. Stephen's Green, Dublin 2, Ireland
(a division of Penguin Books Ltd.)
Penguin Group (Australia), 250 Camberwell Road, Camberwell, Victoria 3124, Australia
(a division of Pearson Australia Group Pty. Ltd.)
Penguin Books India Pvt. Ltd., 11 Community Centre, Panchsheel Park, New Delhi—110 017, India
Penguin Group (NZ), 67 Apollo Drive, Rosedale, North Shore 0632, New Zealand
(a division of Pearson New Zealand Ltd.)
Penguin Books (South Africa) (Pty.) Ltd., 24 Sturdee Avenue, Rosebank, Johannesburg 2196,
South Africa

Penguin Books Ltd., Registered Offices: 80 Strand, London WC2R 0RL, England

This is a work of fiction. Names, characters, places, and incidents either are the product of the author's imagination or are used fictitiously, and any resemblance to actual persons, living or dead, business establishments, events, or locales is entirely coincidental. The publisher does not have any control over and does not assume any responsibility for author or third-party websites or their content.

SEDUCED AT MIDNIGHT

A Berkley Sensation Book / published by arrangement with the author

PRINTING HISTORY
Berkley Sensation mass-market edition / January 2009

Copyright © 2009 by Jacquie D'Alessandro.
Excerpt from *Tempted at Midnight* copyright © 2009 by Jacquie D'Alessandro.
Cover art by Gregg Gulbronson.
Cover design by Edwin Tse.
Cover hand lettering by Ron Zinn.
Interior text design by Laura K. Corless.

ISBN: 978-0-425-22549-3

BERKLEY® SENSATION
Berkley Sensation Books are published by The Berkley Publishing Group,
a division of Penguin Group (USA) Inc.,
375 Hudson Street, New York, New York 10014.
BERKLEY® SENSATION and the "B" design are trademarks of Penguin Group (USA) Inc.

PRINTED IN THE UNITED STATES OF AMERICA

10 9 8 7 6 5 4 3 2 1

This book is dedicated to Cindy Hwang and Leslie Gelbman. Thank you for loving the Mayhem in Mayfair series! And to Collyn Milsted, a wonderful teacher. Thank you for sharing your time, expertise, and stories of England, and for giving me the opportunity to spend time with your students.

And as always, to my wonderful, encouraging husband, Joe. You are brilliant and have so much integrity— I'm so proud to be your wife. And to my fantastic, beautiful son, Christopher, aka Brilliant/Integrity, Junior—I'm so proud to be your mom.

Acknowledgments

I would like to thank the following people for their invaluable help and support:

All the wonderful people at Berkley for their kindness, cheerleading, and help in making my dreams come true, including Susan Allison, Leis Pederson, Don Rieck, and Sharon Gamboa.

My agent, Damaris Rowland, for her faith and wisdom, as well as Steven Axelrod, Lori Antonson, and Elsie Turoci.

Jenni Grizzle and Wendy Etherington for being such great buds.

Barbara Hosea for her wonderful haircutting talent, Andrea Moore, and Kathy Burgess for making me laugh and calling me *Darlin'*.

Thanks also to the wonderful Sue Grimshaw of BGI for her generosity and support. And as always to Kay and Jim Johnson, Kathy and Dick Guse, and Lea and Art D'Alessandro.

A cyber hug to my Looney Loopies: Connie Brockway, Marsha Canham, Virginia Henley, Jill Gregory, Julia London, Kathleen Givens, Sherri Browning, and Julie Ortolon, and also to the Temptresses the Blaze Babes.

A very special thank you to the members of Georgia Romance Writers and Romance Writers of America.

And a very special thank you to all the men and women serving in our armed forces for the sacrifices you and your families make to keep our nation safe.

And finally, thank you to all the wonderful readers who have taken the time to write to me. I love hearing from you!

Chapter 1

London, 1820

From the London Times:

> *Do you believe in ghosts? Mrs. Marguerite Greeley was found murdered and robbed last night in her Berkeley Square town house, in a crime identical to the robbery and murder of Lady Ratherstone only last week. Mrs. Greeley's butler reported hearing eerie moaning sounds coming from her private sitting room where her jewel box was located. Upon entering the room, the butler discovered the body and missing jewels and stated that all the windows and doors were locked from the inside. Similar sounds and locked windows and doors were reported at Lady Ratherstone's home. It seems clear Mrs. Greeley is the latest victim of Mayfair's cleverest, most diabolical, seemingly invisible, and thus far uncatchable criminal. Which begs two questions all of London is asking: Could the thief indeed be a ghost? And who is next?*

After making certain she wasn't observed, Lady Julianne Bradley slipped from the crowded drawing room and walked down the candlelit corridor. Although her heart pounded in anticipation, urging her to hurry, she forced her feet to keep a sedate pace. She had no wish to call undue attention to herself should she happen upon anyone.

Music and laughter, the hum of conversation, and the tinkling of crystal faded as she made her way farther from the center of Lord and Lady Daltry's elegant soiree. She turned a corner then counted the rooms as she passed . . . one, two . . . she slowed as she approached the third door.

The feeling that she was being watched suddenly flooded through her. A heated flush, the sort that always stained her pale skin a telltale red whenever she experienced any sort of nervousness, whooshed upward from her neck, flaming her face.

She turned, scanning the area, and saw nothing amiss. She was alone. *Your imagination is running amok as usual.*

Hoping she didn't look as furtive as she felt, she took one last glance around, then opened the third door. She stepped quickly into the room, closing the door behind her.

"It's about time you arrived."

The whisper came from directly beside her, and Julianne barely squelched the startled cry that rose to her lips. Leaning back against the oak panel, she looked around the shadowed library, illuminated in a curtain of dull gold from the low-burning fire glowing in the grate. Three pairs of eyes scrutinized her.

"We were beginning to think you weren't going to come," said Lady Emily Stapleford, impatiently pulling Julianne away from the door. "At best we have only a few minutes together before someone notes our absence from the party. What on earth detained you?"

"It was difficult to escape Mother," Julianne said. As she did at every soiree, the Countess of Gatesbourne took her duty of advantageously placing her only daughter in the path of every eligible titled gentleman in attendance very seriously. Such contrivances only served to render Julianne more shy than usual, a fact that greatly displeased her mother, who was not shy about voicing her displeasure.

Julianne's three friends exchanged a glance then gave an understanding nod. They well knew the countess's overbearing nature.

"Well, we're just glad you're here," said Carolyn Sutton, Countess Surbrooke, with a smile. "For a moment I thought perhaps a ghost absconded with you."

Julianne glanced at the beautiful newlywed who'd returned to London two days ago after a fortnight-long wedding trip to the Continent with her new husband. Carolyn was practically glowing with obvious happiness. Julianne's admiration for her friend's calm efficiency and serene composure knew no bounds.

"Botheration, Carolyn, not you, too," said Sarah Devenport, Marchioness Langston, in her usual no-nonsense manner—another trait Julianne wished she herself possessed. Sarah shoved her spectacles higher on her nose and frowned at her sister. "You're nearly as bad as the *Times*, not to mention many guests at this party. You can't possibly believe that a ghost is responsible for the recent rash of robberies."

Emily's mouth curved upward in the mischievous grin that so often touched her lips. "Unless he's like the ghost in our latest book selection. Of course, in *The Ghost of Devonshire Manor* the only thing stolen was a lady's innocence. The story was so deliciously real—"

"Which is why I called for this meeting of the Ladies Literary Society now," interrupted Julianne. "The timing of a ghost robber is perfect. I think we should hold a séance, similar to the one in the book, to discover who this thief is."

"I think that's a marvelous idea," said Emily.

"I think perhaps the Devonshire Manor ghost has addled your wits," said Sarah.

"Perhaps," Julianne conceded. "I must admit I haven't been quite the same since I read it." Indeed, the book had ignited a restlessness within her she'd been unable to squelch. "The story affected me strongly. It was haunting—"

"As a ghost story should be," Emily interrupted with a grin.

"Yes, but more than anything, you can't deny it was

extremely"—Julianne cleared her throat then lowered her voice—"*sensual* as well."

"It was indeed," agreed Sarah. "A more apt title might have been *The Haunting of Lady Elaine*."

"*By the Very Delicious Maxwell*," added Emily, fanning her hand in front of her face.

"Yes," said Carolyn. "Maxwell was...oh, my..."

Her words trailed off into a vaporous sigh, and Julianne, Emily, and Sarah all nodded and murmured in agreement. Based on the fact that the Ladies Literary Society's reading selections were far more scandalous than their group's name would suggest—which was no accident—Julianne had known their ghost story would be more than a simple tale of spirits flitting about in graveyards. Yet she hadn't anticipated its deeply sensual protagonist Maxwell, who was a ghost—a fact that didn't stop him from seducing the lovely Lady Elaine. Over and over again. In some very inventive ways.

"If only such a man existed in real life," Emily said. "So strong and brave. Masculine and romantic and—"

"Passionate." The word slipped from Julianne's lips before she could stop it.

"He does exist," Carolyn and Sarah said in unison. "I married him." The sisters looked at each other and shared a smile.

Julianne's gaze dropped to Sarah's midsection, which was just starting to show signs of swelling with the baby she carried. Her happiness for her friends, both of whom had fallen in love and married in the last several months, mingled with undeniable envy. She'd never have the love, joy, and passion that Sarah and Carolyn shared with their husbands.

No, there would be no love match for her. She'd long ago accepted the inevitable—that her father would arrange her marriage, his choice based solely on the advantageous considerations of property, titles, and money. As she'd been reminded practically from the cradle, she had no say in the matter, and complying without complaint to her father's wishes was the least she could do, since she'd had neither the decency nor the sense to be born a boy. After overhearing her parents' conversation earlier today, Julianne feared her arranged marriage was closer than ever.

Still, her heart dreamed of falling in love. Of passion. Of a man who would want her in those same ways and not merely as the product of a business arrangement. A man who would have fire in his eyes when he looked at her...

Even as Julianne tried to erase his image from her memory, a mental picture rose in her mind. Of a tall man with stark features, ebony hair, and dark eyes filled with secrets and mystery. A man surrounded by a veil of tempting, seductive, enticing danger. A man forbidden to her.

Gideon Mayne...

His name whispered through her mind, a silent sigh of longing.

He had fire in his eyes when he looked at her—a look that made her burn to know more, to know everything about him.

"Yes, you both married fabulous, dashing men," Emily said, pulling Julianne from her wayward thoughts, "and very selfishly, I might add, leaving nothing but nincompoops for Julianne and me. No other such magnificent men exist, and alas, Maxwell is but a figment of fiction."

He existed, Julianne knew.

But he could never be hers.

Lady Elaine had suffered the same dilemma regarding her ghostly lover Maxwell in *The Ghost of Devonshire Manor*, and Julianne vividly understood the hopelessness of the other woman's impossible feelings.

"The things that Maxwell did to Lady Elaine..." Sarah gushed out a sigh. "Good heavens, no wonder she never wanted to leave her home."

Julianne bit back a groan as a flash of heat tingled through her body. The story's scandalous nature had conjured all manner of fantasies featuring Gideon Mayne, images she couldn't dispel from her mind.

"My favorite parts of the book were when Maxwell scared off Lady Elaine's various suitors," Carolyn said. "He was quite devilish. And ingenious."

"Very," agreed Sarah. "I especially laughed when he made the vicar's duck entrée dance and quack on his plate."

"Maxwell did those things because he didn't want another man to have the woman he loved and desired so deeply," Julianne said softly. "His pain was so palpable, I could feel it, and my heart broke for him. They both knew that in spite of their feelings, their circumstances rendered them unable to truly be together."

Yes, circumstances no less impossible and unsolvable than those between her and the man she could not stop thinking about.

In an effort to banish thoughts of that which she could not have, Julianne sought to change the subject back to her séance idea of catching the robber. "Certainly if one is going to be haunted by a ghost, Maxwell is the sort to have—"

"Oh, I agree," interjected Emily. "Much preferable to the ghost that haunts my aunt Agatha's Surrey estate. His name is Gregory. According to Aunt Agatha, he's old, paunchy, suffers from the gout, and is wholly unpleasant."

"What makes your aunt believe she has a ghost?" Sarah asked in a dubious tone, pushing her spectacles higher on her nose.

"She's seen him," Emily responded. "And heard him. He groans a great deal. She calls him Gregory the Groaner."

"But how could she hear him?" Julianne asked. "Your aunt Agatha, although a dear lady, is deaf as a tree stump."

"Apparently Gregory flits about in the corridors, complaining of his aches and pains loudly enough for even Aunt Agatha to hear."

"Have *you* seen Gregory?" asked Carolyn.

Emily shook her head. "No, but I did hear some odd groaning sounds the last time I visited."

"Hearing groaning sounds, seeing ghosts, that's one of the things I wanted to discuss," Julianne said. "Based on our book selection, I think we should conduct a séance, similar to the one Lady Elaine held. Only instead of trying to conjure a lover, we'll attempt to summon this Mayfair ghost."

Emily's eyes sparkled with interest. "Ah, yes, you mentioned that earlier, then we went off on a tangent. An excellent suggestion. Of course we won't be successful, but it should prove an interesting diversion. When and where do you suggest?"

"I could host it tomorrow evening," Julianne said. "Could you all come?"

"I wouldn't miss it," Emily said without hesitation. "Who knows what sort of ghost might be summoned or secrets revealed in the dark?"

"I wouldn't miss it either," said Sarah. "Of course, convincing Matthew to allow me out of his sight for an entire evening will present a challenge. He thinks that because I'm expecting I've turned into delicate spun glass—although I can't deny that his constant attention is flattering and quite, um, titillating." She turned to Carolyn. "I imagine your bridegroom won't be anxious to spend an evening without you."

"Hopefully not." An impish grin touched the corners of Carolyn's mouth. "But I'm certain Daniel and Matthew won't object to spending a few hours together at their club. It will be good for them to miss us."

A wave of pent-up emotions washed over Julianne, and she looked down. The gloomy shadows swallowing her feet in the dimly lit room seemed the personification of the future looming before her.

"You're both so fortunate to have husbands who love you so much," she whispered, unable to keep the hitch of wistfulness from her voice.

"Are you all right, Julianne?"

Carolyn's question, along with her gentle touch on Julianne's sleeve, pulled her gaze upward. "I'm fine," she said, offering what she hoped was a reassuring smile.

Emily frowned. "I don't believe you. You seem out of sorts. And preoccupied."

I am. By the same thing that has haunted me for weeks… thoughts of something, someone, I can never have.

Yet she couldn't admit the truth, not even to her closest friends. They'd be shocked and warn her to turn her romantic inclinations toward someone suitable. Advice anyone would give an earl's daughter harboring an impossible fascination for a man whose circumstances were so far removed from her own.

"Has your mother said something to upset you?" asked Sarah.

Julianne grasped onto the excuse and shot her conscience an inward frown. After all, when *didn't* her formidable mother say something upsetting? Indeed, she'd done so only a few hours ago, and on a topic she *could* discuss with her friends. And one that brought reality back with a thump.

"Actually, yes," Julianne admitted. "I overheard her and Father talking earlier this evening about their plans for my future. Apparently the Duke of Eastling expressed interest in me."

"The Duke of Eastling?" repeated Emily, her expression reflecting the same wide-eyed dismay Julianne felt at the name. "But he's...so...so...not young."

"He's only just turned forty," Carolyn said.

"Which is only several years younger than my *father*," Emily retorted. "Besides, His Grace has already been married. And what did he do? Dragged his wife off to Cornwall, that's what. Which is no doubt where he'd want to drag Julianne as well." She turned distressed eyes toward Julianne. "Heavens, you cannot live in *Cornwall*. We'd never see you!"

"His wife died," Julianne said, "a year and a half ago. He's ready to remarry."

"I thought something like this might be in the wind when I saw your mother speaking to him just before he asked you to waltz," Sarah said.

"As did I," Carolyn agreed. "He's very eligible. And rich. And handsome."

"Yes," Julianne agreed. Indeed, most women found the duke, with his blond hair and light blue eyes, very attractive. But to Julianne, his good looks didn't matter. Not when he exuded the same icy, remote, uncompromising demeanor she'd been subjected to her entire life from her father. A shudder ran through her at the thought, and her father's stern voice seemed to echo in her ears, the mantra she'd heard countless times: *The only thing a worthless daughter can do is marry to the advantage of her family.* She longed for warmth and passion. Not chilly politeness and indifference.

"You are one of the loveliest, most sought-after young women in the ton," Carolyn said in a soothing tone, giving her hand a squeeze. "Your father will be entertaining many offers for you. I noted you shared a dance with Lord Haverly. He's a decent gentleman."

"And as exciting as beige spots on a beige wall," Julianne said with a sigh. "He bears the same expression whether he's ecstatic or livid. Indeed, the only way to tell which one he might be is if he's forthcoming enough to say, 'I'm ecstatic' or 'I'm livid.' He spoke of nothing but the new cutaway jacket he just purchased. He waxed poetic about every stitch. I thought I would doze off during our waltz. Besides which, he's bald."

"Not completely," said Emily. "He's just rather thin on top."

"What about Lord Penniwick?" Sarah asked. "You danced with him as well, and he's quite handsome. And he has a full head of hair."

"Yes. But unfortunately his full head of hair only comes up to my chin. He doesn't speak to me—he speaks to my bosom."

"An affliction that affects many men, I'm afraid, regardless of their height," said Carolyn.

"Yes, but there is a lasciviousness to Penniwick's expression that makes my skin crawl. Every time he looks at me, I fear he's about to lick his chops. Then drool."

"Drooling is definitely bad," Emily said, wrinkling her nose. "What about Lord Beechmore? He's extremely handsome *and* tall."

Julianne shrugged. "And is very well aware of his exceptional looks. I cannot see him falling in love with any woman when he is so completely enamored of himself. He's also very aloof."

"People have said *you're* aloof, Julianne," Emily pointed out with her usual brutal honesty, "when you're actually just shy. Perhaps the same can be said about Lord Beechmore."

"Perhaps," Julianne conceded. "But there is no mistaking his conceit."

"Don't forget Logan Jennsen," Sarah interjected. "You spoke with him as well. He's incredibly handsome, incredibly tall, and not the least bit aloof. And he's fabulously wealthy."

Julianne shook her head. "I agree Mr. Jennsen is all those things, but it doesn't matter. Father would never consider him as he's a commoner, not to mention an American."

"Lord Walston has called upon you several times," Carolyn reminded her. "He's attractive and seems quite nice."

"I suppose. But he's just so . . ." She searched for a word to adequately describe the viscount who was, as Carolyn said, quite nice. They'd shared a pleasant conversation, but in spite of his obvious intelligence and kindness, he hadn't lit the slightest spark of interest within her.

"Dry," she finally finished. "He's like unbuttered toast."

"Well, he's the best of the lot, so slather a bit of butter and jam on him," Emily said with a hint of impatience in her voice. "Unless . . ." Her eyes narrowed and filled with speculation, an expression that snaked a fissure of unease through Julianne. "You're finding fault with gentlemen who, while perhaps not perfect, are certainly acceptable—and certainly far preferable to drag-you-off-to-Cornwall Eastling. The only reason I can fathom why you would do that is because your interest lies elsewhere."

A flaming flush scorched her cheeks, and she gave a silent prayer of thanks for the dim lighting. How had their conversation floated into this perilous water?

"My interest lies in conducting a séance," she said firmly.

"I *meant* that your interest lies in a different man," Emily stated just as firmly. "One we haven't mentioned."

Botheration! Of course Emily, whom she'd known since childhood, would see through her diversionary tactic.

"Who is it?" Sarah asked, her face alight with curiosity.

Someone I can never, ever have. Someone who made every other gentleman mentioned pale in comparison. "No one." *No one I can discuss with you.* "I'm just feeling unsettled because I suspect Father will be making his decision within the next year, and all the gentlemen he's considering are so very . . . *civil*." The word seemed to burst from her, opening the floodgates to her frustrations. "I'm so *tired* of polite and restrained civility. I want a man who is interested in what I have to say and who will discuss more than fashion, the weather, and other trivialities with me. I don't want to merely exist—I want to *live*. I want passion. Feelings. *Fire*." Her words sounded desperate, even to her own ears, yet how could they not when desperation was all she felt?

Sarah reached out and clasped Julianne's hand. Behind her spectacles, Sarah's eyes brimmed with a combination of sympathy and concern. "As someone who is extremely fortunate to have those things you want, I completely understand your desire. You deserve that happiness—*every* happiness—and I dearly hope it comes your way."

"I agree," seconded Emily, and Carolyn nodded.

Tears pooled behind Julianne's eyes. For the show of compassion and loyalty. And because she knew the things she truly wanted were, by virtue of her circumstances, out of her reach.

Not wanting to dwell on such a depressing subject, Julianne said, "Thank you. Perhaps all of us hoping will insure a favorable result. As for tomorrow night, shall we say nine o'clock?"

"Perfect," Sarah agreed, while Carolyn and Emily nodded. "But now I think we'd best return to the party. Matthew is no doubt craning his neck about, looking for me, worried that something's amiss. Good heavens, by the time the baby is actually due to arrive, I fear his hair will be standing up straight on end—all of it that he hasn't yanked out—and he'll teeter on the edge of panic."

Julianne smiled briefly at the picture Sarah's words painted of her normally calm, levelheaded husband. Clearly love could make one act in very uncharacteristic ways.

Just then she heard a soft click. She turned quickly and stared at the closed door. "Did you hear that?" she asked in an undertone.

"What?" responded a trio of whispers.

"It sounded like a door being softly shut." She hurried over to the door and opened it a crack. Peeked into the corridor. And found it empty. Relieved, she drew a deep breath,

Chapter 2

Gideon watched Lady Julianne leave the crowded drawing room. She'd timed her exit well; no one else appeared to notice her slip away from the party. Except him. But then, he'd noticed everything she had done since the moment she'd arrived at Lord and Lady Daltry's soiree.

Keeping close to the wall, he unobtrusively made his way to the curved archway through which she'd escaped. A few of the guests looked his way, but with that inborn, innate ability the aristocracy possessed, they clearly recognized that he wasn't one of them, and their gazes didn't linger. No doubt they thought he was one of the hired help. Which he was. Hired to catch a murdering thief.

Could Lady Julianne somehow be connected to the criminal?

His instincts, which had served him well through the years, told him no, yet based on her furtive departure, she was clearly up to something. And he was determined to find out what that something was. For investigative purposes only. Because his training and commitment to his task demanded he leave no avenue unexplored. Certainly not because he was compelled by an irritating curiosity and need to know what she was up to.

He entered the corridor and found it empty. His gaze swept the area, detecting no changes from his earlier scouting. After turning the corner, he noted the four doors. In his mind's eye he pictured the layout of the house he'd committed to memory during his inspection before the party began, when he ascertained all the windows were securely locked.

Slowing his pace, he strained his ears for any sound but heard nothing save the muted hum of conversation from the party.

He silently opened the first door. A swift perusal of Lady Daltry's femininely appointed sitting room proved it empty. He continued on to the second door, behind which was Lord Daltry's private study, and silently entered the room. And instantly knew he wasn't alone. With his back pressed against the paneling, his gaze swept the deeply shadowed chamber. The oversized desk. Hunting trophies mounted on the walls. Tall bookcases flanking the windows.

A low, guttural groan came from the corner. Gideon's gaze shifted. Narrowed. And then he saw them. A woman, whose white blond hair rendered her instantly recognizable as Lady Daltry. She was bent over the arm of a leather settee, her fine gown gathered up about her waist, her bare arse hoisted in the air. And a man. Standing behind her, with his breeches open.

"Spread your legs wider."

The man's impatient demand was met by a rustle of material and a querulous female whisper. "Don't you dare leave me hanging as you did last time, Eastling."

Eastling? Gideon grimaced at the name and focused his attention on the man. Though he could only see his profile, Gideon indeed recognized the duke. His lips were pulled back from his teeth in a grimace of pleasure. Gideon couldn't tell if Lady Daltry was receiving any pleasure, but based on her words, His Grace had fallen short in providing it during their last tryst. As best Gideon could tell, the duke was currently more interested in his own pleasure than that of his partner. Not surprising, based on what he knew of the man. He briefly wondered if Lord Daltry knew or cared about this

tryst. Apparently marriage vows meant little to the peerage.
But he'd already known that.

Neither the duke nor his partner noticed him, and he
quickly exited the room. Bloody hell, now that unappetizing
image of the duke's fingers pressing into Lady Daltry's buttocks was burned into his brain. A shudder rolled over him as
he approached the third door, which led to the library. With
his hand curved around the brass knob, he paused to listen
and heard the unmistakable murmur of muted whispers. He
opened the door a crack.

"It was extremely sensual as well…" The words trailed off
into a sigh, and Gideon froze. He'd recognize Lady Julianne's
voice anywhere. But *sensual* certainly wasn't a word he'd have
expected to pass her lips.

"Nothing stopped Maxwell's seduction."

Seduction? Maxwell? A sensation that felt precisely like
jealousy but couldn't possibly have been seared Gideon. Who
the bloody hell was Maxwell? And who the bloody hell had he
seduced? Surely not Lady Julianne—

"Lady Elaine. Over and over again. In some very inventive
ways."

Gideon frowned, annoyed at his immense relief that Maxwell, whoever the hell he was, had apparently seduced Lady
Elaine, whoever the hell she was.

"Passionate." Lady Julianne uttered that single word, and
an image rose unbidden in his mind. Of him. And her. Locked
in a passionate embrace. Her hands on him. His hands on her.
His mouth on her. Everywhere.

He briefly squeezed his eyes shut to banish the vivid mental picture. Damn it, she wasn't supposed to be talking about
such things. She should be discussing the weather. Fashion.
The latest gossip.

He continued to listen, trying to decipher what they
were talking about. The word *ghost* caught his attention. It
seemed Lady Julianne and her friends thought they knew a
ghost named Gregory? He situated his ear closer to the crack.
And barely refrained from looking toward the ceiling. Good
God, 'twas clear one of their friends, this Lady Elaine, had

performed some sort of séance and conjured herself a ghostly lover and now Lady Julianne and her friends were taken with the idea. Only instead, they wished to summon the ghost criminal and solve the crimes everyone was talking about. Bloody ridiculous. He was half tempted to appear at their séance and—

"Are you all right, Julianne?"

Gideon recognized Lady Surbrooke's voice, and he strained to hear the reply. When he did, his entire body tensed. Eastling? Lady Julianne's father would entertain an offer from that bastard? An image flashed through Gideon's mind... of the duke bending Lady Julianne over a leather settee as he had Lady Daltry. His fingers gripping Julianne's bare flesh. Thrusting between her legs.

A red haze seemed to dull his vision. The thought of that reprobate touching her... He clenched his jaw and tried to banish the image. And succeeded—only to have it replaced with one of himself. Bending Lady Julianne over a settee. Thrusting into her.

Bloody hell.

He continued to listen, his tension mounting as her friends named a veritable stable of purebred lords who would make an acceptable match for Lady Julianne. Haverly? Good God, the man was nothing but a bald bore. As for Penniwick, Gideon considered it a testament to his self-control that he hadn't poked out the viscount's eyeballs after the way he'd ogled Lady Julianne's breasts while they'd danced. Beechmore wasn't shy; he was a cold, aloof bastard with a nasty temper.

As for Jennsen, Gideon suspected there was much more to the man than he presented to the world. And he found himself greatly relieved when Julianne said her father wouldn't consider a commoner. Somehow the thought of Julianne with Jennsen—a powerful man who women obviously found attractive—suffused him an uncomfortable sensation that felt like a cramp. As for Walston—his lips twitched when he heard Julianne's "dry" assessment.

"Your interest lies in a different man. One we haven't mentioned... who is it?"

Gideon strained to hear Lady Julianne's reply. She denied there was another man, but he suspected from her hesitation and her voice that she wasn't being truthful.

So there *was* someone she desired. Obviously one of those fancy-pants titled bastards. An odd sensation invaded his chest. One that felt like a toxic mixture of envy and yearning and jealousy.

"We'd best return to the party..."

The words broke through the fog that had engulfed him. He quickly closed the door, then froze as he heard it click into place. A soft, barely audible sound, but one that seemed to him to reverberate off the walls.

Had the ladies within heard it?

"Did you hear that?" came Lady Julianne's voice.

Damn it all to hell and back again. Cursing his uncharacteristic carelessness, he looked for the nearest escape. With the second door out of the question thanks to the duke and Lady Daltry, and the first too far away, he dashed toward the fourth door and quickly entered. Just as he closed the door behind him—taking extra care not to repeat his error—he heard the third door open.

He swiftly scanned the chamber, relieved to find it empty. Another sitting room of some sort. Bloody hell, how many sitting rooms did these aristocrats require? A body only had but one arse to plop into a chair.

He drew a deep breath and leaned back against the oak panel. A bit too close, that escape.

Of course, given his current mission, he was perfectly within his rights to be wandering the corridors and peeking into rooms. Still, he had no wish to be caught eavesdropping at a door crack by Lady Julianne and her friends. Bloody humiliating, that's what that would have been. An insult to his abilities as a Bow Street Runner to be discovered in such an ignominious fashion. And such detection would make it necessary to converse with Lady Julianne—without time to prepare himself first. Not something he cared to contemplate when the first thing that popped into his mind whenever he thought of her was, *I want you.*

And bloody hell, it seemed as if he thought about her all the time.

Just then he noted a sound in the corridor. He pressed his ear to the crack in the door and heard the quiet rustle of gowns. Once the sound faded, he peeked into the corridor. Lady Julianne and her cohorts were just turning the corner, clearly on their way back to the party. Good. He'd wondered what she was up to, and now he knew. So now he could focus on what he needed to concentrate on: discovering the identity of the murdering ghost thief. Excellent.

Not wanting to return to the party directly on the heels of Lady Julianne's group and risk any chance of it appearing he'd followed them, he decided to recheck the windows to make certain they remained locked. Experience had taught him one could never be too careful or thorough. Yet even while that task should have fully occupied him, his mind was filled with *her*. As it had been from the first moment he'd seen her two months ago. A day he'd rue until his last breath.

The damn woman was nothing but pure distraction. By damn, it was all her fault he'd nearly been caught. All her fault he'd felt compelled to follow her. All her fault he'd even known she'd slipped away from the party. While his watchful gaze had carefully scanned the drawing room, looking for any activities that could be deemed in the least suspicious, his eyes had been drawn to her again and again. The only reason he'd known she left the party was because he was so thoroughly, painfully aware of her. A bloody irritating situation he found himself, unfortunately, unable to control.

Bad enough to have a woman on his mind when he needed to focus on work. But to have this particular woman embedded in his thoughts . . . he shook his head. Bloody hell, it was nothing short of madness, and he was nothing short of a bloody idiot. Might as well be fixated on a damn royal princess. Or on owning a fancy Mayfair town house like the one in which he now stood. Or inheriting a hundred thousand pounds. All things he would never have.

He'd learned long ago not to waste his time and energy chasing after the impossible. Better—and much wiser—to set goals he could actually achieve. A woman like Lady Julianne Bradley was so far beyond his sphere as to be utterly laughable. Indeed, if he were insane enough to admit his ridiculous fascination with her to anyone—something that wouldn't occur without benefit of a severe blow to his head—he'd be laughed out of England.

Yet still she haunted him. Night and day, although the nights were the worst. When he lay alone in his bed, staring at the ceiling, imaging his fingers skimming over her creamy skin. Wreaking havoc with her perfect, blond curls. Memorizing every curve. Her body over him. Under him. His body sliding deep into her silky heat—

He cut off the thought with an exclamation of disgust and moved along to check the final window. Like the others, it remained locked. In an effort to escape his torturous thoughts, he exited the room. His intention to return to the party was waylaid as he approached the third door. The door she'd entered.

Instinct and something else he refused to examine too closely had him slipping into the room. After closing the door behind him he drew a deep breath. And smelled only the scent of beeswax and the leather volumes that lined the walls.

Hoping for a whiff of her, weren't you? his annoyingly honest inner voice asked.

He wearily leaned his head back against the oak panel and dragged his hands down his face. Yes, damn it, that's exactly what he'd hoped—that her scent still lingered. What was *wrong* with him?

Lady Julianne Bradley is what's wrong with you, you oaf.

God help him, as much as he wanted to, he couldn't deny it. From the moment he'd laid eyes on her, he'd wanted her. With a raw, intense hunger unlike anything he'd ever experienced. A hunger that confounded and confused him.

With an effort he pushed off from the door and headed across the room to recheck the multitude of windows. But the task was too mundane, one that allowed his thoughts to remain fixated on the exact thing he wished to purge from his mind. *Julianne.*

Part of him wanted to simply stare at her, drink in the almost shocking flawlessness of her beauty. Never had he seen a more exquisite woman. He was accustomed to ugliness, so used to it that beauty never failed to surprise him. But never more so than her beauty. Because it was so utterly, completely pure. Of course he knew enough of her class to know her outward beauty wouldn't extend inward.

Still, outwardly, everything about her was perfect. Her silky golden blond curls. Her smooth, creamy complexion. The perfectly matched dimples that flanked her gorgeous, perfectly shaped mouth. Her fine, delicate cheekbones. The clear sapphire blue of her eyes. He'd taken one look at her and completely forgotten the murder investigation that had brought him to her home.

But then the other, darker half of his fascination for her had kicked in, one that hit him like a blow to the gut. The one that didn't want to simply admire her from afar but desperately longed to yank her against him, wreak havoc with all that golden blond perfection, and put out this damnable fire she'd inexplicably lit in him.

What the bloody hell was it about her that affected him this way? Yes, she was beautiful, but it wasn't as if he'd never seen a gorgeous woman before. He'd even sampled several upper-class ladies and discovered they were not at all to his taste. Nothing but bored aristocrats looking to relieve their ennui by tupping a commoner. A brief nibble of the forbidden lower class, of a man who didn't require padding beneath his clothes to give the illusion of musculature, that titillated for a few moments before they returned to their fancy homes and neglectful husbands. He'd found those women shallow and spoiled and had forgotten them quickly once the physical passion was spent, as he was certain they'd forgotten him.

So why was he so fascinated by Lady Julianne? Ridiculous as it seemed, part of what continually drew his eye was the way she moved: graceful, yet with an underlying energy. So many ladies of her class were so bloody limp and languid they reminded him of soggy bread. It was as if silk resided under their skin rather than bones. But Lady Julianne walked as if she had a purpose for doing so. Punctuated her words with elegant gestures of her slim hands.

During his previous investigation he'd observed her dancing at several soirees and had been unable to tear his gaze from her. He'd never danced in his life, had never wanted to or even considered doing so. But during those waltzes, while he watched her gracefully whirl and twirl in the arms of some lucky bastard, he'd found himself wishing he were that lucky bastard. That he could sweep her into his arms and lead her around the dance floor. Feel the energy and grace of her while they became lost in the music.

Yet it had to be more than her poise and elegance. *It's those eyes,* his inner voice whispered. The innocence and vulnerability shining in their deep blue depths. Possibly. He wasn't accustomed to seeing innocence in any form. Clearly the novelty of it had affected him. Made him want to admire it. But then, as he damn well knew, he'd want to steal it. Take it away from her. Make it his own.

You're good at stealing. His conscience slyly raised its head from the grave in which he'd long ago buried it. *Money. Secrets. Innocence. Lives...*

He roughly shoved that hated inner voice back to the dark, dank depths of his soul from where it had escaped. He closed his eyes, and his mind instantly conjured Lady Julianne's image. Yes, damn it, it was those eyes. She had eyes a man could get lost in. And every time he'd seen her since that first time, he had to force himself not to succumb to the temptation to drown in those shimmering blue pools. Then there was the way she looked at him...as if she were equally as fascinated with him, something he'd obviously misread. Why would an innocent earl's daughter give a man like him so much as a second thought?

She wouldn't, you dolt. So it's time to forget about her and concentrate on the task at hand.

Right. The murdering ghost thief. A disparaging sound rose in his throat. Ghost indeed. There was no such thing. The person responsible for the recent rash of crimes was just that: a person. A very clever person. A very clever person Gideon had every intention of catching.

"You might be clever," he muttered, "but you're going to make a mistake. And when you do, I'll be right there. Waiting."

And speaking of waiting… He'd finished checking the windows and had lingered here long enough. It was time to continue his search. And he'd best remember he was looking for a criminal and not that fancy bit of aristocratic fluff. She was destined for the Duke of Eastling—his teeth clenched at the mere thought—or another fop of the same ilk. No matter what, a purebred princess like Lady Julianne would never, could never, belong to a lower-class mutt like Gideon. Which was perfect, as he didn't want or need a purebred princess. Plenty of willing women right in his own little unfancy corner of London. All he needed to do was put that distracting woman from his mind. And he would. Starting right now.

He opened the door a crack. After ascertaining the corridor was empty, Gideon slipped from the room. He was about to head back to the party when from the corner of his eye a slight movement at the opposite end of the corridor caught his attention. Turning, he narrowed his gaze at the window marking the end of the long hallway. And saw it again. A slight ruffling of the blue velvet curtain.

With a well-practiced silence he slipped his knife from his boot. Keeping his back against the wall, he cautiously made his way forward, every sense on alert. When he reached the end of the corridor, he quickly discovered the culprit.

The window, which he knew had previously been locked, was now slightly open.

Upon examining the lock, Gideon saw that it had not only been disengaged but very cleverly incapacitated in a way that would make it seem as if the lock were in place should anyone attempt to resecure the window.

He cautiously opened the glass panels. Chilly air blew through the opening. After making certain no one was lurking about in the flower beds below, he stuck out his head and looked down at the narrow walkway along the side of the house. No footprints were visible in the soft, moist dirt.

Leaning back inside, he inspected the sill and carpet below the window. No mud. Which meant that the window had been opened by someone in the house, and no one had used it to gain entry or escape. Yet. If he had to guess, he'd wager someone had opened the window with the intention of returning later and using it to enter the house. Of course, if the *Times* got wind of this, they'd no doubt speculate that a ghost wouldn't leave footprints.

After closing the window, he used his knife to hack off a small triangle of wood from the corner of the sill then wedged the piece between the frame and the sill to create a makeshift lock. He tested his handiwork to make sure it held. Merely a temporary fix, but one that would prevent an intruder from the outside entering until Lord Daltry replaced the lock.

Satisfied, Gideon crouched low and pushed aside the left velvet panel. Nothing save some small balls of dust. He moved aside the right panel, and grim satisfaction filled him at the glint of gold. Reaching out, he picked up the object and turned it over in his hand.

A snuffbox. Enamel depicting a hunting scene, trimmed with gold. Obviously expensive. And obviously not the property of a ghost. A closer examination revealed no initials. Dropped by the person who opened the window? Definitely possible. No dust marred the outside of the piece, so it hadn't been behind the curtain for long.

Gideon rose and slipped the small box into his pocket. First he'd recheck the inside of the house, then head outside to make certain no one lurked on the grounds, tasks that would require all his focus and attention, leaving no room for things he shouldn't be thinking about.

Thank God.

Chapter 3

Julianne and her friends no sooner stepped into the drawing room when a pair of masculine voices said in unison, "*There* you are."

They turned as a group. Matthew, Lord Langston, and Daniel, Lord Surbrooke, stood not three feet away. Their gazes were filled with what appeared to be a mixture of curiosity and suspicion.

"Yes, here we are," said Sarah in a bright voice. She slipped her hand through her husband's arm and offered him an equally bright smile. "And so are you. Where have you been?"

Matthew cocked a brow. "Where have *I* been?"

"Yes. I've been looking for you everywhere. I believe you promised me a dance."

"As I've been standing in this exact spot—which provides an excellent view of the room, by the way—for the past quarter hour and haven't seen a trace of you until now, I'm curious as to where 'everywhere' might be," Matthew said.

Sarah waved her hand in a vague gesture. "Oh, here and there."

"But obviously not *here*."

"Obviously, my darling husband, who simply *must* stop worrying about me lest I'm tempted to cosh you right here in Lady Daltry's drawing room." She shoved up her spectacles. "Don't forget; things are only found in the last place one looks for them."

"I suppose you've been looking for me 'everywhere' as well?" Daniel said to Carolyn. Amusement laced his voice, and Julianne's breath caught at the smoldering, intimate way he was looking at his wife.

"Naturally. Of course, it's nearly impossible to keep track of anyone in a crowd such as this."

Daniel and Matthew exchanged a glance. Then said in unison, "They're up to something."

Sarah raised her chin and gave an injured sniff. "I don't know what you're talking about."

"Oh?" Doubt was written all over Matthew's face. "The four of you nowhere to be found, then sneaking back into the party—"

"We weren't sneaking," Julianne felt compelled to interject.

"Very well," conceded Matthew. "Walking back into the party in a furtive manner." His gaze encompassed all four women, then he turned toward Daniel. "You know what's going on here, don't you?"

Daniel nodded. "Oh yes. They've clearly read another book."

A guilty flush heated Julianne's cheeks, one she prayed neither gentleman would notice, but her prayers clearly went unanswered when Daniel's gaze locked on hers for several seconds. "And by the looks of it, it's another tome steeped in scandal."

"Which could prove very interesting," Matthew said, his tone thoughtful, "especially given the adventures their last two reading selections initiated. What have you literary ladies been reading?"

"I don't know what you're talking about," Carolyn said, mimicking her sister's earlier words.

"You realize I have ways to make you reveal your secrets," Daniel said softly.

A becoming blush suffused Carolyn's cheeks, but she pressed her lips together and remained silent.

"How about you?" Matthew asked Sarah. "Anything to say?"

Sarah pushed her spectacles higher on her nose. "Would you care to dance?"

Matthew chuckled, then leaned closer to whisper something in Sarah's ear. Julianne didn't hear what he said, but whatever it was, it caused scarlet to stain Sarah's cheeks.

"What were you two gentlemen doing while we were... indisposed?" Emily asked in her usual impudent manner.

"Discussing the topic that is on everyone's lips," answered Daniel. "The recent murders and robberies. Several people were wondering if the thief might strike again tonight. If so, he might well be caught."

"Why is that?" Sarah asked.

"There is extra security on the premises," Daniel said. "In the form of a Bow Street Runner. Mr. Gideon Mayne."

Everything inside Julianne stilled for the space of several heartbeats, then thundered back to life. *He's here.* Her gaze immediately scanned the room.

"Hopefully then the scoundrel will be caught," Sarah said. Or at least that's what Julianne thought she said. How could she possibly concentrate when *he* was here?

She'd met the Bow Street Runner two months ago, purely by chance when he was investigating a series of murders plaguing Mayfair. He'd interviewed Julianne and her mother because they'd attended a soiree at one of the victims' homes.

Gideon Mayne had instantly captured her imagination the moment he walked into Julianne's home. Left her speechless. Breathless. He was unlike any gentleman she'd ever come in contact with in her very sheltered existence—not surprising as he wasn't by any stretch a gentleman. The tall, broad-shouldered, muscular Runner possessed a compelling air of competence and strength, mixed with a hint of danger and a large dose of adventure.

Everything about him fascinated her. His sheer size. His sun-browned skin. His thick, dark hair that required a trim. His large, capable, calloused hands. His deep voice that bore a slight trace of hoarseness. His mere presence shrank their spacious drawing room to the size of a hatbox and gave breath to every secret fantasy and romantic dream she'd kept buried in her heart for years. And he'd had the very same effect on her every time she'd seen him since.

He was the personification of the man that had previously lived only in Julianne's most secret, adventurous longings. And a man she hadn't believed existed outside her heated imaginings.

Until he'd stood before her. And nearly stopped her heart. Her heart, which had recognized him instantly. As a man of strength. Passion. Integrity. A man who was trustworthy and capable of getting things done. A man able to make decisions—ones that didn't involve what time he was scheduled to arrive at his club or which card to play at the gaming tables.

A man of adventure.

A man who, given their vast social differences, could never, ever be hers.

How many times had she told herself to forget about him? Hundreds? Thousands? Yet he remained firmly embedded in her mind, filling her with longings that, in spite of her best efforts to suppress them, grew stronger every day. Longings her reading of *The Ghost of Devonshire Manor* had only served to inflame—

Her thoughts cut off at the sight of Gideon. He stood near the French windows leading to the terrace, scanning the crowd with a sharp-eyed gaze. His granite-hewn features, uncompromising jaw, and a nose that had clearly been broken at some point were set with determination. A man looking for something and intent upon getting what he wanted. Just then, his dark gaze settled on her.

And suddenly everything and everyone populating the expanse of parquet floor between them seemed to vanish. Gone were the clinking glasses, the conversations, the laughter, and the lilt of music. The party guests seemed to waver before her eyes then melt away. Julianne heard nothing save the pounding of her heart. Saw no one except the vital, mysterious, rugged man across the room. Felt nothing save the same wild, raw, pulse-pounding exhilaration she experienced every time she laid eyes on him.

Their gazes held for the space of several heartbeats. Something flickered in his eyes. A flash of fire that even from across the room heated her, curled her toes inside her satin slippers. For a single wild instant she thought he meant to cross the room to her. But then he stiffened and only offered her a nearly imperceptible nod before shifting his attention beyond her.

She tried to pry her gaze from him, but she simply couldn't. He gave the room one last sweeping glance, one that avoided her, then he slipped out the French windows.

"Julianne?"

Emily's voice seemed to come from very far away. Julianne blinked twice then turned toward her friend. "Yes?"

"Are you certain you're all right?" There was no mistaking the concern in her friend's voice.

Dear God, she didn't know. All she knew was that everything in her strained in the direction of the terrace. She yearned to go beyond those glass-paned doors and follow the man she'd been unable to erase from her mind. Just to steal one more glimpse. Just to feel the heat of his gaze one more time.

She couldn't, of course.

Forcing her attention back to her friends, she said in what she hoped was a reassuring tone, "I'm fine. Truly. Just a bit tired." Her gaze flicked back to the French windows. *No one would have to know.*

She drew a bracing breath. Straightened her spine. Then firmly shoved aside the guilt and cowardice nudging her. "I see Mother sitting near the potted palms. I think I'll join her for a bit. Find out if she's cast her matchmaking eye on some young, handsome viscount."

"And I believe I hear the start of a waltz," said Matthew to Sarah. "Shall we?"

The couple moved toward the dance floor, followed by Carolyn and Daniel. They'd no sooner moved away than Emily's face puckered as if she'd bitten into a sour pickle. "Botheration, I just caught sight of Logan Jennsen," she whispered.

Julianne turned and noticed the wealthy American, whose fortune guaranteed him a place on every hostess's guest list, chatting with a group of gentlemen near the punch bowl. Emily made no secret of her dislike of Mr. Jennsen, although Julianne wasn't certain of the cause of her antipathy.

"There is just no escaping that uncouth man," Emily grumbled in an undertone. "He's like dust—everywhere and impossible to get rid of. If you'll excuse me..." She hastily melted into the crowd.

Julianne looked at the French windows again then at her mother by the potted palms. She firmly told herself again that she couldn't follow Gideon. If her mother even suspected Julianne would consider following a man onto the terrace, she'd fly into the boughs and never let her out of her sight.

Mother wouldn't have to know, her inner voice whispered. *No one would have to know.*

Everything in Julianne stilled. She'd always longed for an adventure, and this might well be her last chance. There certainly wouldn't be any adventures once she was bound for life to the chillingly forbidding duke or someone of his ilk.

A wave of resentment toward the strict restraints under which she lived, would always have to live, swamped her. A lifetime of breeding, of being raised in the confines of the aristocracy and under the weight of her mother's oppressive thumb enabled her to present the perfect picture of the perfect earl's daughter.

With few exceptions, every minute of every day was planned and scheduled, orchestrated and overseen by her mother's sharp gaze and, when he bothered to notice her at all, her father's forbidding countenance. It was only a matter of time—and she suspected a dismayingly short amount of time—before her life would be taken over and ruled by a husband. A man who no doubt wouldn't give any more thought to her wishes than her parents did.

A strangling emotion gripped Julianne, one she only allowed to escape her soul during the dark of night. That aching mixture of despair, anger, yearning, resentment, and longing. It grabbed her in a vise, nearly choking her with its intensity, threatening to break the facade she presented to the world.

Outwardly, she was the perfectly mannered, impeccably groomed, infinitely demure aristocratic earl's daughter. But inside...inside seethed all the emotions and wants and needs she ruthlessly repressed. Inside lived the daring, bold, adventurous young woman she longed to be. The woman who always knew the right thing to say. The woman who didn't struggle to overcome painful shyness. A woman who was admired for more than her looks, gowns, title, and family fortune. A woman who was wanted. And needed. And loved. Not merely an expensive piece of marriageable chattel to be sold to the wealthiest bidder.

A woman who was free to make her own choices.

Her gaze shifted back to the French windows, to the darkness beyond them. And once again the noise surrounding her dissolved, now replaced by the inexorable ticking of a clock. Of time slipping through her clenched hands.

Before she could stop herself, she headed across the room. Her mind screamed at her to halt, but her feet refused to obey. Her better judgment told her this was a mistake, but her heart refused to listen.

She stopped in front of the French windows. Her reflection in the glass panes showed a young woman whose eyes glittered with a combination of trepidation and excitement. A young woman whose lips were parted in deference to her rapid breaths.

A young woman on the verge of an adventure.

Pausing only to ascertain that her mother remained busily chatting, Julianne slipped through the doors and entered the shadows beyond. She darted away from the circle of light spilling onto the terrace from the drawing room and was immediately swallowed by thick darkness. Heart pounding, she swiftly descended the flagstone steps into the garden below. Once there, she pressed her back against the rough brick wall and fought to calm her shallow, uneven breathing.

Gloom surrounded her, enveloping her in what felt like a suffocating cloak. Her heart stuttered then beat in frantic thumps. After a moment her breathing and heart rate settled, and she forced herself to keep inhaling slowly, deeply, until her vision adjusted to the shadowy gloom.

Clouds obscured both the moon and stars, blanketing the sky in unrelieved black. A brisk, chilly breeze rustled the leaves, biting through the thin muslin of her gown, and the hint of rain hung heavy in the mist-filled air. But she barely noticed the discomfort as she breathed in the heady scent of night.

And freedom.

Peering through the dense dark, she noted with relief that she was alone. Clearly the chilly, moist weather had discouraged the guests from venturing outdoors. All the guests save one: Gideon Mayne.

But where was he?

Eyes and ears alert, she made her way slowly around the shadowy perimeter of the garden, forcing herself to recall that Gideon was close by. Even so, everything inside her urged her to return to the safety of the crowded drawing room, to leave this dark place where unknown evils lurked. Everything inside her except that inexorably ticking inner clock. And her heart, both of which compelled her to continue.

You're not alone, her heart whispered. Yes. Gideon was here. All she needed to do was find him.

When she reached the back of the garden, she paused. With her arms wrapped around herself in a feeble effort to ward off the chill, she looked around but saw no sign of him. Unless he'd hidden himself in the thick privet hedges, or skulked behind one of the enormous trees looming in front of her— she craned her neck to make certain he didn't—he'd either gone into the mews—a dark, dangerous place she wouldn't consider entering—or he'd returned to the house.

Which is precisely what she needed to do. Before she was discovered missing. Or caught the ague from the cold.

Botheration, here she'd finally screwed up her courage, taken some action, and it was all for naught. Her first adventure certainly hadn't turned out the way she'd hoped. Her better judgment told her it was for the best she hadn't found Gideon. God only knows what might have passed if she'd happened upon him here in the shrouded privacy of the garden.

An image of him drawing her into his arms, kissing her with those beautiful lips that in spite of his uncompromising mouth still managed to somehow look soft, flashed in her mind, rippling a heated tingle down her spine.

Swallowing her disappointment, she turned to make her way back to the house.

Suddenly a muscular arm wrapped around her waist with a viselike grip, jerking her backward, trapping her against a body that felt like a stone wall. Her breath whooshed from her lungs. Before she could pull in enough air to scream, she saw the silver glint of a knife. Then felt the cold press of the blade against her throat.

Chapter 4

"If you scream, it'll be the last sound you ever make."

The harsh warning whispered past Julianne's ear, and for several frantic heartbeats she froze, immobilized by terror, chilled to her core with fright. Then sheer panic set in, along with the desperate instinct to struggle, an urge she fought to suppress lest she end up with a slit throat.

Her assailant dragged her deeper into the shadows, behind one of the soaring elms. With a deft move, he turned her, pinning her between himself and the tree. He then captured both her hands in one of his, trapping her with strong, calloused fingers, and raised her arms above her head. Rough tree bark bit into her wrists and her back through her gown. The cold knife blade pressed against her throat. And the heat of him seared her from chest to knee.

Held motionless by the weight of his body and the fear pounding through her, she lifted her gaze to her attacker. And stared.

At Gideon Mayne. Whose stark, angular features appeared set in granite. His gaze raked her face, and recognition flashed in his eyes, followed by a flare of fire that stole what little breath fright hadn't robbed her of. Her relief that he'd recognized her was short-lived, however, when, rather than lowering his knife and releasing her, his forbidding countenance grew even more stern. Was it possible he didn't recognize her after all?

Julianne wet her dry lips then stretched her neck in an attempt to relieve the pressure of the knife. "Mr. Mayne... 'tis I...Julianne Bradley."

He remained silent for several seconds, his gaze boring into hers. Finally he spoke, muttering an obscenity that scorched a blush to her cheeks. She felt him turn the knife a bit, hopefully so that the sharp blade didn't gouge her skin, although he didn't lower the weapon. "So I see. What the bloody hell are you doing out here?"

His voice was a rough rasp that sent another tingle skittering down her spine. With a calm she was far from feeling, she managed to reply, "I'd be delighted to tell you as soon as you remove that knife from my throat."

Instead of instantly complying, he narrowed his eyes. "You're lucky I didn't slit your damn throat."

She raised her brows. "So it would seem. But unless you still intend to do so, I must ask you to remove your weapon."

Without taking his gaze from hers, he slowly lowered the knife, and she swallowed. He did not, however, release her hands or step back.

With her initial fright abated, she became acutely aware of him. His hard body resting against hers. The heat emanating from him. His large, calloused hand holding hers over her head. The fire simmering in his gaze. And suddenly she no longer felt in the least bit cold. Indeed, she felt as if she stood in a circle of flame.

She drew in an unsteady breath and caught his subtle scent. It was crisp and pleasing, and somehow...familiar? Unlike the usual gentlemen of her acquaintance, Gideon didn't smell like any fragrance from a bottle. He simply smelled clean, like fresh soap and warm skin, but with an added dash of dark, elusive danger and adventure. The scent intoxicated her, and she found herself pulling in another long, slow breath.

Her common sense coughed to life, demanding that she

order him to release her. To step back. But her lips refused to form the words.

"The knife's gone, so now you'll answer my question," he said brusquely. "What are you doing out here?"

"I..." *was looking for you. Hoping for a glimpse. Never daring to dream I'd feel you touching me.* "...felt the need for some fresh air."

His scowl deepened. "So you ventured outdoors *alone*?"

His tone clearly indicated how foolish he thought her, and an embarrassed flush sizzled up from her neck. Before she could think of a reply that wouldn't necessitate admitting she knew she wouldn't be alone, knew he was in the garden, he continued, "Where the bloody hell is your chaperone? Don't you know there's been a rash of crimes? That thieves and murderers and all manner of dangers lurk in the darkness? Of all the bloody stupid—"

"I wasn't alone." The truth rushed from her lips before she could stop it.

He went perfectly still, then his expression turned flat. "I see." He gave a quick glance around. "So where is the... *gentleman*?" He seemed to spit out the last word.

A frisson of anger worked its way through her heated awareness of him and the remnants of her fear and surprise. Clearly he thought her not only stupid but promiscuous as well. She hadn't ventured into the garden without careful consideration. As for being promiscuous, nothing could be farther from the truth—at least in deed. Surely her private thoughts and secret desires didn't count. Why, she'd never even been kissed!

She raised her chin and squarely met his gaze. "He's right in front of me. Although based on the way you grabbed me, nearly slit my throat, and continue to manhandle me, I'm not inclined to describe you as a gentleman at the moment."

His gaze roamed over her with bold thoroughness, lingering for several seconds on the skin above her bodice before rising to meet her eyes. A wave of heat swamped her. Had he detected the frantic beating of her heart—a staccato rhythm that was entirely his fault?

"No one has ever accused me of being a gentleman," he said with the hint of a sneer, making it clear that was quite all right with him.

"Do you normally treat women you meet in gardens in such a barbaric manner?"

"I wasn't aware we'd planned an assignation, Lady Julianne."

"You know as well as I that we hadn't."

"Well, then. As for my 'barbaric manner,' I don't trust anyone who's behind me. Something you'd do well to remember, since it's clearly your habit to skulk about in places you shouldn't be."

Annoyance—at herself for being caught in such a mortifying fashion and at him for catching her—stiffened her spine. "I assure you I wasn't skulking. I saw you leave the drawing room and...I wished to speak to you. I knew you could protect me from any dangers lurking in the dark."

"Indeed?" The single word was spoken in a silky whisper that breathed warm against her cheek. "And just who do you suppose is going to protect you from me?"

His question, the speculative intensity with which he was looking at her, as if assessing from which angle to best pounce upon her, stole her breath. She moistened her dry lips, observing how his sharp eyes noted—and seemed to darken at—the gesture. "Do I *need* protection from you, Mr. Mayne?"

Silence stretched between them. Did he feel this same taut tension as she? Could he hear her heart pounding? God knows she could. Hear it and feel it. Reverberating in her ears. Pounding at her throat. Pulsing between her thighs.

Finally he said, "Any woman foolish enough to venture outdoors alone, in the dark, requires protection. For your own sake, I hope you won't do so again." He then released her wrists and stepped back several paces.

Julianne instantly missed his heat. The feel of his strong fingers wrapped around her flesh. His large body trapping her against the tree. His subtle scent surrounding her.

Yet even as she missed his nearness, annoyance had her lifting her chin. "I assure you I wasn't being foolish. As I said, I knew you were out here and wished to speak to you."

One ebony brow hiked upward. "You could have spoken to me in the drawing room."

Under her mother's sharp-eyed scrutiny? Hardly. If Mother suspected for even an instant her fascination with Mr. Mayne, she'd see to it that Julianne never laid eyes on him again.

"The drawing room wouldn't do, as what I wish to discuss with you is of a...private nature."

His eyes glittered in the darkness. She could feel him assessing her. Feel his gaze roaming over her like a heated caress. One that obliterated the air's biting chill.

Setting one large hand against the tree trunk next to her head, he leaned forward slightly and said in a low, rough whisper, "Well, then, my lady, speak up. We have all the privacy you could possibly want right here."

Speak? Dear God, she could barely breathe. His proximity, the warmth emanating from him, his intoxicating scent all conspired to overwhelm her. Rob her of her wits. And even if she were capable of it, she didn't want to speak. She wanted to touch. To rest her fingertips against his rugged, clean-shaven jaw. To explore the texture of his skin. Then slip her fingers into his thick hair. To see if it felt as silky as it looked.

Then taste...to brush her lips against his. To discover if that firm, uncompromising mouth could be...compromised. To experience what she knew in her heart would be an incomparable kiss. Because surely a man like Gideon would know how to kiss a woman. And God help her, she so desperately wanted to be kissed. By him. This man who'd launched countless sensual fantasies.

And then she wanted to bury her face against the strong column of his neck and simply breathe him in. Absorb his heat and strength and delicious scent.

"Well, my lady?"

His warm breath touched her cheek, igniting her skin. Answer...she needed to answer him. Before he concluded she was a bird-witted mute. She searched her mind for something to say and grasped at the first thing that entered her brain.

"The ghost." The two words exploded from her mouth like twin pistol shots. "I...I wish to discuss the ghost with you."

She barely swallowed the horrified *ack* that rose in her throat. Dear God, what was she saying?

"What ghost?"

Botheration, now that she'd embarked upon this perfidious path, there was no turning back. "The one I understand you're trying to find."

"You mean the *murdering thief* I *will* find."

"Er, yes."

"What about him?"

Yes, Julianne, what about him? her inner voice taunted. "Well, I, um...believe he tried to rob my household."

Another horror-stricken *ack* vibrated in her throat. Good God almighty, her mouth had totally run amok. It was as if she had no control over her own words. Her lips parted, and lies spewed forth like steam from a boiling kettle.

His gaze narrowed. "When?"

I haven't the faintest idea. "Last night."

"What happened?"

I lay alone in my bed. And thought of you. "I...I was awakened by strange groaning sounds."

"Did anyone else in the household hear them?"

"Not that anyone said." That much at least was true.

"Did you report these noises to your father?"

"No." As he seemed more interested than suspicious, she warmed to her fabrication and improvised, "I'd assumed what I heard was the wind and actually didn't think of it again until..." *just now.* "Until I read the story about Mrs. Greeley this morning in the *Times.* I checked our valuables and found nothing missing."

He was silent for several seconds, tiny spaces of time during which she wondered if he could smell the stench of her lies rising from her skin like a noxious cloud.

"What made you decide that the sounds you heard weren't actually the wind?" he asked.

The question felt like a bottomless chasm yawning in front of her. One misstep on her part, and she'd fall into the depths of hell—and he'd realize she was lying faster than a horse could trot.

After considering for several seconds, she said, "Upon reflection, I realized that the sounds came from the direction of the corridor rather than outside."

"Did you enter the corridor to investigate?"

Good heavens, the man was full of questions. Not wishing him to picture her cowering beneath her covers like a molly-coddled milksop, she raised her chin and said, "Of course I investigated. I'm not a coward."

"I see," he said, his tone so dry it was clear he didn't believe her claim—which only served to irk her and make her want to prove him wrong. "Was anyone in the corridor?"

"No."

"What if there had been?" He leaned a bit closer, and she drew in a sharp breath. Dear God, he was so...large. Broad. Tall. Had the sun been out, his sheer size would have cast her in a shadow. "What if you'd happened upon the murdering ghost robber absconding with your jewels?" he whispered close to her ear.

Heat sizzled through her, and she had to swallow to find her voice. "I...I would have screamed. Coshed him with my candlestick. As I said, I'm not a coward."

"Brave words from a brave woman. What if he'd coshed you first?"

Unlikely, as I'd have swooned at the first sight of him. "Unlikely as I'd have...stabbed him first with my embroidery scissors." Yes. That's what a brave woman would have done.

"Oh? Like you did to me?"

"Naturally I don't carry my embroidery scissors to formal gatherings."

"But you carry them in your *nightclothes*?"

Blast. He had a point. Thinking quickly she fabricated, "Except for formal occasions, I always carry embroidery scissors. I leave them on my night table before retiring. When I heard the noises, I slipped them into my robe's pocket."

"How resourceful, although I feel it my duty to inform you that such a puny weapon, yielded by such a pu—petite woman, would prove little or no use against a man. Especially one who caught you unawares."

The silky timbre of his voice wasn't lost upon her, nor was his nearly calling her puny. Clearly the man was making sport of her. And clearly he didn't believe she was brave. *You aren't brave*, her annoyingly honest inner voice informed her.

Very well, she wasn't brave. At all. Never had been. Indeed, the bravest thing she'd ever done was follow him into this garden, and look how that had turned out. Obviously she was far from the adventurous, confident woman she longed to be. Her one chance for an adventure, and she'd mucked it up and made a total fool out of herself.

To her horror, her bottom lip trembled. She bit down on it, hard, and blinked back the tears threatening to flood her eyes. Yes, her first adventure had proven naught but a lie-filled calamity. He obviously thought her a foolish, senseless chit, and at the moment she felt like one. Anger—at herself for not listening to her common sense and for starting this crescendo of falsehoods—filtered through her with disheartening humiliation. It was time to abandon this disastrous outing and return to the party. Before she made an even bigger bird-wit of herself.

Before she could move, however, he continued, "Do you know what I think?"

That I'm a liar. And a fool. And you're correct. Some modicum of her shredded pride made her hike up her chin a notch. "No, but based on your tone, I'm certain you're going to tell me."

"I think you'd have swooned at the first sight of an intruder and would have lain on the floor until one of the maids happened by and saw you."

How annoying that he was most likely correct. But she wasn't about to confirm his suspicions. And what was one more lie at this point?

Stretching up to her full height, she said in her iciest tone, "You clearly don't know me as well as you believe, Mr. Mayne. However, if your scenario were correct—and I assure you it is not—then I can only surmise a doctor would have been summoned, and at this very moment I'd be nestled in my bed, rather than here, listening to you laugh at me."

"Assuming the intruder hadn't killed you."

"Yes. Now, if you'll excuse me..."

She made to push away from the tree but found herself caged in when he slapped his other hand on the massive trunk next to her head. "So the rose has thorns," he murmured. "Interesting." Then he shook his head. "I wasn't laughing."

"You most certainly were."

"Then I can only deduce you don't know what laughter sounds like."

"I most certainly do, although I have to wonder if you do. Has anyone ever told you you're very dour?"

Although his expression didn't change, she sensed his surprise at her boldness. Indeed, she surprised herself. But since he already held her in such low regard, she at least could regain some respect for herself by standing up to him.

"Dour? No one who's lived to repeat the sentiment. Has anyone ever told you you're a spoiled princess?"

His question instantly deflated her, draining her momentary bravado. Of course he would think so. He'd only see what everyone else saw. He wouldn't see the daring adventuress lurking beneath the surface who desperately longed to break free from the constraints of her position in society and soar from her gilded prison. He wouldn't perceive the urgency that had driven her to enter the garden or the courage it had taken for her to walk alone into the darkness.

Feeling utterly defeated and suddenly exhausted, she said quietly, "Yes, I've been told I'm a spoiled princess. Actually, it is but one of several similar endearments I'm subjected to every day." Again she made to push from the tree, and again he stopped her, this time by shifting closer. Now no more than six inches separated them.

She leaned her head against the rough bark and looked up at him. She couldn't decipher his expression, but it was clear he wasn't happy.

"You shouldn't have come out here." His voice resembled a growl.

"Yes. That is obvious."

His gaze bored into hers with a heated intensity that

burned her from the inside out. Dear God, the way he was looking at her... as if he were a starving beast and she was a tasty morsel he'd happened upon. And the way he made her feel... as if she were gasping for air and he was the last bit of oxygen on earth.

Holding her breath, she stood in an aching jumble of desperate want, need, apprehension, and anticipation, unable to move, waiting to see what he'd do next.

Just when she thought his hot scrutiny would incinerate her where she stood, his gaze shifted to study each of her features. When he came to her mouth, he lingered for several breath-stealing seconds before slowly raising his gaze back to hers.

"You should return to the house."

Julianne had to swallow twice to locate her voice. "Yes," she whispered.

She should return. She knew it. But apparently her feet did not, as they remained firmly rooted in place. Perhaps she might possibly have convinced her feet to move, but then he lifted one hand from the tree trunk and touched a single fingertip to her cheek. And the only thing fleeing the garden were any thoughts of her leaving.

His finger followed the same path his gaze had just traveled, painting featherlight strokes over her face. The tip of his finger was hard. Blunt. Calloused. Yet infinitely gentle.

She watched him as he touched her, noting the avid way his gaze followed his finger. The muscle that ticked in his square jaw. With his finger lightly circling the outer curve of her ear—a bit of skin she'd had no idea was so sensitive—he leaned in. Brushed his cheek against her hair.

In an agony of anticipation, Julianne remained perfectly still, terrified that if she so much as breathed, he would stop. End this wondrous adventure. She heard him take a slow, deep breath, one he released in a ragged stream of warmth against her temple.

"Delicious," he muttered. "Bloody hell, I knew you'd smell delicious." The last words ended on a low groan. "What is that scent?"

How could he possibly expect her to answer questions?

With an effort, she managed to say, "Vanilla. It...it's my favorite flavor, so I commissioned a perfumer on Bond Street to make it into a fragrance for me."

He pulled in another deep breath. "You smell like the bakeshop: warm, sweet, scrumptious." His lips brushed over her hair, and he groaned again. "You really need to go back, Julianne. Now."

The intimacy of that gravelly voice saying her name, without the formal use of her title, touched something deep inside her. She could no more have left the garden at that moment than she could have held back the tide. She'd longed for a moment like this, and nothing her common sense or conscience screamed at her could deter her.

"No," she whispered. "Not now."

"Don't say you weren't warned."

Perhaps she'd been warned, but she certainly wasn't prepared. For nothing could have readied her for the onslaught of his mouth capturing hers. With a hunger beyond anything even her darkest imaginings could have conjured. His tongue swept along the seam of her lips, demanding entrance, and with a gasp of shocking pleasure, she complied.

The delicious friction of his tongue tangling with hers rendered her light-headed. She'd read of such intimacies, most recently in *The Ghost of Devonshire Manor*, had imagined such a kiss, but the reality...the reality yanked her from her moorings, setting her adrift on a stormy sea of sensation, battering her from all sides.

Heart pounding, knees shaking, she opened her mouth wider, desperate to taste more of him. She'd known he looked like adventure, smelled like adventure. Now she knew he tasted like it as well. Like a foreign land she'd always longed to explore but never thought she'd have the chance to visit.

His hands came forward to cradle her face, holding her immobile while he kissed her senseless. Breathless. She mimicked his every gesture, gliding her tongue over his, reaching up to touch her fingertips to his face—only to lament the fact that she couldn't feel his skin through her gloves. Any worry that her technique was lacking dissipated when he growled low in his throat and pressed his lower body into hers.

Heat whooshed through her at the feel of his hardness pinning her to the tree. Her entire body felt as if it had been awakened from a deep, cold sleep, and for the first time in her life she knew the overwhelming power of desire. She began to tremble, shake with this heady, incredible assault on her senses.

Engulfed in a haze of lust, Gideon deepened their kiss, his mind empty except for the single word pounding through him with every rapid thump of his heart. *Julianne.* Bloody hell, she tasted so damn good. Felt so damn good. Smelled so damn good—like a sweet treat he wanted to gobble up in two big bites.

A shaking sensation worked its way through the fog of want enshrouding him, clouding his better judgment, and he realized it was her. A small corner of his mind had noted with grim satisfaction her initial gentle shivers, but somewhere during their kiss they'd clearly grown into full-fledged shakes. He could feel them vibrating against his thighs, where his body pinned her against the tree. Beneath his hands, which held her head immobile. Against his lips that roughly ravaged hers.

With a groan of self-disgust, he broke off their kiss and stepped back. The instant his hands fell from her face, she slid several inches down the elm's trunk. Muttering an oath, he clasped her shoulders lest she slither all the way to the ground.

Bloody damn hell, now he'd done it. One touch, and he'd completely forgotten the sort of gently bred hothouse flower she was. Scared her to the point she couldn't stand up. What the devil had he been thinking?

Problem was, he *hadn't* been thinking—a constant difficulty around this woman. Bad enough he'd been such an idiot as to kiss her at all. But then he'd kissed her like a pillaging barbarian. No finesse, no gentleness—just taking. It had gone exactly the way he'd known it would if he were ever stupid enough to touch her: ten seconds of tenderness touching her face, then a total loss of the control he prided himself upon. And now he'd clearly frightened the bones from her knees.

He peered at her through the darkness, hoping to hell she wasn't going to fall victim to the vapors, and another groan rose in his throat. Rapid breaths puffed from between her kiss-swollen, moist, parted lips. She just looked so damn... *kissable*.

Yet her eyes remained closed, and tremors still racked her body, arousing his conscience—an inner voice he'd thought long dead—which lashed him with recriminations. For not sending her back to the party the second he found her. For that instant of weakness, of giving in to his overwhelming desire to touch her, taste her. For allowing himself to be drawn into an impossible situation.

That kiss, the feel of her softness pressed against him, her sweet scent surrounding him, her delicious taste flooding his senses, had all but brought him to his knees. That kiss had done nothing to appease his hunger for her. No, instead, his previous cravings paled to nothingness compared to the ravenous appetite for her now scraping at him.

What a bloody idiot he was.

Her eyes blinked slowly open, and she gazed at him with a glazed expression. She was still shaking, but at least she hadn't swooned. Yet. She slowly moistened her lips, a leisurely lick that tightened his fingers on her shoulders and swelled him against his breeches—something he wouldn't have thought possible, as he was already harder than a brick.

"Why... why did you..."

Ruthlessly pushing away the desire clawing at him, he braced himself for a barrage of outraged recriminations—which, in spite of his warning to her, he deserved for the way he'd all but mauled her.

"Stop?"

He blinked. "Why did I *stop*?"

Again she licked her lips—a fascinating gesture he longed to study at length—and gave a limp-necked nod. "Why did you stop?"

"You were shaking. I frightened you."

"I was shaking... but you didn't frighten me."

Realization dawned with another swift stab of lust. She hadn't trembled with fear but with desire. Before he could fully wrap his mind around the idea, she reached out and grabbed his lapels. Yanked hard, but certainly not hard enough to move him had he chosen to remain in place.

But the knife-sharp desire to feel her again cleaved through his common sense, and he stepped forward. His body brushed against hers, and if he'd been capable of levity, he would have laughed at how profoundly that whisper of a touch affected him.

She tilted her head back and looked at him with those beautiful eyes, glowing with what he now recognized as arousal, and whispered, "More." The word was half tremulous request, half impatient demand.

"Given my penchant for summing things up in one word, I must admit that *more* is an excellent choice."

Indeed, perhaps there was a living, breathing man capable of refusing her, but Gideon sure as hell wasn't that man. And even if desire wasn't compelling him to this madness, his own pride would have done so. He simply *had* to kiss her again if for no other reason than to redeem himself—to prove to himself that he could do so without losing control. And to teach this temptress a lesson: that dangers lurked in the dark. That in the future she needed to remain within the safe confines of the drawing room.

Pulling her away from the tree, he turned them so that his back rested against the rough trunk. Spreading his legs, he drew her into the V of his thighs, a place where she fit so perfectly and felt so damn good it seemed as if she were molded precisely for him. He ran his hands down her back, pressing her closer, then lowered his head.

He brushed his lips over hers, once, twice, forcing himself to gently explore where last time he'd simply plundered. He circled her full, parted lips, drinking in her breathy sighs. Shoving back the urgency nipping at him, he slowly sank deeper into the kiss, his tongue savoring the sweet taste of her. Her arms slid over his shoulders, and she seemed to simply dissolve into him, wax melting from the inferno burning inside him.

She squirmed, and his erection jerked, effortlessly breaching the control he'd only seconds ago thought fully reinforced. His hips thrust slowly forward, a movement he was helpless to stop—a fact that irritated and alarmed him. Bloody hell, what was happening to him? What was this woman doing to him?

Grasping her shoulders, he set her firmly away from him, then released her as if she'd turned into a pillar fire. Which it seemed she was—and he was kindling.

"Enough," he said in a rough voice he didn't recognize. She swayed a bit on her feet, and he moved several more steps away lest he be tempted to hold her again—like a spider falling into a deadly web. Damn distracting woman. He narrowed his eyes at her. "I don't know what game you're playing, princess, but I assure you it's one you don't want to play with me."

She stared at him for several seconds, and he could see her gathering herself. Wrapping her arms around her midsection, she lifted her chin to a regal angle. If he'd allowed it to, the unmistakable hurt in her eyes might have taken the edge off his annoyance. But it was far wiser for him to concentrate on that annoyance. At her, for coming out here and tempting him with her incomparable beauty and sweet scent and judgment-stealing kisses. And at himself for allowing her to do so.

"I wasn't playing a game," she said quietly, then added in a flat voice, "And I'm not a princess."

Without another word, she turned and walked away. Keeping to the shadows, he silently followed her, his inconvenient conscience insisting he make certain she arrived at the house safely. She walked with short, rapid steps and kept looking around, clearly nervous. He was sorely tempted to make his presence known but forced himself not to. Not while they were still alone in the dark.

When she reached the terrace stairs, he judged it safe for him to speak. "I'll be calling on your father tomorrow to investigate your claims of the ghost," he said softly from the shadows. "I suggest you apprise him of the story you told me before I arrive."

Her back stiffened, and for several seconds she remained still. Then, without a word or a backward glance, she hurried up the flagstone steps and entered the drawing room.

Chapter 5

"'Oh, what a tangled web we weave when first we practice to deceive,'" Julianne muttered to herself as she paced in her bedchamber the next morning. Streaks of pale pink filtered through the window, shades of the predawn's dark mauve surrendering to a new day. Yet the hint of illumination did nothing to lighten her troubled mood.

"Clearly Sir Walter Scott was far more astute than I when he penned those wise words."

Indeed. If she'd devoted her time to rereading his *Marmion*, rather than scandal-laden tomes such as *The Ghost of Devonshire Manor*, she wouldn't be in such a fix.

Indeed, if she hadn't read *The Ghost of Devonshire Manor*, her thoughts wouldn't be filled with sensual ghosts who ignited fantasies that drove her from parties into the darkness to seek out a fascinating Bow Street Runner who'd...

Kissed her.

The memory slammed into her, halting her nervous footsteps. Dear God, how he'd kissed her. Kissed her until she'd forgotten the chilled air. The impropriety of her actions. How to tell the truth.

Everything except him.

Even the cold slap of humiliation that followed would never cool the heat of that kiss. Never erase the wondrous discovery of Gideon's taste. His scent and heat surrounding her like a warm, male blanket. The intimate press of his hard body against hers. Indeed, she should be grateful for the humiliation she'd felt afterward, as it was the only thing that kept her from clinging to him like an overzealous vine and begging him to never stop. From imploring him to touch her. Everywhere. From giving in to her own overwhelming desire to touch him. Everywhere.

Although she hadn't embarrassed herself quite that much, she'd still managed to immerse herself in an untenable situation. She'd spent a restless night tossing, turning, pacing, trying to figure out a way to avert the disaster of epic proportions looming on the horizon. But like a spider trapped in a poisonous web of its own making, every idea just tied another knot in her tangle of deception. Every idea save one. The only way to extricate herself was to tell Gideon the truth.

She'd have to intercept him before he spoke to her father and admit she'd lied. For the only other option was to lie to Father, to tell him the story she'd told Gideon. She cringed at the mere thought. She knew her father well, knew precisely what his reaction would be. Without proof, he'd simply coldly dismiss her claims, telling her as he so often did that she was nothing but a silly, ridiculous girl who knew nothing and should concentrate on doing the one thing she was good at: sitting on a settee and looking pretty.

Indeed, if her father spoke to Gideon, he'd make that opinion known. God knows Gideon already held her in little enough esteem. To have her own father confirm her general uselessness to the one man she wished regarded her highly was a humiliation she wasn't certain she could bear.

Of course, the prospect of telling Gideon the truth—that she'd followed him into the garden with the hopes of catching a glimpse of him, of talking to him—about anything—was mortifying enough to cramp her stomach. He'd think her an absolute idiot and would no doubt never wish to speak to her again. And she couldn't blame him. But at least she'd be an honest absolute idiot. And since nothing could ever come of their acquaintance, it was for the best. She'd always have the memory of their unforgettable kiss. The most wondrous adventure she'd ever had.

Her inner voice coughed to life. *It was the only adventure you've ever had.*

She pursed her lips. Fine. It was her *only* adventure. But what an adventure it had been. And maybe, perhaps, Gideon *wouldn't* hate her after she told him the truth. Perhaps he'd be flattered and admire her honesty and they could be—

She cut off the thought with a violent shake of her head. Could be what? Friends? Hardly. Not only would her parents forbid such an association with a man they'd view as nothing more than an ill-bred, common nobody, but why would Gideon want to be friends with a woman he believed to be nothing more than a foolish, spoiled princess?

Nor could they ever be anything else. Certainly not acquaintances who met in dark gardens for stolen kisses. She was fortunate no one had come upon them. Mother had noted her absence from the party and had scolded Julianne, even after she'd offered the excuse that she'd felt unwell and had merely found a quiet alcove to rest for several minutes. No, to find herself alone again with Gideon would prove too much of a temptation. It was one thing to want him in the solitary privacy of her own thoughts, where they were not only friends but lovers. It was quite another to try to control her desires when she was with him. Close enough to touch. Especially now that she knew how he tasted. How he felt. How he kissed.

Drawing a resolute breath, she exited her bedchamber. She'd force down some breakfast then position herself in the morning room window seat where she'd see Gideon arrive at the house. She'd tell him the truth and be done with her deceit. And carry the memory of their heated kiss in her heart.

When Julianne approached the dining room, her steps slowed, and she frowned at the muffled sound of her parents' voices coming from within. Botheration. Mother rarely awoke this early, and Father usually took a tray in his private study on those occasions when Mother did come to breakfast early. It was unusual for them to eat together in the morning—a fact that piqued her curiosity, especially after she heard her father say her name.

Angling herself to remain out of sight, she approached the oak door, which stood slightly ajar.

"—have appointments today with Beechmore, Penniwick, Haverly, and Walston," came her father's gruff voice.

"What about Eastling?" Mother asked.

"I spoke to him last night. He's scheduled to arrive directly between the others."

"Excellent. Good for them all to be aware of the competition. But of course you're favoring Eastling."

Julianne held her breath, waiting for her father's reply. When it came, her stomach clenched.

"Naturally," Father said. "The duke's holdings and influence are far more vast than the others'. If we can reach an agreement, the marriage could take place very quickly."

"Not for at least several months. There's a wedding to plan, the banns to post—"

"Eastling made mention of a special license. Said he'd have neither the time nor desire for a fancy affair before returning to Cornwall—with a bride—in two weeks' time. I'll know more after our meeting today, but you'd best prepare yourself to do whatever it is women do in such circumstances—arranging for a wedding dress, et cetera. And do it quickly."

The clink of silverware against china, followed by the scraping of a chair against the floor jerked Julianne from the stunned state into which she'd fallen and spurred her to action. She sprinted across the corridor and had just secreted herself in the small alcove there, when her father emerged from the dining room. Shrinking into the shadows, she willed herself to be invisible. He strode past. Seconds later she heard a door close firmly, indicating he'd entered his private study, as was his habit after breakfast.

For the space of several erratic heartbeats, Julianne remained frozen in place, her ears ringing like a death knell with the echo of her father's words. She pressed her palms against her cramping midsection, but the pressure did nothing to calm her inner tumult.

Dear God, this was worse than she'd thought. If Father's plans fell into place, she'd find herself married to the duke and shipped off to the wilds of Cornwall, all within a fortnight.

A silent scream reverberated through her, shaking her insides until they roiled in protest. Surely she shouldn't be so distraught, suffer such a violent reaction, to news that was hardly shocking; she'd always known she would marry, and in accordance with her father's wishes. Known full well the time was approaching for a husband to soon be chosen.

Yes, but she hadn't known soon would be quite so *soon*. Or that she'd find her prospective groom so unappealing. Or that she'd be forced to live in Cornwall, so far away from her beloved friends and everything she'd ever known.

A calm, inner voice of reasoning tried to insert itself into the panic threatening to overtake her. What difference did it make if her wedding took place in two weeks or two months? As for His Grace, given his wealth and position, he was one of the most eligible bachelors in the kingdom. And although he was past the first bloom of youth, he was far less decrepit than most men of his exalted rank. As for his dour, frosty demeanor, perhaps a young wife could coax him into better humor. She'd be a duchess. The toast of the ton. Mistress of a magnificent estate. She should be ecstatic.

Yet the thought of pledging her life to the duke, of being a wife to him...in word and deed...she squeezed her eyes shut and pressed her hands tighter against her protesting stomach. The thought of him touching her, kissing her, of sharing intimacies with him...a shudder ran through her. When he'd held her during their waltz last night, she hadn't experienced the slightest spark of desire—a fact that was made even more painfully obvious after her passionate interlude with Gideon.

Still, the thought of marrying any of the other prospective suitors scheduled to call today left her equally bereft and empty. None of them were the sort of man she longed for, not only because she didn't find any of them attractive, but mostly because none of them cared a jot about her. Only her money. That and the fact that she looked decorative sitting on a settee.

She could see her life as the Duchess of Eastling stretched before her... years and years of a lonely, passionless existence with a cold, indifferent husband. No adventures, no jolts, no excitement... just day after lonely day.

An image of Gideon rose in her mind, and she had to press her lips together to quell the cry of longing that rose in her throat. A litany of *if onlys* raced through her mind. If only Gideon were a nobleman. If only she weren't an earl's daughter. If only she were free to follow her heart. If only she were brave enough to take what she wanted, to have the sort of adventure she craved. She wasn't foolish enough to believe Gideon cared for her, but neither was he immune to her, at least physically. And certainly she was attracted to him. Painfully so. In a way she'd never been to any other man. And she'd never describe him as boring. He wasn't tainted with the jaded ennui of the gentleman of the ton. And while he wasn't a nobleman, she knew, in her heart, that he was a noble man.

She forced her eyes open and pulled in several slow, calming breaths. Her future would be decided by the end of the day or very soon thereafter, and the Duke of Eastling loomed on her horizon like a gloomy, frosty, dark cloud. Time was short, urging her, compelling her, to do... something. Take some action. Grab what little happiness she could before she was shackled by unbreakable vows and an existence far away.

But how? What could she do? A humorless laugh escaped her. If only she had a ghostly lover like Maxwell from *The Ghost of Devonshire Manor* to assist her. He'd helped Lady Elaine in numerous ways, both in and out of the bedchamber—

She stilled, struck immobile by the idea that sprang to life in her mind. She shook her head, trying to jar the thought loose, but it refused to budge. Rather, it took root and grew at an alarming rate. She mulled it over for several minutes, frowning even as a sense of purpose and excitement snaked through her. The plan was so outrageous she doubted even

Emily would dare it. It would require more courage than Julianne had ever exhibited in her entire life, for she risked a great deal. Indeed, she risked everything.

But if I don't, I'll have...nothing. No memories to hold dear in the long, lonely years ahead. None save those she'd made last night with Gideon. And those wouldn't be enough. She needed more. She wanted...nay, she *craved* more.

For years she'd envied Emily's daring. Sarah's cleverness. Carolyn's calm determination. Now was her chance. Her last chance. Her *only* chance. With only a fortnight of freedom left, she couldn't waste a single day.

Her better judgment and conscience shouted warnings, but she shoved them aside with a ruthless force she hadn't previously known she possessed. After all, what were a few more lies at this point?

After running her plan through her mind once again to make certain all the pieces were in place, she drew a resolute breath and stepped from the alcove. And headed toward her father's study.

Chapter 6

Gideon sat in an obscure corner of Lord Gatesbourne's foyer and seriously contemplated kicking the elegant arse of the next man who walked through the oak double doors. Yes, kicking him—perhaps tossing in a punch or two for good measure— then flinging him on his bruised posterior into the privet hedges. Headfirst. He'd been waiting on this damned uncomfortable mahogany bench that was probably worth more than all his own furniture combined for over an hour. If he had any sense, he'd get up and leave rather than suffering the humiliation of—

Of what? his inner voice jeered. *Waiting on a titled gentleman's schedule?*

Hardly. He'd been doing that for years. Any man foolish enough to work among the rich knew the world revolved around their agenda.

Yet what had his every muscle tensed and his entire body on edge wasn't the lowly bench he'd been relegated to, leaving him with nothing to occupy his time save watching haughty gentlemen come and go, being escorted down the long corridor by the earl's perfectly proper butler, Winslow. No, it was the parade of nose-in-the-air aristocrats themselves that had him ready to commit mayhem. Because he knew exactly why they were here. Every one of the bastards was vying for Julianne's hand.

Lords Haverly and Beechmore had come and gone, as had Lords Penniwick and Walston, although none of them were granted the amount of time bestowed on the Duke of Eastling.

None of them had spared Gideon so much as a glance.

While watching His Grace accept his walking stick and top hat from Winslow, Gideon had noted the shadows beneath the duke's frigid pale blue eyes. The slightly gray cast to his complexion. The man didn't look well rested. Of course, one didn't get much sleep when one was busy lifting the skirts of the fine ladies of the ton.

Just then another man entered the foyer, and Gideon inwardly frowned as but yet another flash of jealousy burned through him—this one more intense than the others. What the bloody hell was Logan Jennsen doing here? Other than gobs of money, what made the American more suitable for Julianne than Gideon himself? Jennsen held no title, nor did blue blood run through his veins.

Gideon had first met Jennsen when he'd interviewed the American, along with dozens of others, in relation to the same murder investigation two months ago during which he'd first met Julianne. He'd instantly known that Jennsen had secrets. The sort of secrets a man didn't share. With anyone. Easy for Gideon to recognize that look in Jennsen's eyes—the same way he recognized it in his own, every time he looked in the mirror. Yet it seemed gobs of money—something Gideon certainly didn't have—could buy an audience with Julianne's father. Bloody hell.

"His lordship will see you now," the dour-faced butler said to the wealthy American.

"Thank you, Winslow," Jennsen replied.

Tucked away on his bench, Gideon watched Winslow lead Jennsen down the corridor. The butler returned to his post a moment later, not offering Gideon anything more than a frown—but one only tossed in his general direction. Normally

Gideon would have been mildly amused by this obvious display of someone who worked for the haughty upper echelons behaving equally as haughty as his employer when faced with someone not of the peerage or great wealth. But not today. Not when he had to force himself to remain seated rather than stalk down the corridor, grab Jennsen by his fancy cravat, and demand to know his intentions toward Julianne.

Bloody hell, he felt as if steam were about to erupt from his pores. Had he thought that merely tossing these bastards on their arses was enough? Ha! What he needed was a sword. With a very sharp point. To hasten their retreat. Toward the Thames. Perhaps a dip in the cold water would cool their ardor. *In that case, you'd best jump in with them*, his inner voice murmured.

Damn bloody pesky inner voice.

But at least it had kept him, for several seconds, from thinking about her.

Julianne.

Her name wound through his mind, coiling around his brain. Indeed, he'd thought of nothing else but her all night. All morning. Every minute until he'd left his Bow Street office, during the long walk to Grosvenor Square—one he'd hoped would clear his head but had not. Her scent, her taste, the feel of her in his arms were tattooed upon his senses, etched so deeply he despaired of ever exorcising them. Bloody hell, how long would it take before he forgot that kiss?

Never, his inner voice whispered. *You'll never forget it.*

Stupid inner voice. He *would* forget it. He *had* to forget it. He knew damn well there was no point in hungering for things he couldn't have. And Lady Julianne was most definitely one of those things.

Still, his heart had beat ridiculously and annoyingly fast as he'd approached the mansion. Would she be at home? Would he see her?

He hadn't, and he firmly told himself he was glad. Yet that hadn't stopped him from listening for her voice, her footsteps, hoping for a glimpse of her every second he'd sat on this damned uncomfortable bench. Had Julianne visited with the gentlemen callers? Gideon clasped his hands between his spread knees, and with his forearms resting on his thighs, he leaned forward and stared at the glossy black-and-white marble tiled floor, as if it held the answer. In his mind's eye he imagined her, perched gracefully on some priceless antique settee, dazzling each man with her beauty. He visualized each man ogling her, looking into her extraordinary eyes, wanting her, touching her. His fingers tightened, and his jaw clenched. Bloody hell, he felt like a volcano on the verge of eruption.

Those extraordinary eyes...did she have any idea how expressive they were? The instant the thought filtered through his mind, sanity returned. Of course she knew. Women always knew that sort of thing and used their wiles to their advantage. Yet something told him she was different, *screamed* she was, especially after last night. Her eyes reflected a sadness, a vulnerability that in spite of his best efforts to ignore, reached inside him. There was nothing calculated in her demeanor, and God knows he'd known women whose every word, every gesture struck him as a devious move in some stealthy chess game. But not Julianne. No, she had an innocence about her that fascinated him. And scared him—because that fascination ran so very deep.

The sound of footfalls broke through his reverie, and he looked up to see Logan Jennsen stride into the foyer. To Gideon's surprise, rather than ignore him as had all the previous callers, the American made his way to the uncomfortable bench.

Gideon rose and accepted the hand Jennsen extended. "Mayne," Jennsen said, his gaze sharp but unreadable. "What brings you here? Another investigation? The murdering ghost robber perhaps?"

"As a matter of fact, yes. And you? Are you another suitor?" Gideon inwardly slapped himself. Damn it, he hadn't meant to ask, and certainly not so abruptly. Or in a tone that resembled a growl.

But Jennsen merely laughed. "God, no. I've no desire to take one of these overly delicate society maidens to wife."

An annoying, ridiculous, and completely inappropriate

wave of relief washed over Gideon. Jennsen's gaze grew speculative, and he continued, "Although, now that you mention it, I must admit there is something about Lady Julianne. She is undoubtedly the most beautiful woman I've ever seen. And there's a sweetness about her yet also a determination."

Gideon's gut tightened in an unpleasant way that resembled a cramp. "Actually, I didn't mention it."

"I understand the Duke of Eastling's in the running. Along with a number of others." Jennsen lifted a brow. "Are you one of them?"

For several seconds, Gideon could only stare, nonplussed. "Hardly. A Runner could never aspire to an earl's daughter."

Jennsen shook his head. "Damn ridiculous, all these society rules and titles you Brits encumber yourselves with. Can't imagine being a slave to a pile-of-bricks estate and some foolish name." He flashed a grin. "Part of my American charm."

Gideon didn't bother to point out that Jennsen's "American charm" rendered him the only man to come through the foyer who'd deemed to talk to him. Although he sensed Jennsen had his own reasons for doing so. He doubted the man ever did anything without a good reason. But what could that reason be?

"There's no pile of bricks *I'm* enslaved to," Gideon said, "but a man's name is important—as is his honor—whether there's a title attached to it or not."

Something flickered in Jennsen's eyes, gone so fast Gideon wondered if he'd imagined it. "Agreed," Jennsen said. "So, how goes your investigation? Have you captured the culprit?"

"No. But it's only a matter of time. Criminals always give themselves away eventually. They make mistakes."

Was that another flicker in Jennsen's eyes? "And you find those mistakes."

It wasn't a question, and Gideon wished he knew what the man was thinking. "Yes. And I don't give up until I do."

Jennsen nodded slowly then said, "That's precisely the sort of skill and dogged attitude I'm looking for. I've a project in the works that requires some investigation. From what I've seen and heard, you're one of the best. Certainly you did an outstanding job with the murder investigation two months ago."

Gideon inclined his head in thanks. "What do you need?"

Jennsen shot a quick look at Winslow, who was occupied giving instructions to a footman. "Someone to make discreet inquiries," Jennsen said in an undertone. "A certain individual has approached me with a business venture. I've been unable to find any unsavory information on this man, and I'm certain there must be something."

"Why do you think that?"

"Because *everyone* has something...if you know what I mean."

Gideon nodded slowly. "Yes, I do."

"Would you be interested in looking into it for me? I'd make it worth your while."

"I'm a bit tied up right now with this recent rash of crimes—"

"I'm not in a rush." A smile that didn't reach his eyes curved Jennsen's lips. "I'm a patient man."

"In that case, yes. Who is this man you want information on?"

"Lord Beechmore. Before I seriously consider his proposition, I need to know more about him. *Everything* about him. Not surface information—I already have that."

"I understand. I'll look into it and let you know what I find."

"Excellent. I look forward to hearing from you."

"Jennsen, before you go..." Gideon slipped the snuffbox he'd found the previous evening from his pocket and held it out, carefully gauging Jennsen's reaction. "Would this be yours?"

Jennsen shook his head. "No. I don't partake of snuff. Nasty habit, if you ask me." Speculation glittered in his eyes. "Since you've asked me about it, the box clearly isn't yours. Where did you get it?"

Gideon debated whether to tell him, then decided it couldn't do any harm. "I found it beneath an open window during Daltry's party."

"May I?" Jennsen asked, holding out his hand. Gideon handed him the box, and Jennsen studied it more closely. "I've seen this piece. And recently. But at the moment I can't recall where or who had it." He handed it back to Gideon. "If I remember, I'll let you know."

After Jennsen departed, Winslow announced, "His lordship will see you now."

Gideon followed him down the corridor, his footfalls swallowed by the blue and gold patterned runner. Gilt-edged mirrors and fine paintings—some landscapes, some dour gentlemen who were no doubt Gatesbourne ancestors—lined the paneled walls. Fresh-cut flowers arranged in crystal vases dotted gleaming tables, their floral scent mixing with a hint of beeswax. Every inch oozed wealth and privilege.

Winslow announced him at the threshold to what he surmised was the earl's private study. Sunlight poured in from the bank of windows lining the far wall, highlighting the masculine mahogany and leather furniture, massive fireplace, and floor-to-ceiling bookcases. The Earl of Gatesbourne sat behind a highly polished desk, watching Gideon approach with all the enthusiasm one might bestow upon a large insect.

"What brings you here, Mayne?"

The curt greeting didn't surprise Gideon. People were rarely excited to receive a call from a Runner. With a negligent wave of his hand, the earl indicated the leather chair opposite the desk. After seating himself, Gideon told the earl the purpose of his visit.

When he finished, the scowling earl remained silent for several long seconds. Finally he said, "Quite frankly, I've never heard of anything so ridiculous as this nonsense about ghosts." He regarded Gideon through narrowed eyes that held not the slightest trace of warmth. Indeed, if Gideon had to describe the earl in a single word he'd choose *frigid*. Everything in his demeanor and tone bespoke of iciness.

"As for this outlandish tale my daughter told you last night and me this morning," the earl continued, "I can only conclude the foolish chit's imagination got the best of her. Just like a woman to blow something as simple as a branch scraping against a window all out of proportion."

Gideon's jaw clenched at the earl's disparaging tone and less than complimentary words about Julianne. They raised an overwhelming urge in Gideon to defend her—a surprise, as he'd questioned her story himself. And because he himself had thought her foolish last night for venturing into the garden alone. Foolish...and achingly desirable.

Yes, if he had to describe Julianne in just one word, that word would be *desirable*. And *foolish* would be reserved for him. Or perhaps *idiotic* was more apt, for giving in to his craving to kiss her, to touch her had surely been the height of idiocy.

"I've instructed my groundskeeper to trim the branches around Julianne's windows so there won't be any further disturbances tonight as there were the last two nights."

The earl's voice roused Gideon from his brown study and he frowned. "Last *two* nights? Lady Julianne heard the moaning sounds again last night?"

"She heard *the wind*. For the last two nights. I assure you she won't hear the sounds again tonight."

Something in the man's tone set off warning chimes in Gideon's mind, and his fingers involuntarily clenched. He was well acquainted with men like the earl. Men who ruled by intimidation. Gideon certainly recognized a bully when he saw one. But he was long past being intimidated by anyone's father.

"While I don't believe in ghosts, given the recent rash of crimes, I think Lady Julianne's claims bear investigating," Gideon said, keeping his tone even and his expression carefully blank—talents honed from years of practice.

Another layer of ice glazed over the earl's eyes. "Nothing is missing from my home. I was not robbed; no one in my household was murdered. There is no proof of an intruder outside of my daughter's frivolous imagination. She should not have mentioned her outlandish story to you. I assure you she won't make such an error again."

Gideon's shoulders tensed. He didn't know how the earl

planned to assure that Julianne didn't make such an error again, but he did know that all his protective instincts were on alert. "Perhaps *you* weren't robbed, but I believe this so-called ghost meant to burgle Lord Daltry last night." After telling the earl about the opened window at last night's soiree, he said, "I checked the area outside Lord Daltry's home early this morning. There were footprints in the flower bed beneath the window. Someone had tried to gain entry. The window, however, had not been opened after I'd jammed it closed. I interviewed Lord Daltry's entire staff this morning. Except for one footman who believes he saw a shadowy figure leaving the garden about an hour after the party ended, no one saw or heard anything."

"So Daltry wasn't robbed, and no one was hurt."

"No. Not yet."

"And neither was I robbed."

"No. Not yet."

"Nor do I intend to be."

"An excellent sentiment, one I applaud. However, the so-called ghost criminal may have other ideas."

The earl pushed his leather chair back from his polished mahogany desk and stood. "My home is secure, and there is no proof that anyone attempted to gain entry. There is nothing here to investigate, Mr. Mayne—"

A knock cut off his curt dismissal. Shooting a dark scowl toward the door, the earl said, "Come in."

The door opened, and Lady Julianne crossed the threshold. And it felt to Gideon as if all the air had been sucked out of the room.

Bloody hell, she literally stole his breath. She wore a high-waisted blue gown that exactly matched her incredible eyes. The garment, although modest, hinted at lush feminine curves. Golden hair framed her beautiful face, the glossy curls upswept except for the artful tendrils that curved next to her cheeks and along her slender neck. Caught in a ray of sunshine, she looked like an angel.

His gaze settled for several seconds on her mouth...on

those lush lips that had parted so eagerly beneath his. Lips he now knew were pillowy soft. And warm. And tasted like vanilla. He felt a sudden urge to squirm and forced his gaze upward, where it collided with hers.

Although he did his damnedest to conceal the flare of desire that ignited in him every time he looked at her, he wasn't certain he succeeded, especially after a scarlet flush washed over her cheeks.

"Did you come to stand mutely in the doorway, Julianne, or is there some reason why you've seen fit to interrupt my meeting?" There was no missing the annoyed chill in the earl's words. Gideon watched her attention jump to her father. She moistened her lips in an unmistakably nervous gesture then ventured several hesitant steps into the room.

"I'm sorry to interrupt, Father, but I wished to speak to both you and Mr. Mayne. Regarding this." She drew what appeared to be a bracing breath then crossed the rug, her steps more confident, and held out a dirty piece of vellum to her father.

"What is it?" the earl asked in an impatient tone.

"A note. I found it on my bedchamber floor just inside the door—as if someone had slid it underneath."

"And why would either I or Mr. Mayne find that of any interest?"

"Because the note is . . . odd."

"What does it say, Lady Julianne?" Gideon asked.

"It says—"

Before she could say, the earl snatched the missive from her and snapped it open. Then he frowned. "What the devil does this mean?"

"May I?" Gideon asked, holding out his hand.

The earl thrust the note at him. Gideon looked down at the crudely printed, misspelled words. "Yor next." He raised his gaze to Lady Julianne. "When did you find this?"

"Just a few minutes ago."

"How long since you'd been in your bedchamber?"

She considered then answered, "At least two hours."

"You're certain the note wasn't there earlier?"

"Positive. I saw it as soon as I opened the door. I would have noticed the pale paper against the dark wood floor if it had been there earlier."

"Do you recognize the handwriting?"

"No."

"Have you ever received a missive such as this before?"

She shook her head. "No."

The earl cleared his throat. "Clearly it was written by someone nearly illiterate. Probably one of the servants dropped it and it was kicked beneath the door."

Gideon raised his brows. "That's an abundance of coincidences, my lord. And I must tell you: I cast a very suspicious eye on coincidences."

The earl favored him with a cold stare. "Then what are you suggesting, Mayne?"

"I'm suggesting that your staff be questioned. Because if one of them didn't coincidentally drop this note, which then coincidentally found its way beneath Lady Julianne's bedchamber door, then we must consider that it's exactly what it appears to be." His insides tightened, and he had to force out the words. "A threat against Lady Julianne. Made by someone who was or still is inside your home."

Chapter 7

Julianne stood in the music room, her fingers restlessly braiding the gold fringe edging the heavy blue velvet drapes. Dust motes floated in the long, gilded rays of sunshine streaming through the windows. Her beloved dog lay curled near the hearth, a tiny bundle of energy temporarily at rest, the tip of her tiny pink tongue sticking out while she dreamed doggie dreams.

With a sigh, Julianne paced to the fireplace. She usually found a profound sense of peace in this room, with its cream silk walls, muted shades of blue and green reflected in the draperies and Axminster carpet, polished cherrywood furniture, and grandly ornate pianoforte. It was her favorite spot in the entire house, the place she considered her sanctuary, cozy in spite of its size. A place she felt calm and safe.

But not today.

No, today restless nervousness jangled through her. What would Gideon discover? And how much longer must she wait until she knew? He'd left Father's study over two hours ago to interview the staff. Surely Johnny was no longer around the household—

Her thoughts were interrupted by a knock. "Come in," she called.

The door opened, and Gideon entered. Their gazes met. And for a single instant she fancied fire flared in his dark eyes and the floor beneath her shifted. Then his expression went blank. Feeling the need to support her less-than-steady knees, she took a single step backward to brace her hips against the pianoforte.

What felt like an eternity but was surely no more than ten seconds passed in silence, a quiet space of time during which her entire body heated under his inscrutable regard. She wished she could read his thoughts. Had he discovered the truth? Did he know what she'd done? Unable to stand the suspense any longer, she asked, "You interviewed the staff?"

Instead of answering, he closed the door behind him. The quiet click reverberated through her, a soft confirmation that they were alone. She should have demanded he leave the door ajar. Instead, she had to press her lips together to keep from asking him to turn the lock into place.

With his gaze steady on hers, he walked toward her, his eyes so intense, she felt like a mouse stalked by a large, hungry cat. Surely she should want to flee, or retreat, rather than longing to run toward him and be devoured.

He halted when an arm's length separated them, a distance she instantly yearned to erase. Indeed, she had to lock her knees to keep from doing so.

"No one saw or heard anything," he said, "nor did anyone claim ownership of the note."

She prayed her relief didn't show. Clearly Johnny was no longer about. Either that or the coal porter was an accomplished liar. Thank goodness.

"What is your theory?" she asked.

Another silence stretched between them, and she found herself curling her fingers against the pianoforte's wood to keep from giving in to the desire to brush back the ebony lock of hair that fell over his forehead.

Finally he said, "Clearly something is afoot. And I intend to find out what it is."

And God help me if he does.

"And I intend to see to it that no harm befalls you." His gaze raked her face. "It appears that note was left as a threat to you. Do you have any idea who might have left it?"

"No." Could he tell that single syllable was an outright lie? She studied his eyes in hopes of finding the answer but instead found herself drowning in their intensely dark depths. And holding her breath.

A muscle ticked in his jaw. "Do you know of anyone who would want to hurt you?"

"No." That much at least was true. "I find it difficult to suspect any of the servants. They've all been with us for years."

"Perhaps more time to build up some sort of resentment. And servants have friends. Families. Cohorts. Aside from them, a parade of suitors made their way through your home today."

Julianne couldn't hide her surprise. "Surely you don't suspect one of them."

"Why wouldn't I? Because they're wealthy? Titled? Men in their positions are capable of criminal acts."

"What possible motive could they have? I'd hardly be a viable bridal candidate if I cocked up my toes." A humorless sound escaped her. "I'm worth much more alive than dead, believe me. But surely the words 'yor next' merely referred to my family's jewels—that they would soon be stolen—rather than as a threat against me. Surely Lady Ratherstone and Mrs. Greeley were killed because they came upon the thief during the commission of the robbery."

"I considered that both women would still be alive if they hadn't happened upon the thief; however, it's just as likely—more so in my opinion—that the ladies both knew their killer. That that's how he gained entry into their homes. And were killed for their trouble. Therefore I think it's rather odd for the robber to give warning to his next victim. To afford your family the time and opportunity to take precautions against an imminent theft."

Julianne frowned. Botheration. Perhaps she'd overplayed her hand. Still, she hadn't asked Johnny to leave the note; the enterprising young man had done that on his own. How could she have known that by hiring the coal porter to make ghostly noises he'd improvise in such a way?

Of course, she could have just ignored his note. Slipped it into her pocket and pretended she hadn't seen it rather than bringing it to her father's and Gideon's attention. But at the time it had seemed the most expeditious way to accomplish her goal—to make her ghost story real enough to convince both her father and Gideon. So that Gideon would investigate. Thus enabling her to spend time with him. It had all seemed perfectly plausible, but now, with Johnny acting on his own without consulting her...she needed to tread carefully so as not to trip into the dark abyss of her own lies.

She cleared her throat. "Yes, a robber giving his victim warning does seem a bit odd, although it's no secret my parents are hosting a ball next week. More than two hundred guests are expected."

"In Lady Ratherstone's case, precisely the sort of occasion after which the criminal struck."

"Perhaps our would-be thief isn't concerned, because he truly is a ghost."

"I'm afraid I don't share your belief in the fanciful. A real, live person left that note in your bedchamber." He leaned toward her just a bit, but it was enough to make her forget how to breathe for several seconds. Not only because of his nearness but due to the unsettling sensation that he could somehow see directly into her soul. Discern each and every one of her falsehoods. "Make no mistake—I will find out who's responsible."

She prayed she didn't sound as breathless as she felt. "Excellent. Yet so far your only suspects are servants who have been loyal to my family for years and esteemed members of society seeking my hand in marriage." She cocked a brow. "Are you always so suspicious?"

"Yes. It's the only reason I'm still alive." He moved a step closer to her. Now only two feet separated them. She could see the fine grain of his clean-shaven jaw, skin her fingers itched to explore.

"Everyone lies, Lady Julianne," he said softly, and she found herself nearly lulled into a trance by the movement of his lips.

Pulling her gaze back to his eyes, she asked, "Even you, Mr. Mayne?"

"*Everyone*, Lady Julianne." Before she could think up a reply, he lifted his hand. And she stared.

Dangling from the end of one long finger were her embroidery scissors. She blinked, and her hand flew to the pocket in her gown. Her empty pocket.

"How did you—?"

"Everyone," he repeated softly. "Although it appears your claim that you carry embroidery scissors was truthful."

"Of course it was." There was no need for him to know that she'd developed her long-standing scissor-carrying habit only that morning. Adopting a very put-upon air, she held out her hand.

"Everyone has secrets," he said, setting the small gold scissors in her palm. His calloused fingertips brushed her skin, and she pulled in a quick breath at the contact. "Facets of ourselves we don't share with anyone else."

She couldn't refute his words, as she'd never shared her inner longings with anyone, not even her closest friends. She'd never heard anyone voice such an opinion, and it prompted her to say, "It's as if there are different people inside us...people known only to ourselves."

"Yes." He inclined his head and studied her. "Who are those different people inside you, Lady Julianne?"

Daring, adventurous women. Who want to know all about you. Who want to touch you. Kiss you. Who want to feel again the magic you made me feel last night. "No one you would recognize, I'm sure. Who are the people inside you?"

Something flickered in his eyes, then a curtain seemed to fall over his features. "No one you would care to know."

She shook her head. "I disagree. I think you're—" She pressed her lips together to cut off her words. Before she admitted too much. Allowed him to see just how intriguing and compelling she found him.

He leaned forward and set his hands on the pianoforte on either side of her. "You think I'm...what?"

Fascinating. She could feel the heat emanating from his body. She drew in a deep breath, and his clean scent flooded her senses. It was all she could do not to arch her back and curve into him. "I...I think you're...wrong. I'd like to know about the people inside you."

"Indeed? Now why would a purebred princess like you want to know about a mutt like me?"

Princess. A flash of annoyance tempered her rapid heartbeat. "I'm a student of human nature; I enjoy studying people." She gave the mere foot of space between their bodies a pointed look. "You have a habit of caging me in, Mr. Mayne."

"You have a habit of allowing yourself to get trapped, Lady Julianne."

Botheration. Had she just thought him fascinating? "Has anyone ever told you you're quite irritating?"

To her further annoyance, his lips twitched with clear amusement. "No one who's ever lived to repeat the sentiment."

Recalling that they'd shared a similar exchange last evening, Julianne's own lips threatened to curve upward. Instead, she adopted a stern expression. "Then allow me to be the first. You're quite irritating."

"You don't fear my reprisal?"

"Not at all. Do your worst."

His eyes seemed to darken. "So...the porcupine has quills. Interesting."

A half-dismayed, half-amused sound escaped her. "Porcupine? That's hardly flattering. I much prefer your 'rose has thorns' analogy of last evening. Do you have any idea what a porcupine looks like?"

"Of course. There's one painted on the sign leading to the Drunken Porcupine pub. I pass it every day on my way to Bow Street."

"And this is what I remind you of? The Drunken Porcupine?"

"Yes. Well, except that you're not drunk. At least I don't think so..." He leaned forward, brushing his cheek against hers, and drew in a slow, deep breath, effectively stalling her own. Then he leaned slowly back. "You smell like dessert, not spirits. Definitely not drunk."

Perhaps not. But dear God, she felt intoxicated. "That's not very...complimentary."

"You think not? I actually meant it as one."

"Indeed? It's not one I've ever heard before."

"Then perhaps you'll remember it. I'm certain you don't need another man to tell you you're beautiful."

In spite of herself, her lips twitched. "I'm certain I don't need another man to tell me I remind him of a drunken porcupine."

A ghost of a smile whispered across his face. "Good. I'm delighted to be in a category unto myself." His gaze lowered to her mouth, and her lips involuntarily parted. When he raised his eyes to hers, his seemed to glow with a banked flame. "About your invitation..." He leaned slowly toward her.

"Invitation?" Dear God, was that breathless sound her voice?

"Yes. You invited me to do my worst." His lips hovered just above hers. "But I'd much prefer to do my best."

Oh, my... Her entire body tensed, humming, tingling with anticipation. Waiting...wanting...

A sharp yip sounded. Then another.

She blinked her eyes open. No lovely male lips hovered anywhere near hers. Indeed, Gideon had stepped away from her and was scowling at the carpet.

"What in God's name..." he pointed toward the floor, "is *that*?"

Feeling bemused—and decidedly unkissed—Julianne followed his gaze and stared down at the white ball of fluff returning Gideon's scowl measure for measure. A ferocious growl rumbled in her pet's throat—or at least as ferocious a growl as something barely larger than a teapot could manage.

Julianne scooped up the bristling, protective bundle of fur, cuddling it close to her chest. "This is Princess Buttercup."

For several seconds the only sound was Princess Buttercup's rapid sniffs as she stretched out her bejeweled collared neck and quivered her nose in an attempt to catch Gideon's scent.

"Princess Buttercup..." Gideon repeated slowly. Then he briefly pinched the bridge of his nose and shook his head. "And just what exactly *is* Princess Buttercup?"

"She is a Maltese."

"A Maltese? I suppose that's some fancy breed of dog?"

His tone raised her hackles and her chin. "Of course she's a dog. What did you think?"

"At first I thought it was a long-haired, yipping rat."

Annoyance rippled through Julianne, and she hugged her baby closer to her chest. "That's very unkind," she scolded, her voice a hissing whisper. "Princess Buttercup looks nothing like a rat."

"She's the size of one." His scowl deepened as it raked over her pet. "Are those *bows* in its hair?"

"Yes. You'd wear bows, too, if your hair hung in your eyes all day long."

"I assure you, I would do no such thing." He craned his neck a bit then asked, "Good God. Is it wearing a...dress?"

Julianne hiked up her chin another notch. "Certainly not. It is a short, tulle *skirt*. She doesn't wear dresses or gowns— they inhibit her walking."

"I suppose next you'll tell me she has a tiara."

"Only a small one. For very special occasions. For every-day outings she prefers hats."

His gaze shifted back to Julianne. "You're joking."

"On the contrary, I'm perfectly serious."

He muttered something under his breath that sounded sus-piciously like "bloody most ridiculous thing I've ever seen."

Irritation pursed her lips. "You're acting as if you've never seen a dog before."

A humorless sound escaped him. "*That*"—he nodded

toward Princess Buttercup—"is not a dog. *That* is a yapping, dressed-up, miniature ankle biter."

Julianne gasped, covered Princess Buttercup's tiny ears with a protective hand, then lowered her voice. "*That* is a completely inaccurate, not to mention unfair, assessment. For your information, dogs are *supposed* to bark. She didn't bite your ankle—although she clearly should have. She's merely very protective of me, and you're a stranger to her. As for me dressing her up, she's the closest thing to a sibling I've ever had, and as we both enjoy it and it harms no one, I can't see that it's any of your concern."

With indignation fueling her, Julianne advanced a step toward him and shot him her most scathing look. "Regarding her size—she cannot help it if she's smaller than normal. She was the runt of her litter, and no one else wanted her. *I* prefer to call her petite."

She pressed a kiss to Princess Buttercup's soft fur. "We've heard Mr. Mayne's opinion of you. Let's see what you think of him." She set her pet back on the carpet. The little dog immediately approached Gideon's boots, which were given a thorough sniffing examination. Julianne grudgingly gave Gideon credit for remaining still, even when Princess Buttercup went up on her hind legs, rested her diminutive front paws on the shiny black leather, and continued to sniff.

Finally the dog circled around Gideon once, then plopped her bottom on the carpet. After a series of sharp yips, she hoisted herself upward, front paws clawing the air, tail swishing, and pranced about.

"Does that mean I pass muster?" Gideon asked, and Julianne thought she detected a note of reluctant amusement in his voice.

"Hmmm...it would seem so," she said, not adding that Princess Buttercup, whom she deemed a very good judge of character, had had a very different reaction to her earlier callers. She growled at all of them and had particularly disliked Lord Haverly. "Actually, that particular move means she wants to be held."

"Then perhaps you should pick her up. Before she trips on her skirt."

"She's prancing for *you*. You pick her up."

Julianne had to bite the insides of her cheeks to keep from laughing at his expression. "*Me?*"

"Yes. You. Surely a big, strong man like you isn't afraid of a...what did you call her? Oh, yes...a miniature ankle biter?"

He frowned. "Of course I'm not afraid. I simply wouldn't want to break the little beast."

"Oh, she's quite sturdy. And quite fierce." She scooped up the prancing dog. "She won't bite you." She stifled the smile threatening to curve her lips. "Probably."

Before he could protest further, she settled Princess Buttercup against his chest. His hands came up, and to his obvious discomfort he found himself with a palmful of panting white fluff.

"Um, I really think—" His words were cut off when Princess Buttercup's eager pink tongue proceeded to bestow a bevy of kisses to the underside of his jaw.

Cuddled in those large, capable hands, held against his broad chest, enthusiastically kissing his skin—for the first time in her life, Julianne found herself envious of her pet.

"Bloody hell, cut that out," Gideon said gruffly, stretching his neck to the side to avoid the barrage of canine adoration. Yet even as he said the words, Julianne noticed how gently he cradled the little dog. How his fingers tenderly stroked her.

And for the second time in her life, Julianne found herself envious of her pet.

"It appears she likes you," Julianne said.

"You sound surprised."

"Actually, I am. She's never taken to any gentleman so thoroughly. Indeed, she normally snaps and snarls at them."

He looked at her over Princess Buttercup's head. "In my experience, dogs are very good judges of character."

She couldn't help but smile. "If that's the case, then, given her reaction, you must be a prince among men."

His gaze seemed to bore into her, heating her from the inside out. "Not even close." Princess Buttercup gave an enthusiastic yip and strained upward. "Does her tongue *ever* stop?" he asked as the bit of pink flicked over his chin.

"When she's asleep."

He bent down and gently set the energetic dog on the carpet. Then rising to his full height, he said firmly, "Sit." Princess Buttercup's tiny white bottom instantly hit the carpet.

Julianne blinked in surprise. "Heavens, you're good at that. She normally never listens to anyone except me." She watched Princess Buttercup cock her tiny head and look up at Gideon with adoring black button eyes, as if waiting for him to tell her what she could do next to please him.

"It's all in your tone," Gideon said. "Dogs respond to the voice of authority."

Julianne pulled her gaze away from her clearly besotted pet—and really, she could hardly blame the beast—to look at Gideon. An odd flutter occurred in her chest when she saw him shoot the dog a quick wink. "You say that as if you own a dog."

"I do." Unmistakable affection flickered in his dark eyes, and a slow smile curved his lips. And she could only stare. Good Lord, the man was absolutely devastating when he smiled. "A *man's* dog."

"Ah. An enormous, drooling beast with plate-sized paws."

"*Any* dog is enormous compared to yours. And Caesar doesn't drool."

"Caesar? What sort of name is that for a dog?"

He hiked up one dark brow. "Asks a woman who shackled her pet with Princess Buttercup."

She hiked a brow right back at him. "And what would *you* have named her?"

He glanced back at the dog, who still looked up at him with adoring eyes. When his gaze returned to rest on hers, Julianne caught her breath at the heat simmering in the dark depths. "Lucky. I'd name her Lucky."

She had to swallow twice to locate her voice, which his intense stare had stolen. "Why Lucky?"

"Because she belongs to you."

The air between them seemed to crackle, and for the space of several heartbeats Julianne simply forgot how to pull it into her lungs. All she could do was stare. And want.

Then he cleared his throat, breaking the spell or whatever it was that had fallen between them. "If you'll excuse me, I must continue with my duties."

She roused herself from the stupor his words and unwavering regard had lulled her into. "Duties?"

"Yes. Before your father departed, he instructed me to make certain all the windows were securely fastened."

"Departed?"

"He left for his club immediately following our interview. You mother, by the way, departed at the same time to call upon friends."

"Fastened?"

"You have a habit of asking one-word questions."

Because you have a habit of making me forget how to speak English. "My habit is to be *concise*."

"I . . . see," he said in a dry tone that made it clear he didn't see at all. "Your father hired me to patrol the grounds this evening in hopes of discovering the source of the noises you've heard the past two nights and hopefully the identity of the person who wrote the note you found. In case there is some threat to you, he wishes for you to stay home for the remainder of the day. He also wanted me to make certain all the windows in the house were secure—which is the task I was undertaking when I entered this room."

"I see." Obviously her parents weren't concerned that Gideon would be in the house with their daughter during their absence. Of course nothing save death would keep Father from his club or Mother from her social rounds, and naturally they would consider a house filled with servants ample chaperone. Besides, Mother and Father wouldn't see Gideon as a threat to her innocence. No, they would view him merely as another person in their employ, no more noticeable or important than a lowly stable boy or footman, neither of whom would ever *dare* behave in an improper manner.

"Have you found all the windows to be secure?" she asked.

"I've so far found them all locked, except one." His darkly intense gaze pinned her. "In your bedchamber."

The idea of him in her bedchamber momentarily unfocused her thoughts, rendering her unable to speak. Then she shook her head. "That is odd. They were secure last night, and I haven't opened them today. Perhaps one of the maids did so."

"Perhaps," he said, although he didn't sound as if he believed it possible. "The window is locked now. See to it that it stays that way. And now, if you'll excuse me, I need to continue my duties."

Without another word, he crossed the room and tested the windows. In order to prevent herself from trotting after him and asking if he required any assistance—which he clearly did not—she busied herself with scooping up, then petting Princess Buttercup.

When Gideon finished his task, he said, "Everything's secure." He then made his way to the door. Before exiting the room, he turned and offered a brief nod. "Good afternoon, Lady Julianne, and you, too, Princess Buttercup." His gaze lingered on Julianne for several seconds. Then he said, "Don't worry. I'll be watching this evening. And I'll put a stop to any mischief making." Without another word he quit the room, closing the door behind him with a quiet click.

Julianne pulled in a deep breath. Her father had hired him. Gideon was here. In her home. He would return this evening. And be outside all night.

Dear God, it worked. Her plan had worked.

Unable to stop herself, she performed a quick twirl. She held Princess Buttercup out at arm's length and frowned at her beloved pet. "He would have kissed me again if you hadn't interrupted," she scolded softly.

The tiny dog whined, then looked longingly toward the

door. Julianne shook her head. "He's gone. But...he'll be back."

Princess Buttercup wagged her tail and emitted a happy yip. Julianne pulled her pet close and dropped a kiss on the soft fur.

"Oh, my, yes. I know exactly how you feel."

Chapter 8

"Do you suppose there are any ghosts in the room yet?" Juli-anne asked, her whisper breaking the unnerving silence. She peered through the dimness at her three guests. The meager glow from the single taper set in the center of the small round table around which they sat, in a circle so tight their knees bumped, was all that relieved the gloomy darkness of her pri-vate sitting room.

The unsteady breath she'd expended to ask her question set the flame to flickering, casting unearthly shadows against the silk-covered walls. Rain splattered the windows, silver streaks blown horizontal by the howling wind that rattled the glass and whistled through the eaves. The entire atmosphere was entirely too spooky. And morbid—although morbid matched her mood quite well.

How was she going to tell her friends about her father's deci-sion, the one he'd informed her of only an hour ago? She could barely stand to think the words, let alone say them out loud. She had to tell them...but by God, she didn't want to.

"I hate to be the one to have to point this out," Sarah said in a loud whisper, "but there are no such things as ghosts."

No sooner had the words been spoken than lightning flashed, followed by a deafening boom of thunder.

"Sounds as if someone or something disagrees with your assessment," Emily said, her voice ripe with amusement. "Certainly Lady Elaine didn't have much difficulty summoning her ghost lover Maxwell at a séance such as this."

"Clearly Maxwell was a more cooperative sort of ghost than the elusive ghost we seek," Julianne murmured. Her gaze moved to the window, noting the inky darkness beyond the rain-streaked glass. Was Gideon out there yet? If not, he would be soon. She hated the thought of him outdoors in such a storm, yet the knowledge that he was so close set her heart to fluttering.

But then another sort of flutter hit her: a nervous jitter in her midsection. What if things did not go as planned? What if Gideon were to discover Johnny during the young man's mission tonight? What if—?

She cut off the litany of useless questions. All she could do was hope for the best and trust that Johnny was as resourceful as she believed. And as fleet of foot as she hoped.

"Are you here, ghost criminal of Mayfair?" Carolyn called softly. "If so, can you give us a sign?"

Four gazes flitted about the room, but no sign manifested itself.

Julianne frowned. That would have been a perfect opportunity for Johnny to play his part. Perhaps he had been detained by the foul weather.

"It seems quite clear our ghost isn't going to join us," Emily said, heaving a sigh that nearly blew out the candle.

"Perhaps he's off robbing another unsuspecting household of its jewels," said Sarah. "Hopefully no one will be killed the next time he strikes."

"Oh, I wonder who will be next?" Emily asked, her eyes wide.

"My parents are attending Lord and Lady Keene's musicale this evening," said Julianne. "Lady Keene's jewel collection is magnificent."

"Yes," agreed Emily, "most of it reportedly gifts from her numerous lovers."

"You shouldn't repeat gossip," Carolyn scolded, the playful wagging of her finger taking the sting from her reprimand.

"I *never* repeat gossip." Emily's devilish smile flashed. "Which is why you must listen carefully the first time I tell you."

After their laughter died down, Sarah said, "If you recall from the book, Lady Elaine summoned Maxwell to her by goading his jealous nature. Perhaps we'd have better success if we did the same." Clearly she was getting into the spirit of the séance despite her nonbelief in ghosts.

"Since I fear none of us possess jewels to better Lady Keene's collection, it will be difficult to incite the ghost's jealousy," said Carolyn.

"Who wants to bother with a ghost criminal when summoning a ghost *lover* would be so much more entertaining?" asked Julianne. "What could we do to incite his jealousy?"

"Describe all the marvelous gentlemen who constantly fawn over us, professing their undying adoration," suggested Emily.

"And who, precisely, might that be?" Julianne asked.

Emily looked toward the ceiling. "You of all people should hardly need to ask, Julianne, based on the number of suitors vying for your hand."

"None of whom have professed undying adoration for anything other than my father's money. I don't matter in the least."

"Well, I could name Matthew as one who adores me," Sarah said, "but I doubt that would incite much jealousy."

"The same for me with Daniel," Carolyn added.

Sarah's gaze grew thoughtful behind her spectacles, and she tapped her chin. "I wonder if Matthew would be jealous if another man were to—"

"Kiss you?" Emily interjected. "Oh, he'd turn green as a lawn in springtime."

"Most likely," Sarah said, not looking displeased at the

notion. "Not that I'd ever allow another man to kiss me. Or that another man would ever want to."

"Logan Jennsen wanted to," Carolyn reminded her in a teasing tone. "He was quite smitten with you before your marriage."

"We were friends, nothing more," Sarah said primly. Then she raised her brows at her sister. "He was quite smitten with *you* before *your* marriage as well."

"Perhaps a bit," Carolyn acknowledged. A small smile played around the corners of her mouth. "I'd already suspected my heart belonged to Daniel, but I knew for certain after Logan kissed me."

Julianne's brows shot upward at Carolyn's unexpected words. From the corner of her eye she noted that Emily's jaw dropped.

"Logan Jennsen *kissed* you?" Emily's voice cracked on the word kissed.

"And Daniel didn't pound him to dust?" Julianne asked. "Or worse?"

Carolyn chuckled. "Unbeknownst to me at the time, they exchanged . . . *words* over the incident."

Emily, who appeared absolutely thunderstruck, looked at Sarah. "You don't seem surprised by this revelation."

"Carolyn told me when it happened."

"Yes, and you immediately told your husband," Carolyn said, shooting her sister a mock frown.

"Well, of course I did," Sarah said in her most prim tone. "I knew Matthew would immediately tell Daniel, and Daniel needed to know." Laughter danced in Sarah's eyes. "He was most seriously displeased."

"I'm certain he was," said Julianne. "What sort of words did Daniel and Mr. Jennsen exchange?"

Carolyn shrugged. "Daniel's never said, and I've never asked."

"How could you not ask?" Julianne wondered. "I'd positively burn with curiosity."

"I thought it more prudent to simply let the matter be forgotten. If *I* asked questions, then Daniel might ask for details, and it's really best I don't give them. Especially as he's considering a business venture with Logan."

"Ah," said Emily, folding her arms across her chest, her expression smug. "So Mr. Jennsen proved himself a repulsive kisser. I cannot say I'm the least bit surprised."

"On the contrary," said Carolyn, shaking her head. "He is an *excellent* kisser." Even in the dim light Julianne thought she detected a blush suffuse her friend's cheeks. "As I said, if my heart hadn't already belonged to Daniel...well, let's just say that Logan most definitely knows how to kiss a woman. And that is the sort of information that's best shared *only* with one's most cherished friends."

Emily's brow nearly furrowed into a knot. "What, precisely, do you mean by *excellent*?"

"I mean that any woman he chooses to kiss will most definitely enjoy the experience. And perhaps even be spoiled for anyone who might come after."

Emily made a disparaging sound and gave a dismissive flick of her wrist. "I find that very difficult to believe. Indeed, I'm shocked you didn't feel the need for a good scrubbing after being touched by that uncouth colonial. After all, how 'excellent' could he possibly be? For that matter, how 'excellent' could *any* man be?"

"Extremely excellent," said Sarah.

"Marvelously excellent," replied Carolyn at the same time.

"Extraordinarily excellent," said Julianne in unison with her two friends. And immediately found herself the recipient of three startled looks.

Heat rushed into Julianne's face, and Emily's eyes narrowed. "And where exactly are you getting your *extraordinarily excellent* information from? Don't tell me Logan Jennsen kissed you as well?"

"Heavens, no," Julianne said, but the nervousness in her voice lent doubt to her words, even though they were truthful.

"But *someone* has kissed you," Emily persisted. "I can tell. It's written all over your face."

"I...well..." Oh, dear. Why hadn't she simply pressed her lips together to keep from speaking? Both Sarah and Carolyn sat on the edge of their seats, clearly eager to hear what she had to say. And Emily's expression made it clear she'd never allow the subject to drop until Julianne answered. Julianne debated lying, but her friends knew her well enough to detect an outright falsehood.

She drew a bracing breath, then said in a rush, "Yes, I've been kissed."

"When?" asked Sarah.

Carolyn leaned forward. "Where?"

"By whom?" demanded Emily.

The eager questions fired at her like pistol shots, ripping gaping wounds in her conscience. She hated to prevaricate with her dearest friends, but she simply couldn't tell them the truth. At least not the entire truth.

After swallowing to moisten her suddenly dry throat, Julianne said, "It was, um, some time ago." True, if one considered last night some time ago. It certainly *felt* as if ages had passed since Gideon had kissed her. "As for where...the garden. And by whom...someone I shall never forget."

"Which means you must recall his name," Emily said, waving her hand in an impatient gesture for Julianne to continue.

Indeed. She feared blurting out *Gideon* every time she opened her mouth, as he so completely filled her mind. "Of course. But since the gentleman and I are fated to different futures, I'd prefer not to reveal it."

Carolyn and Sarah looked disappointed, but Emily appeared positively crestfallen by her refusal. And annoyed.

"Well, isn't this a fine stew," Emily said, her lips compressed in clear irritation. "You've all experienced these wonderful kisses, the sort described in detail in *The Ghost of Devonshire Manor*. Except me. And *you*"—with her beautiful face pulled into a pout, Emily stabbed a finger at Julianne— "won't even tell us who your extraordinarily excellent kisser was. I'm feeling very left out. And infuriatingly unkissed."

Carolyn laid her hand over Emily's. "Someday, very soon, I'm sure, you'll experience a wonderful kiss."

"When you least expect it, some daring, wonderful kisser will sweep you right off your feet," Julianne added.

Emily's lips twitched. "You make him sound like a broom."

"Which rhymes with *groom*," Sarah said with a grin. "He'll kiss you, sweep you off your feet, and we'll be attending a wedding."

"*Humph.*" Emily flounced back in her chair. Then a mischievous gleam lit her eyes. "Perhaps *I'll* kiss *him* and be the one doing the sweeping."

"I'd wager that whomever you finally set your sights on won't stand a chance against you," Sarah said, laughing.

"Yes, perhaps we'd best warn the poor man," teased Carolyn.

"At least give him a head start," joined in Julianne. Then she sobered. "Speaking of weddings...I don't want to cast a pall on our evening, but I suppose there's no point in delaying telling you..." Her voice trailed off, and she stared into the candlelight for several seconds, desperately wishing she didn't have to say the rest, that it was all just a bad dream from which she would soon awaken. "Shortly before you arrived, my father told me he has decided upon a husband for me. It's the Duke of Eastling."

Emily gasped. "Are you *betrothed*?" The word sounded like an obscenity, and as far as Julianne was concerned, it was.

"Not officially yet, but according to Father I will be by next week. He and Mother plan to make the official announcement during their ball." With a heavy heart she told them about the duke's wish for the marriage to take place before his planned returned to Cornwall.

For several long seconds only silence met her announcement. Then Sarah reached out and clasped her hands. Emily and Carolyn did so as well, and Julianne found herself clinging to her friends like a lifeline.

"Have you had an opportunity to spend any time with the duke?" Sarah asked, her eyes filled with concern.

A bitter sound escaped Julianne. "Not very much, but that will be remedied within a fortnight. I'll be spending the rest of my life with him." She lowered her chin and stared at the table. "With a man I barely know, and to whom I'm not the least bit attracted. A man who will take me away to Cornwall." Tears stung the backs of her eyes. "A man who cares nothing for me."

"Well, I simply wouldn't do it," Sarah said, her expression as fierce as her voice. "I would refuse to marry him. Surely there is someone else. Someone you could care for. Someone who cares for you."

Julianne offered her loyal friend a sad smile. "It doesn't matter, as the duke is the man Father has chosen."

"The choice should be *yours*," Sarah insisted.

"We weren't born into the peerage," Carolyn said to her sister. "Our circumstances regarding marriage were vastly different than Julianne's. Our father was a physician, not an earl."

"And Julianne is a woman, not chattel to be bartered away to the highest bidder."

"'Tis the way of the peerage, I'm afraid," said Emily. "You've only been part of this life a short time, Sarah. Very few marriages are love matches. If one is very, very fortunate, love eventually grows."

"And if it doesn't?"

"Thus the prevalence of infidelity in society."

Sarah shook her head, and her glasses slid downward. "Well, that is simply unacceptable. And my earlier statement stands. I just wouldn't do it. I *couldn't* do it. I couldn't possibly share the intimacies of marriage with someone I didn't love. Someone who didn't care for me."

Carolyn put her arm around Julianne's shoulder and shot her sister a frown. "You're not helping, Sarah. How could the duke, or any man for that matter, not adore our Julianne?"

"He'd be an utter fool not to," Sarah agreed. "But what of her feelings for him? Or rather her lack of feelings?" Before anyone could answer, Sarah turned to Emily. "What about you? Do you harbor any hopes of making a love match?"

For several seconds Emily looked down and fiddled with the pale blue trim of her muslin gown. Then she raised her chin. "It has always been my dearest hope, but I fear I'm in a situation similar to Julianne's. My father has lately suffered some...financial setbacks. Although he hasn't yet said anything, I suspect he'll be looking for a wealthy man for me. A *very* wealthy man."

"And if you don't happen to love this *very* wealthy man?" Sarah asked.

"Love has nothing to do with it," Julianne and Emily responded in unison. "At least so far as our fathers are concerned," Julianne added, unable to hide the despondency in her voice. "Which makes me very glad I experienced that wonderful kiss," she continued softly. "Indeed, I was sorely tempted to steal more than a kiss."

"I don't blame you one bit," Sarah said. "Lady Elaine was expected to marry another, but with Maxwell she shared kisses and so much more—"

"Again, that is not helping." Carolyn skewered her sister with another frown.

Sarah cleared her throat, as if swallowing the rest of what she'd intended to say, then settled her concerned gaze on Julianne. "Is there anything we can do? Having married for love, I don't see how anyone could contemplate doing otherwise."

"Visit me in Cornwall?" Julianne suggested, trying not to sound as defeated as she felt.

Her three friends instantly agreed that they would. But in her heart, Julianne knew that once she married the duke, nothing would ever be the same again.

"There must be something more we can do," Sarah persisted.

Julianne shook her head and fought the tears pushing behind her eyes. "Nothing can be done. Except for me to prepare myself for my wedding." The words tasted like sawdust in her mouth.

Sarah's mutterings sounded like, "*Something can always be done.*" Then she cleared her throat and spoke up, "Perhaps a ghost lover like Maxwell can steal you away."

Julianne offered a weak smile at the whimsical suggestion.

If only she *could* be stolen away. Not by a ghost, but by a real man. The only man she'd want to do so.

Gideon.

The party broke up soon afterward, and after waving good-bye to her friends through the rain-slashed foyer window, Julianne made her way back to her bedchamber. The instant she entered the room, her gaze fell upon the leather-bound *The Ghost of Devonshire Manor* she'd set on her dresser just before departing to meet her friends. She'd been idly flipping through the pages then, and now, after closing the door, she picked up the volume and ran her fingers over the gilt lettering on the cover.

"You were quite the devil, weren't you, Maxwell?" she murmured.

She skimmed through several pages, pausing at a random one, and began reading. Ah, yes, one of her favorite scenes, where Maxwell did his best to seduce Lady Elaine, and the lady tried her best to resist the temptation. The sensual ghost eventually managed to push past her reluctance. Just thinking about the scene that followed brought a heated flush to Julianne's cheeks. Indeed, Maxwell's best proved very pleasurable. For both him and Lady Elaine.

"You invited me to do my worst. But I'd much prefer to do my best."

Gideon's words from earlier that afternoon echoed in her mind. Heat scorched her face then raced downward to engulf her entire body. He'd been a hairsbreadth away from kissing her. And if her plan for tonight hadn't gone awry, he'd be inside the house right now, rather than outside.

She set down the book and paced the length of the chamber, her thoughts troubled—now not so much by her impending engagement and marriage but rather a question that had plagued her all evening.

What had happened to Johnny?

She'd not seen the young coal porter since this morning when they'd struck their bargain. Since then he'd drastically changed the script of their little play, first by leaving the note in her bedchamber, then by not making any ghostly noises during the séance. Dear God, she hoped no disaster had befallen the young man. But surely his absence was merely due to the foul weather.

Foul weather that Gideon would be in right now as he guarded the house. If only it wasn't storming—

You'd sneak outside to see him? her inner voice asked with scathing disapproval.

Yes. That's exactly what she would do.

Her common sense berated her. Told her she should send up a prayer of thanks for the rain that kept her inside. Her heart countered that she wasn't made of spun sugar and therefore wouldn't melt if she got wet.

No, she wouldn't melt, but was she brave enough to venture out alone into the stormy darkness?

You wouldn't be alone. Gideon is out there.

Yes, but the perimeter of the mansion was large. What if she couldn't find him? What if, while she searched the rear of the mansion, he was patrolling the front? There was no telling how long she might be alone in the dark.

Perhaps she could entice him inside to warm himself by the fire and dry off. She could offer him something to drink. Several of Cook's delicious biscuits. Her heart sped up at the prospect.

She made her way to the window nearest her bed, pushed aside the heavy green velvet drape, and frowned. It was so dark outside, all she could see was her own dim reflection in the panes. She stepped closer to the window, trying to see beyond the balcony to the ground below and rested her hand against the glass. Chill seeped into her palm, and her insides ached at the thought of Gideon out there, cold, wet, and alone.

Lightning blazed across the sky, and Julianne blinked against the sudden brilliance. Thunder boomed following a series of lightning flashes that illuminated the entire rear gardens of the house. Julianne stared into the brightness. And her blood ran cold.

A hooded figure stood directly in front of her, holding a large knife in one gloved hand.

Her mouth dropped open in shock.

The figure reached out with its other hand and grasped the handle to the French windows. The door rattled. The lightning ended, plunging the room into darkness.

Julianne screamed and ran, the sound of the rattling ringing in her ears.

Chapter 9

Cold rain dripped down Gideon's face and neck, seeping beneath his collar to trickle down his back, a discomfort he ignored as he'd reached his saturation point hours ago and couldn't possibly get any wetter. He could only hope the foul weather wouldn't keep the so-called murdering ghost robber—or whoever had left that note in Julianne's bedchamber—from attempting his scheme tonight. For that's precisely what it would it be—an attempt—as Gideon had every intention of catching the bastard.

Especially now, since the bastard had struck again. The magistrate's disturbing news, spoken to Gideon less than two hours ago, echoed through his mind. *Lady Daltry... robbed of her jewels... and murdered.*

Lady Daltry, who had been alive and well this morning when Gideon had checked for footprints outside the window of her home.

"She's the last one, you bastard," Gideon muttered. "The last one you're going to rob and kill."

Hopefully, the note leaver and the ghost robber were one and the same, so he could put a quick end to this. Not only for the sake of the fine citizens of Mayfair but for himself. He needed a new assignment. To get away from here. From *her*. From the agonizing, overwhelming temptation that strangled him, that he couldn't seem to fight, every time he was near her.

Keeping to the shadows, he slogged through the mud, eyes and ears alert, Caesar at his heels. He often brought Caesar on missions such as this, and the keenly intelligent animal had proven himself a worthy partner. Caesar had taken a bite out of more than one fleeing criminal's arse.

They turned the corner leading to the front of the mansion, and Gideon heard what sounded like a faint cry. He paused, knife at the ready, straining to hear above the thunder growling in the distance. Caesar halted beside him, and he felt the dog's sudden tension.

The sound came again, louder, stronger, and this time unmistakable. A scream. From inside the house.

Julianne.

Gideon raced forward, Caesar on his heels. Heart pounding, he was running up the stone steps, prepared to smash through the door or the window or both—whatever he needed to do to get to her—when the front door swung open.

Winslow, expression anxious, candle in hand—which blew out the instant the oak panel opened—stood on the threshold. Gideon caught a glimpse of Julianne standing in the foyer, clasping a candelabra with both hands, her eyes wide with obvious fright.

"What's wrong, Winslow?" Gideon asked, taking the stairs three at a time.

The butler started, then visibly relaxed when he recognized him. "Oh, I'm so glad you're here, Mr. Mayne. I was just about to call for you. Lady Julianne—"

Gideon pushed past him, leaving a trail of mud and rain on the marble floor, and halted in front of Julianne. The terrified look in her eyes twisted his gut. He took the candelabra from her, noting she was shaking, and passed it to Winslow, who'd shut the door and joined them.

Gideon gently grasped Julianne by the shoulders, absorbing her tremors. "What happened?"

"I...I saw someone. Just outside my bedchamber window. On the balcony." A shudder ran through her, and she briefly squeezed her eyes shut. Twin tears rolled down her pale cheeks. "He had a knife. And he was trying to get in."

Gideon's fingers involuntarily tightened, then he pulled his handkerchief from his pocket, realizing too late it was too wet of be of any use. Still, Julianne accepted it with a nod of thanks. "That's the window that I relocked earlier today after finding it unfastened. What did he look like?"

"I couldn't tell. He wore a black cloak with a hood. I saw him. Then I screamed. And ran. I couldn't stop screaming."

"I heard you." Yes. And his heart had nearly stopped.

Just then two more people rushed into the foyer, both of whom Gideon recognized from his interviews with the servants that afternoon. The first, a strapping young footman named Ethan who, instead of his impeccable livery, now sported bare feet and sleep-flattened hair, and wore an obviously hastily tied flannel robe. Ethan was followed by the cook, Mrs. Linquist, an older, heavyset woman, ensconced from chin to toes in white nightclothes. Her mobcap was badly askew on her frizzy gray hair, and she brandished a small cast-iron pot in one hand.

"Wot's happenin'?" Ethan asked at the same time Mrs. Linquist asked, "Who screamed?"

"Lady Julianne saw someone outside her window," Gideon said tersely. "I want you all to stay right here. Don't move from this spot. I'm going upstairs to investigate. If you see or hear anything, yell. Do not open the door to anyone. Understood?"

They all nodded. Gideon turned to Winslow. "Are you armed with anything besides that candlestick?"

Winslow's eyes widened. "Certainly not."

"Then it will have to do." He looked at the brass candlestick the footman held. "Same for you." After giving the cook and her cast-iron pot an approving nod, he turned to Julianne. "Get those embroidery scissors out of your pocket."

Gideon pointed to the dog sitting patiently next to his boots. "This is Caesar. He'll watch over you while I'm gone." Looking down into Caesar's intelligent brown eyes, he ordered in a low voice, "Guard."

Without another word he strode from the foyer, moving swiftly toward Julianne's bedchamber. He entered cautiously, knife ready, but instantly sensed the room was empty. After assuring himself that was indeed the case, he examined the windows, both of which were securely locked. He stepped onto the balcony but found no evidence of an intruder. He noted the sturdy tree close by. The branches would hold a man's weight. A reasonably fit man could certainly make the climb or use a rope to gain access to the balcony. And Lady Julianne. There was no doubt in his mind that whoever had left the note in Lady Julianne's room had also unlocked her window in order to gain entrance when he returned tonight.

He left the room, then quickly checked the rest of the house, making sure the windows remained locked, inwardly cursing the number of rooms in the household. When he'd satisfied himself that no one had gained admittance, he reentered the foyer. Julianne and the servants remained exactly where he'd left them with Caesar standing before them like a sentry.

"No one has entered the house," he reported, pleased that she'd followed his instructions and noting the relieved looks on everyone's faces. He looked at Mrs. Linquist. "Lady Julianne could use some hot tea."

"Of course she could," the woman said, making clucking noises like a mother duck fussing over her young. "Such a fright she had. I'll see to it at once."

Gideon nodded at Ethan. "Go with her."

"I'll fetch a mop," said Winslow, glancing at the muddy, wet mess Gideon's boots had made of the pristine floor.

After they left, Gideon looked at Julianne. Her eyes were still huge, but they'd taken on a fierce gleam, and she was no longer shaking. She clutched her embroidery scissors to her chest and looked fully prepared to use them against anyone foolish enough to attempt harming her.

Something in his own chest turned over at the sight of her: beautiful and frightened, yet determined and brave. She might have started off screaming, but by God, she'd pulled herself together. Hadn't succumbed to the vapors or tears. He had to lock his knees to keep from giving in to the overpowering urge to take her in his arms.

"What happens now?" she asked.

"I'm going to check outside."

Her eyes widened, and she shook her head. "But what if he's out there? That knife—"

"Given the alarm you raised, I'm certain he's gone. And I have a knife, too."

Her glance flicked down to the blade he held. "His knife is bigger."

Bloody hell, she was *worried* about him. When was the last time anyone had worried about him? He couldn't recall. Still, he wasn't certain if he was more touched by the sentiment or insulted. "I have another knife as well, so he's outnumbered."

She reached out and grabbed his sleeve. "You'll come back?"

He glanced down at her slim, pale hand on his wet, black sleeve. Bloody hell, he liked the way it looked there. Felt there. Not trusting his voice, he jerked his head in a nod. After stepping back, he looked down at Caesar and commanded softly, "Guard." Then he exited the house and, after hearing her lock the door behind him, he made his way to the rear of the mansion.

The rain had tapered off to a relentless, cold drizzle. When he reached the tree outside Julianne's bedchamber window, Gideon crouched down. Even in the dark he could discern the muddy, rain-filled impressions of a man's boot, which meant the bastard had used the tree to climb up. It also meant the man he sought was agile, athletic.

He crouched down to study the footprints. They appeared to be the same size as those he'd discovered beneath Lord Daltry's window this morning. Gideon followed the prints, which led along the perimeter of the garden to a gate leading to the mews. The gate was locked, but a man who could climb a tree to the balcony was certainly capable of scaling the eight-foot wall. Gideon unlocked the gate, but as expected, the mews were deserted. Grim, he returned to the house.

The instant Winslow admitted him, Julianne asked, "Well?"

"It appears he climbed the tree to gain access to your balcony. Since I didn't see him nor did Caesar sense him, I believe he must have known of my presence. He waited until I'd left the rear of the house, then entered through the mews. He would have had ample time to do so before I made my way around the property back to the rear of the mansion. Since he obviously knows which bedchamber is yours, you'll need to sleep in a different room until he's caught—one without a balcony or tall trees outside the windows. Nor an adjoining door to another room that has either. Is there such a chamber?"

She considered then said, "Yes. The room two doors down from mine. Do . . . do you think he'll be back?"

"I doubt he'll attempt to return tonight, although I won't be letting down my guard in case he does. But after tonight . . . yes. I think he'll be back. And I've no intention of allowing him to get away again."

She frowned, clearly troubled. Which was bad, because that made him want nothing more than to reach out and brush his fingers over the furrow between her brows. To reassure her that he'd allow no harm to come to her. And since the urge was so strong, he needed to get away from her. As quickly as possible.

"Winslow, I'll need a list of every person who entered the house today: servants, deliverymen, callers, everyone."

"Yes, sir. I'll consult with the housekeeper in the morning and prepare the list."

"Good. One more thing . . ." He withdrew the snuffbox from his pocket and held it up so both Winslow and Julianne could see it. "I found this last night. Do either of you recognize it?"

He handed the piece to Winslow, who held it up to the candlelight. He frowned, hesitated, then shook his head before passing it to Julianne. "I've never seen it before."

Julianne studied the ornate box for several seconds, then handed it back. "It's not familiar."

Gideon tucked the box back into his waistcoat pocket and turned to Winslow. "If you'll stay with Lady Julianne, I'll return to my rounds."

Before the butler could answer, Julianne said, "You'll do

nothing of the kind. You're soaked to the skin and must be half-frozen." Turning to Winslow, she said, "Please light the fire in the drawing room and instruct Mrs. Linquist to bring the tea there. Mr. Mayne will require towels and—" she turned toward Gideon, and her gaze skipped down his wet length. "Do you have a change of clothes?"

"No. And there's no point, as it's still raining."

"As you've already ascertained that the intruder is no longer about, I see no reason for you to return outside, at least until my parents return home. Besides, since it appears I'm the intruder's target, I'd feel much safer if you remained with me."

Damn it, she had a point. He *should* remain with her. Needed to remain with her and not let her out of his sight for a minute. The thought of what might have happened to her if that knife-wielding bastard had gained entrance to her bedchamber—

He cut off the thought, forcing it from his mind. She was unharmed. But to insure she remained that way, he needed to stay with her until her parents returned home. He had to keep her safe.

Yet one look at her, so beautiful, those huge eyes staring up at him, filled with trust and unmistakable admiration, as if he were some sort of hero, and he knew he was in deep, deep trouble. The need to touch her, taste her, breathe her in, clawed at him with razor-sharp talons. Just who the bloody hell was going to keep her safe from *him*?

Chapter 10

"Thank you, Mrs. Linquist," Julianne said after the cook set down the silver tray bearing the tea service, followed by Winslow, who carried an armful of fluffy Turkish towels.

"Please go back to bed," Julianne said to the kindly woman. "Mr. Mayne will remain in the house, and Winslow will man the door until Mother and Father return."

"Yes, Lady Julianne." Mrs. Linquist turned toward Gideon. "Don't know what we'd have done if ye weren't here, sir. Never have we had such a fright. Very glad ye were about."

"I'm glad as well," Gideon said.

The two servants headed toward the door, followed by Caesar, who planted himself at the threshold.

For several interminable seconds Julianne could think of nothing to say...could do nothing save stare at Gideon. Gideon, whose wet hair glistened in the firelight's golden glow. Whose wet clothes clung to him like a second skin. Who she wanted to touch so much she could barely stand still.

Desperate for something to say other than *I want to touch you so much I can barely stand still*, she nodded toward Caesar. "It appears he's guarding the entryway."

Gideon nodded. "That's precisely what he's doing. If anyone approaches, we'll know."

Which, Julianne realized, meant that in spite of the door being open, they were ensconced in privacy. Exactly where she needed them to be to continue this afternoon's doggie-interrupted interlude.

No sooner had the thought entered her mind than a low growl sounded from the doorway. Caesar jumped to his feet, his gaze fixed on a point in the corridor. With lightning speed, Gideon slipped his knife from his boot then moved to stand directly in front of her.

"Someone's coming," he whispered. "Stay behind me."

"Surely it's just Winslow," she whispered back. She prayed her parents hadn't yet returned.

"Most likely. But I'm not taking any chances."

Another growl sounded from Caesar. Julianne peeked around Gideon's shoulder. A tiny ball of fluff appeared in the doorway. Caesar barked. Once. A low, deep woof. And Julianne could only stare as Princess Buttercup, her little black nose quivering, sidled up to Caesar. Caesar, who could swallow Julianne's diminutive dog in a single gulp.

Alarmed, Julianne started to move around Gideon, but he put out a restraining arm. "Wait," he said softly.

"For what? For your dog to make an hors d'oeuvre out of mine? I think not."

"He wouldn't do harm unless he sensed a threat. A teacup-sized fluff ball dressed in tulle is hardly a threat. He'll no doubt just nudge her out of his way."

"One Caesar-sized nudge could knock her over." Julianne elbowed her way by him, but he wrapped his fingers around her upper arm. She halted, rendered motionless by his touch.

"Just because he's large doesn't mean he can't be gentle," he whispered close to her ear.

A heated shiver raced down her spine. She turned her head, and for several seconds their gazes locked. Then his flicked down to her mouth. Her breath caught. Was he going to kiss her? *Please...*

To her disappointment he instead released her, although her

skin continued to tingle. Somewhat relieved by his words, Julianne watched as the two dogs sniffed each other, her worry dissipating when she noted the pair of vigorously wagging tails. Princess Buttercup nudged Caesar's front leg with her nose then gave the spot a quick pass with her pink tongue. Caesar responded by licking his chops then nudging her rump with his snout. Princess Buttercup then hoisted herself up on her haunches and waved her dainty front paws at Caesar. His answer was a lick to her ear. As if that settled everything, Caesar then planted himself back at his post in the doorway. The Maltese snuggled up against his side, yawned once, then closed her eyes.

Julianne's brows arched upward. "Nudge her out of his way, will he?" She had to press her lips together to contain her mirth at Gideon's nonplussed expression. "Obviously you underestimated Princess Buttercup's charms."

"Obviously." They both watched as Caesar bestowed a gentle lick to Princess Buttercup's head then cast his gaze once more toward the corridor. "Good God, I think he's... *infatuated*."

She smothered a giggle at his shocked tone. "It appears the feeling's mutual."

"But they're so...so..."

"Different?" she supplied helpfully when he appeared at a loss.

"Incompatible."

She shrugged. "Whatever their differences, 'tis clear they worked through them." She shot him a sidelong glance, drew a deep breath, and summoned her courage. "Amazing what a few swipes of the tongue can accomplish."

He turned toward her so quickly she swore she heard his neck snap. His gaze latched onto hers, and the fire that flared in his eyes nearly scorched her where she stood. "Yes, amazing," he murmured, his gaze dropping to her mouth.

Her entire body tensed in anticipation, but instead of pulling her into his arms as she'd hoped, he nodded toward the towels resting on the settee next to the fireplace in which flames snapped. "May I?"

With her tongue—her sadly *unswiped* tongue—tied in

knots, it took her a full ten seconds to find her voice. Dear God, he must think her a nincompoop. A mute nincompoop. She cleared her throat and managed, "Of course."

She crossed to the settee and lifted one of the soft white towels embroidered with the Gatesbourne crest. Botheration, since he hadn't picked up the gauntlet she'd tossed, clearly more drastic measures were called for. She was beginning to understand the frustration Maxwell had suffered with the reluctant Lady Elaine. Thanks to her Literary Society readings, Julianne wasn't ignorant regarding ways to get a man to kiss her. At least in theory. Obviously, in practice was something else altogether.

He approached her slowly, his gaze steady on hers, trapping her as surely as his arms had that afternoon. He looked large and dark and masculine, yet guilt pricked her at his wet, disheveled appearance—which shouldn't have been attractive, yet was. Wildly so. While she'd remained in the dry warmth, he'd gone back into the rain to search for the intruder, during which time her fright had abated enough for her to realize with no small amount of chagrin that tonight's culprit had of course been Johnny.

She'd speak to the young man first thing in the morning—very firmly. Tell him that he mustn't do anything like that again. Good heavens, he'd nearly scared her to death. She'd merely expected him to make some ghostly moans and groans, not frighten her so badly that she temporarily forgot her plan.

Gideon stopped a mere two feet from her. He may have required the fire's heat, but she did not. Indeed, she felt uncomfortably warm. And as if her skin had somehow shrunken several sizes.

He reached for the towel. His fingers grazed hers, and she pulled in a quick breath. She expected him to simply take the towel and withdraw his hand. Instead, when his fingers touched hers, he went perfectly still. His skin was rough and still bore a trace of chill, and another wave of guilt washed over her at the discomfort he'd suffered—but it was nearly drowned out by the heat that suffused her at his touch.

Propriety demanded she step back. Move her hand away from his. Yet she remained rooted in place, greedily drinking him in as if she were parched. Propriety had no place in her plans for this evening.

She moistened her lips, noting his gaze flick to her mouth again and the flames that kindled in his dark eyes. "Like Mrs. Linquist, I'm very glad you're here. I'd never been so frightened in my entire life."

For several heartbeats he said nothing, just studied her with those dark, unreadable eyes. "I won't allow anyone to hurt you," he said quietly, his expression and voice utterly serious.

Her imagination instantly took flight, picturing him dueling ghosts, tossing hooded knife wielders into the Thames, then sweeping her up into his strong arms and carrying her off to his kingdom where they would—

He took the towel from her and stepped back.

Julianne's fanciful thoughts disintegrated, and she blinked, pulling herself back into the present. She picked up another towel from the stack and approached him.

"Let me help." She reached up and pressed the towel against his cheek. And felt his entire body tense.

A muscle in his jaw ticked beneath the towel. Her gaze dropped, and she noted the white-knuckled grip with which he strangled the towel he held.

A thrill of feminine satisfaction raced through her. Clearly he was tempted. And fighting that temptation.

She could feel the tension emanating from him. Sensed him combating what he clearly wanted—or at least what she desperately hoped he wanted: to finish what they'd started in the music room. To touch her. Kiss her.

Determined to see him fail in his struggle, she leaned toward him. He inhaled sharply, and his full, firm lips parted. Just when she thought he was about to capitulate, he practically snatched the towel from her hand then backed up a step. "I can do it," he said, his voice sounding as if he'd swallowed gravel. "Why don't you see to the tea?"

Good heavens, the man actually looked...nervous? Certainly she'd unsettled him. Surely the notion that he was shouldn't delight her so, but it did nonetheless. Why, he looked as if he wanted to bolt from the room.

Her delight instantly wilted. She didn't want him to bolt from the room. Best she not unsettle him *too* much. Therefore, even though she wanted nothing more than to help him dry off, she forced her feet to cross the Turkish rug. "I'll see to the tea."

After settling herself on the settee, she reached for the teapot, wrapping her fingers around the curved silver handle. Unfortunately, she then made the tactical error of glancing toward Gideon. And completely forgot about tea. Forgot about everything save him.

He stood with his back to her, bathed in the golden glow of the fire, his jacket half-on, half-off. She watched in stupefied fascination as he shrugged the garment the rest of the way off his broad shoulders. His cravat and red waistcoat followed, leaving him clad in his white shirt, which adhered to his body as if painted on. Julianne's avid gaze took in the breadth of his shoulders. The play of his muscles as he rubbed the towel over his chest and back, then down his arms, blotting the wetness away.

When he crouched down to spread the clothing he'd removed on the hearth to dry, his damp breeches clung to his backside in a manner that made her mouth go dry. Before she could recover, he stood and turned.

Their gazes collided, and she felt the impact of his intense regard down to her toes. He no longer looked nervous. In fact, he appeared so in command of himself, she wondered if she'd misinterpreted his reaction earlier. If she'd been capable of speech, she would have told him he looked delicious, er, drier, but sadly, anything as complicated as stringing two words together was currently beyond her.

Her knees seemed to have turned to liquid, and she sent up a silent prayer of thanks that she was already seated. How was it possible that he could reduce her to such a boneless state with a mere look? Surely the fact that he could should have frightened her. Appalled her. *Something* other than breathlessly exciting her.

He approached her slowly, the towel dangling from his long fingers. He looked big and dark, deliciously damp and dangerous, and she couldn't have torn her fervent gaze from him if her very life had depended upon it. He stopped an arm's length away from her, and her gaze focused on the fascinating front of his snug breeches with the zeal a starving dog would bestow on a mutton chop. *Oh, my.* Those breeches left no doubt that Gideon was very perfectly and very generously made.

"Are you all right?" he asked.

Her gaze snapped up to find him watching her with an inscrutable expression. Heat flooded her cheeks. *No. I am not all right. You're throwing all my fine plans into utter disarray.* How could she possibly entice him to kiss her when it apparently required all her wits to remember to breathe? "I'm fine."

He studied her for several more seconds, then nodded slowly. "Yes, I can see that you are. Indeed, you appear well recovered from your fright. Remarkably so."

Was that a twinge of suspicion in his voice? Before she could decide, he continued softly, "There's something you're not telling me."

Clearly that *was* suspicion in his voice. She had no doubt that given enough time he would unearth the truth—and be very angry with her when he did. Rightfully so. He'd no doubt never forgive her. Rightfully so. No doubt never want to speak to her again, let alone kiss her. Which meant she needed to do everything she could to insure that time didn't come too swiftly.

Lifting her chin, she said, "Contrary to what you obviously believe, I am not prone to the vapors or artfully arranging myself on fainting couches. I am made of sterner stuff and don't require days to recover from unsettling experiences." She offered him a small smile. "Besides, I feel very safe with you here."

He didn't comment, merely set aside the towel then sat on the opposite end of the settee. She glanced down and noticed that mere inches separated his knee and her yellow muslin gown. Far too little distance to be proper. Far too much distance for her liking.

She cast about in her blank mind for something to say. Something to divert his attention from her remarkable recovery. Something witty and interesting that would engage him. Perhaps draw a smile from those lovely, firm lips—before he laid them upon hers. But his nearness once again rendered her mute with longing and wants so overwhelmingly strong she feared when she did finally speak they would simply just pour out of her like a dam burst free. *Touch me. Kiss me. Put out this raging fire you've started in me...*

He leaned toward her, and what little breath she had remaining expelled from her lungs. She felt herself leaning toward him, as if blown by a strong wind, and her lips parted in expectation.

"It would be much easier if it were in the cup," he said softly.

She blinked. "I beg your pardon?"

He nodded toward the table. "The tea. It would be considerably easier to drink if it were actually poured into the cups."

Julianne jerked her head around and stared at her hand, which still gripped the teapot's handle—the teapot that remained resting on its silver tray. A hot flush of embarrassment and self-directed annoyance rushed into her face, and she quickly lifted the pot. It was one thing for the man's presence to make her forget what she was about; it was quite another to allow his profound effect on her to be so patently obvious.

"Of course," she murmured, filling both cups then passing him one, managing only thanks to years of experience not to slosh the hot liquid over the cup's edge.

She took extra care in selecting a trio of biscuits for his plate, using the time to compose herself. She'd longed for and had gone to great lengths for an opportunity such as this: time alone with him. She had no intention of wasting this chance to get to know him better. Both Gideon the man and Gideon the extraordinarily excellent kisser.

She passed him the plate of biscuits. "Are you feeling warmer? Do you need more towels?"

"I'm fine, thank you."

Yes, he certainly was. Much more than fine, actually. Supremely, extraordinarily fine. Good heavens, he was beautiful even when he chewed a biscuit. Although she couldn't deny he also appeared...displeased? Her heart sank at the thought. Certainly he didn't appear particularly happy about sitting here, sipping tea with her. A depressing state of affairs, as she was nearly giddy with excitement.

A dozen questions sprang to her lips, things she wanted to know about him. Actually, she wanted to know *everything* about him. Where he lived. Where he'd grown up. His family. His likes and dislikes. His favorite color. If he enjoyed reading. The details of his dangerous and adventurous work. If he thought of her even a fraction of the number of times she thought of him.

How it was possible that such a devastatingly attractive man wasn't married or spoken for.

Or was he?

The thought struck her like a cold slap, and before she could stop herself, she asked in a rush, "Are you married?"

He looked at her over the rim of his steaming cup. His eyes narrowed slightly, then he slowly lowered his tea. "No."

A ridiculous wave of relief surged through her—ridiculous because, what did it matter? Whether he belonged to someone else or not was irrelevant. He could never belong to her. Still, in her heart she'd known he wasn't married. Had known he wouldn't have kissed her if a wife waited for him.

"Betrothed?" she asked.

"No. Why do you ask?" His gaze hardened. "Do you think I would have kissed you if I had a wife or fiancée waiting at home for me?"

His words so closely mirrored her thoughts that she wondered for an insane instant if through his intense regard he could actually read her mind.

Don't lose your nerve now, her inner voice whispered. *Carpe diem.*

Yes. If she didn't seize the day, here and now, she might never get another chance. Before she found herself married to a man she didn't love. A man who would plunk her down in Cornwall and likely leave her there to rot. After demanding his husbandly rights. A shudder of revulsion ran through her. Dear God, the thought of the duke's hands on her made her flesh crawl. And spurred her to action.

Drawing all her courage, she answered, "No—I believe you too honorable to kiss me if you were married. Yet, surely dozens of women are madly in love with you."

His gaze seemed to pierce hers. "The way dozens of men are madly in love with you?"

Julianne shook her head. "There is no one in love with me."

"Says a woman whose suitors litter the path leading to her door."

"They wish to *marry* me. For money. They care nothing about *me*."

"They seem quite besotted to me."

"They are. With my very generous dowry."

Something that looked like annoyance flashed in his dark eyes. "You make it sound as if that is all a man would admire about you. Which sounds like false modesty. And a fishing expedition for compliments."

There was no missing the rebuke in his words—one that stung. "I'm not seeking compliments, especially from a man who clearly has a disinclination of bestowing them. Nor do I possess false modesty. I know I am admired for my looks. I simply take little pleasure from that fact."

"Really? Why is that?"

There was no missing his skepticism, and she debated how honest to be with him. She'd planned to use this time to find out more about *him*, yet he'd somehow turned the tables on her. Still, if she told him something of herself, perhaps he would be more inclined to reciprocate. "Do you truly wish to know?"

"Indeed. I cannot wait to hear why a princess such as yourself doesn't wallow in her looks." He leaned back and raised his brows, looking like a man expecting to be entertained by a troupe of jesters.

Vexing man. How did he manage to make her desire him yet wish to shake him at the same time? Annoyance rippled through her, nudging aside her shyness. "Wallow? Has anyone ever told you you're condescending?"

"Condescending?" he repeated in an incredulous tone. "A commoner like me? Never. Has anyone ever told you you've no idea what you're talking about?"

"As a matter of fact, yes. Almost daily. Neither of my parents credit me with the least bit of intelligence. They think the only thing I'm capable of is being decorative—and they demand that I be so. You cannot begin to understand how much I *loathe* being nothing more than an ornament. As if I have no thoughts or feelings. No ambitions." She moved her leg so that her knee touched his. "Or desires."

His teacup froze halfway to his lips. His hot gaze bored into hers for several seconds, then he slowly set aside his cup and rose. He backed several steps away from the settee until he stood before the hearth. Julianne might have been thoroughly discouraged were it not for how his damp pants clung to the irrefutable evidence of his desire for her.

"What are you doing?" he demanded.

She huffed out an impatient breath. Clearly any form of subtlety was lost on this man. "I'm *trying* to get you to show me what you referred to this afternoon—just before we were interrupted—as your best. If you'll recall, you were about to kiss me."

"That... shouldn't have happened."

Her heart sank. "And last night?"

"You know the answer to that as well as I do."

She rose and joined him near the fire, stopping when a mere arm's length separated them. Longing raced through her, and the sense of urgency, of time running out, of her parents soon returning suddenly overwhelmed her. Capturing his hand between both of hers, she gripped his fingers tightly.

"I know what answer I'm expected to give, but it isn't what's in my heart. I... I have this recurring dream... a nightmare, actually. I'm in the middle of a crowd, trapped inside a glass coffin. I scream and cry and pound on the glass, but no one pays the slightest attention. They all just go about their business as if I'm not there. I'm trying to tell people that I'm alive. Tell them what I want, my hopes and dreams, but no one listens. No one cares."

He frowned. "That's just a dream—"

"No. It's *my life*. And I'm tired, so tired of imagining, of dreaming. Of wanting but never having."

An incredulous sound passed his lips. "What are you talking about? You have more than anyone I've ever known."

She felt him tugging his hand from hers, felt her chance slipping away. She tightened her grip, then pressed their joined hands to the center of her chest. "Yes, if you count gowns or jewels or invitations to parties."

"And you don't?"

"As anyone would, I enjoy the creature comforts provided by my position. I've no desire to be cold or hungry. But once those necessities are seen to...fancy gowns and parties are not important to me. Not nearly as much as other things."

"Such as?"

"Love. Laughter. Companionship. Desire. Romance. Passion. *They* are what I long for." She lifted one hand and skimmed her fingers over his brow. Down his cheek, to his firm jaw, his faint stubble rasping against her skin. For several seconds he remained immobile under her touch. Then he jerked away as if she'd burned him.

"Stop that," he said, his voice resembling a low growl.

He was breathing hard, and his eyes glowed like ebony coals. Unable to stop herself, she stepped forward and erased the distance he'd just put between them. She placed her hands on his chest, her palms absorbing the rapid beat of his heart. Looking into his eyes, she whispered, "I can't." Her fingers splayed over the hard muscles of his chest.

He gripped her wrists, halting her explorations. "You're playing with fire."

"Am I? It doesn't seem so."

"One of us has to show some restraint."

"Really? Well, in that case, I congratulate you, as you've shown a frustrating amount thus far." She took another step forward. Mere inches now separated them. His scent wrapped around her: rain mixed with a hint of damp linen and something else she couldn't define except to know it belonged to him alone. She could feel the heat emanating from his body. "This afternoon you were about to kiss me when we were interrupted."

"That was a mistake."

"The interruption? Yes, I agree. One I'd like very much to remedy. Right now."

His fingers tightened on her wrists. "Kissing you was a mistake, Lady Julianne. One I don't want to repeat."

"You didn't mind calling me Julianne earlier...Gideon. And as for you not wanting to repeat our kiss..." She yanked her hand from his grasp and ran it swiftly downward, intending to point to the evidence of his desire. But he moved, setting her slightly off balance, and the back of her hand brushed the hard bulge in his breeches.

"Bloody hell." The obscenity was a low-pitched hiss on his quick intake of breath.

The bulge pulsed against her fingers in a manner so fascinating she couldn't pull her hand away. She swallowed and forced herself to boldly reach for what she wanted so badly. Gideon's passion. Now. Before she was entombed with the duke for a lifetime.

Summoning her courage, she brushed her fingers down his length. "This tells me you want to. Very much. Gideon, the only time I've ever felt free of that glass coffin is when you kissed me."

Instead of pulling away as she feared he might, he gazed at her through half-closed eyes and gave a slow thrust into her hand. The feel of him, so hard and hot, reduced her knees to porridge.

"I'm not some fancy, polite aristocrat with ice flowing in his blue-blooded veins that'll treat you like a fragile bit of glass, Julianne." His voice sounded scraped from his throat.

"To which I can only say thank God."

The raw hunger in his eyes all but devoured her. He wrapped one strong arm around her and jerked her against him. "You want a kiss? Very well, I'll oblige you, Princess. But be warned: you're about to find out *precisely* what a few swipes of the tongue can accomplish."

Chapter 11

Gideon didn't give her time to think, didn't give himself time to think, to reconsider. Damn it, he didn't want to think anymore. Couldn't fight this raw, raging need any longer. All he wanted was to feel. Her. All of her. *Now.*

He slanted his mouth over hers in a hard, hungry, demanding kiss. What sounded like a whimper came from her, but before he could even wonder if he'd hurt her, she proved he hadn't by winding her arms around his neck and pressing herself against him.

He clasped her to him, every muscle straining to get her closer, while his tongue explored the velvet of her mouth. Bloody hell, if heaven had a taste, she was it. Soft, warm, sweet, and delicious. Her body fit against his like a piece of a puzzle he hadn't known was missing. A tiny granule of sanity tried to work its way through the wild, desperate need careening through him but was incinerated when she squirmed against him.

White-hot desire exploded, and with a groan that seemed ripped from the depths of his soul, he ran one impatient hand down her back to curve around her lush bottom, to pull her tighter against his aching body. Possibly, just possibly he might have been able to dredge up the strength to halt this madness if she'd remained passive in his arms. But with her fingers sliding through his hair, her tongue dancing with his, and her body writhing against him, he didn't stand a chance.

His other hand plunged into her hair, scattering pins, sifting through a cascade of soft curls. The seductive scent of vanilla filled his head, overwhelming him with the need to taste.

Without breaking their frantic kiss, he scooped her into his arms then lowered her to the hearth rug, following her down. While his lips continued to ravage hers, he insinuated his knee between her thighs, and his hand found the soft swell of her breast. A low groan sounded. Hers, he thought, but he couldn't be sure.

Needed to touch her... *had* to touch her. He yanked down her bodice until her breasts were freed, and only then did he find the strength to leave her lips. He kissed his way along her jaw then ran his tongue along the side of her neck, gently sucking on the throbbing pulse there.

"Gideon..." his name, whispered on that breathy sigh, ignited even more of the fire in him that he would have sworn couldn't burn any hotter. She arched beneath him, and he dragged his mouth lower. His tongue circled one nipple then drew the tight bud deep into his mouth while his fingers found the other crest. Her hands fisted in his hair and she gasped, then released her breath on a long moan of pleasure.

He kissed and nuzzled his way around her luscious breasts, teasing and licking with his lips and tongue, lightly grazing her soft skin with his teeth, while his hand wandered lower, exploring the curve of her waist and hips through her gown. When his fingers curled over her mound, her heat nearly singed him.

A single word pounded through his mind, the same mantra that had been driving him mad with want for the past two months. *Julianne...Julianne*. His usual control burned to ashes, leaving only a hot, raw, desperate need that demanded to be satisfied. Wanting, needing more, he reached down and slipped his hand beneath the hem of her gown. Skimmed his palm up her stocking-covered leg, over the gentle curve of her calf and thigh. His restless fingers unerringly found the slit in her drawers. The first touch of her slick feminine folds nearly undid him. Bloody hell, she was so wet. So hot.

She groaned again, and he lifted his head. And gritted his teeth against the arousing sight of her. Hair a golden tumble of disarray, moist, kiss-swollen lips parted, eyes glazed and half-closed, nipples erect and wet from his mouth. Bathed in the glow from the fire, she somehow managed to look like an angel and living, breathing sin at the same time.

He lowered his head and brushed his mouth over hers. "Spread your legs," he whispered against her lips.

She splayed her thighs, and he teased her wet folds with a single fingertip. "Wider," he demanded. Once again she did as he bade, her ragged breaths warming his face. She clutched at his shoulders and lifted her hips, and another groan escaped her, this one ending with his name.

"Gideon..."

"Shhhh," he whispered against her ear.

"I...ohhhh, my...I can't. I feel as if I'm going to scream."

"If you do, you'll bring the entire household down upon us." He lifted his head and looked into her glazed eyes. "Neither of us wants that." God knows he didn't. He wasn't nearly done with her.

She pressed her lips together. "I'll try to be quiet but— *ohhhh*—you're making it extremely difficult." She glided her hand down his chest, over his abdomen, and his muscles jumped. "I want to touch you, too."

He pressed his erection against her hip to thwart her eager hand. Bloody hell, it was all he could do not to come as it was. One touch from her, and he'd explode in a heartbeat.

"Not now," he said against her lips. He eased one finger into her tight sheath to distract her and had to grit his teeth to contain the growl that rose in his throat. By God, she was tight. And so damn wet. And hot. And soft. And he was so damn hard he was going to lose his mind. More, damn it. He wanted more. Now. *Now*.

He slipped his hand from her body and, ignoring her sound of protest, moved to kneel between her splayed thighs. Heart pounding as if he'd sprinted to Bow Street and back, he impatiently pushed her gown up to her waist. Quickly unfastened her drawers. Grimly noted that his hands were far from steady.

Desperate need unlike anything he'd ever experienced grabbed him in a vise. He yanked her thin cotton drawers down and off her legs, not pausing or caring when the delicate material tore. If he'd had the mind to do so, he would have been appalled at his lack of control, but he was beyond caring about anything save the dark, wild, reckless need clawing at him.

The instant he'd tossed aside her ruined drawers, he set his hands on her raised knees and urged her legs apart. Damp golden curls surrounded her glistening sex. He inhaled sharply at the sight, and his head filled with the musky tang of her arousal mixed with the intoxicating scent of vanilla. Bloody hell, it was the most delicious fragrance he'd ever smelled. Slipping his hands beneath her, he raised her hips and dipped his head.

Julianne bit her lips together to stifle the cry of surprise and shocking carnal pleasure that begged to escape. The sight of Gideon's dark head buried between her thighs alone was enough to wring a shout of delight from her. But what he was doing with his mouth...his lips...dear God, his tongue. His fingers. All of them relentless. Teasing, licking, flicking, delving, driving her mad. Helpless to do otherwise, she undulated against his mouth, desperately seeking more of the addictive pleasure. Her hands fisted against the carpet, her body tightening, coiling, straining, searching for an answer that remained just out of reach.

Then he performed some sort of magic with his fingers and mouth, and it was as if she'd been tossed into a storm of indescribable pleasure. An endless moan she couldn't contain escaped her as pulsing sensation engulfed her. When the spasms subsided, she lay gasping, boneless, dazed, her breaths coming in short, ragged puffs. Dear God, now she knew *precisely* what a few swipes of the tongue could accomplish.

Magic.

She felt Gideon gently lower her legs to the rug where they simply splayed open in utter, lax abandon. Felt him shift to lean over her, then his warm hand cupping her face. The pad of his thumb slowly brushing over her bottom lip.

"Julianne."

Her name breezed across her face, and with an effort she dragged her heavy eyelids open. And found herself staring into dark, intense eyes that seemed to reach inside and touch her soul.

She raised an unsteady hand and brushed back the dark lock of hair that fell across his furrowed brow. And murmured the word that had haunted her every thought for the past two months. "Gideon."

"Are you... all right?"

"I'm... I don't quite know how to describe it." She traced her fingers over the stark panes of his face, marveling even more at the fact that she could touch him so freely than at the extraordinary way he'd made her feel. "Utterly limp, but in the most delightful way."

"I didn't hurt you?"

"No." Worry suffused her. "Did *I* hurt *you*?"

A whiff of amusement entered his eyes. Leaning down, he brushed his mouth over hers. "No. You were..." He lifted his head, and his gaze drifted slowly over her. When his eyes met hers once more all traces of humor were gone. "Perfect," he whispered. "You were perfect. But—"

She laid her fingers on his lips, halting his words. "Please don't say you're sorry this happened. Because I'm not."

He lightly grasped her wrist and after pressing a quick kiss to her palm, moved her hand away. "Very well, I won't say I'm sorry. But that doesn't change the fact that it *shouldn't* have happened."

He abruptly sat up. Without ceremony he reached out and tugged up her bodice over her breasts that felt swollen and sensitive. Once she was covered, he stood then helped her do the same. She felt slightly unsteady on her feet and grasped the mantel for support.

Frowning, he bent down and scooped up her ripped drawers along with a handful of hairpins then shook his head. Muttered something that sounded very much like, What the bloody hell was I thinking? and raked his free hand through his hair. "We need to set you back to rights," he said in a low, urgent tone. "Now. Before anyone comes—"

A low *woof* from the doorway chopped off his words. They both turned. Caesar was on his feet, staring intently down the corridor. Princess Buttercup stood beside him, giving her best imitation of a fierce growl. Above the canine noise Julianne heard the unmistakable sound of her mother's imperious voice.

"...cannot credit that such a disturbance occurred, Winslow."

"You should have sent for us immediately." Her father's icy words followed by his heavy footfalls crossing the foyer's marble floor sent her stomach careening toward her shoes.

In the blink of an eye Gideon shoved her ruined drawers inside his shirt, then plucked her up and set her on the settee where she landed with a bounce.

He tossed the hairpins onto her lap. "Shove those into your hair," he commanded in a low, taut voice. "Doesn't matter if it's messy."

Trying not to panic, she scooped up her tangled curls and stabbed in pins while he snatched up his waistcoat. He jabbed his arms through the openings and buttoned it with a steady-fingered dexterity she couldn't help but admire, especially as she was shaking all over.

As he shrugged into his jacket, he ordered, "Swoon. And be damn convincing about it."

Swoon? Why, she'd never swooned in her life! But one look at his tight expression had her understanding his command. She nodded and quickly arranged herself on the settee.

Peeking one eye open, she watched him stride across the room and lay a hand on Caesar, who stopped growling at his master's touch.

"Winslow, fetch some hartshorn," Gideon called, his voice filled with urgency as he ran into the corridor. "Quickly! Lady Julianne has fainted. Ah, Lady Gatesbourne, how fortunate you're here. I'm afraid I've little experience in these matters."

Rapid footsteps approached. Julianne heard her mother gasp and her father mutter, "Ridiculous, foolish gel."

Seconds later Julianne's mother patted her cheeks in a none-too-gentle manner. "What happened?" her mother asked in a sharp voice. "Winslow told us in the foyer what occurred this evening but said Julianne seemed quite recovered."

"She did," Gideon said. "We were drinking tea, and all seemed well, but when we began discussing the evening's events, she became agitated. Said something about feeling utterly limp, then just like *that*"—he snapped his fingers— "she went down like a tenpin. I tried to revive her, but she didn't respond. That's when I dashed into the corridor for Winslow."

Just then Julianne heard a breathless Winslow rush into the room. "Here's the hartshorn, my lady."

Julianne had managed to remain unresponsive while her mother tapped her face, shook her shoulders, and rubbed her wrists, but one whiff of the powerfully unpleasant hartshorn had her nose twitching in protest. Putting on what she prayed was a convincing performance, she rolled her head from side to side, enough, she prayed, to explain her disheveled coif. Then she groaned and blinked her eyes open.

"She's come around," her mother said, passing the hartshorn back to Winslow. "Bring some damp cloths and a glass of water," she instructed the butler who instantly departed to do her bidding. Her mother then turned her attention back to Julianne. "Are you all right?"

Julianne blinked several more times then frowned. "Of course, Mother. How are you?"

"Very well. However, I am not the one who swooned."

Julianne widened her eyes. "Swooned? Me?"

Mother nodded and pursed her lips. "I'm afraid so."

"Surely not. I never swoon."

"Well, you did. If you could see yourself you'd know it's true." Her mother's appraising gaze swept over her. "You look a fright."

Julianne raised her hand and slowly pushed back a way-ward curl. "How...distressing." She cast her gaze around the room, noting her father's thunderous scowl, then looked at Gideon.

"Mr. Mayne. What are you doing here?"

Gideon's dark eyes gave away nothing. "You don't recall?"

Pressing her fingertips to her temple, Julianne puckered her brow. Then she nodded slowly. "Yes...of course. How silly of me. We were drinking tea. Then suddenly I felt utterly limp." Her gazed panned over everyone. "And then all of you were staring at me."

Winslow returned, and Julianne's mother placed a damp cloth on her forehead then helped her sit up and drink some water. After several sips her father asked, "Are you recovered enough to walk, Julianne?"

"Yes, I believe so."

"Good." He turned to his wife. "See that Julianne is settled in bed. I wish to speak to Mr. Mayne privately."

Nerves jittered in Julianne's midsection at her father's words and frigid tone. Her gaze flew to Gideon, but his attention was fixed on her father.

"As the intruder tried to enter Lady Julianne's bedchamber via her balcony," Gideon said, "she should not sleep there until this man is apprehended. Given the intruder's apparent dexterity, there should be no balcony or trees near the window nor should it adjoin to a room with either. Lady Julianne indicated there was such a bedchamber two doors down from hers."

"The blue guest room," her mother murmured. "Very well, I'll bring her there." She turned to the butler. "Winslow, see that the room is prepared."

"Yes, my lady."

Winslow departed, and with her mother's assistance, Julianne rose. When her mother attempted to take her arm, Julianne shook her head. "Thank you, but I'm quite all right."

In spite of Julianne's protest, her mother wrapped her fingers firmly around Julianne's upper arm. "Let's not take any chances. After all, we can't risk you falling down and injuring yourself. Especially now."

Julianne's insides curdled. Especially now. Yes—when her betrothal and marriage were imminent. Certainly couldn't have the bride sporting any bruises or a sprained ankle or broken leg.

Anxious to forestall any mention of her upcoming nuptials, she turned to Gideon and looked into those dark, fathomless eyes. "Thank you for all you did for me this evening, Mr. Mayne. I'll never forget it."

His features appeared hewn of stone. He inclined his head and said in an emotionless tone, "It was nothing, Lady Julianne."

His words froze her. Was that merely his way of saying you're welcome—or was he trying to tell her the intimacies they'd shared had meant nothing to him? She longed to search his eyes for some clue to his feelings, but he'd already looked away from her.

With a heavy heart she allowed her mother to lead her from the room. As they passed her father, his scowling gaze raked over her from head to foot. He then turned to stare at Gideon with a narrow-eyed expression clearly meant to freeze the Runner where he stood. The unmistakable suspicion in that expression made her blood run cold.

Dear God, did Father suspect something less than innocent had taken place between her and Gideon in the drawing room?

∽∾

Gideon held Lord Gatesbourne's frigid glare and waited for the earl to speak. Years of practice allowed him to project an outwardly calm demeanor, but it was one at complete odds with his inner turmoil.

Bloody hell. What in God's name had come over him? Now that he could think clearly again, he was shocked by his own actions. He was not a reckless man. His greatest assets were his strength and his control. They'd saved him more times than he cared to recall. Against his enemies. Hardened criminals. Thieves and murderers. Yet somehow he'd let a mere slip of a woman, with bottomless blue eyes that reflected such a compelling combination of hope and heartbreak, knock his legs out from under him. In a way no one ever had before. In a way that both confused and alarmed him. In a way he would have wagered all he owned—modest though that was—was impossible.

Yet, there he'd been, legless. Lost in her. Mindless. Heedless of everything and everyone but her. And apparently helpless to stop it. Double bloody hell.

He had to get out of this house. Away from her. Away from this investigation. He needed to catch the bastard he was after and put an end to this. Get back to his life. And forget about her. As quickly as possible. Before he lost his bloody mind. Or his control again.

Finally Lord Gatesbourne spoke. "I'll have your account of this evening's occurrence, Mayne."

"Of course." He related the events in a calm, precise manner, leaving out nothing except the part where he'd lifted Julianne's skirts and rendered her utterly limp.

"I see," said the earl when Gideon finished his recitation. "So you didn't see this man yourself."

"No."

"In fact no one saw him except my fanciful daughter. Who has also heard moans that no one else heard."

There was no missing the earl's insinuation, and Gideon shook his head. "Given the evidence of the footprints under the tree, there's no doubt someone tried to gain access to Lady Julianne's bedchamber, my lord. I saw her immediately afterward. Her terror was genuine. Plus, do not forget the threatening note found in Lady Julianne's bedchamber and the fact that I discovered the very same window where she saw the intruder unlocked this afternoon."

The earl made a disgusted sound and muttered something about wretched timing that Gideon didn't quite catch.

"I beg your pardon, my lord?"

"Nothing." The earl's eyes took on another layer of frost. "That being the case, I'd like to know how this knife-wielding intruder gained access to my daughter's balcony after I hired *you* to patrol the grounds."

"With such a vast area to cover, it was unfortunately impossible for me to be everywhere at once."

"And why were you not out looking for this scoundrel when the countess and I arrived home?"

"Your daughter suffered a terrible fright. Given there was no trail to follow beyond the mews, I thought it best to remain here and insure Lady Julianne's safety until you returned."

"And you insured her safety by drinking tea and eating biscuits?"

Gideon's gaze didn't waver. "I insured her safety by first making certain all the entrances to the house were secured then not letting her out of my sight. If anyone had been foolish enough to attempt to harm her in my presence, they would have had to get through me—and Caesar—first. And I assure you they would not have succeeded."

The earl jerked his head toward the doorway where Caesar stood at attention. "I take it that large beast is Caesar?"

"Yes. He is a skilled guard dog and has helped me apprehend dozens of criminals."

The earl's scowl deepened, and he commenced pacing in front of the fire. A full minute passed before he stopped directly in front of Gideon. "No harm can come to my daughter," he said fiercely.

A frisson of relief worked its way through Gideon. Finally the man showed some warmth toward Julianne and appeared genuinely concerned for her safety.

"As time is short, you're my best chance to make certain Julianne is kept safe," the earl continued. "Therefore I want to hire you to guard her. You'll follow her everywhere, although it's probably best that she not go about too much. You'll stay here, in the house, and make sure no harm befalls her."

Gideon's every muscle tensed. His first instinct was to flatly refuse. Guard her? Follow her everywhere? Stay here? Bloody hell, he'd go mad. Even more disturbing, however, was the thought that he'd fail to resist her, as he had so spectacularly tonight. The way she stripped him of his control appalled him. Angered him. Indeed, it actually frightened him.

He could tell himself that now that he'd touched her, knew the feel and taste of her, knew that she smelled like vanilla—

everywhere—his curiosity and appetite for her was appeased. But he'd be lying to himself. Because the knowledge of her scent and feel and touch had appeased *nothing*. No, instead it had served only to inflame him further, to make him want her more. This desire for her . . . it went beyond mere hunger. It was a ravenous *craving*. He didn't want to merely hold her, touch her, kiss her. He wanted to devour her. Brand himself on her. Touch her so deeply, make her his so profoundly and thoroughly, he'd haunt her every thought. The way she haunted his.

And he couldn't understand *why*. Obviously he desired her. Bloody hell, what breathing man wouldn't? He'd experienced desire. Lust. Had experienced pleasure with his share of women. Yet as steamy as those encounters had been, they now seemed tepid in comparison to the heat Julianne inspired. Julianne brought out something in him he didn't understand. Something, for the first time in his life, he hadn't been able to control. And wasn't certain he'd have the strength to control in the future. That was very bad—for both of them. It meant he needed to stay far, far away from her and her irresistible allure.

But how could he refuse to protect her? If he did, and something happened to her, he'd never forgive himself. Yet neither could he trust himself. For both their sakes he had to refuse.

"There are other Runners who could—" he began, but the earl cut him off with an impatient flick of his hand.

"From what I hear, you're the best, and I'll have nothing less."

"I appreciate that, but I cannot—"

"I'll make it worth your while financially." The earl named an amount that nearly matched Gideon's yearly Bow Street salary. And therefore raised his suspicions.

"That's a great deal of money," Gideon said.

"It is worth a great deal that my daughter remain safe for the next fortnight."

Gideon's brows rose. "Just the next fortnight? What about after that?"

"Even if the culprit hasn't been apprehended by then,

Chapter 12

With Caesar keeping pace beside him, Gideon walked along the dark street, his thoughts as gloomy as the shadows that surrounded him. Tendrils of fog rose from the ground, and puddles filled the uneven pavement, soaking his boots. The rain had stopped, but a damp chill infiltrated the still air. His strides ate up the ground, each one taking him farther from the Grosvenor Square mansion he'd departed five minutes ago and closer to Covent Garden. To his own modest home. Where he belonged.

She will be married to the Duke of Eastling.

The words clanged through Gideon's mind as they'd ceaselessly done since the earl had uttered them, like rusty chains hobbling criminals on their way to the gallows. The news had stunned him, and he'd gone perfectly still. On the outside. On the inside, it felt as if everything shifted and tumbled. Crashed and shattered. Then the reverberating words were replaced by an agonized *Noooooo!* that had screamed through his head.

It had taken him several seconds to recover, and when he had, anger and betrayal stabbed him like daggers in the back. She'd known. *Known* she was betrothed to another man, yet she'd deliberately set out to entice him. Then a keen sense of self-disgust filled him. He'd done a great many things he wasn't proud of, but by damn, he'd never cuckolded a man. Even if he'd desired the woman and she'd been willing. Even if he'd disliked her husband.

For years he'd been forced to witness the damage and pain that sort betrayal could cause. And he wanted no part of it. How many vicious rows had he listened to while watching the light fade from his mother's eyes after his father came home stinking of some trollop's cheap perfume? More than he wanted to recall. There were bloody few lines he hadn't crossed, but that was one of them. Until she'd deceived him. Not to mention the point of pride and honor that he didn't take things that didn't belong to him. And unbeknownst to him—because she'd deceived him—she belonged to someone else.

Now, on the cold walk home, he passed under a gaslight, the fog shifting eerily in the pale yellow glow, and he heaved out a long sigh. In spite of both the betrayal and self-disgust, an aching, profound sense of loss all but strangled him. Bloody hell, what was wrong with him? Why had the earl's announcement hit him with the force of a blow to the head? He'd seen the parade of suitors tramping through the house. The men who flocked to her at parties. It certainly wasn't as if *he* ever could have thrown his name on the silver platter bearing those of her countless admirers.

Still, the news of her imminent marriage had caught him off guard. And he didn't like being caught off guard.

She will be married to the Duke of Eastling...

Unreasonable, white-hot jealousy ripped through him with a viciousness that wouldn't allow him to deny what it was. Bloody hell, the thought of that bastard putting his hands on Julianne, taking her without a care to her pleasure as he had Lady Daltry at last night's soiree, made him want to break things. Most specifically, that bastard's face.

Fancy gowns and parties are not important to me. Not nearly as much as other things. Love. Laughter. Companionship. Desire. Romance. Passion. They are what I long for.

In his mind's eye he saw her saying those words, the despair and vulnerability and yearning reflected in her expressive eyes. He clenched his teeth so hard he was surprised they didn't crumble to dust. She sure as hell wouldn't get all those things from a cold bastard like the duke.

The only time I've ever felt free of that glass coffin is when you kissed me.

Damn it, the taste of her still lingered on his tongue. In spite of the chill, dank air, he could still smell her. Feel her curves against him, and her warmth surrounding him. It was as if she were tattooed on his senses.

How the hell was he ever going to forget her?

Especially now that he'd agreed to protect her?

He dragged his cold hands down his face and released a pent-up breath that fogged the air. God knows he hadn't wanted to agree. Had wanted to tell her arrogant father that Gideon Mayne couldn't be bought. And he hadn't been bought—by the money. That he could have walked away from. But as much as he cursed himself for it, he couldn't walk away from Julianne when she was in danger. He would find the bastard threatening her and stop him. He'd do his job.

And *then* he'd walk away from her.

She'd marry the duke and move to Cornwall.

And that would be that.

All he needed to do was make sure he kept his damn hands and his damn mouth off her.

But now that he knew she belonged to someone else—that her betrothal wasn't simply something nebulous that would happen *someday*—his tarnished honor demanded there be no further intimacies between them. All he needed to do was hold on to that sense of anger and betrayal he'd felt upon hearing the news, the realization that she'd deceived him, and he'd succeed. Surely he could do that.

Wouldn't have mattered if you'd known, his inner voice taunted. *The evening would have ended the same way. With you lifting her skirts.*

His hands tightened into fists, and he shook his head to dislodge the insidious voice. No. He would have found the strength to resist her had he known.

You wanted her more than you wanted your next breath.

True. But the knowledge that she was betrothed would have cooled his ardor.

Wouldn't it?

Yes! his tarnished honor roared. *Absolutely yes.*

He turned off the main road onto a narrower cobbled street. Almost home. Where he'd climb into bed and get some much-needed rest.

You won't rest, you idiot. You'll lie awake and stare at the ceiling and remember what it felt like to kiss her. To bury your face between her soft thighs.

Heat raced through him, settling in his groin, and he grimaced as he swelled against his breeches. The fact that he hadn't had a woman in two months wasn't helping the situation. Not since he'd first seen Julianne. He hadn't wanted anyone other than her.

His lips compressed into a thin line.

That was going to change. Tonight. And he knew just the place.

He looked ahead, and his gaze fastened on the sign coming up on the next corner. The Drunken Porcupine. He hadn't been to the tavern since he'd met Julianne. In fact, he'd been living like a monk since that night. Well, no more. He quickened his pace, and a moment later, he pushed open the heavy oak door.

Loud guffaws, ribald singing, and the sound of a fiddle spilled out, along with a haze of smoke and the scent of sausage and cooked cabbage. Two months might have passed, but nothing had changed. Booths lined the outer walls, and wooden benches set in front of long, pockmarked tables ran the length of the room.

He made his way through the dimly lit interior, Caesar at his heels, nodding greetings to a few men he knew, returning the glares of several he didn't. When he reached the well-worn bar, he chose an empty stool in the corner that afforded him a good view of the room and put the wall at his back. Caesar settled himself at Gideon's feet.

"Well, look wot the storm blew in."

Gideon turned and found himself the subject of a narrow-eyed stare from Luther, the giant of a barkeep who polished a thick glass mug with the corner of his apron. The dim light reflected off Luther's shiny bald head and glinted on the small gold hoop in his earlobe. The tattoo of a rose decorated a beefy forearm. In spite of standing behind the bar, he still looked very much like the brawny sailor he once was. "Thought mayhap ye'd died and hadn't bothered to tell me."

"Couldn't very well tell you if I had."

Luther considered that, then nodded. "I suppose not. What'll ye have? Yer usual nip o' ale?"

"Whiskey."

Luther made no comment, and seconds later his ham-sized hand set down two glasses in front of Gideon. "I'll join ye," Luther said, pouring a generous shot of amber liquid into each glass. When he finished, he picked up his glass and raised it. "Here's to ye still bein' alive."

Gideon raised his glass. "And you as well."

"Thank ye."

Gideon tossed back the potent liquor in a single gulp then closed his eyes against the scrape of rough fire that burned its way down his throat. When he opened his eyes, Luther was setting down his empty glass and staring at Gideon with a speculative expression.

"Can't recall I've ever seen ye drink whiskey," Luther said.

"I rarely do," Gideon said. "Probably because it tastes so foul." A shudder ran through him. "Jesus. I think my guts are melting."

Luther gave a bark of laughter. "Probably are. Best whiskey in London right here." Then Luther sobered and rested his massive forearms on the bar and leaned forward. "Ain't right that ye stayed away so long, Gideon. Ain't no way to treat a friend."

Gideon met his gaze and gave a tight nod. "You're right. I'm sorry."

Luther nodded his acceptance then flashed a grin. "Especially a friend who's so much bigger than you."

Gideon allowed himself to grin back. Gideon stood several inches over six feet, but Luther was still a half a head taller and probably a good four stones heavier. "I could squash ye like a spider," Luther said, grinning.

"You'd have to catch me first."

"That'd be a problem," Luther agreed, shooting his left leg a rueful expression. A wound sustained in a knife fight on the docks had ended Luther's seafaring ways. "Speedy bastard, ye are."

"It's what keeps me from getting squashed like a spider."

Luther poured them each another whiskey. After Gideon had taken a swig—a much smaller one than last time, although it most likely didn't matter as his insides had already corroded—Luther said, "Interestin' that ye'd stop in tonight."

"Why's that?"

"Someone were here earlier askin' about ye."

"Oh? Who?"

"Gave the name o' Jack Mayne. Said he were yer father."

Gideon's hand froze halfway to his mouth, and his fingers tightened on the glass. An unpleasant cramp seized his insides.

Luther leaned in a bit farther. "Thought I recalled ye once sayin' yer father were dead."

"He is." Gideon slowly lowered his hand but continued to grip the glass. "At least as far as I'm concerned."

Understanding dawned in Luther's dark eyes, and he nodded. "Know a few blokes like that meself."

"What did he look like?" Maybe, just maybe, it hadn't really been Jack Mayne.

Luther considered for several seconds. "Like you around the eyes. Rough. Haggard. Had a jagged lookin' scar here." Luther pointed to his own chin.

Bloody hell. That was Jack Mayne. The fact that he and his light fingers were back in London didn't bode well for the fine citizens who valued their possessions. "What did you tell him?"

"That I hadn't seen ye in weeks and weren't expectin' to."

"He say anything else?"

"Just to let ye know he were lookin' for ye should ye come in."

Gideon nodded slowly and took another sip of whiskey.

Jack must be in dire circumstances to seek out his son. Their last parting four years ago hadn't been pleasant. If they were unfortunate enough to run into each other now, Gideon knew it wouldn't be any more pleasant. He didn't want to throw his own father in Newgate, but unless Jack Mayne had turned over a new leaf—which he very much doubted—he suspected it might come to that. And if Gideon himself didn't do it, one of the other Runners would. For as crafty as Jack Mayne was, someday he'd get caught.

Luther moved down the bar to service other customers, and Gideon cradled his drink between his hands and stared into the amber liquid. Memories he'd refused to let surface pushed at him, but he ruthlessly shoved them aside. After years of practice, he was good at suppressing the unpleasant recollections. Besides, there were other things to think about. Like the reason he'd come here tonight.

When Luther returned, Gideon gave the tavern a look-over then asked casually, "Where's Maggie?"

"She ain't workin' tonight. Off to Vauxhall with some bloke she met a few weeks back. Seems a decent sort." Luther picked up another glass to polish. "She the reason ye're here tonight?"

Yes. No. Bloody hell, he didn't know. "I was just wondering where she was."

"And now ye know." Luther shot him a speculative look. "Don't think she'd a-taken' up with this other bloke 'cept she got tired of waitin' for you. I wager she'd come runnin' back if ye so much as crooked yer little finger."

Gideon didn't respond. He knew Luther was correct. Maggie Price had made it clear from the first time she met Gideon six months ago—on her first night working at the tavern— that she'd like to serve him more than drinks. And on several occasions she had—when Gideon's work-consumed, solitary existence had proven too lonely for even him.

He liked that she didn't ask a lot of questions and didn't make any demands on him. She didn't like to talk about her past, which was fine with him, because he didn't like to talk about his. He'd even been tossing around the idea of maybe pursuing something a bit more frequent between them than the occasional roll in the hay.

And then he'd met Julianne. And all thoughts of any woman besides her had fled. His mind *knew* how bloody ridiculous that was, but try as he might, he couldn't change it. Since he didn't have any logical excuse for not bedding Maggie, he stayed away. He knew she wouldn't have denied him, but she deserved better than to be a stand-in for another woman. She deserved a man who would care for her. For a brief moment he'd thought he might be that man. They got on well together. They pleased each other in bed. He didn't love her, but he liked her. Wasn't that enough?

Given how he'd stayed away and barely thought of her since meeting Julianne, he guessed not.

"Why don'tcha just spit it out?"

Luther's question jerked back Gideon's thoughts. "Spit what out?"

"The reason ye came here tonight. Ye can start with 'er name. And don't say Maggie, 'cause it ain't her who's got ye all tied up in knots."

"What makes you think it's a woman?"

Luther looked toward the ceiling. "Between ownin' this place and havin' been married nigh on twelve years, I know woman trouble when I see it." He nodded toward Gideon's half-finished whiskey. "Must be bad for ye to be swillin' that rotgut."

"You said this was the finest whiskey in London."

"Don't mean it won't rot yer guts. So who is she?"

"Maybe it's Maggie."

Luther shook his bald head. "If it were, ye'd have been out the door on yer way to Vauxhall as soon as I said she were there with another bloke." He stroked his chin and gave Gideon a speculative look. "Is she somebody accused of a crime ye know she didn't commit? Or worse—that she did commit? Well, split me windpipe! Have ye lost yer heart to a murderess?"

Gideon shot him a frown. "She isn't a murderess, and I

haven't lost my heart." He dragged his hands down his face. "Just my mind."

Luther nodded sagely. "Drive ye to the brink, a woman will. If I didn't care for my Rose the way I do, I'd've tossed her into the Thames long ago."

Gideon's lips twitched at the mention of Luther's diminutive wife. Rose was small, but she was very handy with a cast-iron skillet. She didn't tolerate any nonsense from the Drunken Porcupine's clientele. Or from her husband.

"Toss her in the Thames?" Gideon scoffed. "I'd like to see you try. She'd flatten you with that skillet of hers before you ever got her hefted over your shoulder."

Luther rubbed the back of his head as if he'd been coshed. "Yer right about that. Course once I hefted her over me shoulder, it wouldn't be to the Thames but to bed I'd be takin' her." He blew out a gusty sigh. "Ah, well, that's wot happens when ye let a woman get under yer skin and fall in love. As yer clearly findin' out."

Gideon went perfectly still. Took a single careful breath. Then said slowly and distinctly, "I haven't fallen in love." Heavily in lust, but certainly not in love. He might be foolish, but he wasn't a complete idiot.

Luther nodded. "Right. Yer just tied up in half hitches and miserable and so randy ye can barely think."

Since that perfectly described what he was feeling, Gideon felt compelled to admit, "Something like that. I suppose."

Luther let out a bark of laughter then clapped Gideon on the shoulder with an enthusiasm that would have sent a lesser man to the floor. "Well, wot do ye think love feels like, ye horse's arse? Best watch yerself, or next thing ye know, she'll be swattin' ye upside yer head with a skillet. And I can tell ye, *that* hurts like a bugger."

Gideon tried to imagine stunning, aristocratic, ladylike Julianne wielding a skillet and simply couldn't.

Luther planted plate-sized fists on the bar and grinned. "So who's the wench who's finally stolen yer cold heart? Anybody I know?"

Gideon stared into the remnants of his whiskey for several long seconds. Then he lifted his gaze to Luther's. "My heart isn't stolen, but I can't deny I... want her. You don't know her, and I can't have her."

The merriment leaked from Luther's eyes. "Why can't ye have her?" A dumbfounded expression came over Luther's ruddy face. "Don't tell me she's not wantin' *you*? Can hardly spit but find a woman that isn't givin' ye the eye."

"She's getting married." He tossed back the rest of his whiskey. "In a fortnight. Then moving to Cornwall."

Luther nodded slowly. "That's a pickle, all right. But maybe if she cares for ye, she'll call off the weddin'."

"Wouldn't matter." He debated whether to go on, then figured what the hell. Even though he was still miserable, having someone to confide in made him feel just a bit less awful. "She's an earl's daughter."

Luther's eyes widened, then he gave a low whistle. "Well, that's a right mess ye've got there, my friend."

A bitter sound escaped Gideon. "Yes, it is."

"Wot the hell are ye doin' even *lookin'* at a bird like that?"

"Damned if I know. She's nothing but a spoiled, pampered princess."

He said the words fiercely, wanting them to be true, but the instant they passed his lips, his insides cringed. *Fancy gowns and parties are not important to me. Not nearly as much as other things. Love. Laughter. Companionship. Desire. Romance. Passion. They are what I long for.* Yes, she was pampered, as everyone of her class was. But from the first instant he'd seen her, he'd suspected there was more to her. And after tonight he was very much afraid he was right. And he desperately didn't want to be. Didn't want her to be anything more than a spoiled princess.

"Wouldn't expect an earl's daughter to be anythin' else," Luther said. "Must be beautiful to have turned yer head like this."

"Yes." Beautiful and vulnerable and captivating. And completely unavailable. Hoping for some sage, coolheaded advice, something that would slap him out of the lust-induced fog that threatened to choke him, he asked, "What do you do when temptation is about to eat you alive?"

"Temptation? Mostly I try to avoid it." A wide grin split Luther's rough features. "Unless I absolutely can't resist." He grabbed the whiskey bottle and poured another round. "Cheer up, mate. Look on the bright side. Ye've got an entire fortnight to tup her. That'll cure ye of what's ailin' ye. Then the best part is the fancy bird will fly the coop to Cornwall! She'll be out of yer sight and then out of yer mind. Especially after ye find yerself another beautiful bird."

Gideon forced himself to nod, but he knew that even once Julianne was out of sight, it would take a very long time before he got her out of his mind. And he realized what a fool he'd been to think coming here tonight would in any way help him forget her.

Chapter 13

Julianne paced the blue guest room where she'd slept last night—or rather tossed and turned last night—her thoughts a jumbled mixture of vivid recollections of her interlude with Gideon and worries about what had transpired between her father and Gideon after she'd retired. Had her father guessed she and Gideon had shared intimacies? Had he dismissed Gideon—or worse, threatened him? Had he told Gideon about her engagement? Would she ever see Gideon again?

Those plaguing questions had been interspersed with reliving the incredible moments she'd spent in his arms. She'd read of such intimacies in the scandalous selections favored by the Ladies Literary Society, but reading about them and experiencing them were two completely different things. Never had she imagined that she could feel such passion. Incite such passion. Want or need another person so much. Care so profoundly. So that nothing else mattered. But now that she knew, now that she had been offered that intoxicating glimpse, she wanted to see it, feel it, again. She wanted those intimacies, and more.

Therefore it was now time to gather her courage and face

her father. And discover if Gideon, the only man she wanted to share those intimacies with, had been banished from her life even before her wedding.

She exited the bedchamber and headed down the corridor but paused before the door to her own bedchamber. After making certain she wasn't observed, she turned the brass knob and slipped inside.

Bright morning sunshine filled the room, spilling over the gold and green carpet and neatly made bed. Her gaze fell on the window leading to her balcony, and a shudder ran through her. After speaking with her father, she'd have her chat with Johnny. But first she needed to take care of one thing.

She crossed to her wardrobe and opened the double doors. Crouching down, she pulled a book-sized wooden box from its hiding place beneath the old pair of ankle boots she wore when picking flowers in the garden. Then she stuck her hand into the left boot and withdrew a small brass key. She unlocked the box, lifted the lid, and gazed upon her trove of treasures. She lovingly added her newest cherished items to the velvet-lined box: her copy of *The Ghost of Devonshire Manor*. And Gideon's handkerchief.

She'd held the linen square all night against her heart. She raised it now to her lips and breathed deeply. His scent clung to the material, that wondrous smell of starch and adventure and warmth that belonged to him alone. The one that was permanently etched in her memory. Even with her eyes closed, she could have picked him out of a crowd simply by inhaling.

She should return it—after all, he hadn't given it to her to keep. But she simply couldn't part with it. It would serve as a secret reminder in the long, lonely years to come of what, for one magical night, she'd shared with a man who'd captured every aspect of her mind and imagination.

"You are now the most beloved of my treasures," she whispered into the handkerchief. After carefully placing the linen square on top of her other beloved items, she locked the box and replaced it and the key in her wardrobe. As she stood, she caught sight of herself in the full-length cheval glass in the corner. Did she look different? Unable to resist, she crossed to the mirror, watching herself as she moved. Was there a new sway in her step? Surely there must be. She stopped an arm's length in front of her reflection and critically assessed her appearance. Outwardly she appeared the same as always. But inside...inside nothing was the same. And it never would be.

She felt like a new Julianne. One who'd finally experienced something of life. Of adventure. Of passion. One with a secret that lived inside her like a beating heart. Not the sort of secret she could ever share or confide to her friends, but one that burned brightly within her, warming her as if she'd swallowed the sun.

Raising her hands, she brushed her fingertips over her cheeks. Perhaps her skin bore a bit of a glow. She touched her lips that still felt kiss-swollen. Then ran her fingers down her neck, over her collarbone to her chest. Her breasts felt sensitive, and beneath her gown they bore several traces of red where Gideon's stubble had abraded her tender skin. Outward signs, but ones that would remain known only to her.

Still, was there some other outward sign? Something in her demeanor? Something her father might have noticed last night? Her stomach cramped at the thought. She glanced at the ormolu clock on the mantel, dismayed to note the time. Father would be at breakfast now, and she knew better than to disturb him before he'd finished his meal and newspaper. Better to speak to Johnny first then seek out Father. In the meanwhile, she could only pray he hadn't guessed that something improper had occurred. And if he had, surely Gideon had denied it. *It was nothing, Lady Julianne.*

She closed her eyes and drew a deep breath. Oh, but Gideon was wrong. It had been *everything.*

Opening her eyes, she studied her dreamy expression in the mirror. Surely she should be appalled at what she'd done, at the shocking liberties she'd allowed him. She should regret her actions.

But she did not. Instead, she prayed she'd have the opportunity to repeat them.

She drew a bracing breath. Now it was time to face Johnny.
And then her father.

∽

"Yor not an easy man to find."

Gideon halted in the act of adding three folded shirts to his
portmanteau and forced himself not to whirl around. He was
startled, which irritated him. He'd learned his lesson well,
and not many men could sneak up on him unawares. But this
particular man had always had the uncanny ability to move
like a ghost and gain access to places he didn't belong.

The slightly raspy voice hadn't changed in the years since
he'd last heard it. Bloody hell, he'd hoped to never hear it
again. The eggs and bacon he'd finished eating for breakfast a
short time ago suddenly felt like stones in his stomach.

If he hadn't let Caesar outside to explore the patch of grass
that constituted their yard, the dog would have warned him.
But it was too late now. Gideon released the shirts, pulled in
a deep breath, and slowly turned. And looked into dark eyes
that exactly matched his own.

The voice hadn't changed, but Jack Mayne had, and Gideon
had to force his features not to register any surprise. He was
considerably thinner, and his hair, while still thick, had gone
completely gray. Deep lines were etched along the sides of his
mouth, across his forehead, and around his eyes. The last time
Gideon had seen him, he'd been dressed in little better than rags.
Now he wore decent boots, fine breeches, a snowy shirt and
neatly tied cravat, and a superfine jacket. And a bloody top hat.

With that devilish grin Gideon knew so well, his father
doffed his hat and offered a mocking bow. "Aren't ya glad to
see yor old man, Gideon?"

There'd been a time, many years ago, when Gideon the
small boy had indeed been thrilled to see his father. Those
days were long since past.

"Jack," he said, his voice flat. He hadn't called him Father
since the day he'd walked out of the hovel where they used to
live. On the day there hadn't been any more reason to stay.
"What do you want?"

"Why, I want to see my boy! It's been a long time."

Four years, two months, and sixteen days. Not nearly long enough. "You've seen me." Gideon nodded toward the doorway. "Now get out of my house."

"Ah, now don't be like that, Gideon," Jack said. "Nice set of locks you've got on yor doors and windows. Don'tcha wanna know how I got in?"

"No. I just hope you didn't break whichever lock you picked. I'm not in the mood to replace it."

A reproachful look filled Jack's eyes. "You insult me, Son. As if I'd be so careless." He waggled his fingers. "Still the best there is. Of course, it was thoughtful of you to set yor guard dog outside. Wouldn't have cared to have his teeth attached to me arse when I entered the house." He made a sweeping motion, encompassing Gideon's bedchamber, and nodded. "You've come up in the world. Not the fanciest section of London, but far from the worst."

Gideon folded his arms across his chest and stared at the man who he'd had to turn his heart against. While he still had any of it left. "What do you want, Jack?" His gaze raked over his father's clothes. "Is it money? Because if so, you should have worn your rags instead of cleaning yourself up so prettily."

"No, I don't need money," Jack said with an injured air. "I might be gettin' on in years, but old Jack Mayne can still take care of himself. In fact, I recently came into a nice little nest."

"Which means you found a fat bird to pinch. You'd be wise not to forget that we're not on the same sides of the law."

"I'm not likely to forget." Jack gave him a broad wink. "Of course, *yor* the one on the wrong side."

"Just one of many things we disagree on."

"Indeed we do. Talented hands ye've got Gideon. I should know. I taught them everything I know."

"They are indeed talented—at catching criminals and sending them to Newgate. Why are you in London?"

"Heard tell of some fine opportunities here for a man with my gifts, and as ya can see..." He tugged on his lapels and grinned, "I heard right. Figured as long as I was here, I'd give ya a visit."

Gideon didn't have any doubt that Jack's "opportunity" was the sort that could result in a trip to Newgate. "If I hear you've done something, if I catch wind of anything, I—"

"Won't protect me," Jack said. "So you've said a hundred times. Well, I don't need yor protection, boy. And you'd have to go some to catch me doin' anything—if I were doin' anything."

"I'm glad you understand. Now, if you'll excuse me . . ." He shot a pointed look at the doorway.

"Is it off to work yor goin' . . ." Jack slanted his gaze toward the open portmanteau on the bed, "or on a holiday?"

"Work."

Jack nodded. "Yor a busy man. That's good." His brows shot up, and keen interest glittered in his eyes. "I don't suppose yor involved with the case everyone's talkin' about and that's been in the *Times*—that murderin' ghost robber? Now there's a clever bloke."

Gideon's instincts tingled. "Why do you ask?"

Jack gave a nonchalant shrug. "It's a fascinatin' story. Got any leads on who the bloke is?"

Gideon crossed to the bed and grabbed the scuffed leather satchel. "I have to go."

"Course you do," Jack said, nodding in an approving fashion. "Lots of criminals to catch around here, I'm sure."

Gideon looked him in the eyes. "Don't be one of them."

Something flickered in Jack's eyes, then he grinned. "Not to worry. Yor old da is still pretty spry."

Which, Gideon knew, meant Jack didn't think he'd get caught. But someday he would. And Gideon didn't want to have to be the one to catch him.

"I'll be seein' ya around, Son," Jack said. He tipped his hat, then turned on his heel and quit the room. Gideon walked to the doorway and watched as Jack, softly whistling under his breath, left the house.

It wasn't until the door closed behind him and Gideon was

once again alone that he realized he'd been holding his breath and his hands were tightened into fists.

Having Jack Mayne gain access to his house and sneak up behind him was not a stellar way to start his day—a day he'd have to spend resisting, er, guarding Julianne.

Bloody hell, it was doing to be one damn long day.

∞

Julianne stared at Johnny, trying to comprehend what he'd just said. And simply couldn't. "What do you mean you didn't come here last night?"

Johnny wiped the back of one dirty hand over his soot-smudged cheek. He was a strapping young man of two and twenty whose father had been delivering coal to the Grosvenor Square mansion for a decade. When his father passed away six months ago, Johnny had taken over the business. Now his gaze darted back and forth, obviously as anxious as she that they remain unseen and unheard in this recessed corner of the pantry where she'd pulled him.

"I'm awful sorry, milady," he said in an undertone. "My wife, she's been expectin' a baby, and don't ye know he had the bad timing to decide last night was when he wanted to be born. There were no one else to help her, and I couldn't leave. But I'll come tonight, I will, and make the moans and groans. Just like we'd planned."

Julianne felt as if the floor beneath her feet shifted. "You didn't come to the house last night," she said slowly, enunciating each word very carefully, watching his face.

Johnny looked at the ground and scuffed the toe of his dirty boot against the floor. Then he raised his chin. "No, milady. And 'tis real sorry I am."

"You didn't dress in a hooded robe and stand on my balcony?"

Johnny's mouth dropped open. "Glory be, milady. Wherever did ye get a daft idea like that?" His eyes widened, and he instantly looked abashed. "Beggin' yer pardon, I am."

She grasped his sleeves. "Did you write a note and leave it in my bedchamber?"

The young man's green eyes rounded to saucers. "Course not, milady. Why would I do such a thing? And 'tis not much of a letter writer I am."

She wanted to shake him, demand he tell her the truth, but she could see he was. Which meant...

Dear God, it meant that someone else had left the threatening note. Tried to gain access to her bedchamber. Someone with a knife.

A shudder of fear racked her, and she released Johnny to wrap her arms around herself to ward off the sudden chill gripping her. Who would do such a thing? And why? She recalled the crudely written words on the note, Yor next, and another chill ripped through her.

"Are ye all right, milady?" Johnny asked. " 'Tis right pale yor lookin'."

"I'm fine," she lied.

"I'll come tonight. Swear I will."

Julianne frowned. She certainly didn't want to risk Johnny being hurt should last night's intruder return. "No. It's best if you don't."

"A promise is a promise, milady. Besides, with the new mouth to feed at home, I need the extra blunt." His eyes clouded with worry. "Ye'll still pay me if I come tonight instead of last night, won't ye?"

"I'll pay you for *not* coming tonight, or any other night." She reached in her pocket and slipped out two gold coins, which she pressed into Johnny's hand. Johnny opened his fist and gaped at his windfall. "For you. And your wife and baby."

"Thank ye, milady." He dashed off toward the servants' entrance, leaving Julianne alone.

Deeply disturbed, she exited the pantry and made her way up the servants' stairs to avoid walking through the kitchen where Mrs. Linquist would see her. After making certain she wasn't observed, she entered the corridor, smoothed her skirts, then made her way to the foyer.

"Your father wishes to see you at once, Lady Julianne," Winslow said as soon he saw her. "In his study."

Unable to speak around the lump of apprehension tightening her throat, Julianne merely nodded. She walked to the study on legs that felt heavy and wooden, then stood outside the door for nearly a minute before summoning her courage to knock. At her father's crisp order to enter, she opened the door and crossed the threshold. Her father glanced up from his desk then returned his gaze to whatever he was reading.

"Do you intend to simply stand there, or are you going to tell me what you want?" he asked in that frigid voice that only served to make her more tongue-tied in his presence.

Swallowing her trepidation, she approached his desk. When she stood before it, she moistened her lips then said, "Winslow said you wished to see me?"

"Yes. Regarding Mr. Mayne."

Dear God. His forbidding tone and expression loosened her knees. Since he hadn't invited her to sit, she gripped the back of the chair in front of her.

"I've hired him to guard both you and the house until this matter is settled or you're safely married to Eastling and on your way to Cornwall, whichever comes first," her father announced. He glanced up, and his icy blue gaze bored into her. "Your activities will be severely curtailed. If it is necessary for you to go anywhere, Mayne will accompany you. You will continue to sleep in the blue room, and Mayne will take over your bedchamber—in the hopes that whoever tried to gain entrance last night will do so again and be captured. Hopefully tonight, so we can put a swift end to this nonsense." His gaze took on another layer of frost. "That is the way it is to be, and I'll not hear any arguments about it."

It took several seconds for his words to sink in. When they finally did, her heart soared. She looked down at the carpet to hide the triumph and elation she feared glowed in her eyes. "Yes, Father," she murmured, hoping she sounded sufficiently abashed.

"I don't want you discussing this matter, nor do I want His Grace getting wind of it. If he even suspected some knife-wielding hooligan might be after you, he'd no doubt cry off, and I'll be damned if I'll allow that to happen."

"Did you tell Mr. Mayne of my engagement?"

"Naturally. He had to be made aware of how imperative it is that nothing happen to you."

A bit of her elation evaporated. How had Gideon taken the news? Was he angry she hadn't told him herself? Or did he simply not care? She considered appealing to her father to reconsider the marriage but knew it was useless. Any entreaty would only fall on deaf ears. Nothing would disrupt her father's business arrangement with the duke. Instead she asked, "Will . . . will Mr. Mayne be dining with us?"

A look of pure distaste swam across her father's features. "Certainly not. He doesn't have the proper clothes or manners for the dining room. You'll be perfectly safe with your mother and me during dinner. Mr. Mayne will eat in the kitchen with the rest of the hired help."

Julianne's fingers knotted in her gown, and she pressed her lips together to hold back the flood of arguments she wished to present.

"Mr. Mayne is to accompany you everywhere," her father continued, "therefore don't get it into your foolish head to go haring off alone. Given the situation, it's probably best you remain at home today and this evening." He frowned. "Eastling's soiree is tomorrow night, and you'll need to attend. But for today, you're to remain here."

"Yes, Father." Keeping her expression carefully blank, she raised her head. "But what about my usual round of calls with Mother?"

"She can do them on her own today, as she did yesterday. Mr. Mayne will arrive within the hour." Her father's frown deepened. "After he does, I'll be off to my club." Without the slightest flicker of emotion, he returned his attention to his reading, and she knew herself dismissed.

Julianne turned and made her way across the room. It wasn't until she'd exited her father's study and closed the door behind her that she allowed the smile of triumph to curve her lips.

Gideon would be here, in her home, within the hour, hired to protect her. Her plan had worked.

But a shadow instantly clouded over her triumph. Yes, he would protect her, but instead of it being from an imaginary threat created by Johnny, it was from a real threat.

A real threat with a real knife.

Chapter 14

Before presenting himself at Julianne's home, Gideon had several stops to make. The first was conducted in a shadowed doorway on a narrow side street on the outskirts of Whitechapel lined by tall, soot-covered brick buildings. There he slipped a folded piece of vellum and a sovereign into the hand of Henry Locke, whose cunning ability at ferreting out information people wished to keep hidden made him a very useful asset to Gideon. The man would have made an excellent Runner but for his unfortunate habit of picking pockets.

"These are the people I want looked into," Gideon said, giving Henry the list he'd comprised of everyone he knew who had been at Julianne's home yesterday. He would have preferred to conduct the investigating himself, but he couldn't do that and guard Julianne. "There will be more names, but this will get you started."

Henry glanced at the list, and although it contained the names of some powerful society peers, he showed no reaction. "When do you want the information?"

"Yesterday. Until I tell you otherwise, you can contact me at the Gatesbourne mansion in Grosvenor Square."

Something flickered in Henry's shrewd green eyes. "What brings you there?"

"Why do you ask?"

Henry shrugged. "No reason. I'll contact you as soon as I know something." He pocketed the list then slipped out of the doorway. Gideon watched him move like a wraith through the myriad twists and turns of the narrow alleys and disappear from view.

Picking up his portmanteau and giving a soft whistle for Caesar, he made his way back to the main street, where he hailed a hack. After giving the driver Logan Jennsen's direction, he sat back and closed his eyes.

Damn, he was tired. His eyelids felt gritty and heavy, a consequence of his sleepless night. But at least by not going home when he left the Drunken Porcupine, he'd accomplished something: gaining some information about Lord Beechmore that Logan Jennsen would find interesting. The investigative work had kept him from lying in bed, staring at the ceiling, thinking about things he needed to forget. Things he couldn't have.

The hack jerked to a halt and, after instructing the driver to wait, Gideon stood before Jennsen's home and stared at the sheer size and grandeur of the mansion. Bloody hell, the man was rumored to have more money than the entire royal family combined, and he obviously didn't have any qualms about spending it on his home.

A very proper butler answered his knock and several minutes later escorted Gideon down a long corridor. Jennsen's home rivaled that of Julianne's father, except Gatesbourne's house was, in a word, soulless, while Jennsen's was, in spite of the opulence and objets d'art and paintings that lined the walls, welcoming.

When the butler announced him at the door to a well-appointed study, Jennsen immediately rose from behind the massive mahogany desk and walked toward him.

"Mayne," he said, holding out his hand. "You have news for me?"

Gideon shook the American's hand and nodded. "I do."

"That was fast."

"I had some time and made good use of it."

"Surprised you've had any time at all, what with another robbery and murder on your hands. Terrible news about Lady Daltry." His gaze dropped to Caesar, who stood at attention next to Gideon, giving Jennsen a narrow-eyed look. "He's not going to chew off my leg, is he?"

"Only if he needs to. It's best not to make any sudden moves."

"Thanks for the warning. Would you like to sit down?"

"Thank you but no. I cannot stay. I just wanted to tell you what I learned about the matter you wished me to look into. According to my sources, Lord Beechmore recently suffered some serious financial losses."

Jennsen's gaze sharpened. "How recently and how serious?"

"Last month, and very serious. He was involved in some high-stakes gambling on the Continent. He lost not only an enormous amount of money but two unentailed properties as well."

"Do you have an amount?"

"Not for the properties, but the monetary losses were reportedly fifty thousand pounds."

Jennsen nodded. "Anything else?"

"Just that he keeps a mistress in London, which is expensive, and has reportedly fathered a number of by-blows. Apparently he has a fondness for the household help."

Jennsen shrugged. "Not surprising. Based on my observations, the words *gentleman* and *morals* have little to do with each other. Is that all?"

"For now. If I learn anything further, I'll contact you."

"Thank you. I'll see to your payment and include a bonus for acting so quickly. Actually, I planned to call on you today. I recalled where I saw the snuffbox."

Gideon's interest quickened. "Where?"

"Daltry's party. Soon after I arrived. I was standing with a group of gentlemen, one of whom took the box from his waistcoat pocket."

"Do you recall which gentleman?"

"Lord Haverly."

Gideon instantly added Haverly's residence as another stop he needed to make this morning. He thanked Jennsen for the information, then they walked to the study door. Before turning the brass knob, Jennsen remarked, "The *Times* is once again filled with lurid speculation about the murdering ghost robber. Any new developments?"

"Nothing I can discuss. But rest assured, he'll be caught."

Something glinted in Jennsen's eyes. "Not worried that his ghostly self will slip through your fingers, Mayne?"

"Not in the least. He *will* be caught. And punished for his crimes."

"So if I were a betting man, I should wager on you rather than the ghost."

"Unless you're fond of losing your money."

"Can't say I am. Indeed, I'm not fond of losing anything, in any manner, for any reason."

"Neither am I," Gideon said grimly. "And I don't intend to start now."

He left the house and gave the driver Haverly's direction. Fifteen minutes later he was shown into his lordship's dining room.

"Rather early for a visit," Haverly said, looking none too pleased at having his breakfast interrupted.

For a reply, Gideon held out the snuffbox. "Recognize this?"

Haverly's eyes widened. "Of course I do. It's mine. Where did you find it?" He reached for the box, but Gideon pulled his hand back.

"Find it?"

"Yes," Haverly said with a frown. "I lost it. Sometime during Daltry's party. Is that where you found it?"

"As a matter of fact, yes. Specifically, I found it beneath a window. One whose lock was tampered with. A window someone attempted to use to gain access to the house." Gideon's eyes narrowed. "Where, as you know by now, Lady Daltry was robbed and murdered."

Haverly blinked. "And you think I am in some way responsible?"

"Are you?"

"Certainly not." Haverly tossed down his napkin and stood. A red hue colored his face. "How dare you ask such a question. Why would I do such a thing?"

"I'm not certain. Yet."

"Well, I wouldn't. And I didn't. Obviously whoever did either found or stole my snuffbox."

"Rather careless of 'whoever' to drop it after taking the time to steal it," Gideon said, watching him carefully.

"Perhaps it was dropped on purpose. To implicate me."

Gideon set the box on the table. "Perhaps. But rest assured, I'll discover the truth. I'll show myself out."

He left and settled himself in the waiting hack, this time giving the driver the Duke of Eastling's direction.

His Grace was no more pleased to see him than Haverly had been. "I'm leaving in precisely five minutes for an appointment," the duke said, after Gideon was shown into his private study.

"I'll be brief. You're aware Lady Daltry was robbed and murdered yesterday."

"Yes. Terrible tragedy."

"You knew Lady Daltry well?"

"Known the entire family for years."

"You consider Lord Daltry a friend?"

A hint of annoyance flashed across the duke's features. "Of course. As I said, we've known each other for years."

"Did he have any objections to you tupping his wife?"

The flash of surprise in the duke's eyes was nearly imperceptible, but Gideon had been expecting it. "That's an ill-mannered thing to say about a dead woman."

"I was saying it more about you."

"What makes you think we were...involved?"

"I saw you together. At Daltry's party. In his private study. Next time you decide to lift the skirts of a friend's wife and bend her over a chair, you might want to lock the door."

The duke's eyes turned to slits. "If you're suggesting that because Lady Daltry and I enjoyed a private moment together I had something to do with the robbery and her death—"

"I'm merely suggesting the timing of those two events is...curious."

"Then I'm certain you'll also find it curious that I wasn't the only one lifting her skirts. Lady Daltry was a woman of insatiable appetites. Indeed, I wasn't the first man she'd had that night."

Gideon raised his brows. "Now who's saying ill-mannered things about a dead woman?"

"Unfortunately, it appears I must be less than discreet to defend myself."

"How do you know you weren't her first lover of the evening?"

"She told me."

"Did she give you a name?"

"No. But you won't have any difficulty finding former lovers. I'd wager most of the male guests at the party had at one time or another enjoyed the lady's charms." He rose. "Is that all?"

Bloody hell, it was exceedingly difficult not to show his extreme dislike for this man. This man who had everything yet clearly valued nothing. At least not friendship. Or marriage vows. Or a lady's reputation. This man who would be Julianne's husband. Even though she'd deceived him and he was angry with her, the thought of her married to an immoral bastard like the duke made Gideon sick inside. "That's all for now," he said, matching His Grace's chilly tone.

He departed and this time gave the hackney Julianne's direction. As the hack rumbled along the cobblestones toward Grosvenor Square, he wondered how many lies he'd been told this morning.

∞

After surrendering his portmanteau to Winslow—who gave him the list he'd asked for of everyone who had come into the house the previous day—Gideon sat through a brief interview with the earl during which he was reminded of his duties and told he'd be taking his meals in the kitchen. No big surprise there. He hadn't expected the earl to treat him like anything other than what he was. More hired help.

Gideon then wrote a copy of the list Winslow had provided and arranged to have it delivered to Henry. That done, he made his way down the long corridor leading to the music room where the earl told him Lady Julianne awaited, and the earl departed for his club.

Caesar padded silently along at Gideon's side. "Looking for your little princess friend?" Gideon asked, cocking a brow at the dog.

Caesar licked his chops then started to pant. Gideon shook his head. Bloody hell. How the mighty had fallen. And smote by such a ridiculous thing as Cupid's dart no less. "Best turn your attention to a more attainable mutt, my friend. You know you'll find that fancy, tulle-skirted, tempting ball of fluff already promised to a purebred of her own breed."

Caesar shot him a defiant look, and Gideon frowned in return. "Fine. Don't listen. But don't say I didn't warn you. You'd be smart to harden your heart. Just as I've done." Right. He'd allowed his desires to get the better of him once. He wouldn't be allowing it again.

Once? his inner voice asked incredulously. *Once?*

His frown deepened. Bloody well fine. More than once. But it wouldn't happen again. Especially now that he knew she was engaged. And hadn't told him. Had purposely deceived him. Surely that would help him keep his distance.

They were still several doors away from their destination when Gideon's footsteps slowed at the sound of slow, lilting piano notes floating through the air. The melody was hauntingly beautiful, and he was drawn to it like a moth to flame. He approached the room and halted in the doorway, struck still by the sight of her.

She sat at the pianoforte, her back to him, the foreground to a backdrop of golden sunshine that spilled through the tall French windows, gilding her with an almost ethereal glow. Her shiny blond curls were caught up in a simple knot and woven with pale blue ribbons that matched her short-sleeved

gown, a color he knew would highlight her extraordinary
eyes. A single pale tendril bisected her ivory nape—a bit of
skin that looked like creamy velvet his fingers and mouth
itched to explore.

He clenched his hands and pressed his lips into a tight line
to suppress the urge. And forced himself to recall that she
wasn't his. Never would be. Never could be. That she'd lied to
him and enticed him, knowing she belonged to someone else.
His anger resurfaced—thank God—and he latched onto it as
if it were a lifeline and he'd been tossed overboard into storm-
ravaged waters.

Her back was perfectly straight, her head bent slightly forward, her shoulders swaying as she caressed the keys to coax
forth the haunting melody, one that suddenly changed tempo
and mood, shifting from what had sounded like a dreary
winter's day to a burst of spring sunshine. He stood in the
doorway, entranced by the beauty of the music that swelled
around him. Never before had he heard anything so lyrical,
any tune that conjured such clear, vivid pictures in his mind,
and he wondered if his thoughts matched what the composer
had intended.

After several minutes the music changed again, slowing
down, back into the mournful notes he'd heard when he first
entered the room. He imagined the laughter and sunshine
and happiness slipping away, replaced by shadows, clouds,
and sorrow. The tune ended on a desolate note that reverberated through the room until it vanished into silence. It was
the most evocative, beautiful thing he'd ever heard, yet one
that only further emphasized their divergent circumstances.
Women in his world didn't while away their time playing the
pianoforte in their mansions. Nor did they become engaged to
dukes. Or share intimacies with the hired help.

He was about to speak, but before he could, a series of
yips from near the fireplace broke the silence. Gideon turned
and saw Princess Buttercup, who'd clearly been napping
on an oversized pillow near the hearth, rise from her satin
throne and dash toward him and Caesar as if they were her
long-lost best friends. Today the small dog wore a pink tulle

skirt with a matching bow holding her snowy fur out of her gleaming black eyes. She launched herself at Gideon, a blur of canine joy.

Amused in spite of himself, he crouched down and scratched behind her soft, furry ears and tickled her warm tummy. After bestowing a frenzy of kisses on his hand, she abandoned him and turned her attention to Caesar whose wagging tail thumped furiously against the doorjamb. Gideon stood and allowed his besotted pet a moment to reacquaint himself with his lady love, then commanded softly, "Caesar, guard." Caesar immediately ended the frivolity and posted himself in the doorway. Princess Buttercup plopped her bottom next to him and stared adoringly up into his jowly face.

He turned his attention back to the pianoforte. Julianne had risen and stood beside the velvet tufted bench, her hands clasped in front of her. Her sheer beauty struck him insensate for several seconds, but he quickly recovered himself and walked toward her, his boots muffled against the thick carpet. He stopped when six feet remained between them. His gaze raked over her, and he clenched his hands. Bloody hell, her lips still looked kiss-swollen, and his own lips tingled at the memory of that which he wanted nothing more than to forget.

She said nothing for several long seconds, just looked up at him with those big blue eyes that surely would have melted his insides if he hadn't steeled himself against them. Then she said, "My father told me about his arrangement with you. I'm very glad and relieved you'll be here, especially given Lady Daltry's robbery and death."

"He's paying me extremely well."

Disappointment flickered across her features at his cold words, but then her spine seemed to stiffen. "I see. Well, money is the one thing of which Father has plenty, and he's an expert at discovering how much of it is required to get what he wants. He's fond of saying 'everyone has their price.'" She raised her chin. "Clearly he found yours. I'm not certain which of you to congratulate."

A flush of shame heated Gideon's face. Damn it, he'd purposely made it sound as if he'd accepted the job of protecting her because of the pay—as opposed to anything personal between them—and she'd neatly hoisted him on his own petard.

"You're insinuating I was bought."

"I'm not insinuating it. I'm stating it outright." She gave an elegant shrug. "'Tis of no importance. You're in very exalted company. Father's latest acquisition is the Duke of Eastling—as a husband for me. But you already know that."

"Yes. Your engagement is something *you* conveniently neglected to mention." He tried to keep his tone bland and impersonal, but the words came out harsh and abrupt.

Scarlet suffused her cheeks, but her gaze didn't waver. "Would it have mattered?"

No. "Yes. I'm not in the habit of making a cuckold of another man. In fact, I've a strong aversion to it."

"He is not yet my husband."

"He is your betrothed and will be your husband in a fortnight." Anger mixed with unwanted jealousy spread through Gideon like a poison infecting his entire body. "Bad enough that I compromised your innocence. In my ignorance of your engagement, I also compromised my honor. I don't take things that belong to others."

Her bottom lip trembled, and she seemed to deflate, as if all her bravado leaked out of her. "You didn't *take* anything. Still, you're right, of course. I . . . I should have told you, but—"

"There are no *buts*," he broke in coldly. "You should have told me. As for last night—it didn't happen."

Her eyes glistened, twin pools of distress that threatened to melt his resolve like ice left out in the sun. Before he could succumb, he advanced a single step, using his size to full advantage, and pinned her in place with his stare. "It *did not* happen."

To her credit, she didn't back away. She pressed her lips together, jerked her head in a tight nod, then looked at the floor. Silence swelled between them. Then she raised her head, and this time her eyes resembled burned-out ashes, left dead after a fire. "Did my father tell you the engagement will be officially announced at our party here next week?"

"No." Bloody hell, this investigation had better be finished by then, because the thought of being here to witness such an announcement, to see the duke formally claim her, was something he hadn't the stomach for.

"It's going to be the social event of the year," she said, her tone as flat as her expression. "I suppose you think I'm very fortunate."

"Aren't you?" he asked, a bitter edge to his voice.

She looked away, trailing her fingers over the piano keys, then moved to the fireplace where she stared down at the low-burning flame.

"Fortunate...I'll be a duchess. By virtue of marrying a man I barely know. A man I care nothing for and who cares nothing for me. Fortunate...I'll live in a magnificent home. That is hundreds of miles away from my dearest friends and everything familiar to me. Fortunate...I'll have more baubles and gowns than I could ever wear and will never want for anything."

She turned to look at him, and the combination of anger and hopelessness in her eyes seemed to reach inside his chest and squeeze his beating heart. "I'll have everything except a husband's love. A husband I love in return. Laughter. Friendship. Companionship. Passion."

Her expression tore at him, replacing a portion of his anger with an unwanted compassion that compelled him to say something, anything, that might offer some comfort. "Perhaps you'll come to care for him." He forced the words out, and they tasted like sawdust on his tongue.

A humorless laugh escaped her. "Obviously you've never met the duke."

"I've met him." And disliked him on sight.

"Then I fail to see how you can suggest I'd ever come to care for him. If I had to describe him in one word, it would be *humorless*. Still, given his exalted position and handsome visage, most anyone would consider me very fortunate indeed."

"But you are not 'most anyone.'" He hadn't realized he'd spoken the words out loud until she nodded in response.

"Apparently not, as I consider myself trapped. Although not by His Grace himself. In truth, it wouldn't have mattered which of my suitors Father had chosen, as they are all inter-

changeable with the duke: men I barely know who don't care
for me beyond my dowry, nor I for them. None of them inspire
the least excitement. Light the slightest spark within me." Her
gaze flicked to his mouth, and heat shot through him as if
she'd stabbed him with a hot knife. "Do you know what I am
talking about?"

Did he know? Bloody hell, the mere thought of her made
his heart pound. The mere sight of her set him on fire. "Yes,
I know."

She took a small step toward him, and his heart jumped.
"How?"

Because you're here. Close enough to touch. "I've experienced lust. Passion. Desire." His eyes narrowed. "As recently
as last night. As you damn well know."

"What about love? Have you ever been in love?"

An image flashed through his mind. Dark hair, dark eyes.
He shoved it back, but he couldn't deny it. "Yes." And he
had loved Gwen. Yet still, what he'd felt for the woman he'd
known and loved three years ago seemed utterly tame compared to the maelstrom of conflicting, unwanted, confusing
emotions Julianne inspired. But then, what he'd felt for Gwen
had been . . . simple. Uncomplicated. While it had lasted.

"Was it . . . wonderful?"

"No. It was painful." He dragged his hands through his
hair, ruthlessly battering back the memories that shoved at
him. "Your romantic notions are unrealistic and will lead you
only to heartbreak."

"Was your heart broken?"

He pressed his lips together. Bloody hell, how had the
conversation drifted on to these treacherous waters? Time
to change the subject. But then he frowned. Maybe he should
tell her. Give her a taste of what the real world was like. The
world beyond the castle of riches and privilege in which she
dwelled. Maybe then she'd realize how lucky she was. And
quit looking at him with those vulnerable eyes that reflected
her every emotion, that gazed upon him far too frequently
with admiration. Which would certainly help his ability to
resist her.

"Yes, Princess," he said with a sneer. "My heart was broken. By a woman I'd planned to marry."

His revelation clearly surprised her. "What happened?"

Memories rammed into him, and for several seconds he felt crushed under their weight. He opened his mouth to speak, but nothing came forth. Anger and sorrow and guilt clamped his throat shut around the words that still, after three years, remained so precariously sutured. He swallowed, painfully, then the words suddenly poured out of him, words he hadn't spoken since it had happened. "She died. She worked as a maid. I always came to escort her home, but one night I was delayed. Instead of waiting for me, she walked alone. And was accosted by a footpad. She fought back, but he was stronger. And had a knife." His hands clenched, and the fury he'd felt at the time rose in him again. "He stole what little money she had. Then gutted her like a fish. She died in my arms."

"Dear God. Gideon..." Her eyes filled with a combination of horror and sympathy. With her gaze on his, she walked slowly toward him. His instincts warned him not to let her get too close, but he felt as if he were nailed in place. She stopped less than an arm's length from him. He wanted to look away, walk away from her, but he simply couldn't move. Reaching out, she gently laid her hand on one of his clenched fists. "I'm so sorry. Inadequate words, I know, but I don't have any others." She hesitated then said, "The monster responsible... was he apprehended?"

Another wave of dark memories washed over him. "Yes. I caught him. In the act of hurting another woman. She survived. He did not." Gideon had made damn sure of that.

"You saved that woman's life. And undoubtedly many other women's lives by ending his."

"Yes. But I didn't save the life that mattered to me."

She gently squeezed his hand. Heat rushed up his arm, filling him with anger that she could affect him so effortlessly. "I'm sorry your heart was broken in such a cruel way."

Her words yanked him from the past, and he forced himself to recall the here and now: his sense of betrayal. He pulled his hand away from hers and stepped back. "My heart is none of your concern," he said in a harsh voice. "What should concern you is your penchant for lying."

"If you're referring to the duke—"

"You know damn well I am."

"I didn't lie."

"You didn't admit the truth. That's the same thing."

"Actually, it's not." She raised her chin. "Have you admitted everything about yourself to me?"

"Seems to me I just admitted a whole damn lot." Certainly more than he'd meant to. "You know everything you need to know—the whole of which is that I've been hired to protect you and to catch whoever tried to enter your bedchamber last night."

Her gaze again flicked down to his lips. "Based on what you just told me and what happened between us last night... I know more about you than that, Gideon."

Another wave of heat suffused him, this one settling in his groin. "Which you'd be best to forget. As I intend to."

She shook her head and moved a step closer. "I'll never forget."

He sucked in a quick breath, and his head filled with the scent of vanilla. Want and need swamped him, threatening to overwhelm his resolve. He could—and would—remain in control. He could not—and would not—touch her. He looked into her eyes, a mistake, as they reflected a combination of confusion, hope, and such longing it seemed to rip his chest open. And evaporate his anger like a puddle in the desert.

"Will you really be able to forget?" she whispered, her gaze searching his face. "Did what we shared truly mean nothing to you?" Her bottom lip trembled. "Am I that forgettable?"

He had to fist his hands to keep from giving into the choking need to snatch her against him, a fact that bloody well irritated him, a feeling he grabbed in desperation. "As I said earlier—and you agreed—last night did not happen. We shared *nothing.* What is this—another hunting expedition for compliments, Princess? I suggest you ask one of your many admirers, or here's a novel idea—*your fiancé*—to shower you with admiring words. If you can't wait until one of them calls,

go look in the mirror, wallow in your *extreme loveliness*"—
he spat out the last two words as if they were poison —"and
spout your own bloody accolades."

He didn't want to feel like a bastard for his harshness, but
damn it, he did, which only served to irritate him further.
Frustration built in him until he felt like a boiling caldron. He
steeled himself against the hurt he expected to cloud her eyes
and was surprised when unmistakable anger flared instead.
Indeed, she looked as if *she* were ready to boil.

She stepped back several paces. "That is the second time
you've accused me of wallowing in my looks, *Mr. Mayne.*"
Her lip curled when she said his name, as if it tasted bad.
"Allow me to enlighten you as to why a *princess* such as
myself *doesn't* wallow in her looks. After being surrounded
by it my entire life, I am unimpressed by outward beauty. I
find it treacherous in that it can disguise even the most disagreeable character. Rather like a gorgeous tapestry covering
a writhing pit of vipers. As an example, I offer my mother.
She is extraordinarily beautiful, is she not?"

Gideon hesitated several seconds then replied, "I'm sure
most people would say so."

"I assure you they do. Yet unfortunately she is not a kind
woman. Or a warm, loving one. I don't say that to be unkind
myself, I am merely stating a fact. As you've expressed a penchant for summing things up in one word, I'd apply *ruthless*
to my mother."

Gideon couldn't disagree, although *overbearing* was a
close second choice to describe the woman. It had been painfully obvious since his first meeting with her that the Countess of Gatesbourne possessed a thumb the size of the entire
kingdom. And she had no compunction about holding her
daughter beneath that mighty thumb's weight.

"Beauty's other great failing," she continued, "is that it
requires no level of talent or accomplishment. It's nothing
more than an accident of birth."

"Like the fact that you're an earl's daughter. And I'm a
commoner."

"Yes, although I don't think there's anything common

about you. Honor, integrity, compassion, valor...they are important and lasting. And, as far as I'm concerned, they far surpass any class order."

He studied her and couldn't decide if he were puzzled, annoyed, or both. He watched her anger wither, the fire leeching from her eyes to be replaced by what appeared to be embarrassment. He'd be willing to wager that she'd never confessed such things to anyone. He'd certainly never heard any member of the aristocracy utter such sentiments.

"You must think I'm daft," she said, when he remained silent.

He continued to study her, his own anger seeping away in spite of his best efforts to hold on to it, then finally said, "I don't think you're daft. I think you're...surprising." Yes, she was. Disconcertingly so.

The urge to reach out, to cup her perfect face in his palm, a face she claimed not to admire, gripped him with such force he had to step away from her. He moved to the fireplace, putting a safe distance between them, then stared into the flames. "You cannot deny your beauty garners you much attention."

"Yes, but of what sort? My mother uses it to advance her matchmaking schemes. My father barters it to the highest bidder without regard to my feelings. And who gives me attention for it? Gentlemen who pursue me for my fortune. Who merely want an ornament upon their arm."

He sensed her approach, and his every muscle tightened. From the corner of his eye he saw her stand next to him, and he forced himself to remain staring at the fire.

"As far as I'm concerned, beauty hasn't garnered me any attention worth having," she said softly. "Nor has it gained me any true friends, although it has tossed many false ones my way." A humorless sound passed her lips. "Do you have any idea how excruciatingly *hollow* it is to be admired for no reason other than your reflection in the mirror?"

Unable to stop himself, he shifted his attention from the crackling flames to her. At the sight of her, looking so lost and vulnerable, the last vestiges of his anger melted away, leaving a bone-deep, aching emptiness in its place. "Hardly. If I'm admired for anything, it certainly isn't my looks."

She hiked up a brow. "Now who is guilty of false modesty and on a fishing expedition for compliments?"

A sound of disbelief escaped him. "No man whose nose has been broken twice expects compliments regarding his appearance. As for being admired for anything else..." He shrugged. "I'm good at my job. I have to be, or I'd end up dead. Although the criminals I capture aren't particularly complimentary regarding my skills."

"No, I imagine they wouldn't be. Nor, I suppose are they much taken with your good looks." A whiff of mischief twinkled in her eyes. "No doubt they'd like to rearrange them for you."

He rubbed his finger down the bridge of his nose, telling himself it was ridiculous for a man with no vanity to feel so pleased that she thought him good-looking. "Two have succeeded." He shot her a half grin. "Of course, when the dust settled, they ended up looking far worse than me."

"I've no doubt," she murmured. "How long have you been a Runner?"

"Five years."

"Do you enjoy it?"

"It...satisfies me."

"In what way?"

He turned so he faced her fully. "I like righting wrongs. Solving mysteries. Getting dangerous criminals off the streets. Seeing justice done."

"You must have experienced a great deal during those five years. Seen a great deal."

"Yes." Things she would never want to see. Things he wished he hadn't seen.

"And before Bow Street what did you do?"

"I served in the army."

"And before that?"

"Do you always ask so many questions?"

"No. Never. Mother would be horrified at my lack of manners and restraint. However, I find myself insatiably curious about you. Your life."

"There is nothing to know. I have my work. A few trusted friends." He nodded toward the open doorway. "Caesar."

"How did you two come to be together?"

She appeared genuinely interested, and in spite of himself, he found himself relaxing and responding. "I found him."

"Where?"

"At the docks. Saw some bastard toss a basket over the side of a ship just pulling out. I knew something alive was inside, so I rescued the basket. And found Caesar. He was only a few weeks old."

Her eyes went wide with shock. "He would have drowned!"

"That was the point of him being tossed over the side. Easiest way to get rid of unwanted animals."

"How horrible. And cruel."

"Yes. But it happens every day. That and worse. It's a horrible, cruel world."

"Yes, but there is also a great deal of good."

He shrugged. "In my line of work I see far more of the bad."

She studied him, just as he'd studied her moments ago. Then she nodded slowly. "Yes, I can see that. It's in your eyes, the horrible things you've seen. They've hurt you."

Her words both surprised and unnerved him. She couldn't have seen anything in his eyes. He'd learned long ago how to turn his face into an unreadable mask. Before he could even think of a reply, she asked, "I wonder when was the last time you laughed—a real, true laugh that reached deep inside you and all the way up to your eyes. I wager it's been a long, long time."

His brows collapsed in a frown. "Don't be ridiculous. I laugh all the time." Of course he did—when there was something to laugh about. Hardly his fault that catching criminals wasn't a nonstop jest festival.

"Indeed? From what I can tell, the next time will be the first time. But don't worry. I intend to fix that."

"I'm not wor—"

"Where do you live?"

"Live?"

"Yes. Where do you make your home? Sleep at night?"

His gaze swept the chamber. "Nowhere grand like this."

"You like this room?"

"You want the truth?"

"Of course."

He looked around again. He wished he could honestly say he disliked this room, but he didn't. In spite of its size, it was somehow cozy, and he found the pale green and blue color scheme soothing. "I actually like this room. It's not so...ornate as some of the others."

Julianne nodded. "I completely agree. This is my favorite spot in the entire house. Although it's large, I find it warm and cheerful. And comforting. I love music."

"You play very well."

"Thank you." She looked toward the ceiling and heaved an exaggerated sigh. "Mother would tell you I'm a virtuoso."

His lips twitched slightly. "You're not?"

"Hardly. But I strive to better myself. Have you any musical talent?"

"None that I'm aware of. I've never tried to play any instrument and on the few occasions I've attempted to sing, Caesar put up a howl—literally. So I shut my mouth before he decided to bury me in a deep hole."

She made a tsking sound. "Terrible how criticism can discourage budding talent. What were these occasions that prompted you to sing?"

"Drunken revelry, I'm afraid."

She smothered a laugh. "I see. What songs did you sing?"

"Nothing that could be repeated to a lady."

Her eyes lit up, seeming to glow from within. "Nonsense. I've always wanted to learn a bawdy song. All the songs I know are boring. About flowers and sunshine and grass-filled meadows."

"Like the piece you were playing when I arrived?"

"You heard that?"

"Yes. Parts of it were sad. Mournful. But one part was very bright and...meadowy. What is the name of that piece?"

"I call it 'Dreams of You.'"

"What does the composer call it?"

She hesitated, then said softly, "'Dreams of You.'"

He couldn't hide his surprise. "*You* wrote it?"

"Yes." She looked down for several seconds then lifted her chin to meet his gaze. The shyness and vulnerability that had struck him the first time he'd looked at her stared at him now. "No one has ever heard it before. Except me." One corner of her mouth lifted. "And Princess Buttercup."

"Why?"

"I've no desire to bore anyone."

"I wasn't bored." The words slipped out before he could stop them.

"Do you know anything about music?"

"No."

She gave a quick laugh. "There you have it."

"But I know what I like. Just as I'm sure you like flowers and sunshine and grass-filled meadows."

"Why? Because I'm a *princess*?"

Her lip curled with such distaste on the last word he couldn't help but chuckle. "It's not an insult, you know."

Disbelief was written all over her face. "Really? I had the distinct impression it was." She gave an elegant sniff. "You certainly haven't meant it as a compliment."

Without thinking, he reached out and captured her hand. She drew in a sharp breath as he brushed the pad of his thumb over her fingertips. "Hmmm. So the kitten has claws. Interesting."

It took her several seconds to respond, and he realized the folly of touching her. Color suffused her cheeks with a captivating blush, and heat sizzled up his arm. He quickly released her hand, but his fingers curled into a fist to retain her warmth for several seconds.

"Yes, as a matter of fact she does," she said in a breathless voice. "And she greatly prefers being compared to a kitten rather than a drunken porcupine—although she'd much prefer a lioness to a kitten."

He inclined his head. "As you wish, Lioness. And to answer

your question about why I would think you'd like flowers and sunshine and grass-filled meadows, it's because..."

His common sense had him hesitating, screaming at him to shut his mouth. But his lips obviously weren't listening, because seemingly of their own volition they continued to flap and spill out words that would surely appall him later. "...You're a lovely, innocent young woman who should never be touched by anything that isn't equally as lovely and innocent." Including himself.

She blinked. "That sounds suspiciously like a compliment."

"I meant it as one." And damn it, he did. What in God's name was wrong with him? Where had his anger gone? Where was the rod he'd fused to his spine to steel himself against her?

"Thank you. But I'd still like to learn a bawdy song. Will you teach me?"

"You'd be shocked."

"I hope so. I *want* to be shocked. I want to *feel*. Experience something of life."

Her eyes...bloody hell, he felt himself drowning in those clear, blue pools that shimmered with a combination of everything she'd shown him since he'd walked into this room filled with his righteous sense of betrayal and a fierce determination to keep his distance: shyness and despair, vulnerability and unexpected strength. All things he didn't want to see. Wished to hell he hadn't. He didn't want to find anything in her to like. To admire. To respect. It was so much easier to believe she was nothing more than a spoiled, vain princess enamored of her own beauty.

But clearly, she was much more.

Bloody hell.

If all he felt for her was lust, desire, he had a fighting chance to resist temptation. But if he were foolish enough to let himself feel more for her...to care for her...to allow her to scale the walls he'd built around his heart...well, then, he'd be cast adrift on stormy seas without so much as a rowboat in sight.

His anger drained away, leaving him with nothing save a deep, aching want. One that would have to go unsatisfied.

"I have very little time left before my marriage, and I don't wish to spend it in morose reflection or consumed with sadness. I want to *do* something. Toward that end, won't you please teach me a bawdy song? If you do, I'll teach you something in return."

He should have flatly refused. But once again his lips had a mind of their own and asked, "Such as?"

A hint of mischief touched her eyes. "Embroidery?"

"Not very useful on Bow Street, I'm afraid."

"Ah. Then how about fisticuffs?"

"And what do you know about fisticuffs?"

"Absolutely nothing. So I'm afraid that won't do." She tapped her finger against her chin and frowned. Then brightened. "I could teach *you* to play a song on the pianoforte."

"I'm afraid my hands are too clumsy."

"Nonsense. I'll teach you a simple song. About flowers and sunshine and grass-filled meadows." She held out her hand. "Do we have a bargain, Mr. Mayne?"

He knew he should say no. Tell her to just read or sit in the corner. But damn it, he suddenly wanted to teach her a bawdy song. Watch her cheeks turn scarlet and that unexpected impudence to shine in her eyes. As she'd said, only a short time remained before she'd be married and gone. Why not make that time as pleasant as possible for her? Otherwise he'd feel as if he were just tossing more dirt on the glass coffin in which she'd dreamed of herself confined. He could control himself. He would control himself.

Reaching out, he took her hand and shook it. And firmly ignored the jolt of heat that shot up his arm.

"You have a bargain, Lady Julianne. Let the lessons begin."

Chapter 15

"If I'm to learn the melody, you'll need to at least hum it," Julianne said, resting her fingers on the smooth ivory keys.

She looked up at Gideon from her seat on the piano bench. There was no doubt in her mind that the only reason he'd agreed to teach her a bawdy song was to distract her thoughts from the murders. For which she was grateful. Except that his consideration only made her admire him more. Which only made her want him more.

As had his story about the woman he'd planned to marry. The woman who'd been lucky enough to be loved by Gideon. And whom he'd so tragically lost. Whose death he'd hero-ically avenged. He'd shared a piece of himself she was certain he normally didn't allow people to see. Which did nothing to calm the maelstrom of emotions he evoked in her.

Which unfortunately was not good.

At the moment, however, she found herself suppressing a grin. Goodness, he did not look happy. He stood beside her, one large hand resting on the polished wood, scowling at the keys so fiercely she was surprised they didn't yell *eek!* and hop off the instrument and run away.

"Bow Street Runners don't hum," he informed her.

"I'm certain they do if they don't know the words."

"I know the words."

"Very well, if they're too *afraid* to sing the words."

His scowl deepened, and she had to bite the insides of her cheeks to refrain from laughing. "I'm not afraid. I'm being considerate. Of your ears."

"My ears are made of very stern stuff, I assure you." She lifted an eyebrow. "Are you reneging on our agreement?"

"No."

"Excellent. Besides, I don't see what you're so worried about. It's just a song. Indeed, I wonder if you've told me a Banbury tale. I don't see how a tune entitled 'Apple Dumplin' Shop' can be considered bawdy."

A glint she could only describe as devilish entered his eyes, and she caught her breath. Dear God, how was she going to refrain from begging this man to kiss her again? To touch her. To put his hands and his mouth on her. To make her feel as he had last night. She didn't want to tempt him—or beg him—to compromise his honor.

Did she?

God help her, she didn't know. She'd known he was honorable the first time she'd met him, and she deeply admired him for it. But she desperately wanted more of the intimacies they'd shared. Being this close to him and not touching him was torture. But if she forced him into a situation that impinged on his honor, he might leave. And that would be an even worse torture. He was here. She'd enjoy his company—especially the company of this entertaining, teasing man she found utterly captivating. And that would have to be enough.

"Clearly you don't know what an apple dumplin' shop is, Princess."

She looked toward the ceiling. "It's a place where apple dumplings are sold, of course."

"Maybe in your upper-crust world. But in the less fashionable sections of London, it's a woman's…" his gaze drifted slowly down to her chest, lingered for several seconds, then moved back up again. "Bosom."

Heat suffused Julianne, and her nipples hardened into tight peaks.

"Is that bawdy enough for you?" he asked, a hint of amusement lurking in his voice.

"Yes, that will do nicely," she replied in her most prudish voice. "Do you intend to sing it, or must I guess at the words?"

He raised a dark brow. "Has anyone ever told you you're impudent?"

"Has anyone ever told you you're impossible?"

"No."

"Fine. I shall stand alone in my opinion. Now sing."

"Fine." He cleared his throat then began, "Down went my hand in her bodice top, to visit her sweet apple dumpin' shop—"

His rendition was cut off by a mournful howl from the doorway. Julianne smothered a laugh and watched him shoot a glare at Caesar, whose doleful bay tapered off into silence.

"As if you could do better," he muttered to the dog. He then cleared his throat and continued, "Her apples were so plump and merry, and on the top there was a cherry—"

Another deep, mournful howl, this one accompanied by a high-pitched one courtesy of Princess Buttercup, cut off his song. He shot the dogs a scowl surely meant to send them both slinking from the room with their tails between their legs. But instead their tails wagged as they clearly thought this was a grand game. Julianne covered her mouth with her hand to contain her merriment and his gaze snapped to her.

"Are you laughing?" he asked, sounding more than a little threatening.

"Certainly not," she said with as much dignity as she could muster, considering her insides were quivering with suppressed mirth. "I'm merely wondering how a woman's breast could be 'merry.'"

"I've no idea. I didn't *write* the song. Now, do you want to hear the rest of it or not?"

"Heavens, you sound...petulant."

"Bow Street Runners are never petulant. I am, however, becoming annoyed. I'm trying to live up to my end of our deal, yet I'm thwarted by *critics*"—he shot another glare at the dogs in the doorway—"at every turn."

"I think they just want to sing along."

"Which is a problem as dogs cannot sing."

"Hmmm. I think they might say the same about you, Mr. Mayne."

He turned back to her and narrowed his eyes. "Are you casting aspersions on my bawdy song, Lady Julianne? A song, I must remind you, that you insisted I teach you?"

"Not at all. But perhaps if you sang a bit softer..."

He heaved a put-upon sigh. "Very well. Now, where was I?"

"You'd just waxed poetic about her breast being merry."

"Ah, yes. And topped with a cherry." He cleared his throat and sang, more softly, "Nothing in the world could feel so right, as to lean my face in and take a bite—"

Caesar's barking cut off the words this time. Seconds later Winslow appeared in the doorway, his normally implacable features filled with alarm. "Is everything all right, Lady Julianne?" he asked. "I heard the most awful caterwauling. As if someone had dropped an anvil on their toe."

"Everything is fine, Winslow. It was merely Mr. Mayne singing."

Gideon shot her the same glare he'd bestowed upon the dogs. "Actually, it was merely the dogs howling."

"Yes—howling because Mr. Mayne was singing. Nothing to be concerned about. You may return to your post."

"Yes, my lady."

After Winslow departed, Julianne turned to Gideon. "Perhaps you should sing even more softly."

"If I sing any softer, you won't hear a thing."

She swallowed her laughter. "Exactly."

He glared. "Very funny. Has anyone ever told you you're extremely humorous?" Before she could answer he said, "No—I didn't think so." He crossed his arms over his chest and asked in a testy tone, "Do you want to hear the rest of the song or not?"

"I do."

"Fine. Here we go, and this time I'm not stopping."

True to his promise, he continued singing the outrageous song, accompanied by Caesar and Princess Buttercup. Julianne tried to pick out the melody on the piano, but she was laughing so hard she had to abandon the effort. By the time the song hit its last jarring, discordant note, tears of mirth were running down her face.

"How was that?" Gideon asked, looking both proud and smug.

"There...there simply aren't words," she managed to gasp out, wiping her eyes.

"Glad you enjoyed it."

"Oh, I did. I can't remember the last time I laughed so hard." She smiled up at him. "Thank you."

"You're welcome. And now that my debt of honor is paid, I shall expect to be equally as entertained."

"I cannot possibly top that performance. Has anyone ever told you you can't sing worth a jot?"

"No one who's lived to repeat the sentiment. Has anyone ever told you you've an impertinent tongue?"

"No. Most people believe I am shy and aloof. And perfectly ladylike at all times."

"Clearly most people don't know you well."

She nodded and looked into his beautiful dark eyes. And caught her breath at the humor lurking in their depths. She couldn't recall the last time she'd felt so carefree. "Most people don't know me at all," she said softly.

He stilled, and she watched fire flare in his gaze, melting all hints of amusement. His gaze dipped to her mouth, and for several seconds she couldn't move, couldn't breathe, and the air between them seemed to crackle. Then he blinked, as if coming out of a trance, and stepped back. Then turned to stare out the window.

Julianne had to draw in several breaths before she could speak. "Do...do you wish for me to teach you your song now? Or would you prefer to do something else?"

His gaze snapped back to hers. The smoldering heat in his eyes burned her. The secret place between her legs that he'd awakened last night throbbed, and she pressed her thighs together, an action that only served to further inflame the insistent ache.

He appeared about to speak when another woof sounded from the doorway. Seconds later Winslow appeared, bearing a silver salver upon which a trio of calling cards rested. "You've visitors, my lady," he said. "Are you in?"

Julianne took the cards, slowly scanning the names to give herself a few seconds to recover, then smiled. "Yes, of course. Please show them in."

"One moment," Gideon said, approaching her, his demeanor all business. Completely gone was the teasing, amusing man. "Who is here?"

"My friends Emily, Sarah, and Carolyn."

None of the tension seemed to leave him. He gave a tight nod. "All right."

Julianne turned back to Winslow. "Please arrange for tea and refreshments for us."

"Yes, my lady," Winslow said, then quit the room.

Gideon moved to the doorway and issued a soft command to Caesar that Julianne could not hear. Then he and the dog stepped back, with Princess Buttercup joining them. Seconds later, her friends filed into the room, sending Princess Buttercup into a frenzy of tail wagging and joyful yips. Caesar remained at Gideon's side, his nose quivering as he appraised each newcomer. There was no missing her friends' surprise at seeing Gideon.

"Mr. Mayne, what are you doing here?" Sarah asked in her no-nonsense way. Her gaze jumped to Julianne. "Is something wrong?"

Julianne recalled her father's request that she not speak of last night's incident for fear of the duke finding out. But as far as she was concerned, if the duke found out and decided he didn't want to marry her because of it...

"Nothing—" Gideon began.

"Someone with a knife tried to enter my bedchamber last night through my balcony window," she said in a rush. "Father has hired Mr. Mayne to protect me and hopefully catch the scoundrel."

Gideon barely refrained from groaning. Bloody hell, leave

it to a woman to blab out details she shouldn't. Her father would not be pleased, especially if the duke caught wind of it. Although Gideon couldn't deny that he personally didn't give a rat's arse if either Gatesbourne or His Grace were displeased. And with the way servants gossiped, the entire ton would no doubt hear of the incident within a day or two anyway.

For several seconds there was stunned silence, then all four women began talking at once. They moved as a unit toward the settee and chairs by the fireplace, a rainbow of muslin gowns and chattering voices. Gideon inched his way into the background, doing everything a man over six feet tall could to remain as invisible as possible. He didn't want to answer a plethora of questions about the investigation, nor did he wish to listen to four women chat about all the things that upper-class women were wont to discuss: the weather and the shops, bonnets, parties, and all manner of feminine fripperies.

Yet surely this unexpected hen party was good. The interruption came at a moment when he'd found himself nearly drowning in his want for Julianne. Still, at the same time he felt strangely trapped in this room with four women, who—

Were all looking at him with expectant expressions.

Bloody hell.

"Don't you agree, Mr. Mayne?" asked Lady Langston, pushing up her spectacles.

"Agree?"

"That this talk of the criminal being a ghost is nothing but rubbish?"

A sensible female—thank God. "Of course it's rubbish. This man is very real. And very dangerous."

"Are you certain the person you seek is a 'he' and not a 'she'?" asked Lady Surbrooke. "After all, women can be just as evil as men."

"Indeed they can," Gideon agreed, "and while I would not eliminate someone as a suspect based solely on their gender, I believe our murderer and thief is a man."

Lady Emily's intense gaze bored into his. "You will of course make certain nothing happens to our beloved Julianne."

His gaze shifted to Julianne, who sat on the settee. Bloody

hell, she looked so damn lovely, and her eyes seemed to just...swallow him. He dragged his attention back to Lady Emily. "I will not allow any harm to come to her."

A simple, irrefutable statement, yet the depth of its truth hit him like a blow to the head. He would forfeit his own life if necessary to keep her safe. A realization that stilled him. And stunned him.

"As we're all aware of your expertise, that is a huge relief, Mr. Mayne," murmured Lady Surbrooke. She smiled at him, clearly an acknowledgment of his assistance in solving the case two months ago that had threatened her life, and he nodded in return.

They resumed conversing among themselves, and with relief Gideon continued his inching progress toward the doorway. Her friends demanded details of last night's ordeal, which Julianne provided, along with a recitation that made him sound like some sort of hero.

"Mr. Mayne was so brave, and very intrepid, searching and securing the house and grounds in spite of the foul weather," she said, sending a smile in his direction, and he once again found himself the cynosure of all eyes.

"I'd be more worthy of praise had I caught the culprit," he felt compelled to point out, although he couldn't deny that warmth spread through him at her complimentary words.

"Surely you didn't spend the entire night outdoors," Lady Langston said. "Why, you could have caught your death of chill."

"He stayed indoors with me until my parents arrived home," Julianne said.

"Precisely where he needed to be to insure your safety," Lady Surbrooke said with an approving nod.

"Yes, thank goodness you were about, Mr. Mayne," added Lady Emily.

They again resumed chatting among themselves, and he quickly stepped to the doorway. He didn't intend to listen to them, but it was impossible not to. Their long-standing friendship was evident in the way they spoke—finishing each other's sentences, the warmth and teasing and concern in their voices.

Winslow appeared bearing a silver tea service, followed by Ethan the footman, who carried a food-laden tray. Gideon breathed deeply as the tray filled with biscuits and assorted little tarts and cakes went by just under his nose. The scent of vanilla—her scent—filled his head. His mouth watered, and his body tightened in response.

"Please join us, Mr. Mayne," Julianne said.

"Oh, yes, please do," seconded Lady Langston. He wondered if he looked as wary as he felt, because she added, "We don't bite."

"At least not very often," Julianne added.

Deciding they looked harmless enough and that one cup of tea and a biscuit or two couldn't hurt, Gideon joined the ladies, settling himself in the wing chair opposite Julianne. He looked around the group and realized that Julianne's three friends were studying him with a great deal of interest. He fought the sudden urge to squirm in his seat.

"I've never been to a ladies' tea party before," he said, trying to fill the silence while accepting his cup and saucer from Julianne with a nod. "I'm not quite certain what to do."

"It's very simple," Julianne said with a smile, handing him a plate containing several biscuits and small cakes. "You sip tea, nibble on cakes, chat about the weather, then talk about things you're not supposed to."

Her smile was captivating, and he had to force himself not to stare. He noted how at ease she clearly felt in the company of her friends, not exhibiting the shyness he'd observed in her during larger gatherings and parties.

"And what sort of things are ladies not supposed to discuss?" he asked, hoping to keep the conversation diverted from his investigation.

"Anything that isn't the weather," Lady Emily said, wrinkling her nose. "You won't tell on us, will you, Mr. Mayne?"

If Gideon had to sum up Lady Emily in one word, it would be mischievous. "I suppose that depends on what you reveal, Lady Emily," he said in a perfectly serious tone. "If it's too salacious, I might have to turn you over to the magistrate."

Lady Emily's eyes lit up. "Really? How ghastly!"

"Don't encourage her," Julianne said, continuing to serve the tea. "She'd no doubt enjoy such an outing."

"I absolutely would," Lady Emily confirmed. "I would shamefully exploit my newfound friendship with the magistrate and enlist his help in controlling my hooligan younger brothers."

"Shall I toss them in Newgate for you?" Gideon asked casually.

"A splendid idea," Lady Emily agreed. "Although we probably should wait a few years. Little Arthur is only seven, after all."

"Perhaps when he's nine," Gideon agreed.

Lady Emily sent him a dazzling smile that he was certain knocked most men flat. "Perhaps you're not as dour as I thought, Mr. Mayne."

"Perhaps you're more bloodthirsty than *I* thought, Lady Emily."

The ladies all laughed. "You see?" Lady Langston said with a smile, nudging up her spectacles with her index finger. "You find out the most fascinating things at tea parties."

Ten minutes later, Gideon couldn't disagree with that statement. During that time he learned that Julianne's friends were charming, intelligent, amusing, and witty and that the Gatesbourne kitchen produced the most delicious tarts and cakes he'd ever tasted. They chatted about the robberies and murders, all of them expressing sympathy and horror over Lady Daltry's death. They asked him a few questions, but as he didn't have any information to give them, their conversation moved on to other topics. As was his habit, he sat back and listened, studying the group over the rim of his cup.

"Mr. Mayne is awfully quiet," Lady Surbrooke commented, her gaze resting on him with an expression he couldn't decipher.

"I fear I've nothing constructive to add to a debate concerning whether ostrich or peacock feathers are a more becoming decoration on one's turban."

"Then we must change the subject," Lady Emily said. Her

eyes took on a devilish glint. "Tell me, Mr. Mayne, are you fond of reading?"

Bloody hell, he didn't want to turn this party into an interview. Indeed, it was time he resumed his post at the door. He set aside his plate, intending to rise. "I am, but—"

"Have you read *The Ghost of Devonshire Manor*?" asked Lady Emily.

Gideon heard Julianne's small gasp and turned toward her, noting the twin flags of color marking her cheeks, an interesting reaction to be sure. So interesting that he resettled himself in his chair. "No, I haven't. Is it a book you'd recommend?"

"I'm certain Mr. Mayne wouldn't care for it in the least," Julianne said, shooting her friend a repressive look.

"It's really the sort of story that would appeal more to a woman," agreed Lady Surbrooke, who, Gideon noted, was also blushing.

"And why is that?" Gideon asked, finding this entire exchange fascinating.

"Oh, well, you know," Lady Langston murmured, her face even pinker than her sister's. "It's a love story."

"The title suggests it's a ghost story," Gideon said.

"A love story about a ghost," Julianne said, her complexion resembling a setting sun. "Very girly. All very silly, actually. Who would like some more tea?"

"I would," said Lady Langston and Lady Surbrooke in unison, while Lady Emily unsuccessfully tried to squelch a smile.

The talk turned back to the murders and, as Gideon had no desire to be interrogated by Julianne's overly curious friends, he rose. "If you ladies will excuse me for a few minutes, I'll see to Caesar." He turned to Julianne. "I'll be right outside, on the terrace. If you need me, just call." He gave a soft whistle, and Caesar trotted over to him. Princess Buttercup followed as far as her satin pillow, then jumped onto her soft throne and with a sigh closed her eyes, presumably to nap until the love of her life returned.

Gideon opened the French windows leading to the terrace. Caesar trotted through the opening, then dashed down the flagstone steps leading to the garden. Gideon closed the door behind him, glancing into the room. His gaze met Julianne's through the glass, and for several seconds he couldn't move. Could only stare. And try his damnedest to tamp down the flood of wants that surged through him. With an effort he turned away and moved to the edge of the terrace, where he pulled in some much-needed breaths of fresh, cool air. He risked one quick peek over his shoulder and noted that the four women had scooted nearer to each other. Their heads were bent close together, obviously in whispered, furtive conversation.

Alarm bells clanged in his head. What the bloody hell were they talking about?

∽∾

Julianne pulled her gaze away from the French windows through which Gideon had just departed. And found three pairs of wide eyes staring at her.

"Oh my heavens," Emily said.

"Oh my Lord," murmured Carolyn.

"Oh my, oh my, oh my," whispered Sarah.

Julianne wasn't precisely sure why, but heat rushed into her cheeks, and she quickly reached for the teapot. Emily forestalled her by gently grabbing her hand. "How can you possibly think of tea at a time like this?"

"A time like this?" Julianne repeated. "You mean the murders?"

"I mean *that man*," Emily whispered, jerking her head toward the terrace. "Did you not see the way he looked at you?"

Julianne tried her best to keep her features blank, but she wasn't certain she succeeded or if it even mattered, given the heat scorching her cheeks. "What do you mean?"

Carolyn scooted closer and leaned in. "She means that Mr. Mayne clearly finds you... attractive."

Sarah made a snorting sound. "Well, of course he would find her *attractive*. Good God, what man wouldn't? What Emily means is that he clearly finds you more than just merely attractive." She waved her hand in front of her face. "The heat you two generated was enough to steam the air."

"What *Emily means*," Emily said, shooting a frown around the group, "is that until I saw him in this room with Julianne, I'd never seen Mr. Mayne's eyes be anything other than cool and impassive. Dispassionate, really. And they were when he looked at anything or anyone in this room except you, Julianne. When he looked at you, his eyes seemed to—"

"Breathe fire," Sarah broke in.

"He is clearly smitten," Carolyn agreed. "Certainly he desires you." Her gaze settled on Julianne. "And based on the way you looked at him..."

Carolyn fell silent, but her eyes were filled with concern.

Oh, dear. "How did I look at him?" Julianne asked, hoping her dismay didn't show.

"As if his desire for you was mutual," Carolyn said softly. She reached out and clasped Julianne's hand. "You mustn't do anything foolish. Think of the repercussions—"

"Just because he desires her—and truly what man wouldn't," Emily broke in, "doesn't mean she desires him. Heavens, why would she? He's nothing like the men of the ton."

"Which is not necessarily a bad thing," Sarah said.

Emily looked toward the ceiling. "Says the new marchioness. You didn't marry a Bow Street Runner; you married a marquess."

"Because I was *in love* with him," Sarah whispered. "I didn't care a jot for Matthew's title. Or his money—which, as you'll recall, he didn't have any of at the time. I'd have married Matthew if he were a sailor or a—"

"Yes, yes, that's fine for you to say, but you didn't grow up as Julianne did," Emily insisted. "She's the daughter of an earl. Cavorting with a Runner simply isn't done."

"Who says I'm cavorting—?" Julianne tried to break in, but Sarah rolled right over her, saying, "You'd prefer that she marry a man she doesn't love, a man she barely knows, simply because he's a duke?"

"At least the duke is of our class," Emily said.

Sarah straightened her spine and raised her chin. "*I'm* not of your class, Emily. Neither is Carolyn. Our father was a mere physician."

Emily huffed out an exasperated breath. "You're taking this the wrong way, Sarah. I'm not trying to be haughty—"

"Yet you are being so just the same—"

"I'm merely pointing out that the man is a *commoner*—"

"As were Carolyn and I until our marriages."

"But you were both completely respectable."

"What is not respectable about a man who captures criminals and upholds the law?" Sarah demanded.

Emily's lips tightened. "Nothing," she admitted after a long pause. "But he has no business casting his eye on Julianne, who is so far above his station as to be laughable. Why, it's like that odious Mr. Jennsen thinking he was good enough for Carolyn."

"Actually, the problem wasn't that I thought Mr. Jennsen wasn't good enough for me," Carolyn broke in. "It was that my heart already belonged to Daniel." Her troubled gaze rested on Julianne. "But Emily is correct; I was not born an earl's daughter and as such my marriage was a huge social step up for me. What I think we're *all* trying to say," she continued in her calm voice, squeezing Julianne's hand, "is that we're concerned and want what's best for you. One can't fault a man for desiring a beautiful woman like you; it merely shows he has excellent taste. So long as he doesn't act on those feelings. Desire can be a very strong temptation, but you mustn't do something you'll regret. You must be very cautious, especially as he's staying here in the house."

"Cautious?" Sarah repeated softly. "As you were cautious with Daniel, Carolyn? As I was with Matthew?"

Before Julianne could even think of a reply, the French windows opened. She turned and saw Gideon stepping over the threshold. His gaze scanned the group. "Am I interrupting?" he asked.

"Not at all," Sarah said with a bright smile. She stood. "Although it is time for us to depart."

Carolyn and Emily rose, as did Julianne. She escorted her friends to the foyer, where Winslow handed them their shawls and bonnets. As Emily hugged her good-bye, her friend whispered, "Don't forget you're soon to be a duchess.

Which is what you deserve to be. We'll talk more tomorrow night at the duke's party." Next, Carolyn hugged her and whispered, "Don't do anything you'll regret. If you need me, send word."

Sarah merely kissed both her cheeks and followed Emily and Carolyn from the house. Julianne watched them from the open door, her thoughts in a whirl. They were halfway down the path leading to the street when Sarah exclaimed, "Heavens, I left my reticule. I'll be right back."

She walked swiftly back up the path and reentered the foyer and turned to Winslow. "I forgot my reticule in the drawing room, Winslow. Would you be so kind as to get it for me?"

"Of course, Lady Langston."

As soon as Winslow departed, Sarah grabbed Julianne's hand. "Emily and Carolyn are wrong," she said, her bespectacled gaze serious. "I don't believe Mr. Mayne merely desires you, Julianne. I think he is in love with you."

Julianne had to lock her knees to keep them from sagging. "How . . . what makes you say that?"

"I've been watching him—not just today, but at Lord Daltry's party, and even before that, when we first met him two months ago. I suspected he harbored strong feelings for you, but seeing him today solidified my suspicions. He may not realize the depth of his feelings himself yet—men tend to be slower to comprehend matters of the heart. But I'd stake everything I own that he's in love with you." She studied Julianne's eyes. "Do you care for him?"

The love and understanding shining from Sarah's eyes made it impossible for Julianne to lie. "I . . . I cannot deny I'm attracted to him. But it doesn't matter—"

"Of course it matters. Julianne . . . is he the one who kissed you?"

Julianne dropped her chin and looked at the floor. Then nodded miserably and looked up. "Yes."

Sarah gripped her shoulders and gave a grim nod. "I thought so. Thank you for telling me. I know it can't have been easy to share something so personal, nor has it been easy to keep all this inside you. Having recently gone through the same confusing upheaval of emotions, I know." Her gaze searched Julianne's. "Believe me, I *know*. And now that I know the *who*, we can work on the *how*."

Julianne frowned. "What do you mean?"

The sound of footsteps had her turning toward the corridor. Winslow approached, his brow puckered. "I'm afraid your reticule wasn't in the drawing room, Lady Langston. Perhaps you left it in your carriage?"

Sarah's eyes widened, then she laughed. "Heavens, I just recalled I didn't even bring a reticule with me." She gave Julianne a quick hug and whispered in her ear, "Chin up. We'll talk more tomorrow at the duke's party. In the meanwhile, follow your heart, Julianne. Your heart knows what is right. And you'll always, *always* have my love and support."

And then she was gone, leaving Julianne with far more questions than when she'd arrived. But one thought reverberated through Julianne's mind, wrapping around her, refusing to let go.

Was it possible that Sarah was right? Could Gideon be in love with her? A scary question indeed. But not nearly as frightening as the one that followed on its heels: a question she'd deliberately and steadfastly refused to even consider until now, when it hit her too hard to ignore.

Was she in love with Gideon?

Chapter 16

Gideon stood in the foyer, watching the earl accept his hat and walking stick from Winslow, and the countess adjust her gloves. He tried to recall the last time he'd found himself in the company of such a disagreeable couple and came up blank. After eating dinner in the kitchen, he'd walked the perimeter of the house and grounds, making certain all was secure, then checked every last window and door in the house. Everything was locked.

"We'll be home early," the countess said, frowning at Julianne, who stood still as a statue. "Although I can't abide Lady Foy's annual musicale, we must of course put in an appearance." Her gaze raked over Julianne, and she made a tsking sound. "You're to retire early. There are shadows beneath your eyes, and that will never do. You must look perfectly fresh and stunning for the duke's party tomorrow."

"Yes, Mother."

A muscle ticked in Gideon's jaw. Everything about the countess grated on his nerves. Her voice. Her demeanor. And the bloody nasty tone she used toward Julianne. He would have liked nothing more than to stomp across the fancy

marble tiles and stick his nose in her fancy face and tell her
to shut her bloody stupid mouth. She showed not the slightest
bit of sympathy toward her daughter with regard to the fright
she'd suffered, and if her concern stemmed from anything
more than a worry about what the duke's reaction might be,
she kept it well hidden.

And surely the woman must be blind, because he couldn't
imagine how anyone could look more stunning or perfect than
Julianne. Dressed in a pale green gown with her golden hair
pulled into a simple yet lovely style that left soft tendrils surrounding her face and accentuating the slender column of her
neck, she literally stole his breath.

"Your gown will be arriving from Madame Renee's in the
morning," the countess continued, "and you must try it on
immediately to make certain it's perfect."

"All of Madame's creations are perfect," Julianne said quietly. "I'm certain this one will be no different."

The countess's mouth puckered like a purse string, and she
narrowed her eyes. "I'll tolerate no arguments from you, Julianne. You will be prepared to try on your gown the *instant* it
is delivered. Nothing can go wrong for tomorrow night."

Julianne looked at the floor. "Yes, Mother."

"And stop mumbling," the countess snapped. "Botheration,
you not only look haggard, you sound haggard as well." She
heaved out a beleaguered sigh and turned toward her husband.
"Whatever am I going to do with her?"

"Nothing," said the earl, his voice a cold snap in the air.
"In a very short period of time she will no longer be our concern. Just make sure she looks her best tomorrow night." He
turned to Julianne and fixed his icy glare on her. "You'll retire
early, Daughter, and rid yourself of those unbecoming circles
beneath your eyes so that tomorrow night the duke will have
no reason to believe you've any cause to lose sleep."

The earl then shifted his attention Gideon. "You'll see to
it that there are no disturbances tonight—but if there are, this
time I expect you to catch the person responsible."

"That is why I'm here," Gideon said, returning the earl's
frigid stare with one of his own. He didn't doubt his ability to

protect Julianne from an intruder, but he seethed at his inability to safeguard her from the unkind barbs thrown at her by her parents. In spite of his profession, in spite of the violence in his past and that which he lived with every day on London's mean streets, he didn't consider himself a violent man. He used force only when necessary to protect himself or someone else from being made a victim.

But the earl's cold, dismissive unkindness toward Julianne settled like a red haze over Gideon's vision. In his mind's eye he saw himself picking up the nobleman by his perfectly tied cravat and shaking him like a terrier with a rat. Then telling him in no uncertain terms that if he ever heard him speak to her in such a cutting manner again, he'd shove his bloody teeth down his bloody throat. And while Gideon had never committed violence against a woman, the very elegant countess tested his patience to the limit. He would have taken great pleasure in telling the supercilious woman precisely what he thought of her—right after he tossed her into her very elegant privet hedges. A grim smile compressed his lips at the mental image. *I'd wager that would cause a few unsightly shadows beneath your eyes, Countess.*

A light pressure on his sleeve pulled Gideon from his brown study. He looked down and saw Julianne's pale hand resting against his dark jacket. Based on her quizzical expression, she'd just asked him something. He had no idea what.

"Does that meet with your approval?"

He glanced around the foyer and realized that her parents had departed. "Er, yes." Bloody hell, he hoped so, yet he couldn't think of anything she'd ask him to do that he'd deny her.

One corner of her mouth quirked upward. "Where did you go? You seemed a thousand miles away."

I was planting your arrogant father a facer and tossing your condescending mother into the hedges. "I was here. Just...preoccupied." He cleared his throat. "Do you plan to retire?"

She gave him an odd look, one that made him wonder exactly what he'd missed while he was mentally planting that facer. "Yes. As soon as we're finished." She turned to Winslow, who was rearranging a group of walking sticks into a tall porcelain urn next to the door. "Has the ballroom been readied?"

"Yes, Lady Julianne. It is just as you requested."

"Excellent." She turned back to Gideon and offered him a shy smile. "Follow me."

Bloody hell. He didn't know what awaited him in the ballroom, but when she looked at him like that, he'd follow her anywhere—a fact that simultaneously confounded and alarmed him. He gave a soft whistle, and Caesar followed, shadowed by Princess Buttercup, who wore what appeared to be a...tiny fur coat? Good God.

He walked beside Julianne down a series of long corridors, painfully aware of her. Her shoulder brushed his sleeve, and his nostrils flared, pulling in a sharp breath, which only served to fill his head with a tantalizing whiff of her vanilla scent.

She brushed against his shoulder again, and he barely refrained from groaning. He needed to take a quick look at whatever she wanted to show him, then send her off to bed. That way he'd know she was safe, and there would be a wall between them.

Feeling the need to say something to break the tension gripping him, he said, "You're very...patient with your parents."

Bloody hell. Certainly not the most diplomatic thing he could have uttered, but instead of appearing offended, she merely shrugged. "If you were to ask them, they are the ones who are patient with me. I'm a great trial to them, you see."

"In what way?"

She shot him a surprised sideways glance then leaned a bit closer, as if imparting a great secret. "I'm not a boy."

His gaze involuntarily coasted down her luscious form. "Obviously. Why does that make you a trial?"

Her brows shot up. "Because it renders me useless. I cannot inherit the title. Were I not so uncooperative, recalcitrant, and *a trial*, I would have been born what I was supposed to be: a male. Because I choose to be born a useless girl, Father's younger brother Harold will inherit, a fact that galls my father no end, especially as he detests Harold."

The news that the earl didn't like his younger brother didn't surprise Gideon in the least. In fact, it led him to ask, "Does your father like anyone?"

She pursed her lips and considered. "No, I don't think so. Certainly he doesn't like me. He barely tolerates Mother." She snapped her fingers. "His horse. He's very fond of Zeus."

Even though she sounded very matter-of-fact, he sensed her underlying sadness, and sympathy tugged at him. He knew all too well what it felt like to be a grave disappointment to one's father. Of course, in Gideon's case, the feeling was mutual. And he suddenly realized that that was something he and Julianne had in common, for there was no doubt she was disheartened by her father's attitude. She'd accepted it, just as he had with Jack, but accepting something and being happy about it were two very different things.

"Of course, there were times I *was* a trial." She shot him a sideways glanced filled with mischief. "Once, when I was ten, I had the audacity to go about in Brighton without my bonnet, resulting in a sunburn. Mother flew into the boughs, declaring my complexion ruined for eternity."

He sent her a look of feigned shock. "You are indeed awful."

"Yes. Although my retribution didn't do me much good."

"What did you do?"

"The next day I went to the beach and, while I kept my bonnet on, I removed my shoes and stockings and purposely allowed my feet to cook in the sun. I thought I was very clever— getting sunburned where Mother wouldn't see it." She chuckled softly. "I was quite done in my by own cunning when my skin ended up so tender I couldn't bear to wear shoes for the next three days." She gave him a rueful smile. "I'm afraid my private rebellion wasn't very successful."

"Have you had others?"

"Other what? Sunburns?"

"Private rebellions."

She shrugged. "A few here and there. Looking back, not as many as I wish I'd had. But over the past few months I've remedied that somewhat."

"Indeed? How?"

After a brief hesitation she said, "I joined a book club with Emily, Sarah, and Carolyn."

"I hate to be the one to inform you, but that doesn't sound very rebellious."

"Perhaps not."

Something in her tone made it clear there was more to know, but before he could question her further, they turned a corner, and she paused before the first door. He stopped behind her. And clenched his teeth. Her ivory nape was so close...if he leaned forward, he could brush his lips over that tantalizing bit of skin that seemed to beckon, *Kiss me, kiss me.*

He wasn't certain he wouldn't have obeyed the overwhelming urge, but she saved him from doing so by opening the door. Then she looked at him over her shoulder and smiled—a beautiful, shy smile that coaxed the shallow dimples in her cheeks out of hiding. "I hope this meets with your approval."

She entered the room, and he followed. Then halted. And stared.

Flames danced in a huge marble fireplace, casting the room in a soft glow that reflected off the glossy parquet floor. A dozen candelabras, their silver stems glowing with tapers that scented the air with beeswax, dotted the tables in the ballroom, adding to the soft light.

"Are you hosting a ball?" he asked, looking around, noting how the gilt mirrors lining the pale yellow silk-covered walls made the already huge chamber seem enormous.

She stopped in the center of the floor then turned toward him. The soft candle and firelight gilded her as if she'd been touched by an artist's brush. "Indeed I am. Are you ready?"

"For what?"

"Your dance lesson."

He could only stare. "I beg your pardon?"

She laughed. "Your dance lesson. To satisfy my part of our bargain. As I told you in the foyer, I thought it would be more enjoyable than a piano lesson, and, *ahem*, save everyone's ears."

Ah. So that's what he'd missed while mentally planting her father a facer and consigning her mother to the privet hedges. And what he'd inadvertently agreed to. A refusal rose to his lips; it was ridiculous that he learn to dance. Of what possible use would such knowledge be to a Runner? Besides, he'd most likely tread upon her toes and make a complete fool of himself.

But then an image flashed in his mind... of Julianne dancing with the duke at Daltry's party. He vividly recalled how beautiful she'd looked. And how he'd envied the bastard for holding her in his arms. How badly he'd wished for those few impossible minutes that *he* was the man whirling her around the dance floor. Holding her hand in his. Touching the small of her back. Looking into those incredible eyes while the room swirled around them. A useless, foolish dream he'd savagely pushed aside. But now... a useless, foolish dream that could become reality.

"What if Winslow tells your parents?"

She shrugged. "I promised to retire early—not immediately. And teaching a dance is really no different than teaching a song or a card game. 'Tis a lesson, nothing more. And the door will remain open so all is proper."

Right. Except in a dance lesson he'd be able to touch her.

As if caught in a trance, he walked slowly toward her, his boots tapping against the polished wood floor. "What about music?" he asked.

"I'll hum and sing." Her lips twitched. "We won't need to call upon your, um, formidable vocal, er, talents."

He stopped when only two feet separated them, a distance that at once felt far too great and much too small.

In order to appear more imposing—and to make certain he didn't give in to the urge to yank her against him—he crossed his arms over his chest and frowned. "The way you say *formidable* leads me to believe that you mean something else entirely."

Rather than looking intimidated, amusement gleamed in her eyes. "Perhaps I do. *Indescribable* might be a more accurate assessment of your abilities."

"You said earlier I can't sing worth a jot. In other words, I possess no musical talent at all."

A dazzling smile lit her face. "Actually no other words are necessary, as those words are perfect."

He narrowed his eyes. "How is it that you issue such insults yet don't look frightened?"

She made a dismissive gesture. "Pshaw. You don't scare me."

He deepened his scowl and leaned forward to loom over her, more amused than he cared to admit. "No?"

"No. Oh, you can be very intimidating, especially with that frown, which is quite fierce, by the way. But underneath that crusty exterior is..." She tapped her finger on her chin and gave him a thorough look-over. "Porridge."

He leaned back and blinked, nonplussed. "Crusty? *Porridge*?"

"Yes. Indeed, you remind me of a loaf of perfectly baked bread: hard on the outside, soft on the inside."

"I've never heard such rot," he muttered, shaking his head, torn between mirth and masculine indignation. "Loaf of bread. Unbelievable."

She hiked up a brow. "You disagree with my assessment?"

"Heartily."

"Hmmm. You sound...peeved. I assure you I meant it as a compliment."

"To compare me to a loaf of bread?"

"That's not nearly as bad as *you* comparing *me* to a drunken porcupine." Before he could say another word, she snapped her fingers. "That's an even better description of you. You're like a porcupine—all sharp quills on the outside."

"Thank you. So much. And on the inside?"

"Oh, still porridge."

"What sort of porcupine has porridge on the inside?"

"The sort I'm comparing you to."

"There is no such thing as a porcupine with porridge on the inside."

She planted her hands on her hips. A tapping noise sounded, and he realized it was her foot rapping against the wood floor. "Fine. On the inside you're porcupine innards—that are the consistency of porridge."

"Oh, thank you," he said in his driest tone. "That's much better."

"You're welcome. Has anyone ever told you that you don't accept compliments very graciously?"

He couldn't help but laugh. "No, Princess, they haven't. I assure you I can accept them just fine—when one is actually given."

A knowing look came over her features. "Ah. Now I understand. You prefer pretty, flowery words."

"Certainly not. Bow Street Runners don't like anything to do with flowery words."

"Then you'll have to make do with either a loaf of bread or a porcupine with porridge for innards."

"I don't see why, as I don't agree with either description."

"Fine. Has anyone ever told you that just because you disagree you don't need to be disagreeable?"

"Has anyone ever told you you're incredibly fickle? A moment ago I was a perfectly baked loaf of bread. Now I'm disagreeable."

A slow smile curved her lips. "Only because you disagreed with me."

His gaze lowered to her full lips, curved in that captivating smile, and he felt as if he were being sucked into a vortex. Bloody hell, she was enchanting. Literally so, as it appeared he'd fallen under some sort of spell. A spell cast by a beautiful princess, but one who kept proving herself so much more than merely beautiful on the outside. This princess was beautiful on the inside as well.

"Are you ready for your lesson?" she asked. "I thought we'd try the waltz—unless you already know it?"

He shook his head—both as an answer and to shake off the stupor he'd fallen into. "No, I don't know it. But I must warn you: your toes stand in grave jeopardy of suffering as much as your ears did this afternoon."

Her eyes went soft, and his insides seemed to turn to—bloody hell—porridge. "I suspect you'll be a marvelous waltzer. And I'm not the least bit worried about my toes."

"Well, you should be. I'll be like an ox stomping about."

"Then we have our work cut out for us and had best begin. After all, I must retire early. Can't have those unsightly dark circles under my eyes, you know." The grin she shot him was downright naughty, and he found himself smiling in return— and biting his tongue to refrain from telling her that she couldn't look unsightly if she tried.

She reached out and clasped his left hand, lifting it to chin height, elbow bent, then settled her other hand on his shoulder. "Set your right hand on my back," she instructed.

Heat sizzled up one arm and down the other, and for several seconds he felt as if he couldn't breathe. Damn. Maybe this wasn't such a good idea after all. He looked into her eyes. She appeared expectant—and quite annoyingly nothing else. Certainly she didn't seem as if she were about to go up in flames as he did. Well, hell. If she could tolerate this, so could he.

He settled his right hand on her back and forced himself not to drag her closer.

"A bit lower," she said. "Right at the base of my spine."

He slowly slid his hand down, his palm brushing over the smooth material of her gown, his mind's eye envisioning the gentle curve of her back.

"Here?" he asked softly, pressing his palm to the small of her back.

Her breath caught slightly, and grim satisfaction filled him. Good. She wasn't as unaffected as she'd like him to think. Why should he be the only one suffering? Of course, she chose just then to moisten her lips, a flick of pink tongue that increased his suffering far more than he would have liked.

"Yes, right there." She cleared her throat then continued, "The waltz is a very simple dance, and done to a three beat. As the man, you are the leader, and as your partner, I shall mirror your steps."

"Which means you'll be treading on my toes as well?"

"You must cease this worrying about my toes. I'm not as delicate as I look. We'll go very slowly. Now, on the first beat, you step gracefully forward with your left foot. At the same time, I'll step back with my right. Ready? Begin."

He stepped forward, but apparently not gracefully, because his boot landed squarely on her foot.

"Bloody hell," he said, immediately releasing her and stepping back. "Are you hurt?"

"My toe is fine. Not to worry, I have nine others."

"Which I'll no doubt crush on beat two."

"There are only three beats, Gideon. So how much damage can you possibly do?"

The sound of his name coming from her lips gave him the incentive to at least attempt to redeem himself. "Hopefully not much."

Once again she took his hand, and he settled his at the base of her spine. "This time take a smaller step," she said. "We're not trying to get across the room in a single bound."

"Would have helped if you'd said that the first time," he grumbled.

He managed to execute the first step without mishap. "Now what?"

"For the second beat, you're going to step forward and to the right with your right foot—rather like tracing an upside down letter *L*."

He tried but obviously traced too large of an *L*, because his knee banged into hers thigh, a mistake that arrowed heat up his leg. His gaze flicked to hers, and to his annoyance she once again appeared completely unruffled while he felt hot and uncomfortable and as if his clothes had suddenly shrunk.

"Try again," she said, nodding in an encouraging fashion. "Just take a smaller step."

He obeyed, and continued obeying her instructions, which she repeated with unfailing patience, in spite of his many missteps and toe crunches. At first he felt ridiculous and clumsy and utterly ungainly, and the only thing keeping him from quitting was that he couldn't walk away from this opportunity to hold her in his arms. Indeed, he might have done better if he'd had a different teacher—someone whose every touch didn't set his skin on fire. Made it bloody damn difficult to concentrate when a matter of mere inches separated their bodies. Could she feel the heat and desire pumping off him?

Didn't seem possible she couldn't, as it felt to him as if it exuded from his pores like vapor rising from a hot spring.

"Very good," she said, as they made their way around the floor at an excruciatingly slow pace. "*One*, two, three. *One*, two, three. Now let's add a slight turn to the left so we go in a circle."

The slight turn to the left threw him off, and again he stepped on her toes. "Damn," he muttered. "I'm sorry. I'm not usually so inept."

"There is nothing inept about you, Gideon," she said softly.

He jerked his head up from where he'd been glowering at his feet and found her serious blue gaze resting on him with an expression that did nothing to cool his want of her.

"All you need is a bit of practice," she said, giving his hand a gentle, encouraging squeeze. "A quarter hour from now, you'll be waltzing as if you were born doing so."

"Doubtful," he muttered. A quarter hour from now he needed for this lesson to be over. Before he gave in to his ever-increasing desire to forget the bloody waltz and lower her to the hearth rug and end this hunger gnawing at him.

Gritting his teeth, he tried again, counting *one*, two, three, *one*, two, three furiously in his head.

"Excellent," she praised a moment later. "Now you need to do that very same thing, but looking at me—with a smile—instead of glaring at your feet. It is a dance, you know. Not a funeral march."

He raised his gaze, looked into her eyes, and instantly stumbled over his own feet. And stepped on hers.

He uttered what felt like his hundredth apology, but she didn't miss a step, just slowly kept going, around and around, counting softly. After they'd made a complete—albeit extremely slow—circle of the ballroom without mishap, she offered him a beaming smile.

"Excellent. Now we're ready for some music." She began to softly hum a slow melody. After a moment he asked, "What song is that?"

"Just one of the dozens of songs I know about flowers and

sunshine and grass-filled meadows." Her lips curved in a mischievous grin. "Shall I sing 'Apple Dumplin' Shop'?"

He grinned in return. "Shall *I*?"

She laughed. "Good heavens, no. I'll hum another." She began again, and this time he recognized the song as the one she'd played earlier today. "That is the tune you composed," he said. " 'Dreams of You.' "

She stopped humming and nodded. "Yes." Her serious gaze rested on his, and she whispered, " 'Dreams of You.' "

Again she hummed the haunting melody, and with his gaze locked on hers, unable to look away, they slowly circled the floor. He found himself imagining they stood in a crowded ballroom, and he was dressed in the finest evening attire, and he had every right in the world to approach her, an earl's daughter, and ask her to dance. To take her in his arms where she fit as if made for him alone and circle the ballroom while every other man wished he were Gideon. Who was the luckiest man in the world to be waltzing with her. The most beautiful, desirable woman in the world.

She reached the end of the song, and her sweet hum faded into silence. Their steps slowed then halted. Her eyes glowed up at him, and she smiled. And everything inside him seemed to simultaneously melt and go still.

"I hate to say 'I told you so,'" she murmured, "but..."

He had to swallow twice to locate his voice. "Actually, I don't think you hate to say it at all."

"Perhaps not. You are a lovely dancer."

"You are a lovely teacher." Unable to stop himself, he brought their joined hands to his mouth and pressed a kiss to the backs of her fingers. Her breath caught at the gesture, and he felt a tremor run through her, one he longed to feel again.

"Thank you," he murmured against her fingers. "For the most enjoyable waltz I've ever experienced."

A breathless-sounding laugh escaped her. "That was the *only* waltz you've ever experienced."

True. But he knew damn well that even if he'd experienced a thousand of them, that one still would have been his favorite. He wanted to tell her that, wanted to let her know how heartbreakingly beautiful she looked. How incredible she felt in his arms. How easy it would be to simply stand here all night long, just looking at her. Breathing in her subtle vanilla scent. How much he wanted to kiss her. Make love to her. Make her *his*.

Bloody hell, he needed to get away from her. Now. Before a simple dance turned into something very complicated. Something they'd both regret.

The memory of them together flashed in his mind...of Julianne lying on the drawing room hearth rug, her skirts bunched about her waist, his head buried between her silky thighs, and desire slammed into him like a fist to his gut.

He released her and quickly stepped back. "Our bargain is now satisfied," he said, his voice rough with the want he was trying desperately to hide. "And it's time for you to retire."

There was no missing the disappointment that filled her gaze, but he refused to acknowledge it. "Very well," she murmured, "but first I need to snuff the candles."

He suspected that was merely a stalling tactic—no doubt there was a servant whose sole responsibility it was to snuff out candles—but he didn't argue. Instead he walked to the opposite side of the room and grabbed a long-handled engraved brass candle snuffer from a side table and helped the process along.

When they finished, he moved to the door and said, "I'll escort you to your chamber. Make certain the room is secure."

She looked up at him, lit now only by the back glow of the fire, and he felt himself drowning in her eyes. "And then what?"

"And then I'll do my job." He forced his gaze away and gave a soft whistle for Caesar, who'd been patiently standing guard in the corridor with his fur-draped cohort.

"Gideon, I—"

"Let's get you settled for the night," he broke in, his voice coming out harsh. Based on the yearning so obvious in her eyes, she planned to say something he didn't want to hear. Something that would surely tempt his already shaky resolve.

"Now. Before your parents return home and find you haven't yet retired."

He didn't wait for a reply, just began walking down the corridor. She caught up to him several seconds later.

"Gideon, I—"

"I meant to ask you something earlier," he broke in again, this time in desperation. He couldn't risk her saying what he saw in her eyes. Couldn't let her voice the admiration and longing he saw there.

She hesitated then asked, "What do you wish to know?"

"I'm curious about the book that was mentioned at tea. *The Ghost of Devonshire Manor*. The mere mention of it caused a very interesting reaction in you and your friends."

"Interesting?"

"Yes. Lady Emily seemed quite devilish, and the rest of you blushed and were very eager to change the subject. Given my inquisitive nature, I can't help but wonder what it is about the book that would cause such a reaction."

"I...I suppose we were merely surprised when Emily broached the subject. The book was the latest reading selection of our book club, and we normally don't discuss our choices outside our small circle."

"And why is that?"

"Because they are not books that would necessarily be considered...classics. In the classic sense. Precisely."

Understanding and interest dawned, and he nodded. "I see. So they are scandalous."

A scarlet flush washed over her cheeks. "I suppose a certain type of person might think so."

"And what type is that?"

"A person who can read."

He couldn't help but chuckle. "Well, well. Proper Lady Julianne reading improper books. It would seem the *lioness* has not only claws but teeth as well. Interesting."

They entered the foyer where Winslow assured them all was well. After bidding the butler good night, Gideon and Julianne climbed the stairs. When they reached the top, she said, "Since you are so curious, you may borrow the book, if you'd like."

He knew he should refuse, but the thought of having, even temporarily, something that belonged to her, especially something that had brought such a becoming flush to her cheeks, was too irresistible to refuse. "All right," he agreed. "Thank you."

"You're welcome. I'll get it for you now." She stopped in front of her bedchamber door—the room where he would be staying tonight, in hopes of the intruder coming back so Gideon could capture the bastard.

"Wait," he said softly. He entered the room ahead of her. A fire had been laid, bathing the room with a warm, golden glow. He made certain the windows were locked, noting as he made his way around the room that his portmanteau had been unpacked and his personal items were neatly lined up next to a washstand and pitcher filled with water.

He motioned for her to enter. She did so. Then, with her gaze steady on his, she slowly closed the door behind her.

He stilled at the quiet click, a soft sound that reverberated through his head with the finality of prison bars clanging shut. He stood rooted to the carpet, watching as she crossed the room then opened the wardrobe. She crouched down, arose, then walked toward the bed, carrying what appeared to be a wooden box.

"Is that where you keep all your scandalous books?" he asked, forcing a lightness into his voice he was far from feeling.

She shook her head. "This is my Box of Wishes and Dreams. It's where I keep all my treasures and most prized possessions."

His better judgment warned him to keep his distance, but his curiosity to see the contents of the box won out. He approached the bed and looked down.

"I discovered this box several years ago in a shop on Bond Street and instantly fell in love with it," she said, tracing her fingers over the delicately painted design on the lid. It was of a woman, standing in profile, her arms outstretched. In the woman's one hand dangled her bonnet ribbons and in the other her shoes. Her long blond curls and pale blue gown billowed behind her in the unseen breeze as she ran, hatless and barefoot, through a field of colorful wildflowers. The woman's face was raised to capture the sun's golden glow, and a smile filled with pure joy curved her lips.

"She immediately captured my imagination with her carefree exuberance," Julianne said quietly, brushing a single fingertip over the lid. "I could almost hear her jubilant laughter. She was a brave and daring woman, one free of restrictions and rules, and I recognized her instantly."

Gideon's brows rose. "Recognized her?"

"Yes." She looked up and met his gaze. "She is the woman I've always longed to be. The woman who lives in my imagination."

Taking a small brass key, she unlocked the box and slowly lifted the lid. "As soon as I arrived home with the box, I dubbed it my Box of Wishes and Dreams, and in it I keep things I've collected that represent my fondest desires."

She opened the box, and he looked down. And frowned. In spite of her claim not to be enamored of jewelry, he'd expected the box to be filled with glittery gems and other expensive trinkets. He wasn't certain what all those things in the box were, but not one of them sparkled. He leaned closer and recognized the shape of an object on the top.

"A seashell?" he asked, wondering what that could possibly have to do with wishes and dreams.

She lifted the perfectly formed conch shell from the box and held it in her palm. "I found this on the beach at Brighton—a place I dearly love. The shell reminds me of the exhilaration and freedom I experience walking along the sea-washed sand, the tangy salt breezes whipping through my hair."

She set the shell on the bed then lifted what appeared to be a foot-long strip of ragged material from the box. "This is the tail of a kite I flew on that same beach. I recall laughing as it snapped in the briny wind and soared toward the clouds. And this..." she lifted out another object and handed it to him. "A gull's feather that floated through the air while the bird that had shed it had squawked without restraint then spread its gray-tipped wings and floated toward the cobalt water, skimming the white-capped surface."

Gideon brushed a fingertip over the feather and tried to make sense of the odd feeling gripping him. Before he could figure it out, she picked up several more objects. First she handed him a small pencil drawing of Princess Buttercup, asleep on her satin pillow.

"Sarah drew this. She's very talented." Next she placed a small gray rock in his hand. "I found this in Hyde Park while on a walk with Emily. And this leaf—" She placed that on top of the rock, "is from the elm outside Carolyn's town house. They're reminders of my very dear friends."

Her gaze searched his and as always, he felt himself sinking. Like a drowning man, alone in the middle of the sea. "Do you want to see more?" she asked quietly.

Every self-preservation instinct in his body demanded he say no. That he send her off to the chamber where she was to sleep. But then his gaze fell to the box. And he knew he had to see what else was inside. "Yes," he said softly. "I want to see everything."

Again she reached into the box, this time withdrawing two dried flowers. "One from Sarah's wedding bouquet and one from Carolyn's. Because I've always dreamed of a love-filled marriage such as the ones they have." Next she withdrew two pairs of baby booties, one pink, one blue. "I made these," she said, tracing her fingers over the delicately embroidered material. "For the dreams of the children I hope to someday have."

Once again she reached into the box, this time pulling out a folded piece of vellum. "I added this treasure several months ago, soon after the Ladies Literary Society was formed. During our first meeting we discussed the traits we felt constituted the Perfect Man." She raised her brows. "Would you like me to read it to you?"

"By all means."

She unfolded the vellum and recited, "'The Perfect Man is a kind, patient, generous, honest, honorable, witty, intelligent, handsome, romantic, stunningly passionate, make-your-insides-flutter, full-lipped good kisser who can dance, shop, listen, and solicit a woman's opinion, all tirelessly and without complaint." She looked up and met his gaze. "What do you think?"

Not one mention of wealth. Or a title. Or estates. He fought the overpowering need to loosen his suddenly too tight cravat. "I think that's a lot to ask for in one man."

She nodded solemnly. "Yes. But finding the perfect person for you ... I believe it is possible."

Bloody hell, the way she was looking at him ... as if he were that perfect person for her ... made the area around his heart go hollow. With longing. And desire. God knows he was far from perfect. And the absolute opposite of perfect for her.

Needing to break the suffocating silence, he nodded toward the box. "Anything else in there?"

She picked up two slim books. Setting the first one on the bed, she said, "That is *Memoirs of a Mistress*, one of our previous book club selections. The book is scandalously explicit, but I greatly admired the courage of the author. She was a fearless woman who lived as she pleased and enjoyed all of life's passions." She handed him the other book. "This is *The Ghost of Devonshire Manor*."

"And why was it given a place of honor in your Box of Wishes and Dreams?"

"It represents the sort of loving relationship I've always longed for, albeit with a real man rather than a specter. It was a beautiful story of profound love. Of deep passion. Of two people who, in spite of their feelings, given their circumstances, could never be together."

His heart began to pound in slow, hard beats, and his fingers tightened on the leather-bound volume. "So what did they do?"

"They took what happiness they could. Enjoyed each other for the short time it was possible to do so. Then Maxwell, the ghost, had to return to his world, while Lady Elaine remained in hers. And so they parted."

"And that was it? No happy ending?" He tried to insert a

bit of levity and smile, but his face felt like stone. "I thought ladies liked stories with happy endings."

"Not all love stories have a happy ending, I'm afraid."

The air in the room seemed thick and hot. In desperation, he looked down at the book. Opened it to a random page. And scanned the lines.

She lay on the bed, naked, legs splayed to reveal glistening folds he ached to touch. Lifting one hand toward him, she whispered a single word: "Please." And Maxwell knew in that instant that nothing from her world or the after-world would stop him from making love to her. Claiming her as his own. At least for tonight, for they couldn't have forever.

He snapped the book shut and drew in a shaky breath. Bloody hell. It was definitely time to get the hell out of this room, which suddenly felt as if it were the size of a birdcage. And on fire.

"You need to..." His words trailed off, and he stared into the box. One item remained. As if in a trance, he reached in to pull out the folded white square with the dark blue *G* embroidered in the corner.

"This is my handkerchief."

She hesitated then nodded. And suddenly it looked as if her heart were in her eyes, and everything inside him seemed to still and race at the same time. These things, these simple things she called her most prized possessions, her treasures, held no monetary value. Yet they were rich in sentiment. Certainly not the treasures of a spoiled princess. No, they were the treasures of a sensitive, thoughtful, romantic, beautiful young woman. One who'd added his handkerchief to her Box of Wishes and Dreams.

God help him.

"You offered it to me last night," she whispered. "I hope you'll let me keep it. Someday it will be all I'll have of you."

Bloody hell. His heart felt heavy. As if each beat were a blow against his ribs. "Julianne—"

She cut off his words by placing her fingers against his lips. "I want you to know," she said, her gaze steady on his, "that since the moment I met you two months ago, you haven't been out of my thoughts. You're the first thing I think about when I awaken, the last thing I think of before I fall asleep, and you invade every thought in between. What we shared last night was...magical. Incredible. And I want more of it. More of everything. With you. Now. While I still can."

Chapter 17

Julianne saw the fire flare in Gideon's eyes, a heat so smolder-ing it seemed to set her skin ablaze. He'd spoken of his honor, but surely honor had naught to do with him accepting what she wanted to give him, what she desperately wanted to share with him. All of herself. What she needed to do now was set *his* skin ablaze. But in spite of the scandalously explicit books she'd read, she had no experience as a seductress. Having informa-tion and knowing how to apply it in a situation like this were two very different things. All she could do was let him know how much she wanted him. And pray he wanted her as well.

Her fingers still lay across his mouth, and she traced them over his full bottom lip. Then she stepped forward, until her body brushed the length of his. His nostrils flared, and he sucked in a sharp breath. Encouraged, she rose up on her toes, wrapped her arms around his neck, and pressed herself tighter against him. Then nearly sagged in relief. Even if he'd wanted to deny it, he couldn't refute the hard evidence of his arousal.

"Kiss me, Gideon," she whispered against his rigid jaw, the highest spot she could reach without his cooperation. Heart pounding, she squirmed against him, clinging tighter. "Please. Hold me. Touch me. Kiss m—"

Her words were cut off when, with a low groan that sounded as if it were ripped from his soul, he slanted his mouth over hers in a wild, raw, fiercely hungry kiss. One strong arm wrapped around her waist, yanking her closer, banding their bodies together as if they were bound by ropes. His other hand plunged into her hair, scattering pins, holding her head immobile while his mouth ravaged hers. A dark thrill raced through her at the intensity of his kiss. He kissed her as if he wanted to devour her, clasped her to him as if he'd never let her go. His tongue invaded her mouth, a favor she returned, relishing his warm, delicious taste.

Closer. She wanted to be closer to him. To feel more of his hardness. More of his heat. Taste more. Touch more. Just ... *more.*

It seemed as if she could feel her heartbeat everywhere. Pounding in her ears. At the base of her throat. Her temples. Fluttering in her chest and stomach. In her abdomen, pressed so tightly against him. Throbbing in the aching folds between her legs.

Her restless fingers combed through his thick hair, fisting in the silky strands to pull his mouth closer. She heard him groan, then her feet left the floor as he simply lifted her straight up. As if in a daze, she felt him backing up, stopping when he hit the wall. Without breaking their kiss, he spread his legs, curved one large hand around her buttocks, and drew her into the V of his thighs.

And suddenly it seemed as if his hands were everywhere. Skimming down her back to caress her bottom. Plunging into her hair. Dipping into her bodice. Palming her breasts. Teasing her nipples into taut, aching points.

His mouth was equally relentless, trailing hot kisses along her jaw. Licking fire down her neck, his teeth scraping over the sensitive skin.

He reached between them and jerked his shirttails from his breeches, then grabbed her wrists from around his neck and slapped her hands on his chest. "Touch me," he commanded in a raw voice against her lips, his warm, rapid breaths mingling with hers. "Bloody hell, *touch me.*"

She was only too happy to comply. She splayed her fingers then dragged her palms downward, slipping them beneath the untucked linen. The instant she touched his skin, they both groaned. His eyes slammed shut, and he dropped his head back, the muscles of his throat working as he swallowed hard.

Slowly she slid her hands upward, thrilling at how his muscles jumped beneath her touch. His skin was smooth and hot, ridged with hard muscle. Her fingers brushed over his nipples then sifted through the springy curls dusting his skin.

He groaned, lifted his head, and captured her face between his hands—hands she noted weren't quite steady. His eyes burned like dark coals, holding hers captive, his calloused thumbs gliding over her cheekbones while her hands roamed beneath his shirt. The raw hunger and need in his eyes most likely should have frightened her. Instead it exhilarated her. And she wanted more of it.

She dragged her hands lower and brushed them over the fascinating bulge tenting his breeches. A shudder ran through him. "I want to touch all of you, Gideon."

For the space of a single heartbeat he remained immobile, his gaze locked on hers, a muscle ticking in his jaw. Then with a low growl, he ripped open his breeches.

His hard flesh rose between them, fascinating, beckoning. His chest rose and fell with his fast, heavy breaths, and she slowly encircled him with her fingers then lightly squeezed.

"Bloody hell." The words hissed through his lips, and he grasped her shoulders, his fingers tightly gripping her upper arms. She pulled her gaze away from his captivating arousal and looked up. He regarded her through half-closed eyes that glittered like diamonds.

"You feel so...hot," she whispered. "And hard."

"You have no idea." He flexed his hips, a slow thrust into her hand. "Again," he growled, and she wasn't certain if the single word was more an order or a plea.

She obeyed, lightly squeezing him. His eyes slammed shut,

and she looked down, watching her fingers surround his flesh and move slowly up and down his long, hard length, each stroke dragging another deep groan from him. With an agonized sound he pressed forward, grinding into her palm, and to her utter fascination a pearl of dewy fluid emerged from the tip of his arousal. She captured the drop on her fingertip and slowly circled the velvety head with the wetness.

"Julianne..." She could feel him trembling, and her name sounded torn from his throat. But before she could fully marvel that her touch affected him so, he pushed her hands away from him then yanked her toward him, trapping his erection tightly between their bodies, and kissed her. Deeper, more fiercely, impossibly with even more passion than he had before.

A sudden coolness brushed against her legs, and in some hazy part of her brain she realized he'd lifted her skirts. Hooking one hand behind her knee, he raised her leg, settling her thigh high on his hip.

"You taste so damn good," he whispered against her mouth. "And you feel so damn good..." His hand smoothed up her thigh. Curved around her buttocks. His fingers lightly traced between her cheeks, shooting a hot shiver down her spine, then moved lower to find the opening in her drawers.

She gasped at his first touch along her feminine folds.

"You're wet," he said, his voice a growl against her neck. "So beautifully wet."

His clever fingers were relentless, circling, delving, skimming, and gliding, until her every breath turned into a mindless moan. She clung to his shoulders, helplessly writhing against his hand, desperate for more. He slipped a finger inside her at the same instant his tongue entered her mouth, a simultaneous invasion that melted her knees. Need coiled within her, and her hips undulated, desperately seeking the magic she'd experienced last night.

With a deep groan he dipped his knees, curved his free hand around her bottom, and hauled her higher against him. And suddenly his hardness was pressed against her...oh, exactly right *there*. Her head fell back, and a long, guttural moan rattled in her throat. He slipped another finger inside her, stretching her in the most delicious way, and slowly pumped while he flexed his hips, a thrust that shot such intense pleasure through her she could only gasp into his mouth.

Held tightly against him, his fingers stroking inside her body, his tongue delving inside her mouth, his hot, hard shaft pressed against that magically sensitive female part of her, she simply came apart in his arms.

Molten pleasure pulsed through her, dragging a cry from her throat. He broke off their kiss and with a cry of his own he buried his face in the curve of her neck, whispering her name over and over in a voice that sounded as if he'd swallowed broken glass.

For several long seconds they remained locked in place, both breathing hard, and Julianne reveled in the strength of his arms around her. The feel of his rapid heartbeat thumping against her chest. The scent of his skin mixed with the musk of their arousal. She'd never felt so warm and protected and utterly, beautifully *alive*. And for that, she loved him.

Everything inside her stilled as those words echoed through her mind, their truth becoming clearer with each repetition. She loved him. She loved him.

God help her, she loved him.

Hopelessly. Stupidly. Impossibly.

Irrevocably.

For the space of a single heartbeat she tried to deny it but realized it was hopeless to do so. He'd captured her imagination the instant she'd seen him two months ago, and every minute since had only built on those initial feelings.

She felt him lift his head, and she leaned back, wondering if she should confess the depth of her feelings, wondering if she'd even need to, for surely he'd see them reflected in her eyes. Wondering if she might see in his eyes even a fraction of what she felt toward him.

The instant their gazes met, that hope died a withering death. Instead of glowing with tenderness or affection, his eyes looked like flat stones. His mouth was pressed into a grim line, his expression hard.

Without a word he set her away from him. Her rumpled skirts unfurled, brushing down her unsteady legs. With a lump lodged in her throat, she watched him use his handkerchief to wipe away the evidence of his release from his stomach. He then shoved his wrinkled shirt back into his breeches and fastened them, uttering an obscenity when he realized one button was missing, obviously ripped off in his earlier haste. She saw the button on the floor, next to her shoe, and bent to retrieve it. As Gideon didn't notice she'd done so, she slipped the flat disk into the pocket of her gown.

When he finished, he raked his fingers through his hair, hair she'd mussed with her impatient fingers. He then dragged his hands down his face and let them fall limply to his sides, as if he were too exhausted to hold them up any longer.

"I'm sorry," he said through obviously clenched teeth. "I didn't mean to..." He drew in a slow, deep breath. "That shouldn't have happened."

A cold numbness crept into her, pushing aside all the warmth she'd felt just heartbeats ago. "Why?"

Finally a crack showed in the granite of his expression, and disbelief showed through. "Bloody hell, there are more reasons than I have breaths to name them."

"I'll settle for one."

"You know them as well as I do."

"Because I'm getting married."

He shook his head and again stabbed his fingers into his hair. "That's only one of them, the one that has to do with my honor." A bitter sound escaped him. "Or what's left of it." He grasped her by the shoulders, and she saw that his eyes were no longer flat. No, now they were filled with unmistakable anguish. And anger. Although she couldn't tell if he was angry with her or with himself. "I told you—I don't take things that don't belong to me, Julianne. It's a point of pride and honor to me. And as much as I might wish it otherwise, you do not, cannot, will not ever belong to me."

"You are not the only one who would wish it otherwise, Gideon," she said quietly.

He released her and stepped back. "It doesn't matter what either of us might wish. The fact remains you are engaged—"

"Not officially—"

"Irrelevant. It is only a matter of papers to be signed. But even if you weren't betrothed, this...attraction between us is completely impossible. You're an earl's daughter. An aristocrat. A wealthy member of society. I am so far below you socially, I need to stand on a ladder and look up just to squint at the hem of your skirt."

"I told you, the trappings of wealth aren't important to me."

"It doesn't matter. You cannot change who you are. Who I am. And who I'm not. Fancy balls and gowns and jewels might not be important to you, but they're a part of your world. And that is something I'll never be—a part of your world. Your duty is to—"

"Marry according to my father's wishes?" she said bitterly.

"In your world, yes."

"And what is your duty, Gideon?"

"To let you do it. To not steal your innocence—or what bloody little I've left you with. The innocence that belongs to you." A muscle ticked in his jaw. "And your future husband."

"You've taken nothing I haven't freely given."

"Nonetheless, I shouldn't have taken it. I'd resolved I would never touch you. Then, after I did, I resolved it was a mistake, one that couldn't be repeated." He shook his head, closed his eyes, and blew out a long, slow breath. Then he looked at her again. "Clearly it is one thing to resolve not to do something and quite another to follow through on that resolve. But I won't fail again. I will not, *cannot* make the same mistake again."

Mistake. That's all she was, what they'd shared, to him. "You must think me a terrible wanton."

He shook his head. "No. I take full responsibility. I completely lost control of myself."

"A generous and noble offer, but I cannot allow it. I am just as responsible, if not more so, as I desperately wanted you to lose your control."

Julianne reached out to touch him, but he stepped back,

shaking his head. She pressed her empty hands against her midriff, realizing that it wasn't just her hands that were empty. It was everything. Her life. Her heart. Her soul. She felt as if she were trying to hold water in her clenched fists; no matter how hard she gripped, it still trickled through until only emptiness remained.

"Gideon...I have so little time left." She kept her gaze steady on his, fully aware of the desperation creeping into her voice and not caring. "I've been happier in these stolen moments with you than I've ever been in my entire life—"

"Stop. Please." He moved toward her with jerky steps, then cupped her face in his hands. His eyes looked tormented. "God help me, I have no defenses against you. So please don't share any more of yourself, your feelings, with me. Please don't let me see any more of your heart. I don't deserve it, and it's making an already impossible situation even more so." He squeezed his eyes briefly shut then said in a rough whisper, "You have no idea how close to impossible it is for me to walk away as it is."

She reached up and clasped his wrists. "Then don't walk away, Gideon." The words sounded like a desperate plea, but she didn't care. "Let us be together for the next fortnight, until I must leave. I agree it is all we can have of each other. But let us have that much."

His gaze searched hers, and she made no attempt to hide her feelings from him. She let him see all her hopes and wishes, all her wants and needs and desires. All her love. And with her insides jittering with anxiety, she prayed.

Several long seconds passed in silence. Then he slowly released her. And stepped back.

"I can't," he said. "I can't do it to you or myself. If anyone caught wind of this, the scandal would ruin you. You could lose everything."

"And you would lose your honor."

"Yes."

A bitter sound escaped her. There obviously was no point in telling him that, except for creature comforts, she had nothing.

Dear God, how was it possible to hurt so badly when she felt so numb? She managed to jerk her head in a tight nod. "I...I think it's best if I retire now." She pushed the words past the lump clogging her throat, but with the tears pushing behind her eyes she knew her hold on her emotions was tenuous.

Walking as swiftly as she could, she made her way to the blue bedchamber. She heard Gideon walking behind her, heard Caesar trotting next to his master, and Princess Buttercup panting as she jogged to keep up. When they reached her chamber, she scooped up her dog and waited in the corridor while Gideon checked the room.

"All is secure," he said a moment later. "Caesar will remain outside your door. No harm will come to you."

"Thank you," she said tonelessly. No point in telling him the harm had already been done.

And that she'd never, ever be the same.

∽

After seeing Caesar settled in the corridor outside Julianne's door with a command to guard, Gideon entered his bedchamber. He shut the door behind him then leaned back against the oak panel.

Bloody hell. What a night.

He closed his eyes, a mistake, as he was instantly bombarded with the images he desperately wanted, needed to forget. Of Julianne smiling. Laughing. Teaching him to waltz. Lifting her face for his kiss. Succumbing to her climax. Looking at him with her heart in her eyes.

And what had he done to deserve such an adoring look? He had treated her no better than a common doxie and disgraced himself like a green lad to boot.

He forced his eyes open and scrubbed his hands over his face. Damn it, he'd *tried* not to touch her, but his resistance had worn down, and he'd thought what harm could there be in a simple dance? And he might have made it through the evening without falling on her like a rabid dog, but then she'd shown him that damn box. Her Box of Wishes and Dreams.

Looking at those items that hadn't cost so much as a single shilling, those things she regarded as her most valued treasures, had forced him to acknowledge that which he'd adamantly tried to ignore: Julianne was as lovely on the inside as she was on the outside. That she wasn't spoiled and vain but a unique, kind, admirable, vulnerable, and lonely young woman. One with a romantic nature who longed to break free of the social confines she found so suffocating. It was an insight into her character he hadn't wanted to see, to acknowledge, but once it was staring at him so blatantly, he could no longer ignore it.

Any more than he could have ignored her plea for him to kiss her. He pressed the heels of his palms to his forehead. Bloody hell, the way she'd looked at him, touched him, brushed her body against his... it was as if he were gunpowder, and she'd tossed a lit match on him. His control had exploded in a flash fire of want and need and desire so strong, he'd been helpless to stop it. Yet even as he'd given in, dishonored himself and her, a tiny voice in the back of his mind kept chanting, *Just one more touch then I'll stop.* The problem was that when he perhaps could have stopped, he didn't want to. And when he finally realized he *had* to stop, he couldn't. His need, his desire had been so sharp-edged, so deep, he'd been utterly helpless against it.

And then her offer... that heart-stopping offer... that they be together, as lovers, until her marriage. Until she left to start her life as another man's wife. Where he'd found the strength to refuse, he didn't know. God knows he'd wanted nothing more than to take what she offered and damn the consequences—which for him were negligible. But Julianne... she stood to lose everything, her innocence being the least of it. The scandal that would erupt, should anyone discover she'd taken a lover, would ruin her. It would only be that more salacious and sordid if the lover proved a lowly commoner like him.

And what did he stand to lose? Nothing.

Well, nothing except his heart.

You lost that two months ago, his inner voice informed

him with a hollow laugh. He blew out a long sigh, tried to deny it, then shook his head. What was the point in lying to himself? He'd taken one look at those eyes, that face, and he'd lost his heart right then and there. He hadn't been the same, felt the same, since the moment he'd met her.

But unlike two months ago, when he merely desired her because she was the most beautiful woman he'd ever seen, now that desire had turned into something so much deeper. Yes, he wanted desperately to make love to her, but now he wanted more than that. He wanted to simply *be* with her. Talk to her. Look at her. Laugh with her. Walk with her. Wanted it all with a bone-deep yearning and an ache he'd never felt before. Not even for Gwen, a woman he'd loved. A woman he'd planned to marry and make a life with. Julianne touched something deep inside him, a spot he hadn't known was there until she came along and proved its existence. Which could only mean one thing.

He didn't merely lust after her. No, he'd bloody well gone and fallen in love with her.

"*Arghhhhh,*" he groaned, squeezing his eyes shut. Perhaps there was a bigger idiotic fool in the kingdom, but he sincerely doubted it.

Fallen in love with a woman he could never have. A woman who in a matter of days would be married to another man. Another man who would touch her and bring her to his bed. A man who didn't love her but who would have every right to her. A man who would take her far away to Cornwall. A man who could give her everything—except the things she truly wanted.

His hands fisted as a wave of white-hot jealousy washed over him. The thought of that bastard Eastling touching her made him want to break things. An image of his fists rearranging the duke's perfect nose flashed through his mind; yes, that would be a bloody well perfect thing to break.

The image faded, and a sense of sheer despair and exhaustion washed over him, leaving him physically and mentally drained. He badly needed rest but doubted sleep would come. He crossed the room and looked out the window to the gardens below. The moon cast the area in a silvery glow. Would the "ghost" attempt to enter the room tonight? He hoped so, so he could catch the bastard and put an end to all this. Then he could pick up the pieces of his life that had scattered like feathers in the wind on that fateful day he'd first met Julianne. How he was going to do that, he didn't know. Especially right now, when it hurt to merely breathe.

Determined to focus on why he was here, in this room, he crossed to his portmanteau and withdrew a spool of black thread. Moving back to the French windows, he tied one end to the brass doorknobs, then trailed the spool back to the bed. The darkness in the room rendered the thread invisible. After removing his boots, he lay down on the counterpane then tied the other end of the thread around his wrist. He was a very light sleeper, but because he was so tired, he didn't want to take any chances. If he fell into a deep sleep and the door opened, the string would pull on his wrist and awaken him.

He settled himself in the bed and stifled a groan as her scent surrounded him, inundating his senses. Closing his eyes, he turned his face into her pillow and breathed deeply. Vanilla. And Julianne. Bloody hell, he'd never get any sleep.

For a long time he lay there, staring at the ceiling, listening for the least sound that might be out of place, his thoughts a torturous swirl of recalling moments he needed to forget, futilely yearning for things he couldn't have, uselessly wanting things to be different. If only Julianne were the daughter of a barber or baker. If only he were a nobleman.

If only things were different.

Eventually his eyes grew heavy, and he must have slept, for the next thing he knew, he was bolting upright in the bed, breathing hard, sweat dampening his skin, the dream so fresh in his mind, so vivid, he had to blink several times to realize it was indeed a dream. His gaze flew to the French windows. They remained closed and locked, a filter to the first mauve streaks of dawn staining the sky. Then he looked at his wrist to which the thread remained tied and undisturbed.

He swung his legs over the side of the bed and ran shaking fingers through his hair, widening his eyes to keep them from

Chapter 18

With the disturbing dream still lingering in his mind, Gideon dressed then exited his bedchamber. Caesar greeted him with a quiet woof, an indication that all was well, and Gideon crouched down to give the loyal dog a good rubbing.

"So the princess still sleeps," he murmured, pushing aside an image of Julianne in bed.

Caesar licked his chops and sent a longing look toward the door, and Gideon shook his head. "Ah, I see. You thought I was referring to *your* princess rather than mine." He frowned at his unfortunate choice of words. *Mine* was the one thing Julianne could never be.

"I'm headed to the kitchen, where I'll scare up something good for you. Then you can go outdoors for a while and smell every blade of grass you care to smell. Does that sound good?"

Caesar made a noise that sounded like a grunt of approval.

"Excellent." Gideon stood, murmured, "Guard," then made his way to the kitchen where he was greeted by Mrs. Linquist, who was very relieved to hear his report that there had been no disturbances the night before.

Gideon had just finished his breakfast of eggs, ham, and coffee when Ethan entered the kitchen. "Someone to see ye, Mr. Mayne," the footman said. "Says his name is Mr. Henry Locke. I showed him to the morning room. Are ye available?"

"Yes, thank you." Hopefully Henry had some news for him. After securing Mrs. Linquist's promise to see that food was brought to Caesar, Gideon followed Ethan from the kitchen. The footman escorted him to an elaborately decorated chamber with a distinctly feminine flare. Henry sat perched on a ridiculous little chair with a pink velvet cushion, eyeing the multitude of trinkets in the room. Gideon could almost see him running a tally in his head as to their value.

"You have news for me?" Gideon asked the moment the door closed behind Ethan.

"Yes," Henry said. His gaze scanned the room. "Quite the palace yor set up in here, Gid." His eyes glittered, and he flashed a smile. "Best ye not get used to it."

"Don't worry. I know where I come from. What have you found out?"

"Been checking the names on the list ye sent me. Nothing out of the ordinary with any of the servants. All have been with the family for over a year, some for more than a decade, except a footman named Ethan Weller, who was hired on eight months ago."

"He's the one who escorted you to this room."

Henry nodded. "Seemed a decent lad, but as ye know, looks can be deceivin'. Other than him being employed here the shortest amount of time, nothing stood out about him." He looked down to consult the list he held. "The three delivery people who were here have all been in business for years and are well respected. One of them, the coal porter, a young man named Johnny Burns, seemed a bit nervous when I questioned him, but that could be 'cause the missus just had a baby. Tends to make a man jumpy."

"How jumpy?" Gideon asked, narrowing his eyes.

Henry shrugged. "Enough so I noticed it. But like I said, the wife just popped out a babe. That's enough to put any man off, if ye ask me."

"What about the gentlemen callers?"

Henry's eyes lit up. "Ah, now that's where things get interestin'."

"In what way?"

Henry again consulted his list. "First, there's Lord Beechmore. Good thing the man has his looks, because he doesn't have much else. Likes to gamble, Lord Beechmore does. Unfortunately for him, he's not real lucky. Owes a lot of money to a lot people. Had some recent financial setbacks."

Information Gideon had already discovered. "So marrying a wealthy heiress would work out nicely for him."

"Based on how much he owes, I'd say it's *essential* he marry an heiress. As for Lord Haverly," Henry's lips flattened into a grim line, "apparently his lordship likes to rough up his women. Heard from one doxie that he hurt her pretty bad."

Gideon clenched his hands and swallowed his revulsion. "Bastard."

"Agreed. Then there's the Duke of Eastling. His first wife died a year and a half ago, after only ten months of marriage."

"How did she die?"

"Reports said suicide. She left a note claimin' she were distraught over losin' the baby she carried."

"You sound skeptical. Any reason to believe that's not the case?"

"The duchess's maid, who the duke dismissed right after the funeral, told me the real reason her mistress was upset, and subsequently lost her baby, was she found out her husband had been dippin' his wick in other wells. Lots of other wells."

Gideon clenched his jaw. He tried to dredge up some inkling of sympathy for a man who'd lost his unborn child and wife, but came up empty. The only one he felt sorry for was the unfortunate duchess who was married to the adulterous bastard. A habit the duke would no doubt continue after marrying Julianne, a fact that coated Gideon's stomach with hot fury.

Henry continued, "The maid also said that even though the duchess was saddened over the state of her marriage and losing her child, she just couldn't believe she would take her own life. And then there was the way she died. Put a pistol in her mouth and pulled the trigger. Maid insisted she'd never do that. Claimed the duchess had a fear of firearms."

Gideon mulled that over. Was it possible it hadn't been suicide? Had the duke had a hand in his young wife's demise? But why would he? The death had been ruled a suicide, a note had been left, and losing a child was certainly something that could send a woman into a deep melancholy. Gideon knew from experience that people often couldn't credit that their loved one would end their own life. But why would she shoot herself if she were afraid of firearms? Was he casting a suspicious eye on the duke because the man deserved it? Or was he allowing his personal dislike and jealousy of the man who would marry Julianne to color his thinking? He hated the thought of that bastard touching her, of cheating on her, but that didn't make the man a murderer. In truth, Gideon hated the thought of *any* man touching her.

Unable to come up with any answers, he instead asked, "What about Penniwick?"

"He'll apparently tup anything that stands still long enough. Has fathered a number of by-blows. Found the mother of one of them. A former mistress he deserted when she became pregnant. Apparently Penniwick refused to acknowledge he was responsible. She claims the child is his and couldn't be anyone else's. She also claims Penniwick stole two bracelets and a necklace from her."

Gideon's brows raised at this interesting piece of news. "Did she report the thefts?"

Henry shook his head. "No. The pieces were paste, although she says Penniwick didn't know they were. She decided the laugh was on him." Henry folded his paper and tucked it into his waistcoat.

"What about Lord Walston?"

Henry shook his head. "Couldn't find the slightest whiff of scandal or bad behavior about the man."

Gideon's brows rose. "Nothing?"

"Nothing. From all the praise I heard of him, he's a candidate for sainthood."

"Which means there must be *something*."

"Exactly. Don't worry. I'll find it. Just need to dig a bit deeper."

"And Logan Jennsen?"

"Another one I'll need to dig deeper on. Heard rumors of some scandal in America, but no details as of yet."

Gideon cleared his throat. "Anything on Jack Mayne?" He'd added the name to the bottom of list, dreading any information but needing to know.

Henry looked decidedly uncomfortable. "You, um, know he's, um..."

"A thief. Yes. Tell me something I don't know. Like what he's been up to lately and why he's in London."

There was no missing Henry's relief that he wasn't shattering some pristine image a son might have of his father. "Haven't found anything other than that, but I'll keep lookin'."

After thanking Henry, Gideon escorted him to the foyer. He then climbed the stairs, intent on checking on Caesar. When he turned into the corridor leading to Julianne's bedchamber, he halted.

Caesar lay on his back, his left back paw twitching in delight as Julianne, who knelt beside the beast, gave his belly a vigorous rub. Caesar was making sounds that Gideon guessed were the canine equivalent of *Bloody hell, that feels so good.* Princess Buttercup lay sprawled on her stomach, her tiny front paws set possessively on Caesar's tail.

"Oh, you like that, don't you?" Julianne crooned.

Caesar made an answering sound that surely translated to *I do, I do, I do. Please don't ever stop.*

Gideon found himself pressing his hand against his own stomach. He vividly recalled the incredible feel of her hands caressing him there. And thinking, *Please don't ever stop.*

Just then she looked up, and their eyes met. Everything inside him stilled—except his heart, which seemed to hiccup then double its normal rate. Images from last night bombarded him, tying his tongue in knots, rendering him for several seconds unable to do anything except stare. And want. With a soul-deep ache.

Her gaze slid away, and he realized he'd been holding his breath. After giving Caesar a final pat, she stood and offered Gideon a formal nod and a serious expression. "Good morning, Mr. Mayne."

An acute sense of loss washed through him. Damn it, he didn't want to be Mr. Mayne. He wanted to be Gideon. He wanted to be smiled at. He wanted—

Things he couldn't have.

She was perfectly right, putting things back on a formal level between them. Obviously she'd accepted his decision, which was good. Excellent. His mind, his common sense knew it, yet he still felt unreasonably displeased.

Caesar jumped to his feet and trotted over to Gideon, followed closely by his furry white shadow who today was adorned in a glittering collar and a pair of bright yellow ear bows. After greeting both dogs, which was returned sedately by Caesar and most effusively by Princess Buttercup, Gideon returned his attention to Julianne and said, "Good morning." He couldn't quite bring himself to formally call her Lady Julianne.

He didn't bother to ask if she'd slept well. He could see by the violet shadows beneath her eyes that she hadn't. Her eyes...bloody hell, looking into them actually hurt. They reminded him of a flame that had been doused with water— utterly extinguished of light. Indeed, her eyes held such a bleak expression it was all he could do to refrain from snatching her into his arms and telling her everything would be all right.

But that would be a lie. And no lie would change the truth of their impossible situation.

"I take it there were no disturbances during the night?" she asked.

"None."

And of course they both knew what that meant: that he would remain here to watch over her. Another awkward silence stretched between them. Finally she said, "If you'll excuse me, Mr. Mayne, I'll continue to the dining room for breakfast."

"I'll escort you."

She merely nodded and began walking. As she passed him, the scent of vanilla teased his senses, and his fingers curled inward. With a low whistle to Caesar, Gideon fell into step beside her. The only sound as they moved along the corridor was the rustling of Julianne's gown. They were halfway down the long, curved staircase when Julianne's mother entered the foyer and asked Winslow, "Has my daughter shown herself yet?"

Before the butler could answer, Julianne said, "I'm here, Mother," and hurried the rest of the way down the stairs.

"Finally," the countess said, her gaze raking over Julianne and looking none too pleased. Her attention flicked to Gideon. "Mr. Mayne. Did you capture the hooligan who tried to rob us?"

Gideon noted he was the hooligan "who tried to rob us" rather than the hooligan who'd threatened their daughter. "I'm afraid the hooligan is still at large," he said in a cool voice. "However, the good news is that no further attempt was made on your daughter's life, and she is safe."

The countess's eyes narrowed. "And you will make sure she remains so."

"Yes, I will."

Clearly satisfied that her wishes would be carried out, she returned her attention to Julianne. "Your gowns have just arrived from Madame Renee's."

"Gowns?" Julianne asked, sounding puzzled. "More than one?"

"Yes. By virtue of the exorbitant bonus I paid her, Madame was able to complete enough work on your wedding gown to send it along for its first fitting. Isn't that marvelous news?" Not waiting for an answer to what she clearly considered a rhetorical question, the countess continued, "Madame herself is here to oversee the fitting. She awaits us in my private sitting room. Come along." She turned and headed toward the corridor, clearly expecting Julianne to follow.

"Lady Julianne was just about to eat breakfast," Gideon said, stepping in front of Julianne to block her progress.

The silence in the foyer was deafening. The countess turned and looked at him as if he'd sprouted a third eyeball in the center of his forehead. If he hadn't been so irritated, Gideon would have laughed at her expression.

"I believe you've quite forgotten yourself, Mr. Mayne," the countess said coldly. "Julianne can breakfast after her fittings."

"And how long will these fittings take?"

"It doesn't matter," Julianne said, stepping around him to wade into the tension. "I'm really not hungry."

"If she doesn't eat," Gideon said, his gaze steady on the countess, "she could become weak. Ill. She might even swoon at the party tonight."

The countess's lips puckered as if she'd bit into a lemon. "We can't have that." She heaved a sigh. "I'll arrange for some biscuits you can nibble during the fitting, Julianne. Of course, if you'd arisen earlier, we could have avoided this. Come along now."

She swept into the corridor, and Julianne followed, with Gideon right behind her. When they reached the door to the sitting room, the countess stopped and frowned at Gideon. "What are you doing?" she asked in a hushed voice, her hand on the brass knob.

"I am accompanying Lady Julianne, thus insuring her safety."

"You cannot mean to come to the fitting."

"I most certainly do."

The countess's eyes flashed, and she sizzled a look at him clearly meant to incinerate him on the spot. "Well, you cannot. A man at a fitting is completely beyond the pale. Besides, if you were there, Madame would have nothing but questions, and we want to keep this unpleasantness as contained as possible."

Gideon had to bite his tongue to keep from telling her that she was clearly the authority on "unpleasantness." He personally didn't care if Madame asked questions or if the countess was displeased. But as he didn't want to make things any more unpleasant for Julianne, he turned to her and said, "I'll be right outside this door. If you need anything or have a problem, you call for me."

"I won't have you skulking in the corridor, Mr. Mayne, where anyone might see you," the countess said, looking down her nose at him—quite a feat as he was easily a foot taller than her. "It is ridiculous to think any harm could come to Julianne during the fitting." She nodded toward the next door. "You may wait in the library. There is an adjoining door between the two rooms should an emergency arise." Without another word she grabbed Julianne's arm, opened the door, and propelled her daughter inside. She then followed like a ship under full sail. As she proclaimed in a singsong voice, "Here is the bride-to-be, Madame," she closed the door in Gideon's face.

Gideon glared at the oak panel with enough heat to set it ablaze. Then he pulled in a deep, calming breath and set about his business. After giving Caesar a brief respite outdoors, Gideon entered the library. Crossing the fancy carpet, he grasped the back of a chair and carried it with him, setting it close to the wall. Then he turned the knob of the adjoining door and cracked it open. A French-accented feminine voice drifted through the crack "Zee gown, eet is perfection."

Satisfied, he settled in his chair, Caesar at his feet. Princess Buttercup jumped onto his lap and, after turning in several circles, found a comfortable spot and snuggled in. With his fingers lightly petting the small dog, Gideon leaned closer to the door to listen. And wait.

Two hours later, during which time the weather had been discussed at length and the countess had plied Madame Renee with countless questions regarding her exclusive clientele, the dressmaker and her seamstress finally took their leave. To which Gideon could only say thank God. A soft knock sounded on the cracked door, and it was pushed slowly open. Julianne stuck her head through the opening and offered him a rueful smile.

"You managed to remain awake through all that?" she asked.

"I did," he said. *Barely*, which he didn't add. He glanced

down at the tiny dog asleep on his lap. "Princess Buttercup, however, isn't made of such stern stuff."

"That's why she's named Princess Buttercup, as opposed to Captain Canonball."

"I see. What is next on your agenda for today?"

Before she could answer, the door leading from the corridor opened, and the countess entered. "Lords Penniwick, Beechmore, and Walston are here to see you," she said to Julianne, completely ignoring Gideon, who scooped up Princess Buttercup and stood.

Julianne frowned. "Me? Whatever for?"

Annoyance flashed in the countess's eyes, eyes Gideon noticed were the same stunning blue as Julianne's. But her mother's lacked warmth and kindness and any hint of vulnerability—all the things that made Julianne's eyes so extraordinary.

"They are *suitors*, Julianne," the countess said, her voice laced with impatience. "Naturally they're going to call upon you."

"Even though I'm to marry the duke?" Hope flared in her expression. "Or am I not to marry him?"

"Of course you're going to marry the duke. However, until the papers are signed and the formal announcement is made at our party next week, the other suitors are not to be discouraged." A cunning look settled over the countess's features. "It is good for His Grace to know that other gentlemen remain interested. And besides, if some tragedy were to befall the duke before the final arrangements were in place, we wouldn't want to have discouraged all the other suitors prematurely."

In spite of the fact that Gideon could easily name a number of tragedies he wouldn't mind befalling the duke, his stomach turned at the cold, dispassionate sentiment behind the countess's words.

The countess turned to Gideon. "I can see by your expression that you think to be present during Julianne's visit with her suitors."

"Yes. Especially since one of those suitors could be the man we're looking for."

The countess looked affronted. "Ridiculous. They're *gentlemen*. And I'll not have you interfering."

Gideon's gaze pierced hers. "And I'll not have anyone preventing me from doing the job I was hired to do. Clearly you need to be reminded, Countess, that if any harm comes to Lady Julianne, there won't be a wedding at all. To anyone."

The countess looked as if she wished to argue further but instead said, "Although I'd planned to use the drawing room, I suppose I can have the gentlemen shown into my sitting room next door. You may remain here, out of sight, and keep the adjoining door ajar as you did earlier. I will remain with Julianne throughout the visit." She raised her chin. "And *that* will simply have to do, Mr. Mayne."

Gideon's gaze didn't waver. "Only on the condition that Caesar remain in the sitting room, next to Lady Julianne, throughout the visit."

The countess shot Caesar a dubious look but acquiesced. "Very well. Come along, Julianne."

They entered the sitting room through the adjoining door, and Gideon followed with Caesar. After giving the dog instructions to guard, he returned to his chair in the library. A moment later, Winslow announced the three gentlemen. After the initial pleasantries were exchanged, one of the men, whose voice Gideon recognized as belonging to Penniwick, said, "I say, Lady Julianne, that's quite a large dog you have there." A nervous laugh. "He looks capable of biting off a limb or two."

"He's actually capable of ripping out one's throat," Julianne said, sounding so cheerful Gideon had to smile. "We thought it best to have some extra protection, given the rash of crimes lately, didn't we, Mother?"

"Oh, um, yes." The countess adroitly changed the subject to the weather, and for the next quarter hour Gideon listened to blah, blah, weather, blah, blah, fox hunt, blah, blah, party. Good God. It was all so excruciatingly polite. So excruciatingly boring. No wonder Julianne chafed against the stringent class rules that confined her. He looked over at Princess Buttercup, asleep on a satin pillow near the fireplace, oblivious to all the blah, blah. That was one damn lucky dog.

Just when he thought he would have to endure more meaningless blather, Julianne asked, "What do you gentlemen think of these dreadful murders and robberies? Have you any theories as to who might be responsible?"

Gideon moved quickly and applied his eye to the crack in the door. All three gentlemen looked surprised at the question. Penniwick, Gideon noted, appeared...fidgety?

"Really, Julianne," the countess said with a false-sounding laugh. "No one wants to discuss such unpleasantness."

"I don't mind," Beechmore said, making Gideon wonder if he was also deathly bored of speaking of the weather. "Obviously the culprit is a very clever fellow not to have been caught so far."

"He's a fool, if you ask me," said Lord Walston. "Surely he must know he'll get caught eventually."

"Not if he's careful," said Penniwick in a brusque voice. "No clues have been found, no suspects named."

"Perhaps there have been clues found that the authorities haven't reported," Julianne said.

Gideon watched all three men's reactions. Beechmore seem surprised, Walston confused, and Penniwick again fidgeted.

"That's enough of such a dreadful subject," the countess broke in with an exaggerated shudder, shooting her daughter a warning look. "Would you gentlemen like tea?"

They refused, and a few moments later took their leave. As the countess showed them out, Julianne approached the adjoining door. "Did you glean anything from their reactions when I mentioned the murders?"

"Perhaps. That was clever of you."

"I'm not the nincompoop everyone seems to think I am."

"I've never thought you were a nincompoop." His lips twitched. "I thought you were a spoiled princess."

A grin lurked around her lips. "Yes, I know. Although you'd best be careful, as such flowery words might swell my head."

"I said I *thought* you were a spoiled princess. I no longer do."

Although it looked as if she wanted to question him, she merely murmured, "I'm glad."

Just then the countess sailed across the threshold and fixed her angry gaze on her daughter. "Really, Julianne, you are such a trial. Why on earth would you bring up the murders?"

"I thought it would be helpful to Mr. Mayne to hear how the gentlemen responded."

"And it was helpful," Gideon added. "Thank you, Lady Julianne."

"Well, I won't have it. Lord Haverly is here, and there will be no talk of murders or robberies during his visit. He's brought that American, Mr. Jennsen, with him. I suppose we'll have to entertain him as well, although why he's here, I cannot imagine. He certainly couldn't think himself in any way suitable for an earl's daughter."

With that, the countess swept back into the sitting room with an imperious, "Come along, Julianne."

Gideon watched through the crack in the door for the duration of Haverly's and Jennsen's mercifully brief visit. Jennsen didn't say much, and Gideon found himself very curious as to why the American was here. And with Haverly. His curiosity was satisfied within moments of their departure from the sitting room. Gideon planned to wait in the library until Haverly and Jennsen left, but a moment later, a knock sounded. At his bid to enter, Winslow entered.

"Mr. Jennsen would like to see you. Shall I send him in?"

"Please. But first, where is Lady Julianne?"

"The dining room, with the countess, for their midday meal. Caesar is with them."

Gideon nodded. Jennsen entered a moment later and crossed the room to extend his hand to Gideon. "I waited for Haverly to leave before I asked to see you," Jennsen said.

"I know you arrived together. I didn't realize you two were friends."

"We're not. However, I've learned that it's useful to remain close to those you are suspicious of."

"Why are you suspicious of Haverly?"

"I simply added one plus one and arrived at two. It was his snuffbox you found beneath the window at Daltry's party. Less than twenty-four hours later, Lady Daltry was discovered robbed and murdered. Which makes me believe the snuffbox, and therefore its owner, could somehow be involved in your investigation. Unfortunately, I didn't learn anything of interest from Haverly, but I intend to keep at it."

"While I appreciate your efforts, I prefer not to involve outsiders in my work. Especially as it could be dangerous."

Jennsen nodded. "Understood. And a very noble sentiment. But you are going to have to set it aside in this case, as I'm not letting go of this. In fact, what I've come to tell you is that I spent the morning in a meeting with Lords Surbrooke and Langston. As you can imagine, both are very concerned for their wives' safety, as well as Lady Julianne's. The three of us are therefore offering our services to you."

"Thank you, but—"

"You might as well accept it, Mayne, because you're not going to deter us. Certainly not Surbrooke or Langston, who are like rabid dogs when it comes to any thought of their wives being endangered, especially as they both suffered through dangerous situations in the past several months. Therefore, we've determined that we shall be three extra sets of eyes and ears in the ton for you. Fists, knives, and pistols as well, if needed. That being the case, it would be helpful to know if there's anyone in particular we should be watching. Aside from Haverly."

Gideon kept his gaze steady on Jennsen. He knew very little about this man. Certainly not enough to completely trust him. Especially since Jennsen had visited the house the day of the evening Lady Julianne was attacked. Yet his instincts told him Jennsen wasn't the man he sought. Still, if Jennsen were the guilty party, it couldn't hurt for Gideon to lead him to believe his suspicions lay elsewhere.

As for Langston and Surbrooke, he didn't know them well either, although he couldn't deny there was something to be said for men who clearly loved their wives as much as those two did. And Surbrooke especially had proven himself more than capable during the murder investigation two months ago during which his wife had nearly lost her life.

Except when directed to by his superiors, Gideon preferred

to work alone. *What about Henry?* his inner voice asked. *You often rely on him for help.* True. But Henry was a trusted informant he'd known for years. Still, having a few members of the ton on his side could prove useful. And bloody hell, he'd do anything, *anything*, to keep Julianne safe.

"Three extra sets of eyes and ears might be helpful," he admitted.

Jennsen nodded. "Good. Now, who should we concentrate them on?"

"I'm currently looking at everyone who was in or entered this house the day before yesterday."

Jennsen's expression didn't change. "*I* was in the house then."

"Yes, I know."

"So I'm a suspect." A statement rather than a question.

Based on him being at the house that day, he was. But Gideon couldn't dismiss his instincts that insisted Jennsen wasn't involved. "I'm satisfied you're not the man I'm looking for."

Jennsen flashed a grin. "Although you don't sound as certain about that as I'd like, I'm delighted to hear it."

"There are others, however, who have not yet been cleared to my satisfaction. Some who I expect will be at the duke's party tonight. Therefore, in addition to Haverly, if you, Langston, or Surbrooke were to observe Lords Penniwick, Beechmore, Walston, or the duke himself saying or doing anything suspicious, I would like to know."

"Interesting group," Jennsen murmured. "Consider it done. I'll see you this evening."

Jennsen took his leave, and Gideon headed toward the kitchen for something to eat, passing by the dining room on his way. He observed through the open door that Julianne and her mother were still inside, and he continued on. He enjoyed a bowl of hearty stew, then made his rounds through the house, rechecking all the windows. Afterward he headed outdoors and walked the perimeter of the house and grounds. The day was sunny, with the barest hint of chill in the air. And nothing seemed amiss at the Gatesbourne mansion.

After he completed his rounds outside, Winslow opened the double oak doors for Gideon, and he paused just inside the threshold. The duke stood in the foyer, removing his gloves. He barely spared Gideon a look, then jerked his gaze back. And narrowed his icy blue eyes. "What are you doing here, Mayne?"

Recalling Lord Gatesbourne's directive that the duke not know about the attack on Julianne, and not wishing to do anything that would cause Julianne's father to dismiss him, Gideon answered, "What I've been doing all along: investigating the murders and robberies."

"*Here?*"

"It is necessary that I interview everyone who knew the victims. What brings you here?"

The duke's gaze chilled. "That's hardly your concern."

"I disagree. Until this criminal is caught, everything is my concern."

His Grace slapped his gloves into Winslow's hands. "I'm here to call upon Lady Julianne."

"I see. Before you meet with her, I have a few questions I'd like to ask you."

"I don't see why. I've already answered your questions and told you everything I know."

"These questions are regarding your deceased wife."

The duke stared at him for a full ten seconds before replying. Then he turned to Winslow. "Mayne and I would like to converse in private. May we make use of the library?"

"Of course, Your Grace." Winslow escorted them down the corridor.

After being shown into the library, the duke said to the butler, "After Mr. Mayne leaves, I'd like to see Lady Julianne."

"Yes, Your Grace."

As soon as Winslow withdrew and closed the door, the duke turned to him. "I can't imagine what you would want to ask about my dead wife."

No, but you're apparently curious enough to find out and make sure we had privacy when the questions came. "Let me first say I am sorry for your loss." When the duke's only reply was a frosty glare, Gideon continued, "I understand Her Grace committed suicide."

"Yes."

"She was distraught over miscarrying a child."

"Yes. Unless you can explain why questions about her death are necessary, I refuse to listen to any more of this." He started toward the door.

"I've received reports of rumors she didn't die by her own hand."

The duke stopped as if he'd walked into a wall. He slowly turned. The gaze he leveled on Gideon was the coldest he'd ever seen. "And I suppose it is your duty as a Runner to dig up those filthy, untrue rumors?"

Gideon's gaze didn't waver. "It's been my experience that rumors oftentimes are true, or at least partially true."

"Clearly you've been listening to the whispers of disgruntled servants who were dismissed after my wife's death. Not the best source for the truth." His gaze drilled into Gideon. "You think I killed my wife?"

"Did you?"

"Let me ask *you* a question, Mayne. My wife was young, desirable, and beautiful. What possible reason could I have for killing her?"

"That is indeed a very interesting question. Here's another one: Why would a woman with a deep fear of firearms choose to end her life with a pistol?"

There was no mistaking the anguish that flickered in the duke's gaze. For several seconds he looked like an empty shell. A man who'd lost everything. A man who'd deeply loved his wife. Certainly not the expression of a man who would have killed her. Then his face hardened, and he looked Gideon over as if he were something he'd scraped off the bottom of his expensive boots. "I don't know. And I'll thank you to never mention this painful subject to me again. As there is nothing more to say on the matter..." He finished crossing the room and opened the door. "On your way out let Winslow know I'm ready to see Lady Julianne."

"Very well." Gideon quit the room then returned to the

foyer, where he delivered the message to Winslow. As soon as the butler headed toward the dining room, Gideon strode down the corridor and entered the sitting room next to the library. He positioned himself near the adjoining door, which remained ajar.

And waited.

Chapter 19

Julianne stared at the duke, his words tolling through her
mind like a death knell. Did she look as horrified as she felt?
She could only thank God she was already seated, because his
statement left her shaking.

"I...I beg your pardon?"

"I'll be announcing our engagement at my party this
evening."

Nausea and panic warred within her. "But...why? My
parents have everything planned to make the official announcement at their party next week."

"My plans have changed, and I'm needed back in Cornwall sooner than I'd anticipated. We shall make the official
announcement tonight. I already have the special license;
therefore, the wedding will take place in two days. We'll leave
for Cornwall immediately after the ceremony."

Two days...Dear God. She squeezed her eyes shut. She
felt dizzy. As if she weren't inhabiting her own body. As if
this nightmare were happening to someone else, and she was
just watching it from far away.

He lifted her limp hand where it lay lifeless in her lap and pressed a kiss to the back of her fingers. She opened her eyes and found him watching her. Through those cold eyes she'd have to look into for the rest of her life. He was a good-looking man. So why didn't she find him in the least bit attractive? His eyes were actually quite the perfect shade of blue. So why did they appear so chilly to her?

"I know this comes as a surprise." He offered her a smile. "But not an unpleasant one, I hope."

She had to press her lips together to contain the hideous laugh that threatened to escape. Unpleasant? That was the most lukewarm word she could imagine to describe this entire revolting debacle. She could scream and rail and refuse, but in the end she'd lose. And really, what difference did it make if she married him in two days or two weeks or even two hours? Gideon didn't want her for any period of time. Since her marriage to the duke was inevitable, it was better to just get it over with as quickly as possible.

"I know we don't know each other very well, Julianne," he said quietly, "but that will change. I'm sure you'll love Cornwall. As for the rushed wedding, I'm afraid it can't be helped."

"In two days," she agreed, feeling as if a noose had just been put around her neck. "Have you told my parents?"

"I told your father at the club before coming here. If you'll ring for the servant to summon her, I'll speak to your mother now."

"Of course." Somehow she managed to rise and pull the bell cord. Her gaze fell upon the slightly ajar door leading to the sitting room. Gideon. He'd heard everything. As soon as she left this room, he'd appear. And she couldn't face him. Couldn't face anyone. She needed some time alone.

When Winslow appeared a moment later, she said, "Will you please tell Mother the duke wishes to speak with her? And that I've gone to my room to rest. To be refreshed for tonight's party."

"Yes, Lady Julianne."

After Winslow withdrew, Julianne, still engulfed in a numb fog, turned to the man who would be her husband in two days and offered him a curtsy. "If you'll excuse me, Your Grace..."

He offered her a formal bow. "Of course, my dear. You must get your rest. You've a big evening ahead of you." He smiled. "We both have."

Unable to do more than nod, Julianne quit the room. Not wanting to risk seeing her mother or Gideon, she gathered up her skirts and broke into a run, heading away from the foyer and taking the servants' stairs. By the time she reached the top, her breath was hitching, and sobs she couldn't contain were clogging her throat.

It was over. All her hopes. All her dreams. Her time had run out.

The only word that kept pounding through her mind as she hurried down the corridor toward her bedchamber was escape. Escape. But it was a futile, useless word. There was nowhere to go. Except to Cornwall. As the Duchess of Eastling.

Another sob broke from her throat. Lifting her skirts higher, she dashed the last few feet to her bedchamber. As soon as she closed the door behind her and locked it, she leaned against the oak panel and buried her face in her hands. Tears leaked between her fingers, matching the pain pouring from her heart.

If only she could run away. But she knew if she did, she'd be found. And anyone who might assist her would then face her father's retribution. Which she knew would be swift. And ugly.

She sank to the floor, wrapped her arms around her bent legs, and rested her forehead on her knees. No sooner had she done so than a knock sounded on the door, and the knob rattled.

"Julianne...please open the door." Gideon's low, quiet voice drenched her eyes with a fresh supply of tears.

"I...need to be alone. Just for a little while."

"I heard what happened. I know you're upset. Open the door. Please."

She shook her head, then realized he couldn't see her. "Just a few minutes to myself."

He was silent for several seconds. "Will you at least go into the blue bedchamber?"

She lifted her head and realized that out of habit she'd entered her own bedchamber, the one Gideon was using. "The windows are locked. No one can get in through the balcony."

Another silence, then, "Is there anything I can do for you?"

"Yes. You can leave me alone for a little while."

She heard him sigh. Imagined him raking his hands through his hair. "All right. For a little while. Caesar will be right outside the door while I arrange for some tea to be brought up for you."

"Thank you," she murmured.

"And then you will need to open the door."

She heard his muffled footfalls against the carpet as he walked away, then silence. After several moments her silent sobs tapered off, and her shaking ceased, leaving behind exhaustion and a sense of calm finality. Everything was settled. No more wishes. No more dreams. She knew what she had to do.

She rose to her feet and crossed the room with slow, deliberate steps. From the corner of her eye she noticed Gideon's hairbrush and comb on her dresser, but rather than detouring to run her fingers over them, she continued toward her destination.

She knew what she had to do.

❧

Gideon handed a hastily scribbled sealed note to Winslow. "How quickly can that be delivered? It is of the utmost importance."

Winslow glanced at the direction written on the note. "Within the quarter hour."

"Can the messenger wait for a reply?"

"Yes, Mr. Mayne."

Gideon nodded his thanks then headed toward the kitchen to arrange for tea for Julianne. Julianne . . . who right this minute he knew was crying, and there wasn't a damn thing he could do about it. Bloody hell, it was enough to make a man go mad. If she didn't open the door when he went back upstairs, he might have to consider breaching the lock. To ascertain for himself that she was all right.

He waited while Mrs. Linquist put the tea tray together. When she finished, he insisted on taking it up himself. As he entered the foyer, Winslow handed him a note. "Your reply, Mr. Mayne."

Gideon read the brief message, and a sense of relief washed through him. "Thank you, Winslow."

He continued on to Julianne's bedchamber. Caesar sat like a sentinel outside the door and gave a quiet woof as Gideon approached. He knocked on the door and said, "Your tea has arrived. May I come in?"

When he received no answer, he knocked louder. "Julianne? Can you hear me?"

Silence. A sick feeling tightened his stomach. He quickly set down the tea tray and turned the knob. Still locked. "Julianne. Answer me." He could hear the edge of fear in the sharply spoken words.

He rattled the knob again. "Julianne, can you hear me?"

When he received no reply, he took several steps back then ran forward, putting all his weight into ramming the door with his shoulder. The panel gave way with a splintering crack, and Gideon dashed into the room.

His frantic gaze swept the chamber, jerking to a halt at the sight of Julianne on the floor in front of the fire. He reached her side in three strides and crouched down beside her. She sat with one arm wrapped around her upraised knees. With her free hand she fed a piece of paper into the hungry flames. Silent tears dripped down her face, and she softly hummed a tune he recognized as "Dreams of You."

He was so damn relieved to find her unharmed that for several seconds he couldn't even speak. He reached out an unsteady hand and lightly touched her shoulder. Julianne?"

She slowly turned her head toward him. The emptiness in her eyes made his heart hurt. "I knew you'd come for me," she whispered.

He nodded to give himself a few seconds to collect himself. His gaze shifted, and he stilled at the sight of the open box beside her. Her Box of Wishes and Dreams. At least half the contents was gone. He looked at the dancing flames consuming the paper she'd fed them, and his heart felt as if it were bleeding. "Julianne . . . sweetheart, what are you doing?"

"They're gone."

"What are gone?"

Her bottom lip trembled, and a tear slid down her pale cheek. "Wishes and dreams. All gone."

Bloody hell. This was killing him. She was killing him. Feeling utterly helpless, he brushed back a loose curl from her cheek. Then he reached out and slowly closed the box. Picked it up and returned it to the wardrobe.

He returned to her, crouching beside her, not certain what to say or do. He slipped his handkerchief from his pocket and pressed the linen square into her cold hand. Footsteps sounded in the corridor. He looked over his shoulder at Lady Langston, who was walking across the room, her eyes troubled. Turning back to Julianne, he said, "Lady Langston is here to see you."

Julianne blinked then frowned. "She is? Sarah is here?"

"Right here," Lady Langston said, coming forward. She lowered herself to the hearth rug on Julianne's other side, managing the feat so gracefully one could easily forget she was expecting. She took Julianne's hand and held it between both of hers.

Julianne's eyes flooded with tears. "How is it that you happen to be here just when I need you the most?"

Lady Langston smiled and took the handkerchief to dab at Julianne's tears. "Mr. Mayne sent me a note relaying that you needed a friend. So here I am."

Gideon could tell she hadn't delayed a moment in getting here. Her hair was disheveled, and her hands bore telltale charcoal stains. She'd obviously been sketching.

Julianne gave a huge sniffle. "That was very nice of him."

Lady Langston smiled at him over Julianne's head. "I believe he is a very nice man. And clearly very worried about you. As am I. Mr. Mayne carried up a lovely tea tray. Why don't you and I have a cup and talk?"

Julianne nodded. "All right." She turned to Gideon. "Thank you. For giving me my time alone. And for bringing Sarah to me."

Bloody hell, it was all he could do not to drag her into his arms. Hold her tight. Kiss away every tear. As it was, he couldn't stop himself from reaching out and brushing at the moisture beneath her eyes. He wanted to scold her for frightening him, but he didn't have the heart. He wanted to tell her he loved her and that the thought of her marrying Eastling was as much an anathema to him as it was to her. But since he couldn't say that, he merely said, "You're welcome." And then he stopped touching her. While he still had the strength to do so.

He rose and made his way to the corridor, where he picked up the tea tray. When he returned, Lady Langston was standing. "Set it right there on the hearth rug, if you please, Mr. Mayne," she said. "We'll enjoy our tea there, like an indoor picnic." After he did so, she clasped his hand between both of hers. "Thank you for sending for me."

"I'm glad you were able to come." He glanced down at Julianne, then raked his free hand through his hair. "I knew she needed someone."

"You're very perceptive. And I can see, very concerned. But please don't be. I'll take good care of her."

He nodded. "Caesar will remain outside the door."

She released his hand and pushed up her glasses. "What's left of the door. You broke it down?"

"When she didn't answer..." His voice trailed off, and he shrugged.

"How is your shoulder?"

"Fine. Much better than the door. While you're enjoying your tea, I'll see about arranging repairs."

Lady Langston nodded, and after one last look at Julianne, Gideon quit the room and headed toward the stairs. As soon as he turned the corner and was out of sight of Julianne's chamber, he stopped. Leaned against the wall. Dropped his head back and closed his eyes. Drew in a shaky breath.

For a horrible few seconds when she didn't answer him,

he'd thought he'd lost her—that when he broke through that door he wouldn't find her alive. That another woman he loved was gone. His heart had seemed to stutter then halt, and every cell in his body had screamed an agonizing *No!*

Thank God that worry had proven fruitless. But it had given him a taste of the agony to come. Because she'd be married in two days. Gone in two days. Lost to him forever in two days, as surely as if she *had* died. And that agony he'd experienced for those few horrible seconds was what he would live with every day.

In just two days.

After dragging in a few more breaths, he pushed off the wall and continued toward the stairs, determination coursing through him. He had to discover the murderer's identity before then. If he didn't, there was every chance the danger would follow Julianne to Cornwall, where he wouldn't be able to protect her. And the thought of that was even more torturous than that of her belonging to someone else.

He'd almost reached the foyer when the brass knocker sounded. He paused on the stairway while Winslow opened the door. The sight of Henry standing on the flagstones had Gideon hurrying down the remaining steps.

"Mr. Locke is here for me," he told Winslow. He tensed at Henry's troubled expression. Clearly his friend had news for him...news that wasn't good. Bloody hell, was it concerning Jack Mayne? "Is the library available for us?"

"Yes, Mr. Mayne. Follow me, please."

Gideon headed down the corridor, cursing the ridiculous formality of the butler's escort. It wasn't as if he didn't know where the damn library was located. The instant Winslow departed, closing the door behind him, Gideon said to Henry, "You have news."

"I'm afraid so."

Henry's tone filled Gideon with dread. Dread that he was about to hear his father's name. He braced himself for the blow.

"There's been another murder and robbery, Gid."

It took Gideon several seconds to absorb the news, and

he was ashamed of the relief he felt that Henry's visit didn't have to do with Jack Mayne. "Who?" he asked. "When, where, and how?"

"Vivian Springly, Viscountess Hart. According to the magistrate, she died only within the last few hours from a blow to the head. She was discovered in her private sitting room by a maid. Nothing appears to have been disturbed in the house, except her entire cache of jewelry—which she kept in her private sitting room—was gone."

"Who was home at the time? Was anyone admitted to the house?"

"There was no one at home except the viscountess. The entire staff had the afternoon free."

Gideon frowned. "Was that usual?"

"Happened once a week for the past month, according to the maid."

"Most likely she had a lover," Gideon said. "Any idea who?"

Henry shook his head. "Maid said her mistress was very secretive about it."

"Where was her husband?"

"Dead. Viscount Hart died three years ago after being thrown from his mount."

"Why was the maid at the house when she'd been given the afternoon free?"

"Said she'd come back because she'd forgotten her money."

"Or because she wanted to catch a glimpse of the secret lover."

"Most likely," Henry agreed. "Instead, she caught a glimpse of the dead viscountess through the open sitting room door."

"Anyone besides the magistrate there?"

"Simon Atwater," Henry said.

Gideon nodded at the name of his fellow Bow Street Runner. Atwater was a good man, thorough and intelligent.

"One thing I think you'll find interesting," Henry said. "The viscountess has a connection to one of the names on the list you gave me."

Gideon's interest quickened. "What sort of connection?"

"She is—was—Lord Penniwick's sister."

And that, Gideon decided, was very interesting indeed.

After thanking his friend for the information and getting Henry's promise to keep him informed of any new developments, Gideon escorted his friend back to the foyer and bade him good-bye. He then turned to Winslow. "I need to speak to Lord Gatesbourne as soon as he arrives home."

"His lordship returned just moments ago, Mr. Mayne. I'll see if he's available."

Winslow headed down the corridor, and Gideon paced the foyer, his mind racing. He was convinced these were not haphazard crimes committed upon random victims. Something connected them. Something that would lead him to identify the killer. Perhaps this latest crime would provide the clue he was looking for.

Winslow returned a moment later. "His lordship will see you now." He escorted Gideon to the earl's private study where he was greeted by Julianne's father's frosty gaze.

"Well?" the earl asked. "Dare I hope this interruption means you've some good news?"

"No. Another murder and robbery has been committed." He quickly related the story Henry had told him, concluding with, "There has to be some connection between these crimes."

"Of course there is," the earl said. "They've all been perpetrated upon wealthy members of society. Their jewels stolen, the owners killed so as not to be able to identify the thief."

Gideon shook his head. "No, I mean something more. I don't believe these are random crimes. There must be something that links these particular victims..." Pieces of the puzzle shifted in his mind, clicking into place in a pattern he hadn't seen before. Bloody hell, why hadn't he thought of this earlier? He fixed his gaze on the earl's. "Something that *you* are somehow connected to."

"Me?" the earl repeated coldly.

"Yes. All of the victims have been women. Lady Julianne's life was threatened. I think—"

"That all those women are somehow connected?" the earl broke in. He shook his head. "Impossible. While Julianne might have been acquainted with the *ladies* who were killed, I assure you she had nothing whatsoever to do with Mrs. Greeley."

"Lord Jasper's mistress." Gideon nodded. "I agree. But I'm not thinking the connection is between the victims, but rather the victim's families." He nodded toward the earl's pen set. "May I have a piece of vellum and use your pen?"

The earl nodded his consent, withdrawing the vellum from a drawer and sliding it across the shiny mahogany surface to Gideon. Gideon carefully wrote the victims' names then listed their immediate family members. Lastly he added Julianne's name as an intended victim, with the earl and countess as her family members. When he finished, he handed the list to the earl.

"Please add any family members to the list I'm not aware of. Do you see any connection between the family members, anything at all, no matter how remote it might seem?"

The earl studied the list at length, while Gideon watched him. For several minutes his expression remained completely impassive. Then a frown bunched between his brows.

"You've discovered something?" Gideon asked, leaning forward.

"Perhaps." He circled some names. When he finished he handed the list to Gideon. "This is a group of investors who joined together about a year and a half ago for a business venture."

Gideon perused the names while Gatesbourne continued, "Besides me, you'll see Lord Daltry—"

"Whose wife died the day after his party," Gideon broke in. He continued down the list. "Lord Jasper, whose mistress, Mrs. Greeley, was killed. Lord Ratherstone's wife died, and the latest victim, Viscountess Hart, is Penniwick's sister." Gideon's instincts tingled with grim excitement when he noted the Duke of Eastling's name. "The duke's wife also died, a little over a year ago," he murmured.

The earl seemed startled then nodded. "That is correct. I'd quite forgotten, although she committed suicide."

"Tell me, is anyone on this list related to Lords Beechmore or Haverly?"

The earl nodded. "Ratherstone is Beechmore's uncle. Jasper is Haverly's father."

Gideon felt as if bells clanged in his head. His gut told him he'd found the link. "It cannot have escaped your notice that each of your daughter's suitors is either on this list or, in Beechmore's and Haverly's case, closely related to someone on it."

"Which proves what?" the earl asked.

"Nothing—yet. Except I find it very curious. And coincidental. And I don't believe in coincidences. Tell me, does Lord Walston have any close female relations?"

"A sister and a mother. One of them, or perhaps both of them, is traveling. In Italy, I believe. There are aunts and cousins, of course."

Gideon ran his finger over the final three names. "Count Chalon, Mr. Tate, and Mr. Standish. Who are they?"

"Friends of Eastling's."

"You are acquainted with them?"

"No. They all reside in Cornwall. Eastling's known them for years."

"Wealthy, are they?"

"Extremely. Which is why they were allowed to invest."

"Tell me about this investment," Gideon said.

"It had to do with the development of a fleet of fast ships guaranteed to cut travel time significantly. We were all keen to invest."

"How did you hear of it?"

"At my club. Actually, we were all there, except the Cornish fellows."

"Who spoke of it first?"

The earl considered then answered, "Penniwick approached me about it. At that time, Walston, Eastling, and Jasper were already involved. It seemed an excellent opportunity, and I invested."

"What was the outcome?"

"Unfortunately, the whole thing went belly up."

"So you all lost money."

"Yes."

"How much?"

"Ten thousand pounds."

Gideon stared. "Altogether, or each of you?"

"Each of us." He shot Gideon a cold stare. "Investing is a rich man's game, Mayne. None of us put in more than we could afford to lose, and we all understood the risks going in. Sometimes these things go your way, and sometimes they don't."

Gideon could only inwardly shake his head. He couldn't imagine ever possessing such an enormous sum. Nor, if he did, doing anything to jeopardize it.

"So what is your theory?" the earl asked. "That someone is targeting us?" He nodded toward the list Gideon held.

"It is certainly a good place to start. I'm going to see what I can find out about the men who live in Cornwall. See if there have been any crimes committed against their families. Did any of the other investors know them?"

"Not that I'm aware of. Only Eastling, who vouched for them."

Gideon nodded. "I'm going to warn Lord Walston to be on guard. You should also consider that your wife might be in danger."

The earl's brows rose. "Julianne was this madman's target last time."

"Yes, and he failed." Thank God. "He might switch his attention to your wife."

"Who would do this?" the earl demanded. "And why?"

"I'm not certain yet. But I intend to find out."

Before it was too late. But he felt hope now as he hadn't before. Because he not only believed that women connected to the men on the list were being targeted, he strongly suspected one of the men on the list might be the murderer, targeting the others. Given the amount of money involved, it was certainly possible. But why not simply steal the jewels? Why kill the women? What sort of twisted mind was preying on the innocent?

Four of the men were already victims. Walston and Gatesbourne were the only two who hadn't been robbed or suffered the murder of a close female. Perhaps Count Chalon, Mr. Tate, and Mr. Standish fell into that group as well, but that would take some time to ascertain—something he'd assign to Henry right away. The duke's wife had died, but not recently, and supposedly by suicide. Nor had the duke been robbed.

Gideon's gut told him one of those men was guilty. Now all he had to do was figure out which one.

Before the bastard had the chance to strike again.

Chapter 20

⚜

Glass of punch in hand, Julianne stood with Emily, Sarah, and Carolyn and surveyed the crowd milling about the duke's richly appointed drawing room. Dressed in her new sapphire blue gown from Madame Renee, she felt like a freshly bathed lamb being led to the slaughterhouse. Conversation hummed around them, the news of Lady Hart's shocking murder on everyone's lips, including her trio of friends. At least that's what Julianne surmised they were discussing, as she was too distracted looking about to be certain.

Her gaze fell upon Gideon, and her breathing hitched. He stood near a pillar, about fifteen feet away, deep in conversation with Matthew, Daniel, and Logan Jennsen. As if he felt the weight of her stare, he looked toward her. And for Julianne everyone else in the room faded away. God help her, she was miserable. And frightened. And so in love with him she could barely think properly.

He'd told her he'd remain close by during the party, and she felt comforted by his presence. He'd also told her that under no circumstances was she to venture out of his sight—a directive she had every intention of following. She thought of poor Lady

Hart and the other victims, and a cold shiver ran down her spine. She didn't want to meet a similar end.

Gideon had been particularly insistent as he'd been forced to relegate Caesar to the kitchen. When he'd arrived with the dog, the duke had flatly refused to allow Caesar entrance, stating that he didn't allow pets in his house. That the beast could wait for Gideon in the kitchen, or Gideon could leave as well.

"Is something amiss, Julianne?" Carolyn asked.

She forced her attention back to her friends. *Only everything.* "No. I was just thinking about…"—*all the things I want that I cannot have*—"these terrible crimes. And the announcement that will be made this evening."

Emily nodded. "I cannot believe that the wedding will take place in two days."

"Neither can I," Julianne murmured.

Silence swelled between them, then Carolyn said in a too bright voice, "You'll be a beautiful bride."

"Stunning," Emily agreed.

"And we'll all come to visit you," Carolyn said.

"Of course we will," Emily added quickly. "And you'll come to London for the season."

"And we'll write letters," Carolyn promised, giving her hand a quick squeeze.

"Lots of letters," Emily agreed. She nudged Sarah, who'd remained silent and looked troubled, with her elbow. "Won't we, Sarah?"

"Yes," Sarah said quietly.

Because Julianne knew her friends were trying to make her feel better, she tried her best to smile but feared the effort was less than successful. "Thank you. That sounds lovely."

And she wished with all her heart that she meant it.

From his post by the pillar, Gideon maintained an excellent view of the room. His gaze fell upon Julianne and, as always, his heart seemed to cough several times at the sight of her. She was listening to something one of her friends said, and his throat tightened. She looked so damn beautiful. And so damn sad. She should be smiling. All the time. She should be happy. Always.

Just then her lips curved upward, and his heart coughed once again. Bloody hell, when she smiled, she was so lovely it almost hurt to look at her.

"They're all four grinning," came Logan Jennsen's voice from directly beside him. Gideon turned. Logan was talking to him but looking at Julianne and her friends. "Makes one wonder what they're discussing."

"Something they're not supposed to be, no doubt," Lord Surbrooke said, joining them.

"Gives me shivers just to think about the mischief they could be concocting," Lord Langston chimed in. "Of course, so long as they remain in our sight, they can't get into *too* much trouble. I think." He turned to Gideon. "Jennsen's told you that Daniel and I want to help in any way we can. That we intend to do so."

Gideon nodded. "Lord Langston—"

"Matthew, please."

"And Daniel," Lord Surbrooke added. "We've been keeping an eye on the gentlemen Jennsen mentioned," he said in an undertone, "but so far the worst thing I've seen is Beechmore filching extra glasses of champagne."

"I was wondering," Gideon said, "have any of you heard of Count Chalon? It's a French title but he's lived in Cornwall for years."

"Never heard of him," said Matthew, while Daniel and Logan nodded in concurrence.

"And I spent a year in France before coming to England," Logan added. "Who is he?"

Instead of answering, Gideon asked, "How about a Mr. Standish or a Mr. Tate, both also of Cornwall, both wealthy and from well-respected families."

"Common names, but still I don't know of them," Daniel said.

"How wealthy?" Logan asked.

"Enough so that a loss of ten thousand pounds wouldn't distress them."

Logan's brows rose. "So extremely wealthy. Interesting that their names are unfamiliar to me, as I've made it my business to know about those in such advantageous financial positions."

"They don't spend time in London."

"Still, seems odd we've never heard of such wealthy gentlemen," Daniel said.

A humorless smile curved Logan's lips. "Exactly. Doesn't matter if they spend time in London or not. You can't hide that kind of money. At least not for long. I'd be interested in meeting these gentlemen."

Gideon was about to reply when, as if pulled by some force, his gaze shifted to where Julianne stood. She was looking at him, and he completely lost his thoughts as all his attention focused on her. For several seconds no one else existed. Then Lady Surbrooke said something to her, and she looked away from him. And he pulled in a breath he hadn't realized he'd held.

He quickly recalled his own conversation, and said, "Meeting those gentlemen—yes, I would be very interested in doing so as well. At the very least I'd like to know more about them. If you hear anything, please inform me."

Just then the music changed to a waltz. "Ah, a chance to hold my wife in my arms," Matthew said with a grin. "If you'll excuse me."

"Same for me," Daniel said. They departed together and led their wives to the dance floor, while Jennsen wandered off, murmuring, "I'll leave you to your duties."

Would the duke ask Julianne to dance? Gideon's stomach tightened at the thought. Julianne remained where she'd been before, chatting now with her mother and Lady Emily. He scanned the room but didn't see the duke. In fact, he hadn't seen the duke for at least a quarter hour.

As if the thought of him conjured up the man, Gideon's gaze fell upon him, entering the room from a side door set in the dark wood paneling. The duke looked a bit flushed, Gideon noted. And furtive. His jaw tightened with the grim certainty that within the next few minutes a woman would enter the room from that same doorway looking equally as flushed and furtive.

Unfortunately, he was proven correct when, less than two minutes later, a woman Gideon didn't recognize but whose skin bore a noticeable blush and whose gaze shifted in a stealthy manner slipped into the room. His hands clenched into fists, and he imagined them pummeling the duke to dust. The man was not only an immoral bastard but a blind fool. How could any man blessed to have Julianne as his betrothed even look at another woman?

Probably now, when his temper hovered so close to the surface, wasn't the best time to speak to the duke, but nonetheless, Gideon approached him. Making certain Julianne wasn't out of sight, Gideon stepped directly in front of the duke and said, "A moment of your time, Your Grace."

Clearly annoyed at Gideon's peremptory tone, the duke said, "My patience with you is running thin, Mayne. With both you and your questions. What is it now?"

Only years of practice at schooling his features into an expressionless mask enabled Gideon to hide his distaste. Did the duke know or care that the faint smell of sex and women's perfume clung to him?

"Tell me about Count Chalon, Mr. Tate, and Mr. Standish," Gideon said, watching him closely.

Surprise flickered in the duke's cold eyes, followed by annoyance, and for a few seconds Gideon thought he meant to refuse to answer. Finally he said, "Clearly you've heard of our unfortunate investment. The gentlemen are friends from Cornwall whom I've known for years. They all hail from well-respected families and are wealthy in their own right."

"Except that they're all ten thousand pounds less wealthy now. As are you."

Eastling shrugged. "Sadly, not all investments go the way we might hope."

"That is a great deal of money."

The duke's dismissive gaze flicked over him. "I suppose it would seem that way to you."

"I'm certain it would seem that way to *anyone*. The count is French?"

"Yes, although he settled in Cornwall years ago. All three men eschew London and society." Another shrug. "I felt some measure of guilt for encouraging them to join in a venture that failed, but they knew the risks."

"I'll need their directions in Cornwall. If you'd write them down by the end of the evening, that would do."

The duke's brows rose. "Very well. However, all three are currently traveling on the Continent."

"What of their families?"

"None are married, although Mr. Standish is a widower."

"Any sisters? Mothers?"

The duke's annoyance was clearly growing. "Neither Mr. Standish nor Mr. Tate have sisters, but both have brothers. Their mothers are deceased. The count has a sister who lives with their mother in France. And now, Mr. Mayne, I'm afraid I must see to my *guests*." The way he emphasized the word left no doubt that Gideon did not fall into that rarified category. "If you have any further questions, you'll need to schedule an appointment to see me." The duke turned on his heel and walked away.

Gideon watched him go. And again wondered if his deep dislike and suspicion of the duke was truly deserved or the result of Gideon's feelings for Julianne.

After making certain Julianne was still chatting nearby, Gideon approached Lord Walston, who proved much more cooperative than His Grace.

"Terrible about poor Lady Hart," Walston said.

"You were friends?"

Did something flicker in Walston's eyes? Before Gideon could decide, the viscount said, "Yes. I knew her husband very well. Awful tragedy, his death, and I know her brother, Penniwick, of course. Have you any leads yet in Lady Hart's murder?"

"Actually, I'm convinced that the guilty party will be taken into custody within the next two days."

Walston's eyes widened. "I say. That's good news."

"Yes. What can you tell me about the three gentlemen from your failed business deal, Count Chalon, Mr. Standish, and Mr. Tate?"

There was no missing Walston's surprise or confusion. "Well, I...I don't know anything about them really. Never met them. Friends of Eastling's, so you might ask him."

"It didn't concern you that you'd never met them?"

Walston shook his head. "No. It's not always possible to actually meet all the parties involved in every deal, you know. Eastling vouched for them, and they put up their money. That was good enough for me."

"You have one sister, I believe?"

Walston blinked. "You do ask the most unusual questions. Yes. She's visiting me from Dorset. Loving every moment of being in Town. Finds life on her husband's remote estate rather dull."

"Given the rash of crimes, I suggest you keep a close eye on her." Watching Walston carefully, he added, "Especially as the most recent victims have all been women in some way related to the gentlemen who were part of that particular failed business venture."

Walston blinked. Then frowned. "Have they? I say, I had no idea. Yes, yes, thank you. I'll be certain to watch over Celia." His frown deepened, and he looked around the room. "That is, if I can find her to begin with. Always wandering off, she is." His face brightened. "Ah, there she is. If you'll excuse me..." He gave a vague wave then headed off toward the opposite side of the room, and Gideon quickly lost sight of him in the crowd.

For the next two interminable hours Gideon kept his post by the pillar, maintaining his view of the room. He caught snippets of conversation, many of them about Lady Hart. The guests were clearly reveling in the gossip, enjoying the champagne, music, and dancing. But where was the duke? Gideon hadn't seen him since he'd walked away, telling Gideon to schedule an appointment. Odd, seeing as he was the host and would be announcing his imminent marriage very soon. Indeed, Gideon was surprised the announcement hadn't already been made. As much as he didn't want to hear it, dreaded doing so, part of him wanted it over with.

So, where the bloody hell was His Grace? Lifting the skirts of some other woman? A red haze seemed to blur Gideon's vision. Bastard. With a Herculean effort he tamped down the desire to search every room of the house until he found the duke, then beat him to a bloody pulp. Come to think of it, he hadn't seen Walston in quite some time either. Or Penniwick. Haverly and Beechmore had seemed to disappear for a time as well. Damn crowded party. It was nearly impossible to keep account of everyone.

He allowed his gaze to drift back to Julianne. As she'd promised, she hadn't left his sight, a bittersweet blessing as it was nearly impossible not to stare at her every second. He watched her now, standing with her mother, who appeared displeased about something, which didn't surprise Gideon in the least. Had the woman ever been pleased about anything? Someone claimed the countess's attention, and she turned away from Julianne. It seemed as if a shudder ran through Julianne, and in the space of a heartbeat Gideon was at her side. Touching her arm, he drew her a few feet farther away from her mother. "Are you all right?" he asked in an undertone.

"I'm fine. Just felt a bit of a chill."

"Do you need a wrap?"

She offered him a smile. "No, thank you." Then she leaned just a bit closer...close enough for him to catch a tantalizing whiff of her delicious vanilla scent. "Stop glowering. Anyone watching will think I've made you angry."

He wiped his expression clean. "I wasn't glowering."

"Very well. You were merely frowning strenuously."

"Has anyone ever told you you're very cheeky?"

Amusement bloomed in her eyes, the first he'd seen all evening, and it filled him with a warmth he couldn't put a name to. "Never. I'm delighted you think so. I've always wanted to be a cheeky sort of girl."

He frowned. "I wasn't being complimentary."

"You most certainly were. And you're glowering again."

Again he smoothed out his features. "You're feeling better." On the surface, at least, although not deep down, he suspected.

"Talking to Sarah earlier helped. She is a good listener and a steadfast friend. Thank you for sending for her."

"You're welcome. I would—" He pressed his lips together to cut off his unguarded words. "Go back to your mother. I'm going to return to my post."

She stayed him by touching his arm. "What were you going to say, Gideon?"

He hesitated, then said in a low voice only she could hear, "I would do anything for you."

For the space of a single heartbeat his gaze touched hers, and it took all his will not to touch her. Instead he forced himself to return to his pillar. Once there he drew in a much-needed deep breath, then resumed scanning the room. Almost immediately he saw the duke, who was just entering the drawing room. Once again he appeared slightly out of breath, and Gideon's hands fisted. He was torn between watching the doorway to see which woman would walk in and watching the duke, who approached the musicians. After several minutes passed, however, no one else had entered through the doorway His Grace had used, and the musicians struck up a waltz.

Gideon watched in an agony of futile jealousy as the duke escorted Julianne to the dance floor. Bastard didn't deserve to even touch her. Hands clenched, he recalled every moment in her arms as she'd taught him the dance—a skill he would never have the opportunity to share with her at a party.

He was vaguely aware of the other couples swirling around the floor, but his gaze remained attached to Julianne and her future husband. The duke was as smooth as Gideon had been clumsy, leading Julianne expertly around the room. And the way the man was looking at her...bloody hell, the bastard's eyes didn't look cold now. The heated glint in them made Gideon clench his teeth.

"Bastard is looking at her like she's candy, and he has a craving for sugar," muttered Logan.

Gideon's brows raised, and he slanted a look at Jennsen. The other man was staring at the dance floor, his face resembling a storm cloud. Well, bloody hell. Was Jennsen simply outraged on Julianne's behalf, or was there something more to this?

"Yes, but she *is* beautiful, and they're soon to be married—"

Jennsen's head snapped around so fast, Gideon swore he heard the man's neck crack. "Married?" he repeated, staring at Gideon. "Are you certain?"

Bloody hell. Could Jennsen be harboring an attraction for Julianne? If it weren't for the fact that it only served to increase Gideon's jealousy, he might almost feel sympathy toward him. "Yes. The duke is going to make the announcement tonight."

Logan frowned. "The duke? Why would *he* make the announcement?"

Gideon discreetly sniffed, wondering if Jennsen might be foxed, but he didn't discern any scent of spirits about him. "Because the duke is the man Lady Julianne is going to marry."

"Lady *Julianne*?" For several seconds he stared at Gideon with an utterly blank expression. Then, to Gideon's amazement, color rushed into the American's cheeks. "Oh, um, yes. Of course." He gave a laugh that sounded decidedly forced. "If you'll excuse me, Mayne, there's something I must attend to." With no further explanation, he moved off. Gideon's attention returned to the dance floor, and he wondered who Jennsen had been talking about, because he clearly hadn't been referring to Julianne.

His gaze had just located her when the music ended. She and the duke stood near the French windows leading to the terrace at the far side of the room. With his jaw clenched, Gideon watched him raise her hand to his lips, then excuse himself. Daniel and Matthew and their wives stood nearby, as did Lady Emily and...was that Penniwick with her? Indeed it was.

Gideon looked at Julianne and stilled. She was looking at him. Bloody hell, looking at him as if he were the only man in the room. As if she were saying she wished she'd danced the waltz with *him*. Just as he wished he'd been the one to lead her to the dance floor.

Someone jostled him, yanking Gideon from his thoughts, and he realized with a jolt how many people stood between him and Julianne. Far too many. He couldn't effectively guard her with so much space, so many obstacles between them. He started making his way toward her. He noted her friends moving away from her, heading toward the punch bowl, but Julianne remained where she was, near the French windows.

Gideon frowned and, keeping his gaze on her, tried to move quicker through the crowd. He didn't like her standing by windows, but he couldn't tell her to move. What seemed like a sea of bodies still separated them. He saw her craning her neck. And then she saw him. Looked at him with those beautiful eyes. And he wondered if she could see his desire for her. His feelings for her. If everyone could see it. Because bloody hell, his love for her beat so strongly through him he wasn't certain he could hide it any longer.

In two days' time you won't have to hide it anymore. Because she'll be gone.

In an irony of timing to that depressing thought, the insistent tapping of silverware against crystal sounded from behind him and had the hum of conversation quieting.

"Your attention, everyone, if you please," came the duke's voice over the noise.

Gideon's steps faltered. He saw Julianne's back stiffen, and his every muscle tensed. Here it comes. The words that would make it official. The words he didn't want to hear. Words he wasn't sure he had the strength to listen to. Yet he didn't have a choice but to do so.

"Ladies and gentlemen, your attention, please," the duke commanded. The room fell silent. Gideon continued to make his way through the crowd toward Julianne, the need to be close enough to protect her urging him on.

"I don't wish to alarm anyone," called the duke, "but I've just discovered the Eastling jewels are missing! The murdering ghost robber must be in our midst! Ascertain that your valuables are accounted for—"

His words were cut off as pandemonium broke out. Shouting and several high-pitched screams rent the air as a swarm

Chapter 21

Fighting down the panic that threatened to overwhelm him, Gideon pushed his way through the surging, shouting, anxious crowd. Many people tried to waylay him, but he shook them off, cursing each second-long delay.

By the time he broke free and ran through the open French windows onto the flagstone terrace, he judged nearly four minutes had passed. Most likely Julianne's abductors had either a horse or carriage nearby. Probably in the mews. Pausing only long enough to slip his knife from his boot, he sprinted across the grass toward the back of the garden, gaze scanning, ears straining. Up ahead, near the gate leading to the mews he saw something pale against the dark ground. Heart pounding, he raced toward the object.

He halted and with a combination of hope and dread he bent down to retrieve it. And found himself holding one of Julianne's satin slippers, the intricate beadwork matching that of her gown. He grimly tucked it into his jacket and opened the gate. Bloody hell, which way had they gone? He looked to his right. Empty. Looking to his left, he saw something on the ground, visible in the moonlight, about thirty feet away. He ran toward it then bent down to scoop it up. Julianne's other shoe. Had she inadvertently lost them while struggling with her kidnappers or purposely kicked them off to provide him with clues? Gideon didn't know, but he was grateful just the same.

He raced through the alleyway, halting when he reached the street. No sign of a horse or carriage. Now where? Toward the park? The river?

His gaze fastened on an object about twenty feet away, on the ground beneath the dull yellow haze of a gaslight, and he raced toward it. He was still more than a dozen feet away when he recognized it as Julianne's reticule. He quickly opened it and discovered only two items: a handkerchief and a button...a button he recognized as the one he'd ripped from his breeches in his haste last night. She'd found it. And kept it with her. He ruthlessly shoved aside all the emotions that evoked and frowned. Odd that the reticule was directly under the light. Almost as if it had been purposely placed there.

He looked ahead and saw something beneath another gas lamp in the distance. He raced ahead. And his suspicions were confirmed when he discovered a woman's white lace glove. Just like the one Julianne had worn tonight.

These clues were simply too perfectly placed. Someone wanted him to find them. Which meant it was either Julianne trying to lead him to her.

Or her abductors, trying to lead him into a trap.

∞

Julianne closed her eyes and tried to fight off the panic pressing in on her by pretending she wasn't engulfed in suffocating darkness. That the hood covering her head wasn't really there. By concentrating on figuring out a way to escape. And she couldn't do that if she succumbed to the terror threatening to swallow her.

In the blink of an eye, one of her abductors had grabbed her from behind and clamped a beefy hand over her mouth. Before she could even assimilate what was happening, a foul-tasting rag was stuffed in her mouth, a hood dropped over her head, and she was swiftly carried away.

Two men. There were two men. Both very strong. One held her around her knees, the other around her shoulders. She tried to kick and claw, twist and squirm, but they held her too firmly.

Running, they were running, and between the jouncing and foul rag and the hood engulfing her and the fear strangling her, nausea rose in her throat. She heard what sounded like a gate opening and closing. Her reticule was wrenched from her wrist, her shoes and gloves yanked off.

Then she felt as if she were being heaved upward like a sack of potatoes. She landed on her stomach with enough force to knock the wind from her lungs. After several seconds she managed to pull in an unsteady breath. The smell of leather and horseflesh assaulted her. Dear God, she'd been tossed over a saddle. Rough ropes quickly bound her hands behind her back and her ankles together.

"Ye just keep quiet and still." The rough whisper, muffled by her hood, sounded next to her ear. "Unless ye want yer friends to suffer needlessly."

Someone mounted the horse, and she was lifted as if she weighed no more than a feather and laid facedown across hard thighs. The horse took off at a gallop and a hand pressed into her back to keep her in place. She heard another horse following closely behind, clearly the other kidnapper.

Gideon...Gideon would come after her, and she didn't know if she were more terrified that he would find her or that he wouldn't. If he didn't, God only knows what these two men meant to do with her. But if he did find her, with two kidnappers and only one of him, Gideon could be overpowered.

Her body bounced against the saddle, each jounce shooting pain through her. It seemed as if they rode for an eternity, but it couldn't have been more than a quarter hour before they slowed down. After another few minutes they stopped, and Julianne was pulled down and slung over a burly shoulder. She thumped there for another minute or so, and with each bump against the man's wide back, her dread grew. But along with that dread came an unexpected surge of fury. By God, she wasn't going to allow these ruffians to hurt her—or Gideon, if he found her—without a fight.

She heard the squeak of a door with unoiled hinges opening. A few minutes later she was lowered to the ground where she landed with a less-than-gentle thunk. She forced herself to remain still. Perhaps if they believed her unconscious they'd remove the hood. Or speak freely in front of her. And if she discovered a way to lash out at them, she'd have the element of surprise on her side.

"Ye didn't hurt her, did ye?" asked one of the men. "'Cause we ain't supposed to hurt her."

A statement that lent her a bit of comfort.

"Naw. She just bounced about a bit," said the second man.

"But she's one o' them delicate ladies. And she ain't movin' none. Ain't her but the Runner we're supposed to kill."

A statement that struck utter terror in her heart.

"Maybe she can't breathe with that hood," the second man continued, sounding a little worried. She felt a hand clasp her shoulder and give her a slight shake. "She ain't movin'." A second later, the hood was pulled off. Julianne forced herself to remain immobile and keep her eyes closed. She felt rough fingers press against her neck.

"She's alive," the man said, clearly relieved. "Just swooned."

"Good. Then we don't need to worry about her. Let's keep watch for the Runner."

Their footsteps echoed, moving away from her, and Julianne peeked her eyes open. She was lying on the wooden floor of what, based on the crates stacked around her, appeared to be a warehouse. About twenty feet away, a sliver of moonlight spilled through one dirty window, a pane of glass her abductors were looking through.

Julianne wriggled her fingers and feet, but she was securely bound. If only she had something sharp to cut through the ropes. If only she had her embroidery scissors!

Moving carefully so as not to make any noise, and keeping her eyes on her abductors, she worked to free her hands. The men were engrossed in their whispered conversation, which she unfortunately could not hear.

As she tried to escape her bonds, she also used her tongue

and teeth and lips to push the rag from her mouth. If she couldn't get free, at least she could scream out a warning to Gideon when he arrived.

The rough ropes bit into her skin, stinging her flesh, but she kept sawing her wrists back and forth, one painful stroke at a time, still working on the rag. She soon managed to get the rag out of her mouth but held it between her teeth in case her kidnappers looked her way. Elation filled her at her success, but unfortunately, loosening the rope wasn't going as well. Her fingers were numb and stiff, the rope coarse and stubborn. Sweat trickled down her spine, and her arms ached from her frantic efforts.

Just then the unmistakable squeak of the unoiled door opening sounded, and Julianne's heart stuttered. There was no doubt in her mind who had arrived.

Clearly her abductors knew as well, because they both left their post by the window and moved silently toward her. Her stomach turned when she saw they both carried knives.

Pulling in a mighty breath, she spat out the rag and yelled, "There're two of them, Gideon! They have knives, and they mean to kill you."

A flurry of obscenities came from her kidnappers, and they ran toward her. One of them, a bearded man with dark, matted hair and small, close-set eyes, growled at her, "Shut up," while trying to stuff the rag back in her mouth.

Julianne furiously twisted her head back and forth to thwart him. "If you think you're going to kill Gideon Mayne, you're a fool," she taunted, desperate to keep his attention on her as long as possible. "He could slice you into pieces while blindfolded and shackled."

The man went suddenly still and stared at her. Then he muttered a foul word and turned toward his accomplice. "Christ, Will," he said in a hissing whisper, "did ye hear that? The Runner wot's comin' for her is bloody Gideon Mayne."

Even in the darkness Julianne could see that the man named Will paled. "Damn me to hell and back," Will whispered. "Wot are we gonna do, Perdy?"

"I don't know. But I know wot we *ain't* gonna do."

Will swallowed audibly and nodded. "Right." He cleared his throat then called out, "Listen here, Gideon Mayne. We want to talk to ye. We haven't hurt the lady, and we ain't gonna hurt you neither."

"Don't believe them, Gideon. They said they were going to kill y—"

Her words were cut off when Perdy clapped his hand over her mouth. "Shut up or I'll—ouch!" He jerked his hand back and glowered at her. "Damn minx bit me."

Taking advantage of his surprise, Julianne pulled her bound legs to her chest then gave a hard kick. Her heels connected with Perdy's midsection, and he let out a grunt as he fell back onto his buttocks.

"Wot the hell are ye doin' over there?" Will ground out. "Can't ye take care of one tied-up woman?"

"Course I can," Perdy grumbled. He grabbed Julianne by the hair, and pain shot through her scalp. She let out a cry, and he stuffed the rag back in her mouth, then rose to his feet.

"There's a pistol trained on both of you," came Gideon's voice out of the darkness. "If either of you so much as blink, I'll blow a hole right through your heart. Whichever one is left will get my knife in his gut."

Both men froze. "Put down your knives," Gideon ordered. "Nice and slow. Right by your feet."

Will coughed then said, "There's something ye should know—"

"If you speak again before I tell you to, whatever you say will be your last words," Gideon said in a deadly voice that sent shivers down Julianne's spine. "Now do as I said. Before I get angry. And kill you anyway."

Working frantically, Julianne managed to spit out the rag and pulled in a deep breath. She didn't want to speak and distract Gideon, so she just kept yanking on the ropes, noting with grim satisfaction that she'd made some progress.

She watched both men set their knives on the wooden floor then slowly rise.

"Good," said Gideon from the darkness. "Now kick them toward the crates."

After the knives skidded across the floor, Gideon ordered, "Facedown. On the floor. Hands behind your head."

After they'd obeyed, Gideon said in a chilling voice, "If you move, I won't hesitate to kill you." Then he said softly, "Julianne, are you hurt?"

"N...no. But I'm bound." She gave a mighty twist of her wrist, and it slipped free. "*Was* bound," she corrected, her voice filled with satisfaction, as she pulled the rope off her. "I just managed to free my hands."

"Excellent. You gentlemen are very fortunate the lady isn't hurt. Now, one of you—and only one of you—is going to tell me who you are and why you kidnapped this woman."

"Um, well, it's like this," said the one named Perdy. "This bloke came to us earlier tonight, said he'd pay us handsome to grab the lady from the party."

Julianne didn't hear Gideon moving toward her, but suddenly he was next to her, his fingers lightly pressing against her mouth, his lips next to her ear. "Don't speak unless I ask you something, and then just go along with whatever I say," he whispered. He leaned back, and his gaze fastened on hers. Fear and relief rushed through her, but she firmly shoved them aside and nodded. In a single slice he cut the ropes binding her ankles, then pulled her to her feet.

With one strong arm wrapped around her waist, he loudly said to the kidnappers, "Tell me about this bloke who hired you." He then immediately whispered to Julianne, "Can you stand on your own?" At her nod, he released her and scooped up the ropes from the floor. Then he pressed something into her hand. "Take this knife," he whispered directly in her ear. "If anyone comes near you, stab them. Except me."

Julianne's fingers curved around the handle, and she nodded, praying she wouldn't have to use the weapon.

"Bloke didn't give his name," Perdy said.

"What did he look like?"

"Couldn't tell. It were dark, and he wore a hooded cape.

A dandy he were, though. Had one of them rich bloke voices. Gave us a gold watch and some blunt, said we'd get the rest after the job were done."

"How much more?"

"Twenty quid."

"And what precisely was the job?" Gideon asked.

"Kidnap the lady. Use her as bait to get the Runner here." Perdy hesitated. "Then kill the Runner."

"And what was to become of the lady?" Gideon asked in a silky voice.

"We were to let her go. Leave her in Hyde Park. Unharmed."

"My lady, I believe you are proficient with a pistol, are you not?" Gideon asked her.

"I am *very* proficient with a pistol, Mr. Mayne," Julianne replied, hoping she sounded proficient as opposed to scared out of her wits.

"Excellent. I am going to tie these men. If one of them makes any sudden moves, I want you to blow his head off."

"I'd be delighted," she said in the same voice she used to accept invitations to dance.

"No need to be blowin' anybody's head off," Perdy said quickly. "We ain't movin'. Are we, Will?"

"Hell, no. Jacko would have our head if we did."

Julianne sensed Gideon stiffen, and she wondered who Jacko was, but before she could think on the matter, Gideon nudged the closest man's hip with his boot. "What's your name?"

"Perdy."

"And your friend's name?"

"Will."

"Perdy, I'm going to tie up Will. If he moves, I'm going to stab him. If you move, the lady is going to blow your head off. Any questions?"

"No," both men answered in unison.

Julianne watched Gideon work, and all she could think was, *Please don't make me blow his head off*, which was really quite ridiculous, as she didn't even have a pistol! Still, she gripped the knife in both hands, knowing that if either man tried to hurt Gideon, she'd do whatever was necessary to protect him.

Once both men's hands and feet were bound, Gideon searched their pockets. He pulled a gold watch from Perdy's pocket and held it up to the meager bit of light from the window. He then rolled both men onto their backs, rose, and glared down at the abductors turned prisoners.

"This the watch he gave you?" Gideon asked.

Perdy nodded. "Yes."

"Why were you to kill the Runner?"

"Bloke didn't say. But he never said the Runner were Gideon Mayne," Perdy said in a rush. "If he had, we wouldn't have taken the job."

"Swear we wouldn't have," added Will.

"Why not?" asked Gideon.

"Why, we couldn't kill Jacko's son," Perdy said, while Will nodded. "Done us both a good turn, yer father has—"

"Several good turns," broke in Will. "Didn't know *you* were the Runner the bloke meant. Yor pa's salt of the earth."

"Right," said Perdy. "Helps a lot of us in St. Giles and those down by the docks as well."

"What do mean, 'helps'?" Gideon asked in a sharp voice.

"Gives us money," Perdy said. "Food. Gets us medicine. Liquor. Whatever we need."

"He saved my boy's life, he did," Will added. "So sick little Billy were, we were sure he was a goner. Jacko got the medicine that made him better. Sure as hell I'd never be the one to harm a hair on Jacko's own son's head."

"Anybody stupid enough to try wouldn't live long to tell the tale," Perdy said. "Jacko would see to that."

For several seconds silence pulsed in the dark room. Then Gideon crouched down near the men. "You made a serious error tonight," he said in a low, deadly voice, "and you're very, very fortunate that the lady wasn't hurt. Because if she were, *you* wouldn't live to tell the tale. I know your names, and I know what you look like. I never want to hear of you or see you again. Ever. Is that clear?"

Both men nodded, then Perdy asked, "W...wot are ye goin'

to do with us?" He gave a nervous laugh. "Don't forget—we didn't harm neither of ye."

Gideon stared down at the two men. Everything inside him wanted to pummel them to bloody pulps for touching Julianne. They might not have hurt her, but they *could* have. And they'd certainly frightened her. And the bastards had shaved at least a decade off his own life from the scare. If he lived to be one hundred, he'd never forget seeing her being grabbed and pulled from the room.

"If you'd tried to kill me, I assure you you wouldn't have succeeded," Gideon said coldly. He believed that absolutely, but it irked him that the fact that he was Jack Mayne's son could have in any way saved him. "And if you'd in any way harmed the lady, you'd be dead, regardless. As it is, I'll let the magistrate know where you are. Enjoy your wait until he arrives."

"Aw, now that ain't no way to treat us after we didn't try to kill ye," Will protested. "Plus, ye took our watch."

"I could still shoot you in the head, if you'd prefer," Gideon said pleasantly. "In fact—"

"No, no, that's all right," Perdy broke in. "We'll just stay here. And wait for the magistrate to find us."

"As you wish." Without another word, he turned. He wanted to get Julianne as far away from here as possible. Ascertain for himself that she was indeed all right. And then he'd find the bastard behind this. And make that bastard very, very sorry.

He went to Julianne and handed her her slippers. Once she'd donned them, he took her hand and led her swiftly through the maze of crates. A moment later the cool night air struck them, and Gideon drew a deep breath. He paused long enough to look at Julianne. Her hair and clothes were disheveled, her face as pale as wax, and her eyes the size of dinner plates. She still clutched the knife he'd given her as if her very life depended upon it. He wanted nothing more than to pull her into his arms, but he had to get her away from here. Somewhere safe. Where he could get all the details of her ordeal and send off a message to the magistrate. Somewhere he could have a few moments to himself to recover from a terror that all but paralyzed him.

He took the knife from her and slipped it into his boot. A shiver ran through her, and he yanked off his jacket. "Put this on," he said, helping her slip her arms through the sleeves. "Are you all right? Can you walk?"

"Of course," she answered, actually looking insulted. "I'm not the delicate princess you think I am."

If he'd been capable of doing so, he would have smiled at her umbrage. Indeed, she'd proven herself quite the warrior tonight. He grabbed her hand and walked swiftly, dodging in and out of narrow alleys until they emerged on a wider cobbled street. He saw a hack on the corner and immediately hailed the driver. Seconds later they were ensconced inside. He gave the driver his direction and they were on their way.

Sitting across from her, Gideon reached out and clasped Julianne's shoulders, his gaze searching. "Are you certain you weren't hurt?"

She swallowed and nodded. "My wrists hurt a bit," she said in a slightly trembling voice. "From the ropes."

His gaze instantly dropped to her hands. And his fury flared. Her delicate wrists were badly abraded. He snatched his handkerchief from his waistcoat pocket and pressed it gently against the raw skin, which seeped blood. The sight of her injuries, the rage it inspired, rendered him momentarily speechless.

"They said they meant to kill you," she whispered. A look that could only be described as fierce entered her eyes. Indeed, she suddenly looked like an avenging fury. "I wasn't going to let them hurt you."

Bloody hell. His heart just…melted. "I can see that."

"They put a hood over my head and stuffed an awful rag in my mouth," she said, the words coming quickly between rapid breaths. "I pretended I'd swooned while I worked on loosening the ropes and spitting out the rag. As soon as the door squeaked, I knew it was you. There were two of them and only one of you, and I was so frightened." She drew in a shaky breath. "I would have shot them, you know. If I'd had to. And, well, if I'd had a pistol. I would have used that knife."

Unable to stop himself, he raised her hands and gently pressed his lips against her fingers. "You may have been frightened, but you, my darling princess, were absolutely magnificent."

"I was?"

"Beyond magnificent. You were brave and determined, courageous and dogged. If I had to choose one word, it would be *fierce*."

A bit of color washed into her pale cheeks. She moistened her lips. "I . . . thank you. I believe that is the nicest thing anyone's ever said to me. I knew you would come for me."

Gideon nodded, unable to speak around the sudden lump in his throat. He brushed his lips over her scraped wrists and pulled in a deep breath. And almost smiled. Bloody hell, in spite of all she'd been through, the scent of vanilla still clung to her skin. He looked into her eyes and spoke the simple truth. "I never would have stopped looking for you, Julianne."

Her bottom lip trembled, and tears pooled in her eyes. "I know," she whispered. "Thank you. But about all those nice things you said . . . most of all, I was just very scared." A tear spilled over to trail down her cheek followed by several more, and a breathy sob escaped her. "I don't feel very fierce or determined now. In fact . . . oh, dear, I think I'm going to cry."

The tears overflowed in earnest, and with a groan, Gideon shifted to sit next to her. He pulled her into his arms, and she buried her face against his neck. Feeling utterly helpless, he held her close. Brushed his lips over her soft hair. Whispered words he hoped would soothe her. And with every breath, he fell deeper in love with her. His fiercely brave, terrified princess who escaped her ropes, spat out her gag, screamed to warn him, and would have stabbed anyone who'd tried to hurt him. Bloody hell, she wasn't a princess. She was a . . . gown-clad warrior.

After a few minutes her sobs subsided, and he leaned back to dab at her wet eyes with his handkerchief.

"I've gone through more handkerchiefs with you in the last

few days than I normally use in a month," he teased, hoping to coax a smile from her.

She took it from him and gave her nose a mighty blow. "You might want this one washed before I return it."

"Keep it. You might need it again."

"I hope not. I don't want to cry again." Her gaze searched his. "You were marvelously clever. Pretending you had two pistols. And gloriously brave."

"I'm glad you think so, but I think it only fair to tell you that I was also never so frightened in my entire life." He touched his fingers beneath her chin and lifted her face. "When I saw those men grab you . . ." He briefly closed his eyes, and a shudder ran through him. "If anything had happened to you—"

She touched her fingers to his lips. "But it didn't. Because of you."

He shook his head, dislodging her fingers. "If I'd been closer to you, they wouldn't have been able to grab you in the first place. Why were you standing there all alone? Why didn't you walk to the punch bowl with you friends?"

"The duke told me to wait there. He was going to fetch a diamond ring from the ducal collection then come back and announce our engagement. Instead it appeared he discovered he'd been robbed." She offered him a tremulous smile. "And you saved my life."

Damn it, the way she was looking at him, as if he were a hero, half shamed him because he hadn't kept her from being snatched, and half made him feel so bloody good he couldn't speak. His gaze dropped to her lips, and a groan rose in his throat. There were reasons, so many reasons, not to kiss her, but God help him, he couldn't think of even one of them.

He leaned toward her. Her lips parted. And the hack jerked to a halt.

Julianne blinked then looked out the window. "Where are we?"

"Somewhere safe." He alighted then assisted her. After paying the driver, he said, "There's an extra bob in it for you if you'll deliver a message for me. Wait here. I'll be right back."

The driver agreed, and Gideon escorted Julianne up the short walkway. A moment later they entered a small foyer. Julianne's eyes widened. "Is this your home?"

"Yes." He tried his best to sound casual and shove aside the knowledge that it was sorely lacking in comparison to the mansion in which she lived. "It's safe and was closer than Grosvenor Square. Come."

He led her to his study and quickly lit the lamp on his desk. "Please sit down and make yourself comfortable. I need to write a quick note to the magistrate." He completed his task, sealed the note with wax, then wrote the direction on the outside. The entire time he was aware of Julianne looking around the room. When he finished, he excused himself to give the note to the hackney. He then gathered some cloths, bandages, salve, and a bowl of water. Before reentering the study, he paused in the doorway. Julianne stood before the unlit fireplace, lightly trailing her fingers along the mantel.

The sight of her in his home did something to his insides. Filled them with a sensation he'd never experienced before. By virtue of her aristocratic birth she shouldn't look right here, yet somehow, in the soft light of the single lamp he'd lit, she appeared as if she belonged precisely where she was. Standing before his hearth. Touching his mantel clock, whose ticking was the only sound in the room.

She must have sensed his presence, because she turned. Their eyes met, and he felt as if he'd been punched in the heart. How he was going to get her out of here without breaking his vow to himself, he didn't know. He wasn't even sure if he cared anymore.

Pushing off from the doorway, he slowly approached her. "I want to clean and treat your wounds then bandage your wrists."

"All right." She sat on the sofa, and after setting down his supplies, he retrieved the lamp from his desk and settled himself next to her.

"I didn't know you lived in a house," she said as he gently washed her raw skin with a dampened cloth.

When she winced, his jaw clenched with suppressed fury

at the bastards who had tied her. "Oh? You thought I lived in a cave?"

She gave a short laugh. "No. I imagined you in bachelor's rooms."

"I bought the house several years ago. We never had one when I was a child, and I wanted somewhere permanent. A place to call home. Somewhere that was...mine." He applied the salve, forcing his gaze to remain on his task, fearing that if he looked into her eyes, he would be lost.

"Those men mentioned a Jack Mayne," she said softly. "They said he was your father. And that he'd helped them. Is your father a...philanthropist?"

A humorless sound escaped Gideon. "Not exactly." Although based on what Will and Perdy had said, there was clearly more to Jack Mayne than Gideon knew.

"Your parents," Julianne said, her voice filled with hesitancy. "Are they anything like mine?"

"An earl and a countess? Hardly."

"No. I meant were they...good to you?"

An image of Jack Mayne materialized in Gideon's mind's eye, kneeling down so he was on eye level with his young son. *Just slip yor fingers into the bloke's coat pocket, light and easy, and bring me back wot's in there.* Then of his mother, thin, pale, her coughing worsening until every breath became a struggle and rattle in her lungs—

He blinked away the image and shrugged. "I wasn't beaten or abused, if that's what you mean. My mother died when I was fourteen. She'd been sick for a long time."

"You loved her very much."

Her death was an ache that had softened with time but one he knew would never completely fade. "Very much. And like you, I am a great disappointment to my father."

"How could any father be disappointed in such a fine son?"

"How could any father be disappointed in such a fine daughter?"

"Because she wasn't a son. Why was your father disappointed?"

He hesitated then said, "I chose the army and Bow Street rather than follow in his footsteps."

"But surely there is nothing nobler than fighting for your country and upholding the law. What was his trade?"

Gideon debated not telling her then inwardly shrugged. They were Jack's sins, not his. "Pickpocket. Petty thief. He was also very good picking locks."

He felt her start of surprise. "Your father was a...thief?"

"Yes." As far as Gideon knew, Jack still was one. "He's never quite forgiven me for joining what he calls the wrong side of the law, and I've never quite forgiven him for...well, many things." Mostly the pain Jack's countless infidelities had caused Gideon's mother.

"Based on what Perdy and Will said about your father, about him helping them and others, perhaps he's changed his ways."

"If he's given anyone anything, I doubt he obtained it through legal means."

"It shows a great strength of character that, given your upbringing, you didn't fall into a life of crime."

There was no missing the admiration in her voice, and he risked looking up from his bandaging task. That same admiration was shining in her eyes, and he quickly looked down again. Because he knew what he said next would erase it. "I did fall into it." The words felt rusty on his tongue, as he'd never admitted them to anyone before. "For a time. When I was too young to make my own decisions."

"But you changed," she whispered.

"Yes. I wanted to become someone who I could look at in the mirror and not cringe."

"And have you become that person?"

He pondered, then said, "I like to think so."

"Would it make any difference if I told you that I think you're wonderful? Extraordinary?"

Bloody hell, it made a huge difference. No matter how much he didn't want it to, it did. "Thank you. But you don't know me very well."

"I disagree."

"Which doesn't surprise me. We're very different and don't agree on very much."

"Again, I must disagree. I think we're actually very much alike. Where it really matters. In our hearts."

He pressed his lips together to keep from replying. To keep from revealing what was in his heart. If she had any idea how badly he wanted to tell the entire world and all its dictates and rules that conspired to keep them apart to go to hell, how much he wanted to selfishly steal her away from her rarified world and make her his, she'd run screaming from the room. As well she should.

Instead he said, "If by saying we're alike you mean that *you* are extraordinary, then I agree. You are." And he was going to miss her every day of his life once she was gone. He tied off the second bandage and said, "I'm sorry this happened to you."

"I'm not."

His head jerked up at that. And this time he found himself imprisoned by those eyes, unable to look away. "Why do you say that?"

She offered him a small smile. "Because if it hadn't, I never would have seen your home." She rose and held out her hands. "Will you show me the rest of it?"

Gideon hesitated. Not because he was embarrassed of his house. In fact, he'd worked hard to purchase it and was very proud of it. Obviously it didn't compare to what she was accustomed to, but then not much could compare to the Gatesbourne mansion on Grosvenor Square. No, this was a matter of survival. His home was his sanctuary. Already he knew he'd think of her from now on every time he entered his study. Would see her standing before his fireplace. Sitting on his sofa. If he showed her the rest of the house, she'd live in all those rooms as well. Rooms she'd never visit again but where her presence would continue to haunt him long after she left. The best thing to do, the smart thing to do, would be to take her home. Immediately.

Instead he rose. And took her hand. And showed her his house.

"It's delightful," she said, walking around the dining room then the sitting room. "Cozy, warm, and charming."

"I'm not much of a decorator, I'm afraid."

"I think it's better to have only a few very meaningful things than many items that are decorative but hold no sentimental value."

They continued to the small drawing room, the kitchen, and pantry, then through three empty bedchambers. She remained silent, and he wondered what she was thinking. When they came to the last room, he said, "My bedchamber." She entered the room without a word and walked slowly around, trailing her fingers over his dark blue counterpane and cherrywood furniture. He stood just inside the doorway, taking slow, careful breaths while his heart beat hard and fast and his entire body ached with love and desire and so damn much want he thought he would burst. He never should have brought her here. Because now that she was here, he never wanted to let her go.

After she'd walked around the entire room, she came to stand directly in front of him. And looked at him through solemn eyes. "Do you want to know what I think of your home, Gideon?"

"If you care to tell me."

"I think it is the loveliest house I've ever been in. It is cozy and delightful and a real *home*. It is the perfect reflection of its owner in that it is wonderful. In every way."

Bloody hell. How was he to answer that? He couldn't even find his damn voice.

"Do you know what I want, Gideon?"

No, he didn't. But he damn well knew what he wanted. And he could sum it up in one word: Julianne. In his arms. In his bed. Under him. Over him. Surrounding him. And all the reasons he couldn't have it were fleeing at an alarming rate. Still unable to locate his voice, he shook his head.

"I want to seduce you."

Chapter 22

I want to seduce you. Five little words. That's all it took to melt what was left of Gideon's resistance. He couldn't have her forever. But he could have her for right now. He needed to return her to her family. But not just yet. He tried to live his life with honor, but with this woman he knew, irrevocably, that love was stronger than honor.

He had to swallow twice to find his voice. "I don't think you'll find that a difficult task to accomplish."

"I hope not. Because I'm not quite certain how to go about it." She stepped closer, until only inches separated them. Then she rested her hands against his chest. And with that single touch, all that remained of his good intentions disintegrated to dust.

"Done," he whispered, pulling her into his arms. "I'm seduced."

He covered her mouth with his, and every rational thought fled. *Julianne, Julianne...* Her name pounded through his head, matching the rhythm of his heart, which surely beat hard enough to bruise his ribs. The delicious taste of her filled his mouth, and he pulled her tighter against him, plunging impatient fingers into her soft hair, wanting to touch, taste, everything at once, ravenous for her. A bit of common sense broke through the haze of need consuming him, warning him to slow down. Reminding him she was a virgin. That he should savor. Seduce. Slowly. But it was damned difficult to do when she was yanking at his shirt and squirming against him.

With a groan he broke off their kiss, then dragged his mouth down the length of her neck. Her head dropped back, and he traced her pulse with his tongue as he slowly eased her gown from her shoulders. Down her arms, then over her hips. It pooled at her feet, leaving her clad only in her chemise and stockings.

"Don't move," he said softly, then walked toward the bed.

"What are you doing?"

For an answer he struck a match and lit the lamp on his bedside table. "Giving us some light." He rejoined her and sifted his fingers through her hair. "I want to see you. All of you."

"And I want to see all of you. Right now."

Gideon smiled. "I like this impatience of yours. It nearly matches mine."

"*Humph.* You don't *seem* the least bit impatient."

"Only because I'm trying my damnedest to make this last more than fifteen seconds." His gaze swept over her chemise, and he groaned. The material was so fine he could see her coral nipples. "If it makes you feel any better, the effort is nearly killing me."

He slipped his fingers beneath the straps of the flimsy chemise and slowly slid the material downward, his gaze devouring each bit of creamy skin as it was revealed. When the garment slid off her hips to join her gown, he took her hands and helped her step from the mound of material.

Wearing nothing but her stockings, shoes, and a furious blush, she was ... "The most beautiful thing I've ever seen," he whispered. He reached out and circled her breasts, brushing his thumbs over her tight nipples. "The softest thing I've ever touched." He leaned down and drew one taut nipple deep into his mouth, absorbing her gasp, loving the feel of her hands in his hair, the way she arched her back, offering more of herself.

He kissed his way to her other breast, whispering, "The most delicious thing I've ever tasted." While his lips and tongue and mouth explored her breasts, his hands skimmed the length of her smooth back, the luscious curve of her hips and buttocks.

"Gideon..." She wriggled against him then fisted her hands in his hair. "This is exceedingly unfair."

"What?" he asked, lazily circling her nipple with his tongue.

She yanked on his hair until he raised his head. "I am *naked*."

He skimmed his hand down her torso and tangled his fingers in the golden curls at the juncture of her thighs. "Not exactly." He crouched down and removed her shoes, then leisurely rolled off each stocking. Then he stood, slowly dragging his hands up her body. "*Now* you are naked. And there is nothing unfair about it."

"Except the fact that *you* are fully clothed. A problem I would like solved *immediately*."

"Has anyone ever told you that you're very demanding?"

"Has anyone ever told you that you're infuriatingly *slow*?"

"My clothing can be removed in less than thirty seconds," he said, reaching for his waistcoat.

She stayed his hands with her own. "Oh, no. You undressed me. I want to undress you."

"Very well." He spread his arms. "Be my guest."

Satisfaction, mixed with a hint of uncertainty, flared in her eyes, and she set about working on the buttons of his waistcoat. He watched her, her brow furrowed with concentration, and the wave of love that washed through him nearly drowned him. Unable to keep from touching her, he slowly combed his hands through her silky hair.

"You're distracting me," she said, glancing up at him.

"Would you like some help?"

She shook her head. "I want to do it."

"What happened to your impatience?" he teased.

She looked up again, this time her gaze serious. "It's still there. But I want to savor this. Remember every moment. Every touch."

And just like that, she managed to cut him off at the knees. He remained still, in an agony of anticipation as she finally slid his waistcoat off his shoulders. Drew his shirt from his breeches. He helped her pull the shirt over his head, then fought to remain still as she ran her hands over his shoulders, chest, and abdomen. Everywhere she touched felt as if fire burned beneath his skin.

She stepped forward and pressed her lips against the center of his chest, dragging a deep moan of pleasure from him. When she kissed her way across his skin to circle his nipple with her tongue, his head dropped back, and he groaned. Bloody hell, he didn't know how much of this he was going to be able to take.

"You like that?" she asked, flicking her tongue over him again.

"Yes. God, yes. If you expect conversation..." His words turned into a moan when she drew his nipple into the heat of her mouth.

"If I expect conversation...what?" she whispered, her fingers tracing the sensitive skin just above his breeches.

A heated shiver raced through him. He spoke the only word he could manage. "Huh?"

A delighted sound came from her. "Hmmm. I believe I detect a crack in the marblelike exterior. Indeed, I think the granite has a pulse. Interesting."

Bloody hell. Using his own brand of comparisons against him. If he'd been able to speak coherently, he surely would have told her how annoying that was. Perhaps he would have tried anyway, but just then she pressed her palm against his erection. He sucked in a sharp breath, one he released with a low groan as he thrust helplessly into her hand.

"I want these breeches off, Gideon."

Thank God. Without an instant's hesitation, he stepped to the bed and sat to jerk off his boots. He would have wagered that no man in history had ever removed his breeches faster. After he'd tossed them aside, he stood.

She reached out and brushed her fingers over his jutting arousal. Clearly encouraged by the low growl of approval that vibrated in his throat, she stroked the length of him, tentatively at first but then with growing confidence as his breathing turned choppy and erratic. When she wrapped her fingers around him and lightly squeezed, he knew he was done.

"Can't take any more," he managed in a hoarse whisper, gently grabbing her hand. Bending his knees, he scooped her into his arms and laid her across the bed. He ran his hands up her smooth legs, urging her thighs apart. Golden curls surrounded her glistening sex, her folds wet and swollen, a sight that literally brought him to his knees. Dropping down at the edge of the bed, he pulled her toward him. Draped her thighs over his shoulders. Slipped his hands beneath her. And lifted her to his mouth.

Her groan of pleasure filled the room, echoing through his head. He'd never expected to be able to touch her like this again, and he savored every second, determined to bring her as much pleasure as he could. Circling and teasing, licking and thrusting, tasting, delving, he pushed her until she cried out with her climax.

When her tremors subsided, he kissed his way up her torso. Explored the indent of her navel. Discovered a trio of tiny birthmarks dotting her stomach. Nuzzled her soft breasts. Laved their taut peaks.

Shifting her higher on the bed, so her head rested on his pillow, he settled himself between her thighs. She looked up at him through eyes hazy with arousal and framed his face between her hands. "Again," she whispered. "I want to feel that magic again."

Propping his weight on his forearms, he brushed the head of his erection along her wet folds and prayed he'd last long enough to grant her request. Unable to wait any longer, he eased inside her. When he reached the barrier of her maidenhead, he paused, then thrust.

A startled cry escaped her, and he gritted his teeth, determined not to move. But bloody hell, it was nearly an impossible task. She was so tight and he was so hard... he released a shuddering breath. "Did I hurt you?" he asked, praying he hadn't.

She shook her head. "No. I was just...surprised. I feel... filled. With you." She pressed her pelvis into his, and her eyes drifted closed. "It is...delightful. Incredible. Delicious. Extraordinary. I cannot possibly choose just one word."

Bloody hell, he couldn't even think of one word. He slowly withdrew, nearly all the way, before sinking deep inside her again, his breath a hiss of pleasure at the hot, slick friction. Another leisurely withdrawal, followed by a slow, deep thrust, again, and again, his muscles straining with the effort of holding back. She writhed beneath him, her movements awkward at first, but then she caught his rhythm.

"Open your eyes, Julianne."

Her lids blinked open, and her blue depths pulled at his soul. "Wrap your legs around me," he ground out. She did as he bade and he thrust deeper. Harder. Faster. She moaned his name and arched beneath him, her inner walls pulsing around him, and he clenched his jaw against the intense pleasure. With an effort that nearly killed him, he withdrew and gathered her into his arms, pressing his erection tightly between them. Burying his head in the fragrant space where her neck and shoulder met, he let his release roar through him, groaning her name over and over, like a prayer.

For a long moment he simply lay there, breathing her in, catching his breath. Then he raised his head and stilled. At the sight of Julianne, her hair spread about her like a golden halo, her lips parted and swollen from his kiss, her eyes heavy-lidded with the look of a woman well loved. Which is exactly what she was. Well loved. With everything he had. His heart. His soul. And it killed him that through no fault of either of them, that simply by accidents of birth, that wasn't enough.

He cupped her cheek in his hand and brushed his thumb over her plump lower lip. Then he lowered his head and kissed her.

"Gideon..." she breathed against his mouth.

He lifted his head. "Julianne."

"That was...you are..." She breathed out a long hum of pleasure. "Oh, my."

"Yes, it was. And yes, you are."

And now it was over. He had to take her back. To her world. To her family.

And her fiancé.

She reached up and brushed his hair from his forehead. Then looked at him through very serious eyes. "How?" she whispered. "How am I going to live the rest of my life without knowing this again?"

A lump swelled his throat. Christ. Now he knew what it felt like to die inside. "I wish I had the answer. Because I need to know it as well."

Only there was no answer. Just his life stretching out before him. A life that didn't include Julianne.

❧

When the hack pulled up in front of the duke's town house, Julianne had to force herself to exit the vehicle. Lights blazed from every window, and based on the shadows moving past the panes of glass, it was clear the house was still crowded. She didn't want to leave the intimate interior where Gideon had held her hand during the entire ride. Where his leg had rested against hers and he'd pressed his lips against hers in a kiss that had tasted unmistakably of good-bye.

But in her heart she'd resolved that it wasn't good-bye. Not yet. He would still be in her house for two more days. Two more nights. And she intended to see to it that they spent as many hours together during that time as possible.

Gideon had just helped her alight when the front door opened. Standing in the foyer were her father and a man she recognized as Charles Rayburn, the magistrate, whom she'd met two months ago when he and Gideon were investigating the last spree of crimes plaguing Mayfair.

Mr. Rayburn hurried down the steps, followed by Julianne's father. "What in God's name—" began her father, but Gideon cut him off, saying tersely, "Lady Julianne was kidnapped from the party." He gave a quick description of her ordeal, leaving out, she noticed, any mention of Jack Mayne and the kidnappers' plan to kill Gideon himself. He concluded his story with, "I sent a message to your office, Rayburn, giving you the kidnappers' location."

Mr. Rayburn nodded. "Simon Atwater is here. I'll send him to see to them." He turned to Julianne. "A harrowing ordeal to be sure, Lady Julianne. I'm relieved you're all right. Let's get you inside. There are a lot of worried people in there."

Julianne's father, who until now had remained silent, said to Gideon, in a low, furious voice, "You were supposed to keep my daughter safe, Mayne."

"I *am* safe, Father," Julianne said quickly. "Thanks to Mr. Mayne. He saved my life. No one else even realized I'd been kidnapped."

Her father's gaze never left Gideon. "If you'd been doing your job properly, the kidnappers never would have touched my daughter."

"You're right," Gideon said. "I accept full responsibility."

"Nonsense," Julianne protested. "There was complete pandemonium when the duke made the announcement he'd been robbed—"

"Which only further proves his incompetence," her father stated coldly. He narrowed his eyes at Gideon. "Kidnappers and thieves running amok, and you did nothing."

"He rescued me," Julianne said tightly. "Or do you consider that nothing, Father?"

"Please, let us go inside," Mr. Rayburn said, gently taking Julianne's arm. She wanted to shake him off, scream at all of them that she didn't want to go inside. That she wanted to leave. Now. With Gideon.

But instead, she allowed herself to be led up the path into the house. The duke strode into the foyer, his normally dispassionate features filling with obvious relief at the sight of her. "Julianne, my dear." He clasped her hands and raised them to his lips. "I was so afraid—"

His words cut off, and he seemed to freeze in place when he looked beyond her. She glanced over her shoulder and realized he was staring at Gideon.

"Mr. Mayne rescued me," she said quickly, before the duke could blame Gideon for her ordeal as her father had.

"That's right, Your Grace," agreed Mr. Rayburn who quickly repeated the kidnapping story Gideon had related. When he finished, the duke kissed her hand then murmured, "Thank God you're all right. We must get you home—"

"I want to see Sarah, Emily, and Carolyn first," Julianne said, surreptitiously wiping the back of her hand against her gown to rid herself of his touch. "If they're still here."

A muscle ticked in the duke's jaw. "They are. But so are many of the other guests..." His gaze raked over her. "And you're looking rather worse for your ordeal, my dear. Wouldn't you rather—"

"No, I wouldn't. I want to see them. Now, if you please."

The duke clearly wasn't pleased, but he acquiesced. "As you wish."

As they filed down the corridor, Julianne asked Mr. Rayburn, "Did you capture the robber or recover His Grace's jewels?"

"I'm afraid not. I've been interviewing the guests one at a time, which is why so many are still here. Of course, many also remained out of concern for you, hoping for news."

When they entered the drawing room, the hum of conversation stopped for several seconds, then voices exploded, and Julianne found herself surrounded by a sea of faces. Mr. Rayburn held up his hands and demanded silence then once again repeated the story of her ordeal. When he finished, Julianne was engulfed in hugs and well wishes and bombarded with sympathy and questions, while Gideon was congratulated for his quick action. Julianne's mother kissed her on both cheeks, told her she was very grateful she hadn't been hurt, then told her they should leave as soon as possible as she looked a complete fright.

Sarah, Emily, and Carolyn all hugged and kissed her.

"I swear I paced a hole in the duke's hearth rug," Emily said, giving her nose an unladylike blow.

"How dare you frighten a pregnant woman that way," Sarah scolded, pulling off her spectacles to dab at her teary eyes.

"I thought Daniel was going to nail my slippers to the floor to keep me from ruining whatever part of the carpet Emily left intact," Carolyn said, wiping her eyes with a lace hankie. "Are you certain you're all right?"

No, I'm not all right. For a brief, perfect, shining moment, in Gideon's arms, she had been. And she greatly feared she'd never know such happiness again. She mustered up a smile, hoping to erase her friends' troubled expressions. "I'm fine."

"Mr. Mayne was incredibly brave," Sarah said. She squeezed Julianne's hand. "We owe him a debt that can never be repaid."

A lump clogged Julianne's throat, and to her mortification, tears filled her eyes. Carolyn saw her distress and quickly led her to a nearby quiet sitting room that afforded them privacy but from where they could still be seen. After they settled themselves on overstuffed chairs, Julianne said, "Actually, there is more to the kidnapping story than you've heard." She proceeded to tell them the rest, only leaving out any mention of Jack Mayne.

When she finished, all three women looked at her with round eyes. "Heavens, Julianne," Carolyn said. "You were simply marvelous!"

"Incredibly brave," added Sarah.

"I was scared witless," Julianne corrected.

"I would have swooned on the spot," Emily decreed.

"You?" Julianne laughed. "You would have given those kidnappers an ear blistering so severe they would have promptly returned you and begged your pardon for disturbing your evening."

"I'm sure Mr. Mayne was impressed with your bravery," Sarah said.

Julianne felt a blush warm her cheeks. "He said he was. However, most likely he was merely grateful not to have a swooning female on his hands."

Emily looked at Julianne's wrist then frowned. "That looks like a bandage showing above your glove."

More heat flooded Julianne's face. "Mr. Mayne did that. My skin was chafed from the ropes."

Emily's brows shot upward. "He just happened to have some bandages with him?"

Julianne tried to think of a plausible excuse but realized nothing but the truth would do. "No. We made a stop on our way back here. At Mr. Mayne's house. He bandaged me there."

"You went to his house?" Emily's voice dropped to a whisper. "Alone?"

"Of course alone," Sarah broke in impatiently. "Did you expect them to bring the kidnappers along?" She turned to Julianne. "What is his home like?"

"It's...lovely. Cozy, neat. Just...perfect."

"I'm glad he had the knowledge to tend to your wounds," Carolyn said.

"Don't tell your mother that part of the story," Emily warned. "She'll fly into the boughs."

"I've no intention of telling her anything," Julianne said quietly. She looked into the drawing room, and her gaze found Gideon. He was talking to Mr. Rayburn and looking very serious.

"Why, Julianne...you're *blushing*," Emily said. She drew in a sharp breath, and her gaze bounced between Gideon and Julianne. "Good heavens. You *like* Mr. Mayne."

It felt as if the sun itself burned from her cheeks. "Of course I like him. He saved my life."

Emily shook her head. "No. I saw the way you just looked at him."

"And how was that?"

"With your heart in your eyes." Emily's own eyes looked troubled. "You're in love with him, aren't you?"

For several long seconds Julianne remained silent. Emily was a dear friend, but she was also an earl's daughter, and she knew what her reaction would be if Julianne were to admit the truth. Carolyn would no doubt share Emily's horror. Sarah, Julianne knew, would be more understanding. For all the good that did her.

"Is it true?" Carolyn asked, her eyes filled with concern. "Do you love him?"

"It doesn't matter," Julianne said, plucking at a loose thread on her ruined gown.

"Of course it matters," Sarah said in a fierce whisper.

"No, it doesn't," Emily insisted. "She is betrothed to the duke."

"The announcement wasn't made," Carolyn pointed out.

"But they're going to be married in two days!" Emily said.

"Perhaps she doesn't want to marry the duke," Sarah said. "Perhaps she'd prefer to marry Mr. Mayne."

Sarah's whispered words hung in the air, stealing the breath from Julianne's lungs. They were words she hadn't even dared say to herself, let alone speak out loud.

"*Marry Mr. Mayne?*" Emily repeated in an aghast hiss. "Instead of a *duke*? Are you daft?"

Sarah fixed Emily with a skewering stare. "Have you ever been in love, Emily?"

A scarlet blush colored Emily's cheeks. "No, but—"

"Then, with all due respect, you have no idea what you're talking about," Sarah said firmly. She turned to her sister. "Would you have married Daniel if he weren't an earl? If he were, say, a baker?"

"I see the point you're trying to make—" Carolyn began, but Sarah cut her off. "Yes or no, Carolyn. Would you have married him if he were a baker?"

"Yes. But," she added quickly, "I'm not an earl's daughter."

"You were a viscountess by virtue of your first marriage. And as a viscountess you still would have married Daniel if he were a baker?"

Carolyn let out a sigh. "Yes."

"Why?" Sarah persisted.

Carolyn shot her an annoyed look. "You sound like a barrister."

"Then answer the question."

Carolyn folded her hands in her lap then said primly, "Because I love him."

A triumphant smile lit Sarah's lips. "And there you have it."

"And there you have nothing," Emily said. "This is not some game, Sarah. If Julianne were to go against her parents' wishes and not marry the duke—and to throw him over for a Bow Street Runner? Good God, the scandal would ruin her. She'd be disinherited. She'd lose everything."

"She'd lose money," Sarah agreed. "Material possessions. And most likely any relationship with her parents. But she wouldn't lose everything. She wouldn't lose *me*." Sarah raised her chin and grasped Julianne's hand. "I never aspired to a title, but since I have one, I won't hesitate to use it shamefully. The Marchioness Langston stands firmly behind Julianne. No matter what."

Hot tears pushed behind Julianne's eyes at Sarah's steadfast loyalty.

"Julianne hasn't actually said she'd prefer to marry Mr. Mayne," Carolyn said. She reached out and brushed back a lock of Julianne's hair. "Is that what you want? If you had the choice, would you choose to marry Mr. Mayne?"

Julianne drew in a deep, shuddering breath, then whispered, "To quote Themistocles, 'I choose a man without money rather than money without a man.' If I had a choice, I would choose Gideon. I would rather be ostracized from society and share a life of modest means with him than live in the grandest splendor with anyone else."

"Well," said Emily, sitting back with a plop and looking stunned. "Isn't that quite something."

Sarah patted Emily's hand. "I know it seems shocking now, but you'll understand after you fall in love."

Emily shook her head. "Oh, no. I've no intention of falling in love. Look at this poor girl." She waved her hand in Julianne's direction. "Look what love has done to her. She's miserable."

"I am miserable," Julianne agreed.

"I'm in love, and I'm not miserable," Sarah said. "Neither is Carolyn."

"You seem to be forgetting something," Julianne said. "Mr. Mayne has not said anything about loving *me*. Nor has he expressed any interest in marrying me."

"Well of course a Bow Street Runner would never think to ask an earl's daughter to marry him," Emily said with a sniff.

"I wonder what would happen if he *did* think to do so?" Sarah mused.

And suddenly Julianne wondered the same thing. Would Gideon want to marry her? Yet even as hope flared in her chest, it was instantly extinguished. Her parents would never agree. The banns would have to be posted for three weeks... she'd be long since married to the duke by then.

Unless she simply refused to marry the duke. Yet if she did, she could well imagine her father forcibly dragging her before the vicar. If she ran away... but where could she go? She couldn't involve Sarah in such a scheme. It was one thing for Sarah to recognize a friend who married below her family's expectations but quite another to house a runaway bride. The scandal would then affect Sarah, Matthew, their unborn child...

Yet, here she was, wasting energy on all these useless thoughts. Gideon hadn't expressed any desire to marry her. Hadn't said he loved her. She knew he cared, knew he desired her. But that didn't mean he wanted to marry her. And unless he did, there wasn't any decision for her to make.

She turned, her gaze seeking him out. He stood in the drawing room, now deep in conversation with Logan Jennsen, Matthew, and Daniel. All four men looked extremely serious. Gideon, especially, seemed very tense.

What on earth could they be talking about?

Chapter 23

After ascertaining that Julianne was safely ensconced in the small sitting room chatting with her friends—away from the windows and where he could see her through the open door—Gideon pulled Charles Rayburn aside and told him about the kidnappers' plan to kill him.

"Appears you've stepped on someone's toes," Rayburn said when he finished.

"Yes," Gideon agreed. "The question remains, whose?" Just then he spotted a familiar face across the room and he nudged Rayburn. "That woman, with the dark hair wearing the rose gown. Who is she?"

Rayburn craned his neck. "The one standing with Walston and Penniwick?"

"Yes."

"That's Lady Celia. She's Walston's sister, visiting from Dorset."

Gideon froze. For several seconds it seemed as if he couldn't even breathe. Snippets of conversation and facts of the investigation flashed through his mind: pieces of a puzzle that he hadn't yet been able to put in the proper formation.

And then, like gears turning in perfect unison, those snippets and facts clicked into place. He took a moment to carefully review, to make certain he wasn't mistaken. Then his gaze settled upon the person he sought. The last clue to the puzzle. Standing across the room, looking elegant, chatting with friends. And Gideon knew he was right.

"Is something amiss, Mayne?" Rayburn asked. "You look as if you've seen a ghost."

Gideon turned toward him. "I have," he said, his voice grim. "Now I all have to do is catch it." And now was the perfect time. But he had to act quickly. His mind racing, he swiftly formulated a strategy. "I have a plan. But we'll need help." Once again he scanned the room, halting when he saw who he was searching for. "Follow me."

He walked to the far end of the room, Rayburn on his heels, halting when he reached the trio standing there. "I know who the murdering ghost robber is," Gideon said in an undertone to Matthew, Daniel, Logan, and Rayburn. "We have the opportunity to catch the person here. Now. I have a plan. Do you want to help?"

"Yes," Logan said without hesitation.

"Count me in," said Matthew.

"Me, too," added Daniel.

"Good," said Gideon. "Here's what I want you to do."

༄

Gideon approached Lord Haverly. "A moment of your time, Haverly, if you don't mind," he said, nodding toward the corner to afford them some privacy.

"What do you want?" Haverly asked, looking none too pleased at being pulled away from his conversation.

Gideon held out his hand. "I believe this belongs to you."

Haverly's eyes widened, and he reached for the gold pocket watch resting in Gideon's palm. "Where did you find it?"

"In the pocket of one of the men who kidnapped Lady Julianne."

"Indeed?" Haverly's eyes shifted. "Then what makes you think it's mine?"

"The fact that your name is engraved on the inside was a rather telling clue," Gideon said dryly.

Haverly's skin turned a mottled red. "Bastards. Not only are they kidnappers but thieves as well."

"They claim they didn't steal it. They say it was given to them. As partial payment for kidnapping Lady Julianne."

Now all the color drained from Haverly's face. "Surely you don't believe it was I who commissioned them."

"Wasn't it?"

"Certainly not! Why would I want to kidnap Lady Julianne? I want to *marry* her."

"Perhaps because she's going to marry someone else?"

"That is a reason to be disappointed. Not to kidnap her."

"Then how do you explain how the kidnapper had your watch?"

"Obviously, he stole it from me."

"When did you see it last?"

Haverly frowned. "Earlier this evening. When I first arrived. I consulted it just before entering the party."

Haverly's answer only served to confirm to Gideon that his theory was correct. He nodded toward the man approaching them. "The magistrate is interested in speaking with you."

Without another word, Gideon walked away. Scanning the crowd, his gaze fell on his next quarry, who, he noted, was watching Haverly and Rayburn. Gideon crossed the room, halting in front of the duke.

"I've some news," Gideon said. "Is there somewhere private we can talk? Your study perhaps?"

The duke's sharp gaze assessed him, then flicked back to Haverly and Rayburn. He nodded in their direction. "What's going on there?"

"That's partly what I want to discuss with you. It seems Haverly's in a bit of a...bad situation. But I don't wish to discuss it here."

"My study then," he agreed and led the way into the corridor. A moment later they entered a darkly paneled room that smelled of fine leather, beeswax, and tobacco. A fire burned in the grate, casting the room in flickering shadows. The duke settled himself in the leather chair behind a massive mahogany desk, then indicated Gideon take the chair opposite him.

"I prefer to stand," Gideon said.

"Very well. What did you want to discuss with me?"

"A new development. Haverly's watch was given to the kidnappers as partial payment for abducting Lady Julianne."

Something flickered in the duke's eyes, something Gideon recognized but that was gone so quickly he might have missed it if he hadn't been watching for it. Then the duke's gaze turned glacial. "You're saying he's responsible? That bastard." His fist slammed onto the mahogany desk. "All those murders, all those robberies. Thank God you've stopped him. I trust Rayburn is taking him into custody?"

"Actually, no."

The duke frowned. "Why not?"

"Because although the watch belonged to Haverly, he isn't the person who hired the kidnappers."

"Then who did?"

"*You* did."

The duke stared at him for several seconds then laughed. "You think *I* hired those men to kidnap Lady Julianne? Really, Mayne. I suspected you were incompetent, but this is—"

"I don't *think* you did. I know it. Absolutely. Will and Perdy, the men you hired, are very observant fellows. Fellows who spend a great deal of time studying the wealthy people they target. They recognized your voice, Your Grace," he lied without batting an eye and without the slightest twinge of remorse. "And in spite of the hood you wore, they recognized *you*."

The duke cocked a single brow. "No one will take the word of two criminals over mine. They couldn't possibly have seen anything in the dark."

Gideon slowly smiled. "I never said it was dark."

For several seconds the duke didn't react, then pure hatred flared in his eyes. He shrugged, a casual gesture, but Gideon saw the tension in his shoulders. "I merely assumed it would be dark."

"No, you knew it was. Because you were there. Tonight.

Paying them with Haverly's watch. Which you stole. Just like you stole his snuffbox the night of Daltry's party."

The duke leaned back in his chair and chuckled. "This is quite a story you've concocted, Mayne." He waved his hand in a rolling motion. "Please continue to entertain me."

"With pleasure. You stole Haverly's snuffbox and watch to implicate him. You purposely left the snuffbox near the window you left open during Daltry's party. Your plan was to return later that night to steal Lady Daltry's jewels."

The hatred in the duke's eyes had gone from a mere flare to a steady burn. "I have no idea what you're talking about."

"Yes, you do. When you returned later that night, you found the window locked. How do I know? Because *I* locked it. Your plan was thwarted, but you didn't worry. After all, you'd already killed Lady Ratherstone and Mrs. Greeley and gotten away with it. Who would suspect you?

"The day after the party, you waited until Daltry went to his club, then you returned to the house and robbed and killed Lady Daltry. She would have let you in through some little-used servants' entrance to avoid detection. Just as you robbed and killed Lady Hart earlier today. You knew she'd be alone in the house as you'd been having secret trysts there regularly for the past month."

Gideon set his hands on the desk and leaned forward until he was eye level with the duke. "Walston's sister, Lady Celia, was to be your next victim."

"Celia? Now I know you're mad. I barely know her."

"You know her well enough to have had sex with her earlier this evening."

The duke narrowed his eyes. "There's no way you could prove that."

"Are you calling the lady a liar?" Gideon asked softly.

Gideon could read the cold calculation in the duke's eyes, could almost see his mind racing at the implication that Lady Celia had admitted their tryst, an implication he had no way of knowing was false. Discovering that the woman he'd seen enter the room after the duke earlier tonight was Walston's sister had made everything finally click in Gideon's mind. Except for Gatesbourne, whose daughter was being threatened, and the three men from Cornwall no one but the duke knew anything about, Walston was the only man on the list who hadn't yet had a woman important to him robbed and murdered.

The duke steepled his fingers and touched them to his chin. "I am calling you mistaken, Mayne. Not only are you incompetent, you're insane. What possible reason would I have for robbing anyone? For killing those women?"

Gideon straightened, then said, "The oldest motives in the world: money and revenge. All revolving around the failed business deal between you and nine other men."

Gideon could see by the duke's expression that he'd hit his mark. Pressing his advantage, he continued. "At first there were only seven of you. You, Gatesbourne, Walston, Penniwick, Daltry, Jasper, and Ratherstone. You each put up ten thousand pounds in a venture guaranteed to quadruple your money. But you saw a chance to gain even more. You brought in three more investors—your friends from Cornwall, Count Chalon, Mr. Standish, and Mr. Tate—who each put up ten thousand pounds."

Gideon paused for several seconds, then said, "But there was no Count Chalon, Mr. Standish, or Mr. Tate. You made them up. Your greed led you to lie to your friends. To put up the monies for the fictitious Chalon, Standish, and Tate, money your heiress wife had brought to your marriage, so that you would reap the rewards four times over.

"But the investment went bad. You wanted to stay in, wait for things to turn around, as that forty thousand pounds was all you had. Yet one by one, the others pulled out. They felt the pinch of their ten-thousand-pound loss, but you, you lost four times as much. An amount that left you on the brink of financial ruin. And it was all their fault. If only the others had stayed the course, you would have been one of the richest men in England.

"Instead, your wife found out what happened. What you'd done. Found out you'd tried to cheat your friends and lost all the money she'd brought to the marriage. Between the disillusionment of discovering her husband's true character, the reality of social and financial ruin, and the heartbreak of losing your child, she killed herself."

Unmistakable anguish twisted the duke's face. "She was so young. So lovely."

"You loved her."

"I adored her. And she was *mine*. And they stole her from me. *No one* steals from the Duke of Eastling." Where his eyes had always seemed cold, they now burned with a combination of fervor and hatred. "If it wasn't for them pulling out of the deal too soon, none of it would have happened. I wouldn't have lost everything. I wouldn't have lost Amelia."

"So you made them pay," Gideon said softly.

"Yes." The word sounded ripped from his soul. "Damn it, yes. They *had* to pay. All of them. They *owed* me. I wanted them to feel the grief I felt. So I took from them what they'd taken from me."

"Women they cared for."

"Yes."

"And the jewels...they were merely to distract from the real crime of the murders. To make it seem as if the jewels were the real motive, that the victims were killed in order to gain their valuables. Very clever."

The duke inclined his head. "Thank you. Although one can never have too many jewels, and I needed the money I gained from selling them on the Continent. Those bastards deserved some financial setback. It would have taken me years to ruin them all financially, if I'd even been able to do so. But I could cause them grief like..." he snapped his fingers, "...*that*."

"And Lady Julianne?"

A chilling smile curved the duke's lips. "I needed to marry an heiress. And quickly. Before word of my dire financial situation got out."

"What did you hope to accomplish by climbing up to her balcony and trying to enter her bedchamber?"

"That was merely to frighten her. To establish that someone was after her. So that when she died a few months from now, no suspicions would be cast in my direction. And she had to die. So that just in case anyone ever linked the crimes together, it would appear that the woman dearest to me was also murdered."

Gideon had to fight to tamp down the wave of fury that threatened to engulf him. "Making you a victim rather than the murderer."

"Yes."

"You knew after I questioned you this evening that I was suspicious."

The duke frowned. "Yes, and very inconveniently. Required me to think quickly."

"So you stole Haverly's watch, left the party, and hired Will and Perdy to kidnap Julianne and kill me. It's not difficult to find men willing to do your bidding if the price is high enough. Must have been a nasty shock when I returned with Julianne."

"Very unpleasant indeed," the duke agreed.

"You left Julianne by the French windows after your dance. Told her to wait for you there, while you fetched her engagement ring. Knowing that as soon as you made your false announcement of your jewels being stolen that chaos would reign."

"And I knew you'd be watching her," the duke said. He picked up his quill pen and twirled it between his fingers. "Knew you'd go after her."

He twirled the pen again, and it fell. As he bent down to pick it up, Gideon said, "She was the bait to lure me away, so the kidnappers could kill me. Because you suspected I was getting too close to the truth."

"It would seem I was right about that." In a lightning-fast move, the duke stood and raised a pistol, aiming it directly at Gideon's chest. In a heartbeat Gideon realized he must have pulled it from a drawer in his desk when he bent to retrieve his pen. "And now it seems I'm going to have to do myself what those incompetent fools failed to do. Put your hands on top of your head, Mayne."

Gideon slowly obeyed. "You realize you'll never get away with this."

"I don't see why not. I'll simply say we were talking when

the hooded ghost murderer burst into the room through the French windows. In the ensuing scuffle you were, tragically, shot."

"No one will believe that."

"On the contrary, no one will doubt the word of the Duke of Eastling."

"*I'll* doubt the duke's word," came Charles Rayburn's voice from behind Gideon.

Gideon didn't turn around, but he knew the adjoining door between the duke's study and the library had just opened. And the magistrate had entered the study. Gideon knew Rayburn's pistol would be trained on the duke.

"I will also doubt the duke's word," came Matthew's voice.

"As will I," said Daniel.

"And me," added Logan.

Gideon knew they were all standing behind him. And he prayed none of them would get shot.

"We heard everything, Your Grace," Rayburn said. "All of us. It's over. Put down your weapon."

Hatred burned in the duke's eyes as he glared at Gideon. "This is all your doing. If not for you, no one would have known."

Gideon shook his head. "You would have been caught eventually."

"*No*. Haverly would have been blamed. If you hadn't ruined everything." A sick smile curved his lips. "I may have failed, but I'll at least have the satisfaction of making sure you don't see another day."

In the blink of an eye Gideon threw the knife he'd hidden up his sleeve. In the same instant both Rayburn's and the duke's pistol shots rent the air.

Chapter 24

Julianne froze at the sound of pistol shots. For the space of two rapid heartbeats, she and her friends stared at each other. Then she stood so quickly she knocked over her chair and dashed toward the door, Sarah, Emily, and Carolyn close behind. She raced down the corridor, barely registering the sounds of running footfalls and anxious voices of the other guests pouring in behind them. All she could hear was her heart pounding in terror. *Gideon…dear God, Gideon.*

She knew, *knew* that those shots involved him. What if he were hurt? What if he were—

She couldn't even bring herself to finish the thought. He had to be all right. Had to be. *Had* to be.

A door just ahead opened, and the magistrate stepped into the corridor, quickly closing the panel shut behind him.

"We heard shots," Julianne said, stopping in front of him. She grasped his arm, her fingers digging desperately into his sleeve. "Gideon." His name burst from her lips on a hoarse, terror-filled whisper. "Where is Gideon? Is he—"

"Mr. Mayne is fine." His gaze touched on Sarah and Carolyn. "As are your husbands. Mr. Jennsen as well."

Julianne heard her friends gasp. "Matthew is in that room?" Sarah asked weakly, reaching out for Julianne's hand.

"And Daniel?" Carolyn whispered.

"Yes. And they are all perfectly fine."

Before he could say anything more, a crowd surged in behind them with shouts of, "What's happening?"

Mr. Rayburn held up his hands and demanded silence. Once the crowd quieted, he said, "All is well. There is no need for alarm. If you'll go back to the drawing room, I'll explain everything."

Amid much murmuring, the group turned around to do as the magistrate bade them. But Julianne again grabbed Mr. Rayburn's sleeve. "I'm not leaving this corridor until I see for myself that Mr. Mayne is unharmed."

"And our husbands," Sarah added. "And Mr. Jennsen as well."

"I'm afraid you can't go in there," Mr. Rayburn said in an undertone, nodding toward the door.

"Why not?" demanded Emily.

After making certain the crowd was far enough away that he couldn't be overheard, he said, "You have my word that Mayne and the others are unhurt. The duke, however, is dead."

Before Julianne could even react to the news, the door opened.

Matthew and Daniel, wearing identical grim expressions, entered the corridor. With cries of relief, Sarah and Carolyn went to their husbands and were enfolded in tight embraces. Logan Jennsen appeared next. He nodded at Julianne, then at Emily, who murmured, "Mr. Jennsen."

Julianne craned her neck, and when she saw Gideon walking toward her, her relief was so strong she had to brace her hand against the wall for support. When he entered the corridor, heedless of their audience, she grabbed his hands. "You're all right."

His gaze seemed to burn into hers. "Yes."

"When I heard the shots I thought..." She squeezed his hands and blinked back the tears that rushed into her eyes.

"I know. I'm sorry you were worried. But it's all over now."

"Mr. Rayburn said the duke is dead."

A muscle ticked in Gideon's jaw. "He is."

The magistrate cleared his throat. "Mayne, if you'll escort the ladies and gentlemen into the drawing room and make the necessary explanations, I'll take care of things here."

Gideon nodded. Julianne held his arm as they walked down the corridor, unwilling to let him go, unable to keep from touching him. When they entered the crowded drawing room, however, he left her in the care of her friends and addressed the assembled group.

Julianne listened in shock and disgust to the story Gideon told. Gasps and cries of disbelief punctuated the tale of the duke's horrific crimes. By the end, everyone was clearly stunned yet relieved that the mystery of the murdering ghost robber had finally been solved and that no one else would suffer.

With the explanations finished, Gideon urged the stunned crowd to make their way home, and a slow exodus started toward the foyer. Julianne scanned the room and saw Sarah and Matthew talking quietly nearby. Daniel and Carolyn also stood close together, deep in conversation. Emily and Logan Jennsen stood near the punch bowl, making what appeared to be stilted conversation.

Just then Gideon joined her, pressing a glass of punch into her hand, which she gratefully accepted.

"Are you all right?" he asked.

"I'm...shocked. And grateful. That you weren't hurt. That he was stopped." A shudder of revulsion trembled through her. "That I hadn't married him." She took another sip of punch then added, "You were wonderfully brave and clever."

"Thank you."

"I'm very proud of you."

What looked like a cross between confusion and surprise crossed his face. He lifted his hand, as if to touch her, then seemed to recall himself, where they were, and lowered his arm. "I don't believe anyone's ever said that to me before."

"I'm also very angry with you."

He blinked, then his lips twitched. "Now *that* I've heard before."

"You took a terrible risk."

"No. I took a calculated risk. I didn't have proof; that would have required a trip to Cornwall and weeks, if not months, to obtain. But the duke didn't know that. And I knew I was right. I didn't doubt for a minute that when confronted with the truth, he would confess. I went into battle armed. And came out uninjured. The brandy decanter, which took the duke's shot, didn't fare as well, I'm afraid."

"You're making light of the danger you placed yourself in."

"Only because you're making too much of it. I'm very handy with a knife, plus I had Rayburn and the others at my back." He paused, then said, "Julianne, I—"

"*There* you are," came her mother's voice. "The carriage is being brought around. I swear this ordeal is going to be the death of me." She commandeered Julianne's arm and lowered her voice to a whisper. "Your father is absolutely livid."

"Why?" Julianne asked.

Her mother raised her gaze to the ceiling. "For heaven's sake, Julianne, have you not realized the implications? With Eastling dead, all the plans for your marriage are in ruins."

Julianne pulled away from her mother. "Yes, that is a tragedy," she said in an arid tone. "However, I for one am pleased that I didn't end up married to that murdering madman."

Her mother blinked. "Oh. Well, yes." She quickly recovered her aplomb. "I believe Haverly was your father's second choice, so that's most likely the way it will go."

Cold dread filled Julianne. Even though she knew the answer, she found herself asking, "The way what will go?"

"Your betrothal. But don't worry about it now. There's plenty of time to discuss it tomorrow." She turned to Gideon. "It appears we no longer require your services, Mr. Mayne.

I'll see to it that your belongings are packed up and returned to you tomorrow."

And suddenly it hit Julianne that the investigation was indeed over. Which meant that Gideon wouldn't be guarding her any longer. He wouldn't be coming back to Grosvenor Square tonight. There wouldn't be any more nights. Any more days. No more time. No more Gideon.

Her mother once again commandeered Julianne's arm. "Come along, Julianne. The carriage is waiting."

Once again Julianne shook free. "I'll join you in a moment, Mother."

Her mother heaved a sigh. "If you feel you must speak with Mr. Mayne, I'll wait."

Julianne lifted her chin and spoke to her mother with a firmness she couldn't recall ever using before. "As the man saved my life, I do want to talk to him. And I shall do so without you listening."

Her mother's lips pursed as if she'd sucked on a lemon. Julianne knew she couldn't claim there was need of a chaperone as at least a dozen people still lingered in the room. Finally the countess nodded. "Very well. You may have two minutes. Then I'll expect you in the carriage."

After her mother left, Julianne turned to Gideon. There were so many things she wanted say, but all the words stuck in her tight, dry throat. Words she wished she had the courage to utter. *I love you. Do you love me? I want you. Do you want me, too? I want to marry you. Do you want to marry me?* She hoped he might speak, but he remained silent, just looking at her with an expression she couldn't read.

Nerves assailed her, and she pressed her suddenly damp palms against her gown. Moistened her lips. Then began, "If you need your belongings tonight, you may come to the house—"

"No," he said quickly. So quickly it was clear he didn't want to return to the house. "Having them sent to me is fine."

Julianne felt her time running out, and a sense of panic seized her. Unable to think of a way to delicately ask what she wanted, needed to know, she simply whispered, "Will I see you again?"

Her heart beat in painful thumps waiting for his reply, trying to read his unreadable eyes. And then suddenly she *could* read them. Saw his answer. And his regret. And it felt as if her heart ceased beating. And instead began to bleed.

"The investigation is over," he said quietly.

She had to swallow twice to find her voice. "Which means that you and me...what we shared...is over as well." She'd found her voice, but it was utterly flat. And seemed to come from very far away.

"I'm afraid so. Julianne, I hope you know—" His words cut off and he raked a hand through his hair. "I want you to know that I...I'll never forget you."

She looked up at him and hid nothing. Let him see her heart and the depth of her love for him. Offered herself with her eyes. And he saw it. She knew he did. And so she waited. Until she couldn't stand the silence any longer. Then she asked in as steady a voice as she could muster, "Is that all you have to say to me, Gideon?"

Gideon stared into blue eyes filled with so much hope and yearning and love it actually hurt to look. He could tell her that he loved her, would always love her, but what good would that do either of them? He could tell her that if their situations were different—if she weren't an earl's daughter, or if he were a peer—he'd marry her in a heartbeat. But again, what good would that do? Their situation *wasn't* different.

But he had to say something. He reached out and gently took her hand. And forced himself not to dwell on the fact that it was the last time he would touch her.

"I hope," he said quietly, his gaze steady on hers, "that all your wishes and dreams come true."

For several seconds those blue eyes gazed into his. Then all the hope and yearning leaked away, breaking his heart in the process. She slowly withdrew her hand from his.

"I wish the same for you," she said in a broken whisper. "Good-bye, Gideon."

And then she turned and walked away.

Leaving him with a broken heart and a shattered soul. And a very bleak future.

∞

The following afternoon, Gideon sat in his study, doing the same thing he'd been doing since finally arriving home just before dawn: staring at the mantel. Thinking. Of things he needed to forget but knew he never would. Remembering. Her every word and touch that were branded in his brain. Aching. With a bone-deep pain he despaired of ever ridding himself of.

He blew out a long, tired sigh. If he had to sum up this situation in one word, it would have to be *how*. *How* had he allowed himself to fall so deeply, so hopelessly in love? *How* was he going to get through the next day, the next week, the next year, without her? *How* was he going to stand thinking of her married to someone else?

How the bloody hell was it possible to hurt so badly yet still breathe?

He'd tried to dull the ache with whiskey, but after the first hour realized the folly of that, since there wasn't enough whiskey in the kingdom to make him forget Julianne. So he'd capped the decanter and tried to concentrate on his headache rather than his heartache. And failed completely.

Caesar came to him and plopped his head on Gideon's knee, his soulful eyes filled with canine misery. Gideon scratched behind the dog's ears. "You lost your lady love, too, didn't you, boy?"

Caesar made the most pitiful sound Gideon had ever heard from the beast.

"I know exactly how you feel."

Caesar shifted his eyes to the whiskey decanter, and Gideon shook his head. "Take it from me, it doesn't help. It tastes foul and just gives you a bloody headache. And you don't get your woman back."

Caesar let out a mighty sigh, one Gideon was tempted to emulate, except it hurt too much to breathe that deeply. He dragged his hands down his face, grimacing at the rough scrape of his unshaven jaw.

The brass knocker on the front door sounded, rousing Caesar, who dashed from the room barking crazily, as if grateful to have something to do other than mope. Gideon hauled himself out of his chair and made his way to the foyer, wondering who was calling yet not really caring. His portmanteau had been delivered hours ago by Ethan. He'd hoped there might be a note from Julianne, but there wasn't. And although he was disappointed, what more was there to say?

When he reached the foyer, he quieted Caesar, then opened the door. And raised his brows in surprise at the sight of Matthew, Daniel, and Logan standing on his steps.

"You look like hell," Logan said.

Gideon blinked. "Uh...I'm not quite sure what to say to that except I feel like hell, too."

"It shows," Matthew said. "May we come in? There's something we need to discuss with you."

Gideon opened the door wider. "Of course." He led them to his study, where long rays of afternoon sunshine slanted through the windows. Once they were all seated, Matthew said, "I had a very interesting conversation with my wife on the way home in the middle of the night. It prompted me to call upon Daniel early this morning—"

"And it turns out I'd had a similar conversation with my wife on the ride home."

Logan cleared his throat. "I have no wife and therefore had no such conversation, but Daniel and Matthew were kind enough to include me in their plan."

"What plan is that?" asked Gideon.

"That depends on you. On what you decide to do about this." Matthew pulled an envelope from his waistcoat pocket and held it out to Gideon.

Gideon hesitated then took the envelope. "What is it?"

"One way to find out," Daniel said.

Mystified, Gideon opened the envelope and withdrew the contents. Scanned the paper. Frowned. Then read the words more carefully. Finally he looked up. And found three sets of serious eyes resting on him.

"This appears to be a special license," he said.

"That's because it *is* a special license," Matthew confirmed. "Arranged for today by the three of us at the Archbishop of Canterbury's London office in Doctors Commons."

"How did you manage this?" he asked, his gaze shifting back to the document, unable to quite believe what he was holding. He once again read the names *Gideon Mayne* and *Lady Julianne Bradley* printed on the official document.

"It took a bit of doing," Daniel said.

"Yes, but there isn't much an earl, a marquess, and a very persistent American can't accomplish if they set their minds to it," Logan said with a slight smile.

"But *why* would you do this?" Gideon asked. His gaze shifted between Matthew and Daniel. Surely a marquess and an earl wouldn't approve of a match between him and Julianne. Yet impossibly, based on the paper he held, it seemed they would.

"Because apparently Carolyn would have married Daniel if he were a baker," Matthew said. "And Sarah was willing to marry me even when it looked as if I'd be floundering in massive debt the rest of my life. And because of Themistocles."

Gideon shook his head, utterly confused. "Who?"

"A powerful Greek statesman during the fifth century BC. His daughter was torn between two marriage offers—one from a man of modest means with great character, the other from a man of her social class who was of questionable character. When her friends posed a similar question to Julianne, she unhesitatingly quoted Themistocles, 'I choose a man without money rather than money without a man.'"

Everything inside Gideon stilled. His heart. His blood. His breath. Then they leapt back to life with a force that rendered him speechless.

"We wanted you, and her, to have a choice," Daniel said.

"Before her damn father marries her off to some other useless Lord Something-or-Other," Logan said. He grinned at Matthew and Daniel. "No offense intended."

Matthew uttered something under his breath that sounded like *Bloody American*, then said to Gideon, "Everything is being readied for the ceremony to take place at my house at five o'clock. With us, our wives, and Lady Emily serving as witnesses."

Gideon could only stare. "*Today?*"

Matthew nodded then consulted his watch. "Today. In precisely one hour and nineteen minutes." He slipped his watch back in his waistcoat pocket. "The only things missing are a bride and groom."

Gideon looked down at the paper clutched in his hands. A piece of paper that had the power to give him everything he wanted. Everything he hadn't dared hope could be his. It appeared Julianne wanted him. In spite of his lack of social status and fortune. Not that he was poor. Yet neither was he rich. He nodded his chin at the special license. "This must have cost a fortune."

"Consider it a wedding gift," Logan said.

"She'll lose her family," Gideon said.

"Yes," Matthew agreed. "But she won't lose her friends."

"We can promise you that," Daniel said, and Logan nodded his agreement.

Hope burst through Gideon, so strong, he was grateful he was sitting down, because he felt a bit unsteady.

"I wouldn't have dared to ask her," he said quietly.

"Which is why we're here, meddling," Matthew said, "at our wives' behest."

"Right," Daniel said. "Because we're not normally meddlers, you know."

Logan looked toward the ceiling. "You Brits. Always talking in circles." He fixed his gaze on Gideon. "Well? What's it going to be?"

Gideon drew a deep breath. Then smiled. "The only thing missing now is a bride."

❧

Forty-five minutes later, freshly shaven and wearing his finest garments, Gideon entered the foyer of the mansion on

Grosvenor Square, Caesar at his heels. "I'd like to see Lady Julianne, please," he said to Winslow.

"I'll see if she's at home," the butler said. His gaze flicked down to the small bouquet of flowers Gideon clutched but made no comment. He headed down the corridor, and Gideon had to force himself not to pace. Winslow returned a moment later and said, "Lady Julianne is in the music room. She'll see you now."

Gideon and Caesar followed Winslow's straight back, and with every step, Gideon's heart thumped harder. "Mr. Mayne," Winslow announced at the door.

Gideon crossed the threshold, barely noting Winslow's departure as his gaze settled on Julianne. She stood next to the pianoforte, wearing a pale aqua gown that made her eyes look even bluer than usual.

He walked slowly toward her and wondered how the hell he had ever been foolish enough to walk away from her. He was only halfway across the room when a series of sharp yips came from the hearth. Princess Buttercup, dressed in an aqua ruffled collar that matched Julianne's gown, had caught sight of Caesar. Caesar in turn had caught sight of his love, and a joyful canine reunion of sniffing and licking and grunting and yapping took place before they both plopped down on the hearth rug.

"Hello, Julianne," he said, wading into the silence.

Now that less than six feet separated them, he could see that she'd been crying. Yet in spite of her puffy, reddened eyes, she was still the most beautiful thing he'd ever seen.

"Hello, Gideon." Her hands were clasped in front of her so tightly her knuckles showed white through her skin. "You wished to see me?"

"Yes." He took a quick look at the mantel clock, noted the time, then cleared his throat. "You asked me last night if I had anything else to say to you, and I realize I didn't say everything I wanted to. Everything I needed to."

"I see. Would you like to sit down?"

He shook his head. Went to plunge his fingers through his

hair only to recall the flowers he clutched. "These are for you," he said, holding them out. Bloody hell, he'd clearly strangled the damn things, for they looked decidedly wilted.

But in spite of their less-than-perfect condition, a trembling smile curved her lips. "Thank you," she said, burying her face in the droopy blooms. "I adore daisies."

He hadn't known that. Hadn't even noticed they were daisies. He'd simply bought the flowers from a young girl selling them because, well, wasn't a man supposed to bring flowers when he proposed? Bloody hell, why hadn't he asked Matthew or Daniel for instructions when he'd had the chance?

She looked up at him with solemn eyes. "What did you wish to say, Gideon?"

"I...I...." He let out a long breath. "I wish I was good at pretty words, because God knows you deserve them, but I'm not. So I can only tell you plainly." He stepped closer to her, stopping when less than an arm's length separated them, then took her hand, noting that his weren't quite steady.

"I love you, Julianne. Love you so much I just...ache with it. I think I loved you even when I thought you were nothing more than a spoiled princess, although I convinced myself I didn't. But then, as I discovered that you weren't a spoiled princess at all, realized the kind, loving, generous, brave, and wonderful woman you are, I couldn't deny to myself any longer that I'd fallen completely, utterly in love with you."

He pulled in a deep breath then continued, "I'm not a rich man, and I don't have a title. But I offer all I have, all I am, all my love, my heart and soul, to you."

He dropped to one knee before her. "Julianne, will you do me the honor of marrying me?"

She looked down at him, her eyes huge, her face pale. For several of the longest seconds of his life he endured the loudest silence he'd ever heard. Then her lips trembled and she smiled the most beautiful smile he'd ever seen.

"Yes," she whispered. Then laughed. Then sobbed. "Yes!

Yes!" Laughing, crying, she pulled him up, and he yanked her into his arms and kissed her. And all the places inside him that only an hour ago had seemed so empty filled to overflowing with a happiness he'd never thought possible.

She leaned back and framed his face between her hands. "I love you," she whispered. "From the first moment I saw you, you took my breath away. And now, when you tell me how you feel about me, instead of telling me I'm beautiful, you called me kind. Loving. Generous. Brave. Wonderful. You have no idea how much that means to me."

"Well, you *are* undeniably beautiful. Just in case you thought I didn't think so."

She smiled through the tears streaming down her cheeks. "Am I really going to be your wife?"

"Am I really going to be your husband?" He pulled out his handkerchief and dabbed at her wet eyes. "I brought three of these," he teased, waving the handkerchief before her.

She laughed. "Good. Princess Buttercup was miserable, you know."

"Caesar as well." He rested his forehead against hers. "Me, too."

"Me, too," she concurred.

He lifted his head. "You know your parents will never accept this."

"Then that is their loss," she said without hesitation. "I choose you. Now. Always."

"Are your parents at home?"

She shook her head. "Mother is off on her social calls, and father is at his club."

"I'll speak to them afterward, then."

"Afterward?"

"After the wedding. Which, if we don't want to be late for, we'll need to hurry, because it's starting in…" he glanced at the mantel clock, "twenty-four minutes."

Her jaw dropped. "Wedding? *Our* wedding? In twenty-four minutes?"

"Did I not mention that?" He shook his head. "Sorry. I was

a bit rattled." He quickly told her about the special license and the planned ceremony at Matthew and Sarah's house, concluding with, "When I asked you to marry me, I suppose I should have added, *now*. Will you marry me *now*?" He looked into her glowing eyes. "Will you?"

Her smile could have lit a dark room. "Yes!" Then she sobered. "But first, there's something I must tell you. Something I should have told you before. I . . . I lied to you, Gideon. That first night I claimed to hear ghost noises? I actually didn't. I did so because I wanted you to investigate. Wanted to see you again. So then I hired Johnny Burns the coal porter, to make ghostly sounds, but his wife had a baby and he couldn't make it and then a real ghost came to the balcony and—"

He touched his fingers to her lips to stop the rapid flow of words. "You did that just so you would see me again?"

She nodded. "I'm sorry," she mumbled against his fingers. "I shouldn't—"

This time he silenced her with a long, deep, tongue-dancing kiss that left them both breathless. "A clever ruse to get me back into your life. Have I told you how much I love you?"

"Yes, but I suspect I'll never grow tired of hearing it."

"Good. Because I intend to tell you ten times a day."

She heaved a sigh. "Only ten? I shall perish from neglect."

"Fine. Twenty. Has anyone ever told you you're . . . wonderful?"

She smiled into his eyes. "Yes. The man I love."

He was about to kiss her again but recalled the time. After a glance at the clock, he grabbed her hand and started toward the door, giving a whistle for Caesar, who trotted after them, Princess Buttercup following faithfully. "The wedding is now scheduled to start in nineteen minutes. Matthew loaned me his carriage. It's waiting out front, so we can be on our way immediately."

"I just need to run to my bedchamber for a moment," she said. "I'll meet you outside."

Epilogue

Gideon stood in Matthew's drawing room, sipping a glass of champagne, and reached out to touch his hand to his wife's back. His *wife*. Who stood next to him, laughing at something Carolyn said. His wife, who looked absolutely radiant and still clutched the wilted daisies he bought her. His wife, who had refused the fancy wedding bouquet Sarah had waiting for her and instead insisted on being married carrying the strangled flowers Gideon had given her. His wife, who turned to look at him with all the love he could ever hope to see shining in her eyes.

Matthew's butler approached Gideon. "Excuse me, sir, there's a gentleman to see you. He's waiting in the foyer. Said to tell you his name is Jack."

Gideon went still then nodded. After excusing himself to Julianne, he followed the butler from the room. They were halfway down the corridor when a door on the right opened, and Lady Emily emerged.

"Oh!" she exclaimed, clearly startled to see him. "I didn't know you were…I wasn't expecting…" Her face turned scarlet. "I'm just returning to the party." She hurried off.

Curious, Gideon stuck his head through the doorway from which she'd emerged. It was the library. And in the middle of the room stood Logan Jennsen. Brushing his finger over his bottom lip and looking as if he were in some sort of trance. Interesting.

Gideon cleared his throat. "Is there a problem?"

Logan turned toward him and frowned. "Ten minutes ago I would have said no. Now...I'm not so sure." He approached the doorway and gave Gideon a hearty clap on the back. Gideon noticed Logan's hair appeared a bit disheveled. *Very* interesting. "Nothing I can't handle," Logan said with a small smile. "But I definitely could use a brandy. See you back in the drawing room."

Gideon continued to the foyer, where he found himself staring at a very nattily dressed Jack Mayne.

"Could you excuse us for a few minutes, please?" he asked the butler.

After the servant withdrew, Gideon said, "What are you doing here?"

"Heard there was a wedding." He flashed a grin. "Was going to come in through the window and surprise ye, but decided this were better. More proper. And I wanted ye to have this." He held out his hand. In the palm rested a plain gold band. "I know it ain't fancy, but it were yor mother's. Thought ye might like to give it to yor bride."

Bloody hell, a damn lump clogged Gideon's throat. With all the servants in this house, you'd think they'd be able to keep up with the dust. He took the ring and slipped it into his pocket. "Thank you."

"Yor welcome. Congratulations, son. I wish ye every happiness." He tentatively extended his hand. Gideon hesitated, torn between what he knew his father was and the fact that, regardless of it, he was still his father. He reached out and shook his hand.

"Heard ye caught that murderin' ghost robber. Good for you. Nasty business." He shot Gideon a speculative look. "Surprised ye didn't think I might be yor ghost."

Actually, the thought had crossed Gideon's mind, but he'd quickly discarded it. "You're many things, but you're not a killer."

Jack nodded. "Glad ye know it. After all, a man has to have his standards, ye know."

"Yes, I know."

Silence stretched, then Jack said, "Well, I guess I'll be goin'."

"Before you do—I met a couple of friends of yours," Gideon said. "Will and Perdy. They told me some interesting things about you." He fixed a steady stare on Jack. "Were they true?"

To Gideon's amazement, Jack appeared to blush. "Wot they say?"

"About you helping people."

Jack shrugged. "Oh, that. That's nothin' but a hobby of mine. Just tryin' to be neighborly."

Gideon could tell there was more to it than that, and the realization hit him with a shock. "You really are helping people."

Another shrug. "I suppose."

Suspicion instantly set in. "Where are you getting the funds and supplies to help them?"

A devilish gleam lit Jack's eyes. "Ye probably don't want to know the answer to that, Son. You bein' on the wrong side of the law and all."

Gideon shook his head and pinched the bridge of his nose. "You know, there are other ways to get money from rich people to help your cause."

"Oh? How's that?"

"Have you ever considered *asking* them for it?"

Jack's expression was so nonplussed, Gideon had to laugh. "No, I can see that's never crossed your mind."

"Don't be daft," Jack said. "Why would they just give it to me?"

"Because, believe it or not, some of them are very generous. And kindhearted. If you ever decide you'd like to do things legally and would like some help, let me know."

Jack nodded slowly, then more vigorously. "I'll do that. You bet I will. And now, I'll let ye get back to yor wedding."

Gideon watched him walk toward the door, his emotions in a whirl. Just as Jack reached for the doorknob, he asked, "Would you...would you like to come in? Meet my wife?"

Jack stilled. And then it seemed as the dust affected him as well, as his eyes turned misty. "I'm touched ye'd ask, Son. I'd love to meet her. But today's yor day. For you and her. We'll do it some other time. I'll be in touch. In the meanwhile, don't do anything I wouldn't do." After a final devilish grin, he was gone, closing the door quietly after him.

"There you are," came a soft voice behind him.

He turned and saw Julianne walking toward him. "We've been married less than one hour, and already you've deserted me," she scolded with a smile. "Whatever am I going to do with you?"

He snatched her into his arms and gave her the kiss he'd been dying to give her since they arrived. When he finally raised his head, he said, "I can't wait to show you all the different things you can do with me."

"Oh, my," she breathed against his lips. "I knew life with you would be an adventure." She brushed back his hair. "Did I hear you talking to someone?"

"Yes. My father." He took the ring from his pocket. "He gave me this. It was my mother's. Would you like to wear it as your wedding ring?"

"Oh, Gideon. It's lovely. Yes, I'd be honored to wear it." She slipped off the borrowed ring from Sarah they'd used during the ceremony, and Gideon slid the band in its place.

She looked at the plain, thin gold band as if he'd offered her the crown jewels. And bloody hell if he didn't fall in love with her all over again.

"I love you," he whispered. "If I had to sum it all up in one word, it would have to be *happy*. I'm just so damn happy."

She smiled into his eyes, hers filled with love and joy. "And if I had to sum up in just one word what you are, what you've done, what you've given me, that word would be *everything*. Absolutely...everything."

Turn the page for a preview of
the next historical romance featuring

The Ladies Literary Society of London
by Jacquie D'Alessandro

Tempted at Midnight

Coming soon from Berkley Sensation!

I held him in thrall, my lips hovering just above his. I could feel his heat, smell his desire, sense his pulse pounding at his throat. Need poured through me at the thought of my fangs puncturing his skin, his hot blood flooding into my mouth. And even though I afforded him the opportunity to push me away, to escape the impossible, dangerous situation in which he found himself, I knew he was exactly where he wanted to be...

The Lady Vampire's Kiss *by Anonymous*

"Do you see anything suspicious?"

Logan Jennsen paused beneath one of the soaring elms lining the gravel path in Hyde Park and slipped his watch from his waistcoat pocket, his casual actions in complete contrast to his tension-laced voice.

"Suspicious in what way?" Bow Street Runner Gideon Mayne asked in an undertone.

Logan made a pretext of checking the time. "No one

appears to be paying the least bit of attention to me, but I can't dismiss the strong sensation that someone's watching me."

He noted how Gideon's sharp-eyed gaze immediately scanned the area as he too pretended to consult his own time-piece. Thanks to the bright afternoon sunshine after more than a week of gray, dismal January weather, the park was crowded with pedestrians, riders, and elegant equipages.

"From your tone I gather this isn't the first time it's happened," Gideon said, slipping his watch back into his pocket then bending down. He brushed a bit of dirt from the toe of his black boot, but Logan knew the Runner's gaze was further observing their surroundings.

"No. This is the third time in as many days. Which is why I asked you to meet me here. I hoped you'd see what I was missing."

"I don't see anything out of the ordinary," Gideon said, rising. "Yet. So let's keep walking."

That was one of the things Logan liked about Gideon and the reason why he'd asked the Runner to meet him—the man didn't waste time with unnecessary questions such as *Are you sure?* Or suggestions like *Maybe you're imagining it.* Over the past several months Logan had hired Gideon to perform investigative work relating to his business ventures and had been extremely impressed with the results. So much so, he was considering hiring him on a full-time basis, provided he could tempt Gideon away from Bow Street. But Logan was confident he'd prevail. As he knew, every man had his price. And Logan had the money to pay it.

They stepped back onto the path and continued walking. "Anything else unusual going on?" Gideon asked, his tone as casual as if he were discussing the weather.

Logan considered for a few seconds, then said, "Two nights ago an intruder tried to board one of my ships. The first mate gave chase, but the man got away."

"Any description of the man?"

"Only that he could run like the wind and clearly knew his way around. Otherwise, it was too dark."

"You make any new enemies lately?"

A humorless sound escaped Logan. Based on the work Gideon had performed for him over the last few months, the Runner knew damn well that along with wealth such as Logan's came an influx of people who didn't necessarily wish him the best.

"Not in the last few days—that I know of. Or so I'd thought. Until my instincts began screaming that I'm being watched."

"Never ignore your instincts," Gideon said quietly.

Good advice, although Logan didn't need it. Listening to his instincts and acting upon them were how he'd escaped the poverty into which he'd been born. What had kept him alive through more harrowing experiences than he cared to recall. And he intended to listen to them now, even if Gideon couldn't confirm his suspicions.

"A man in your position...lots of people are going to be looking at you," Gideon said.

"They have been," Logan said dryly. He'd quickly grown accustomed to being the cynosure of all eyes after his arrival in London nearly a year ago. "The members of society regard me as if I'm some exotic, predatory bird who's landed uninvited in their cozy nest. The fact that I'm an American only serves to cast more rancor and suspicion my way. I'm well aware the only reason the ton tolerates me in their lofty ranks is because of my wealth."

"Does that bother you?" Gideon asked.

"It occasionally annoys me but mostly amuses me. As much as the esteemed peers would like to send me packing on the first ship back to America, they're even more anxious to seek my advice on financial matters and investment opportunities." A grim smile lifted one corner of his mouth. "Since there are numerous such opportunities in my own companies, I take full advantage of their unwilling interest in me—which has proven very profitable all around."

Then he frowned. "But this recent feeling...it's different. A sense of menace." Indeed, it raised the hairs on the back of his neck and slithered eerie dread down his spine even on this bright, sunshine-filled day.

"In my experience, such a sense should never be ignored."

"Nor in mine," Logan agreed.

Gideon turned toward him. "You've felt this menace in the past?"

Too many times. "Yes, but not recently. And not since my arrival in England."

"Do you know what—or who—caused it in the past?"

Logan's jaw tightened. He'd never forget. "Yes."

"Perhaps this episode is from the same source."

He shook his head. "Impossible."

Gideon's eyes narrowed. "It would only be impossible if that source was . . . permanently extinguished."

Logan met the Runner's gaze. "As I said—impossible."

Gideon studied him for several seconds with an inscrutable expression, then gave a quick nod and returned his attention to their surroundings. Logan liked that Gideon accepted his word and didn't press him for details. Especially as it had saved him the trouble of lying. While he knew the lies he'd told countless times would slip from his lips once again without hesitation, he couldn't deny his relief in not needing to utter them now, particularly to this man he regarded as a friend. He knew all too well the havoc lies could wreak on friendships. As a result, it had been a damn long time since he'd had a friend.

The path veered into two forks just ahead. When Logan struck out toward the right, Gideon asked, "Do you have a particular destination in mind, or are we just taking a turn around the park?"

"Park Lane," Logan said. "I've a meeting. With William Stapleford, the Earl of Fenstraw."

He felt the weight of Gideon's stare.

"You don't seem pleased about it."

Damn. Was his discomfort so transparent that anyone could notice it? Or was Gideon's observation simply the result of him being extremely perceptive? He hoped the latter.

"I'm not pleased," he admitted. "There are financial matters the earl and I need to discuss, and I suspect it's not going to be pleasant."

Indeed, he knew damn well his discussion with the earl would be most *un*pleasant. Yet just as unsettling, if not more so, was the possibility of seeing Fenstraw's daughter, Lady Emily.

Lady Emily.

Logan's jaw tightened. Was it possible his sense of dread was somehow connected to his imminent arrival at the earl's town house, courtesy of either the earl himself or his daughter? He hadn't seen her for the last three months as the entire Stapleford family had retired to their country estate. But they'd arrived back in London yesterday, and Logan knew it was only a matter of time before he and Lady Emily ran into each other at some function or another.

An image of the woman he'd been attempting—and irritatingly, failing—for months to forget flashed through his mind, and he bit back a growl of annoyance. Damn it, *why* couldn't he forget her? She was beautiful, yet beauty rarely captured his attention for more than a fleeting moment. He'd always preferred the unusual to utter perfection. And Lady Emily's gorgeous face and form were undeniably utter perfection.

Of course, her shiny dark brown hair *was* shot with those unusual deep red highlights that seemed to capture and reflect every bit of light in a room. She stood out among the pale blonds preferred by so many men of the ton like a glossy ebony stone on a whitewashed sandy beach.

And her eyes *were* an unusual shade of green. Rather like viewing an emerald through an aquamarine. Every time he looked into her eyes he felt as if he were gazing into a fathomless sea whose bottom was a verdant lawn. He'd observed those clear, sparkling eyes twinkle with intriguing mischief and warmth while she was in the company of her friends, but turn arctic whenever her gaze collided with his.

From the first time they'd met ten months ago, she'd looked down her aristocratic nose at him, and he'd dismissed her as but yet another pampered, spoiled, supercilious society diamond, the exact sort of woman he had no liking or use for. He'd take a fun-loving, bawdy, unspoiled barmaid any day over these stick-up-their-arse, blue-blooded society chits who, with their fancy gowns, glittering jewels, and supercilious airs, clearly believed themselves superior to mere mortals.

Yet, as he'd become better acquainted with Lady Emily's circle, he found himself drawn against his will to that devilish gleam in her eyes and wondering what sort of mischief a proper earl's daughter could wreak.

Then he'd found out.

Three months ago. At Gideon's wedding to Lady Julianne Bradley—an event that had turned society on its ear. And prompted—at Lady Emily's suggestion—a brief, private interlude between her and Logan. An interlude that had led, at her initiation, to an unexpected kiss.

That damn kiss had turned him inside out. And utterly shocked him as until that point she'd made it abundantly clear she regarded him with all the liking of something foul she'd scrape off the bottom of her dainty satin slipper. And instantly—or as soon as he'd recovered the wits she'd very effectively stolen—filled him with suspicion as to her motives. He didn't for a minute believe her claim that she merely wanted to satisfy her curiosity. Why would he when up until then she'd gone out of her way to avoid him, so much so he wasn't certain if her avoidance more aggravated or amused him?

No, it seemed much more likely that she'd discovered her father owed him a fortune and had decided to play with Logan, attempt to lure him into forgiving the debt. As if a mere kiss—or anything else she might offer—could accomplish that goal. He *never* allowed personal feelings or pleasures to interfere with business.

Still, her sudden turnaround had thrown him completely off balance. If he'd been able to think clearly, hell, if he'd been able to form a coherent sentence, he would have demanded the truth from her regarding her motives. But speech had been beyond him and she'd left the room before he'd gathered his incinerated wits. And that single kiss, which within seconds had burned out of control, had lit a fire in him he'd been unable to extinguish. And had rendered her frustratingly unforgettable.

The day after the wedding and that damn kiss, she and her family had departed for the country, and she'd been out of his sight ever since.

Unfortunately, she'd not been out of his thoughts.

"Does that meet with your approval?"

Gideon's voice yanked Logan from his reverie, and he turned toward the Runner. And found him staring at him with an inquiring expression. "I beg your pardon?"

One of Gideon's dark brows hiked upward. "I said I'll accompany you the rest of the way to Lord Fenstraw's town house, then spy around outside for a bit. See if anyone's lurking about or if anything strikes me as odd."

"Thank you. I'll of course compensate you for your time."

Gideon's lips twitched. "Then I suppose I shouldn't tell you that the task is no hardship as it gives me an excuse to wait around to accompany my wife home. She's visiting with Emily right now, along with Sarah and Carolyne. A book club meeting. The Ladies Literary Society or some such."

Gideon's statement distracted Logan from his concerns of being watched, and his pulse jumped in the most ridiculous way at the knowledge that Lady Emily was indeed at home.

"I must admit I find myself very curious about what goes on at those book club gatherings," Gideon muttered.

Logan raised his brows. "At the *Ladies Literary Society*? What's there to be curious about regarding women chatting about Shakespeare and such?"

"They're not reading Shakespeare."

"Oh? What are they reading?"

"Stories that could make a courtesan blush. In fact, one of their previous selections was actually written by a courtesan. Very interesting information in that one. Some of it damn near made *me* blush."

Logan didn't believe anything could make a man like Gideon blush. He also found it difficult to imagine Gideon's very demure and proper wife reading such salacious material. And unsettlingly arousing to think of Lady Emily doing so.

A thought struck him and his steps slowed. Was it pos-

sible that Lady Emily's claim of curiosity had been her true
motive in kissing him? Had her scandalous readings left her
wondering what it would be like to experience such intimacies? Hell, if that was the case, what else might she be curious
about? Heat that had nothing to do with the bright sunshine
sizzled through him.

But then his suspicions returned. Even if curiosity had played
a part, clearly something more was afoot—and he had no doubt
that that something had to do with the money her father owed
him. Otherwise, why choose *him* to satisfy her curiosity—a
man she obviously didn't like? Immediately on the heels of
that question came a mental image of her...kissing a man who
wasn't him. A lightning bolt of something that felt exactly like
jealousy, but surely couldn't be, tore through him.

He blinked away the disturbing mental picture, then asked
Gideon, "You don't object to Julianne reading such sexually
explicit books?" he asked.

"Hell no. And if you had a wife, you wouldn't object to
her reading them either." Gideon slanted him a brief sideways
glance. "Trust me on that."

Logan didn't doubt him, and much to his annoyance, he
found himself imagining Lady Emily...reclined in his bed.
Wearing nothing save a wicked grin. Looking at him over the
top of a salacious novel. "Quite the mischievous group, aren't
they?" he murmured, pretending his skin didn't feel uncomfortably tight.

"Very much so," Gideon agreed. "Especially Emily. Got
the devil in her eyes, that one."

Hmmm. Yes, she did. And she also read sexually explicit
books. How utterly unexpected. And disturbingly arousing.

"What was their latest selection?" he asked—merely to
continue the conversation and make it appear to anyone who
might be watching that they were simply two friends out for a
walk. It wasn't as if he were really curious. Or would consider
purchasing his own copy to read.

"*The Gentleman Vampire's Lover.*"

"Did you read it?" Logan asked.

"I did."

"And? Was it good?"

Gideon's lips twitched slightly. "Let's just say I found it very...stimulating. You might want to ask Emily about it."

Logan turned to stare at Gideon. "Why the hell would I want to do that?" The question came out much sharper than he'd intended.

Gideon shrugged. "Something happened between you two after my wedding ceremony. In the library. Based on what I observed, I thought maybe it was something...good."

Logan suddenly recalled that Lady Emily had literally bumped into Gideon when she'd fled the library following their kiss. How Gideon's amused voice asking *Is there a problem?* had yanked him from the stunned trance he'd fallen into. And Logan's assurance it was nothing he couldn't handle.

Something good? *It wasn't good, it was great. Incredible.* He cleared his throat. "You thought wrong."

Gideon said nothing and Logan wondered what the other man was thinking. Like a damn sphinx, Gideon was—silent and inscrutable. Logan supposed that was useful for his Bow Street job, but it sure as hell was frustrating otherwise. Couldn't read his thoughts worth a damn.

"I like her," Gideon finally said.

"Who?" Logan asked, although he knew damn well.

"Emily. She and Julianne have been close since childhood, and she's been a good friend to my wife."

"In what way?"

"Julianne's an only child, and her parents..." Gideon's words trailed off and a muscle ticked in his jaw.

Logan nodded. "I've met the earl and countess. I'm no more fond of them than you. Very cold, overbearing people." Who'd disinherited and banished their daughter when she'd gone against their demands to marry a titled gentleman and instead wed Gideon, a lowly commoner. As far as Logan was concerned, it was no loss to the newlywed couple, and he greatly respected Lady Julianne for choosing the man she loved over everything else.

"Those are actually polite ways to describe Julianne's parents. Emily brought laughter and fun into what would have otherwise been a very lonely childhood for Julianne. I find myself fond of anyone who makes my wife smile."

Logan shook his head and chuckled. "Good God, that little bastard Cupid shot you with an entire quiver of arrows. I can practically see little hearts floating around your head, like a love-induced halo."

"No halos on me. But yes, that little bastard Cupid got me but good. And damned if it wasn't the best thing that ever happened to me." He shot Logan a sideways glance. "Why aren't *you* married? Hard to believe some matchmaking mother hasn't clubbed you over the head and forced you to the altar."

"The fact that I'm an uncouth colonial gives them pause, although I've no doubt my wealth would balance that out in the end. Plus, I seem to posses an unfortunate penchant for being attracted to women whose hearts are already involved elsewhere."

"That must be difficult."

"Indeed. Several lovely women have slipped through my fingers since my arrival in London."

"No, I meant about your wealth. Never knowing if your money is the attraction. It's a problem Julianne knew her entire life. One I've never known. Nor would I care to." He flicked a glance at Logan. "Can't say I'd want to be in your position."

A huff of surprise escaped Logan. "Well, that's not something I'm used to hearing. I've become accustomed to being envied. In fact, I can't ever recall anyone *pitying* me because of my wealth."

"Before Julianne, I would have said you're too bloody rich to pity. But money never brought her true happiness. I've never been wealthy, yet I didn't really know what happiness was until I met her."

"So you're saying it's not money or things but people that make the difference."

Gideon shrugged. "Seems that way to me."

Interesting. Logan knew damn well people sought his acquaintance based solely on his money. God knows it was the only reason with most of the arrogant, puffed-up British peers, and he couldn't deny he'd grown more suspicious and

cynical as his wealth had grown. But having spent his forma-
tive years barely one step above abject poverty, he was very
adept at sidestepping frauds and fortune hunters.

He also knew damn well that at this point there was no
chance he'd find a woman who wasn't attracted to his money.
The best he could hope for was a woman who was at least
honest about it and who found him equally as attractive as his
wealth. A woman he could respect and admire, who wasn't
haughty and supercilious and fond of staring down her aristocratic nose at him, and who set his blood on fire. It had so far
proven an impossible combination to find. While money made
most aspects of his life easier, there was no denying it complicated his personal relationships. And caused him to view
people and their motives through suspicious eyes, although
he'd done that long before he'd had two coins to rub together.
That wary mistrust had saved him more than once.

"We're nearing the Fenstraw town house," said Gideon.
"So far I've observed nothing unusual."

Logan yanked himself from his brown study and realized
that Park Lane was indeed just ahead. His gaze scanned the
row of town houses across the thoroughfare and settled on the
aged brick facade of the one belonging to Lady Emily's father.
He now knew she was home, but would he see her?

Logan expelled an exasperated breath. Why the hell did
he care?

Once again, the memory he'd been trying so hard to erase
slammed into him with such force his footsteps faltered.
Of soft, plush lips opening beneath his. Of lush, feminine
curves pressed against him. Her taste and scent inundating
his senses. The flood of unwanted, unexpected desire that had
nearly drowned him.

He briefly squeezed his eyes shut and shook his head to dispel
the unsettling mental picture that wouldn't let him go. Damn it,
this simply wouldn't do. And it suddenly occurred to him that he
hadn't kissed or touched another woman since his interlude with
Lady Emily. Good God, no wonder he couldn't get her out of his
head. He'd been more celibate than a monk.

What he needed was a woman. To put out this unwanted

fire Lady Emily had started. To ease his body and fill his mind with someone else other than her. Yes, that was a perfect plan and he deserved a thump on the head for not thinking of it before now. There was a soiree this evening at Lord and Lady Teller's house. He'd make it a point to attend and find an attractive woman and seduce her. If he couldn't find one at the party who interested him, he'd damn well visit every pub in the city until he did. No woman at a pub would look down her nose at him.

"We'll separate here," Gideon said after they crossed Park Lane. "If I see anything suspicious, I'll report to you immediately. Remain on your guard and let me know if you sense anything else. Until we determine if there's a threat to you, don't go out unescorted. Or unarmed."

Logan's gaze flicked down to his boot where his knife was sheathed. "I'm always armed."

"Are you going out this evening?"

"I am. And I'll be careful. Although, as neither of us observed anything amiss, I'm wondering if I'm merely tired and preoccupied. If you'll come to the house tomorrow morning, I'll see to your payment and let you know if anything happens this evening."

Gideon nodded. "All right. Good luck with your meeting."

Logan drew a deep breath and nodded. There was business to attend to with the earl. Business that had nothing to do with Lady Emily. Her motives for kissing him were highly suspect; although, it didn't really matter what those motives had been. He was forewarned and had no intention of falling prey to whatever devilish plot she'd concocted. He had no desire to see her, no desire to speak to her regarding what had transpired between them, and certainly no desire to repeat it.

If he kept telling himself that enough, surely it would become fact.

He was about to turn to walk up the flagstone steps leading to the double oak doors of Lord Fenstraw's town house when the sense of menace he'd felt earlier hit him like a blow to the head. Senses on alert, his gaze scanned the entrance to the park across the street. And riveted on a man standing in the shadow cast by a soaring elm. A man whose gaze was fixed on Logan.

Everything inside Logan seemed to freeze. His breath. His blood. His heart. No...it couldn't be.

For several stunned seconds all he could do was stare. A carriage crossed his line of vision, and when it moved on an instant later, the man was gone. Logan's gaze darted about, but he couldn't find any sign of the man.

"Are you all right? You look like you've seen a ghost." Gideon's low voice broke through Logan's shock.

Damn it, it felt as if he had. "I thought I saw someone..." his words trailed off and he shook his head, feeling foolish. Yet undeniably shaken.

"Who? Someone watching you?"

There were so many people in the park. Of course the man wasn't who Logan had thought. That was impossible. A slight resemblance combined with a trick of the shadows. "Just someone who looked like a man I once knew."

"Maybe it was him."

"No. That man...died. Years ago." He looked at Gideon. "I once heard that everyone has a double somewhere. Seems it might be true."

"Which man is it?" Gideon asked, looking toward the park.

"He's gone. It was nothing. And I'm due for my appointment." After one last look toward the now deserted area around the elm tree, Logan forced back the unwanted memories the sight of the man had threatened to release and made his way up the flagstone walkway to the earl's town house.

Enter the rich world of
historical romance
with Berkley Books.

Lynn Kurland

Patricia Potter

Betina Krahn

Jodi Thomas

Anne Gracie

Love is timeless.
penguin.com

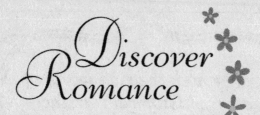